KU-863-122

HEADS OR HEARTS

WITHDRAWN

C016174379

ACKNOWLEDGEMENTS

Kudos to Severn House for resurrecting the mouthy and recalcitrant Quint Dalrymple after fourteen years in the void; the company has form on that count, having already successfully revivified Alex Mavros. Particular thanks to Edwin Buckhalter and Kate Lyall Grant for their personal interest and support.

Yet more of the fizzy stuff to my indomitable champion, Broo Doherty of the DHH Literary Agency. She sees the texts first, poor woman, but always looks on the bright side.

And, of course, eternal love to Roula, Maggie and Alexander. Where would I be without them? In Kay's Bar, probably . . .

P. Johnston, 2015

HEADS OR HEARTS

Paul Johnston

This first world edition published 2015
in Great Britain and the USA by
SEVERN HOUSE PUBLISHERS LTD of
19 Cedar Road, Sutton, Surrey, England, SM2 5DA.
Trade paperback edition first published 2015
in Great Britain and the USA by
SEVERN HOUSE PUBLISHERS LTD.

Copyright © 2015 by Paul Johnston.

All rights reserved.
The moral right of the author has been asserted.

British Library Cataloguing in Publication Data

Johnston, Paul, 1957- author.
  Heads or hearts.–(A Quint Dalrymple mystery)
  1. Dalrymple, Quintilian (Fictitious character)–Fiction.
  2. Murder–Investigation–Fiction. 3. Referendum–
  Scotland–Edinburgh–Fiction. 4. Edinburgh (Scotland)–
  Fiction. 5. Suspense fiction.
  I. Title II. Series
  823.9'2-dc23

ISBN-13: 978-0-7278-8503-6 (cased)
ISBN-13: 978-1-84751-605-3 (trade paper)
ISBN-13: 978-1-78010-656-4 (e-book)

To my sister Claire,
with love, admiration and gratitude

Except where actual historical events and characters are being
described for the storyline of this novel, all situations in this
publication are fictitious and any resemblance to living persons
is purely coincidental.

All Severn House titles are printed on acid-free paper.

Severn House Publishers support the Forest Stewardship Council™ [FSC™],
the leading international forest certification organisation. All our titles that
are printed on FSC certified paper carry the FSC logo.

Typeset by Palimpsest Book Production Ltd.,
Falkirk, Stirlingshire, Scotland.
Printed and bound in Great Britain by
TJ International, Padstow, Cornwall.

PROLOGUE

Woke up this morning, got myself a croissant. And a cup of half-decent coffee. And a banana.

Actually, I've been waking up numerous mornings and getting those previously unavailable comestibles from the corner shop. Independent Edinburgh in 2033 has become almost citizen-friendly. That doesn't make up for the previous three decades of austerity and gritty bread, but it means life for the masses has become more tolerable.

Which, of course, is the point. The Council of City Guardians is full of wise guys and dolls. Widespread unrest and verbal, even physical abuse of the tourists were completely unacceptable. First they tried locking people up. Then they realized that the way forward was to bring a little happiness into the long-suffering citizens' lives. It didn't take much: a smattering of democracy ('Elect Your Own Ward Representative!'), the opening up of the tourist zone to locals on Sundays, better food and drink. Cinemas even show films that were long banned on the grounds that they would incite civil diso-bedience – *The Wild Bunch*, *1900*, *Alphaville* . . . As for books, almost anything has come into the city's libraries. Elmore Leonard is popular, probably because his criminals are so convincing – Edinburgh folk have a taste for people who break the law. Then again, the sainted Elmore didn't approve of prologues.

Even the blues, previously prohibited as subversive, have been made available, the Council's thinking no doubt being that twelve-bar wailing and bawling is more to be pitied than bothered about. Their loss. It turned out that blues enthusiasts are all over the place, nursing battered cassettes and the ancient machines to play them. Exchange clubs immediately sprang up and my ears were blown, both by songs I hadn't heard since I was a student and by musicians I'd never come across. Life is almost worth living again.

Here's the but. Nothing good or even mildly bearable lasts. There's always some genius who thinks he – and males are inevit-ably the overwhelming majority – can take things to the next even more wonderful level. Actually it was several demented specimens, not all of them from Edinburgh. Suddenly the 'S' word was back in fashion. Since the Enlightenment Party won power in the last election thirty years ago and cut the city off from its neighbours, Scotland had become a ghost, a fossilized memory, a cry of anger and frustration carried away on the wind.

Now it was back in a big way. Initially I was with the old bluesman Taj Mahal – 'Done Changed My Way of Living' often enough, thanks. Then sitting on the fence became hazardous as the pointed posts dug in. It was make your mind up time. There was to be a referendum on whether the former capital should take its place in the reconstituted nation. That's right: citizens who for decades hadn't been allowed to choose their sexual partners were going to be trusted with voting for their and the city's future. People in high places were either smoking top-grade tourist dope or there was something distinctly fishy going on.

As a detective I've always had a nose for herrings – red (or any other colour), kippers (we get those now, once a month) and salmon (don't be ridiculous). In this case everything came down to heads and hearts. Fish have them. I'm not so sure about the people wielding power in the country where I was born and raised; born, as it happens, in 1984.

ONE

There was a pounding on the door.

'It's open, ya loud lout,' I shouted.

Davie appeared, his black hair turned to rat's tails by the deluge outside, and careered across my small living room.

'This is for you.' He dropped a package in brown paper on my belly.

'Ooh-yah!' I extracted the contents. 'Talisker? Where did you get that?' Even City Guard barracks weren't supplied with whisky not made locally.

'Wouldn't you like to know?' The big man sat down hard on my armchair, recently given new covers by the Supply Directorate but still sprung like a Model-T Ford with 200,000 miles on the clock. 'Shit!'

'Not there, if you don't mind. My bathroom, resplendent with new fittings and fitments, is at your disposal.' Until recently, citizens had been forced to use communal bath-houses because of water shortages brought about by the Big Heat, climate change's version of the Edinburgh summer. Now that the Big Heat had become the Big Wet, flats have been re-plumbed and we can use as much water as we like. Until the two-minute timer kicks in.

'I don't need any more water, thanks,' Davie said, shaking his head and leaving spatters all over the wall behind him. 'Bloody summer.'

'It's symptomatic of life in the city.'

'What's that supposed to mean, Socrates?'

I raised an eyebrow. 'That's no way for a senior auxiliary to talk. I know Plato debates are only monthly and non-compulsory now, but still . . .' The Council of City Guardians had originally consisted of university professors who followed the Greek philosopher's thinking – at least, the bits that suited them. None of the original rulers were on the Council any more and flux was the rule, even when it came to the Edinburgh Enlightenment's most hallowed principles.

'Everything's turned into its opposite,' I said. 'Summer, until a couple of years ago as dry as the Mediterranean in August, is now

wetter than the Indian sub-continent in the monsoon season. The
Council doesn't imprison many people these days – it just gives
the average criminal a month in the luxury New Bridewell rehabilitation facility, with as much pampering as they can take. Citizens
can start their own businesses and vote for their own ward reps – not
that the local barracks commanders let the said reps do anything to
rock the rowing-boat of state. Citizens can even walk round the
tourist zone and marvel at the things they can't afford.'

'They have vouchers to spend, and not just on food,' Davie said.
He pointed to the ugly beige device on my wall. 'And they all have
telephones like that one.'

'Which aren't tapped by the Guard, oh no, never.'

He ignored that. 'And they get free holidays.'

'To camps down at Portobello, where the sea is completely unpol-
luted by sewage, honest. And there's still no TV, smoking or private
cars.'

'Are you going to open that bottle?' Davie demanded.

I got up and looked out the window. I could hardly see the tene-
ments on the other side of Gilmore Place through the rain.

'All right, what is it you want? You wouldn't have come here in
this downpour just to drink Tali . . . yes, you would.'

Davie laughed. He looked younger, thanks to the Council's
reversal of the rules governing male facial hair. Previously male
citizens had to have their hair cut to a maximum of half an inch
– no metric measurements in the 'perfect city' – and weren't
permitted facial hair, while auxiliaries, the Council's bureaucrats
and enforcers, had to wear beards as if each one was an ancient
philosopher – though at least the females didn't have to wear face
wigs. Now auxiliaries have to be clean-shaven, while citizens can
wear their hair to any length – even those who work with tourists
– and do what they like with their facial hair. That has led to a male
civil population with either moustaches Wyatt Earp would have been
proud of or beards down to their sternums. Not to be left out, women
can wear their hair in any style, leading to an eruption of salons
across the city – all part of the Finance Directorate's private business initiative. I've managed to resist temptation, keeping my now
worryingly grey hair short, though my stubble is only occasionally
under control. I opened the whisky and inhaled.

'Peaty and sweet,' Davie said, picking up a couple of glasses
from my dresser.

'And all the way from the Isle of Skye.' I added a dribble of water from the jug I always have on the coffee table – although Talisker didn't, citizen-issue whisky needs heavy diluting.

We imbibed and luxuriated in silence.

'Which begs the question,' I said eventually.

'How did it get here?'

'Very good, guardsman.' Although Davie was a senior commander, I'd never got out of calling him by the rank he had when we first worked together in 2020.

'Patronizing tosser. If you must know, it comes from a crate donated to the Guard by the Lord of the Isles.'

'For your admirable services in keeping him safe while he was in the city.'

'What's wrong with that?'

'Apart from the fact that he's a scumbag aristocrat who ran away when the crofters revolted back in the early 2000s and has only come back because oil's been found in the waters off the Hebrides?'

Davie scowled. 'I just do what I'm told. Unlike the great Quintilian Dalrymple, who plays at being the protector of ordinary citizens while screwing up official investigations.'

I grinned. 'Love you too, big man.' It was true that I use what clout I retain to twist auxiliaries' arms and find missing citizens, put right cases of mistaken identity, get innocent citizens off – there were no courts in the City of Eden, so Guard personnel often did what they liked – and catch the odd ward rep who'd tapped into his inner Mafioso.

Davie took another sip. 'I know you do some good, Quint, but it's nothing compared with what you could do if you worked with us.'

'Oh, so that's what this is,' I said, pointing at the bottle. 'A bribe. Really, guardsman, I thought you were above that kind of behaviour.'

'Screw you. The public order guardian told me to get you back on board. Council orders.'

'Does she know about the Talisker?'

'Er, not exactly.'

'What if I tell her?'

'Give it a rest, will you? I'm serious.' Suddenly my old friend looked troubled, which was not in his character.

'What's happened?'

Davie looked down. 'I can't tell you unless you sign up.'

'So it's like that, is it, Hume 253?' I used the barracks number that was formerly the only way auxiliaries were addressed. Now they have their names on badges. Until recently I'd never known that Davie's surname was Oliphant.

'Yes, it is, citizen. Are you in or out?'

'Out.' Although I'd been the Council's chief investigator in numerous major cases over the years, I always went back to my own clients. Working for citizens was generally more fulfilling – and substantially less life-threatening.

'You're just guilty,' Davie said, meeting my eyes. 'Who helped set up the City Guard? Who wrote the *Public Order in Practice* manual that's still used in auxiliary training? Eh, Bell 03?'

I sat back in my man-eating sofa. There was no getting away from my earlier life. I'd joined the Enlightenment when I was a student, fought for it through the drugs wars and been one of the Guard's chief ideologues. Then, a couple of decades back, I lost my faith in the system and dropped out.

'Low blows, Davie.'

'Don't care. We need you.' He fixed me with a fearsome glare. 'I need you.'

I turned my eyes to the cascade of water on the window. 'That's very touching. But you can't expect me to drop everything at some whim of the Council. I've got cases, people who depend on me.'

'This is no whim of the Council, Quint. Trust me, you're going to be stuck with this one way or the other. Why not get in at the start?'

'That big, eh?'

'Potentially.'

'So tell me.'

'No chance. The guardian will have my balls for haggis.'

'How can you be afraid of a woman called Doris?'

'I'm not afraid of her, but she's my boss.'

'The recently appointed Doris Barclay. I remember her when she was Knox Barracks commander. She was wound tight, but no more than most of her kind.'

'She remembers you too. Not hugely favourably, it has to be said.'

'Great. But why no written order?'

Davie shook his head. 'Nothing's being written about this, not even Guard reports.'

I had to admit it was enticing. The Council's Edinburgh is the ultimate bureaucratic state, with information stored about everything – formerly in hand-written archives and more recently, in some directorates, in computers bought on the cheap from the warring states that formed after China tried one economic coup too many and disappeared in the biggest financial crisis in history. If the guardians themselves were avoiding written records, a meteorite of excrement was heading for the wind turbine – they've been put up on the Pentlands in recent months in a belated attempt to go green.

'How about a clue?'

'No.'

'Take me to the crime scene?'

'There isn't one. Well, there is, but it isn't clear what the crime is.'

I stared at him. 'Are you pulling my—'

'Certainly not.' Davie got up. 'Am I taking the whisky or leaving it?'

I caught his eye. 'Can I trust you on this? Is it really going to be worth my time?'

'How do I know? It looks like the beginning of a massive case, but these things sometimes fizzle out.' He picked up the bottle. 'I have a feeling this one won't.'

I grabbed the Talisker.

'All right, I'm in. But I'll be out the minute it gets boring.'

Davie laughed grimly. 'Ever the boy adventurer. What age are you next birthday?'

I kicked the back of his leg. The prospect of the big 5-0 was scaring the shit out of me.

'Where are we going?'

Davie was at the wheel of a new and shiny white Korean 4x4. The Guard's fleet of ancient Land Rovers had finally been put out to grass – or rather, handed over to the wards to run, spare parts not included.

'Wait and see.'

'I told you I was on board.'

'Don't you always say that an unprejudiced mind is essential when encountering evidence and scenes?'

The windscreen wipers were on full blast but I could still hardly see anything of the road ahead. Fortunately Davie was a skilled driver, something he was inordinately proud of. He swerved smoothly past a couple of drenched citizens on their bikes, then a bus full of workers going home. We passed the revitalized Market District, buildings whose foundations had been laid in the early years of the century finally completed. That was all part of the city economists' master plan to turn Edinburgh into a tax haven and financial services hub. States in Europe and around the world were getting back on their feet after decades of in-fighting and extreme disorder. We'd been starved of international news, the Information Directorate providing only stories that put independent Edinburgh in a good light. I remembered that offshore banking, low-tax regimes and unregulated markets had been part of the problem that tore the world's economy apart when the man and woman on the street finally had enough of being urinated on.

'Edinburgh as the Cayman Islands? Jersey? Liechtenstein?' I said.

'If you say so.' Davie turned on to Dalry Road.

'Yet another component of the Council's topsy-turvy world. The Enlightenment banned money, remember?' I laughed. 'Though that didn't stop them taking it from tourists.'

'We had to survive somehow,' Davie growled. 'Anyway, the year-round festival wasn't much of a change from before.'

'I don't remember there being marijuana clubs, legalized brothels, a racetrack in Princes Street Gardens and gambling venues all over the city.'

'Neither do I.' Davie shrugged. 'I know the system isn't perfect, but it's getting better.'

'You might be right,' I conceded. 'Then again, what's this big case?'

'Not long now.'

He clammed up and I looked at the shabby surroundings. We were out of the centre now and, despite the Council's efforts to improve citizens' lives, the built environment isn't pretty. Davie bore right and then took a sharp turn. The rain was lighter now and I made out a large maroon sign:

Welcome to Tynecastle, Home of Heart of Midlothian
Football Club
Hearts, Glorious Hearts!

'Uh-huh,' I said. 'Is there a game on?'

'It's five-thirty on a Tuesday,' Davie said. 'Match days are Sundays.'

'Oddly, I knew that.'

'Didn't think you were a fan.'

'I'm not. I was a Hibee when I was a kid, before match-fixing and doping ruined the sport.' The Enlightenment banned football soon after it came to power, preferring rugby. That was one of many unpopular decisions.

'You supported Hibernian?' Davie said in disgust.

'Don't tell me you're a Jambo. You're a rugby player.'

'Was. Knee's knackered, remember? Aye, I was a Jambo, still am. We lived up the road when I was a kid. Screw Hibs. Bunch of left-footers.'

'May I remind you that sectarianism was proscribed by the first Council, guardsman? And religion heavily discouraged. There can't be more than a few hundred Catholics in the city now.'

Davie pulled up by the south stand. 'You'd be surprised. Since freedom of religion was enacted a couple of years ago, organized religions are making quite a comeback.'

'I'd noticed. None of which explains why we're here.' I looked around. There were no other Guard or official vehicles present – only club vans. 'On our own.'

'Some of my men are inside dressed as groundsmen. You'll do as you are – citizen-issue donkey jacket as usual. I've got a full-length rain jacket.' He pulled it on after he got out.

'Is there an umbrella?' I asked forlornly.

Davie laughed and led me into the complex. A door was open but the only person around was a guy in a tracksuit who was obviously a guardsman. I can spot their air of authority no matter how much they try to disguise it.

'Come on,' Davie said, tossing me a maroon-and-white-striped umbrella. 'What, don't you want it?'

'Bit late. Haven't you got one in green and white?'

'What do you think?'

He opened a door, led me down some concrete steps and suddenly we were on the pitch. I remembered a dire Edinburgh derby I'd attended with my old man when I was about ten. Hibs got stuffed.

The seating in the stands was new and the stadium in surprisingly good nick. It had taken the Council long enough to realize that football was an effective opiate of the people, but they're making up for it now. There was even a sign for free pies above a stall.

Two men were standing under umbrellas like mine in the centre circle, garden forks resting against their hips. There was a large plastic box at their feet. I felt a tingle in my spine.

'What's in the box, Davie?'

'Wait and see.'

We squelched over the sodden grass, though it wasn't as bad as I'd been expecting. Surely the Recreation Directorate hadn't run to an efficient drainage system?

'Step back, guardsmen,' Davie ordered. He turned to me and watched as I pulled on a pair of the latex gloves I always carry in my back pocket. 'Never unprepared, Quint, eh?'

I raised the stump of my right forefinger at him, the rubber hanging down pathetically, then squatted and took hold of the opaque plastic box. A deep breath and I lifted it.

'What the . . .'

'You know what it is,' Davie said grimly.

'I do. A human heart, the arteries roughly severed but the parts of the exterior that are visible otherwise intact.'

'Aye. Pleased you signed up now?'

I looked up at him. 'I don't remember signing anything, but I will if you want me to. Right now.'

TWO

We were out in the open, as the person or persons who'd left the organ on the centre spot would have been. The rain had probably obscured the view from the buildings around, but someone could have seen what happened.

'We can't ask questions,' Davie said after a pair of crime-scene technicians, also disguised as groundsmen, had removed the heart and the turf below. 'Council orders. They're worried about publicity.'

'What if someone talks to the media?' There were quasi-free newspapers and radio stations in the city now.

'They're being monitored.'

'Of course.' There would be undercover auxiliaries in every news outlet.

'Who found it?'

'A groundsman, surprise, surprise. He was in before anyone else – the place didn't open till midday today – and he did the right thing.'

'Called the Guard. How do you know he didn't tell his boss first?'

'Because he's terrified. I've got him up in the castle. The recreation guardian's honorary chairman of the club – of all the clubs in the Edinburgh Premier League, of course – which helps.'

'It didn't occur to anyone to take the heart for examination?'

Davie grinned. 'We're not that useless without you. The medical guardian's had a look. Taking into account the ambient temperature, she couldn't be specific about how long it's been there or when it was removed from its host body. She recommended that it be left in situ for you.'

'Did she?' Sophia, the medical guardian, and I were on-off lovers, more on than off in the year since my long-term partner Katharine Kirkwood had illicitly left the city. 'Well, she knows how I work. It's still full of holes, and I don't mean the heart, jackass. Who had access to the stadium? Who witnessed the heart being left? Where's the body it came from? We need to talk to people.'

'The guardian's worried about drawing attention. As for witnesses, the feeling is that anyone who saw it being put on the centre circle will call it in.' Davie headed quickly back to the stand before I could point out how unlikely that was. Citizens still didn't trust the authorities. I looked around as I walked. There were several buildings whose top storeys overlooked the pitch. Were we being observed now?

'So why I am involved?' I asked, brushing water from my scalp.

'Come on, Quint. The city's opening up, tourism's back to the numbers we had before the Chinese crash, Edinburgh may become the capital of Scotland again. This is the last thing the Council needs.'

'And I'm the first thing?'

'Unlikely though that might seem. So where to?'

'Your place of work, I suppose, since I can't knock on doors here.'

'Your supposition is my command.'

Back in the 4×4, I turned to Davie. 'Is there anything you aren't telling me?'

'Yes. The medical directorate's recently started doing heart transplants.'

'Ha-ha.' The likelihood of the resource-starved infirmary being able to provide such complex surgery to the citizen body was minimal. Besides, Sophia would have told me. Or would she? 'You are joking?'

Davie glanced at me. 'Er, yes.'

'On second thoughts, let's go and see the medical guardian. It wouldn't be the first time people in the infirmary were up to no good.'

'No, it wouldn't,' Davie said ruefully, hitting the accelerator hard.

The infirmary is a Victorian building in what had been the university area in the southern centre of the city. Its towers and vanes give it a Gothic air, especially with the stone walls darkened by the rain. There are some more modern parts, not least a steel chimney pointing skywards like that of a first-generation steamship long run aground. There were crowds of citizens in the waiting areas even though it was early evening. Appointments were made until 9 p.m., meaning that riots by those needing treatment were avoided – and that the doctors and nurses were permanently exhausted. That went for the medical guardian too.

'Hello, Sophia McIlvanney,' I said as we were ushered into her office. I never miss an opportunity to use auxiliaries' surnames because I know how much it irritates them; they prefer the titles that make clear their superiority.

'Hello, Quint,' she replied, brushing back a strand of white-blonde hair. There was a time she'd been known as the Ice Queen, but she'd lost that quality for me. Among other things, sex is a great leveller. 'You're here on an affair of the heart.'

'I should be so lucky. But yes, if you want to put it that way.' I tried to avoid looking at the scar beneath her right eye. She caught me out, of course, and I felt my cheeks redden.

'Come on. I've got the pathologists waiting.'

Soon we were all gowned and masked up, even for the single organ. I was happy enough as the air in the morgue is always pungent.

'Go ahead,' Sophia said to her subordinates.

They leaned over the organ, which had been washed of blood either by the person who had cut it out or by the rain, and started speaking. I let the words flow over me – aorta, anterior interventricular branch, pulmonary veins, coronary sinus – waiting to pounce when something struck me. For a time nothing did. Then I heard 'serrated edge' and raised a hand.

'So a serrated blade was used to cut the arteries and so on?'

'That's right,' said the taller of the masked figures. 'Strange. Any professional would use a straight edge.'

'Though the cuts display a reasonable degree of medical knowledge,' said his short colleague.

'Reasonable meaning what?' I asked. 'City Guard medical orderly level?' Like all auxiliaries, they're issued with knives that have serrated blades.

Davie was looking at the ceiling, while Sophia's eyes narrowed.

'As far as I know, medical orderlies are not trained to remove hearts,' she said. 'Kindly suppress your customary suspicion of auxiliaries, citizen.'

'The person or persons who removed this heart were careful not to cut or otherwise damage the exterior,' the taller of the pathologists said. 'That suggests medical knowledge.'

'Did it come from a male or a female?' I asked, after they'd measured the organ.

'Male,' they said in unison.

'Fully developed,' put in Sophia. 'It's about twenty-five per cent larger than a female's.'

'Also, there's no evidence, at least externally, of aortic or venous disease,' said the shorter pathologist. 'So we're probably dealing with a young, healthy male, though that's subject to what we find when we open the organ up.'

After more talking to the microphone that hung above the table, the men looked at Sophia and she nodded.

'Cutting across aorta and aortic valve cusps,' the tall pathologist said.

I let the words roll over me again. This time nothing made me intervene.

'Subject to tissue and other tests, this heart belonged to a young man in good physical condition,' said the shorter doctor.

'Are there any tests that will show how long since it was removed?' I asked.

'To within a period of hours, yes,' Sophia said.

The tall pathologist raised a hand. 'My working hypothesis would be that it was removed within the last twenty-four hours, taking into account the freshness.'

'It couldn't have been frozen?'

He looked at me as if surprised by the question and then shook his head. 'The texture of the tissue suggests not.'

'Anything else we should know?' I said.

There wasn't. The donor had been young and healthy, which somehow made what had happened to him even more of a disgrace.

'Can you give me a lift to the Council meeting, commander?'

'Of course, guardian,' Davie said.

'Citizen Dalrymple's presence is required there as well,' Sophia continued.

'Brilliant,' I mumbled.

We went out into the infirmary yard, the rain having miraculously let up.

'What are you complaining about?' Davie said, under his breath. 'You'll find out more about what's going on.'

I laughed. 'That isn't the way it works, my friend. I'm usually the one whose lemon gets squeezed.'

Sophia gave me a curious look. Her knowledge of the blues was minimal and sexual innuendo wasn't her strong point.

We drove down to what had been the Scottish Parliament for four years spanning the millennium – before public anger at the greed and fecklessness of politicians brought the system down. Edinburgh was lucky. Most parliaments in Europe, including Westminster, were blown up or burned down. Organized crime had been taken over by its disorganized but extremely violent sibling and drugs wars erupted across Europe and the USA. Edinburgh got the Enlightenment and then the Council of City Guardians. There was little crime but even less joy.

'What do you think, Sophia?' I said as we approached the weather-stained relic of democracy near the ruins of Holyrood Palace. The monarchy had been a major target of the mob. Prince Charles should never have married that Colombian drugs heiress. 'Is Edinburgh going to be part of Scotland again?'

'That's up to the citizens,' she said, keeping her eyes off mine.

'Right. No tampering with the ballot boxes by the Council next year.'

'That's an outrageous thing to say, Quint.' Now I got the full benefit of her Medusa-stare. 'I could have the commander here lock you up.'

I laughed. 'Then what would your colleagues do about the heart at Heart of Midlothian?'

'Don't imagine you're indispensable, citizen.' She opened her door and got out. She might have been winding me up, but I couldn't be sure.

'What age are you?' Davie demanded.

'Too old to rock and roll, that's for sure.'

'Arsehole. Show guardians some fucking respect.'

'That, big man, is a two-way street.'

I left him behind and went into the building. It could do with some serious maintenance, but the Council claims it's directing all the resources it can to citizen facilities. But what about the Market District? No expense was being spared there. Still, Davie was right. My life would be much easier if I kowtowed to our lords and mistresses. Then again, someone had to stand guard over the guardians.

A guardswomen in full dress uniform opened the door to the main chamber for me. The fifteen guardians were in their seats in the semicircle, looking down at me.

'Citizen Dalrymple,' said the senior guardian, a gung-ho sociologist in his early forties, who was in charge of the Supply Directorate as well as being this year's numero uno. 'Welcome back.'

'Thanks, Fergus,' I said, taking in the disapproving faces above. 'Call me Quint.'

That was unlikely to happen, at least in Council. In theory everyone in the city can now be addressed by their first name, but you took your life in your hands if you called guardians what their parents had. The city's leaders still call each other by their titles, at least when there are citizens around.

Fergus Calder's smile took a hit, but he persevered. 'You have some thoughts to share?'

I shook my head. 'I was the last to know about this case, so I'll speak last. Tell me everything you know.'

There was a wave of tutting and harrumphing, then the public order guardian stood up. She was wearing the standard tweed jacket, but had gone native with a kilt in her clan tartan. Unfortunately the Barclays wear a yellow weave that blinds and nauseates in equal measure.

'Citizen Quint's involvement in this case has been ordered because it is potentially highly problematic.'

'How do you make that out, Guardian Doris?'

She did me the honour of ignoring that.

'Not only is the city expanding its international profile, but there must be no threat to the Scotland referendum next spring.'

Her colleagues nodded, their expressions serious.

The guardian gave me a glance that did not bode well. 'Although the senior guardian was made aware of the case from the start, this meeting is the first opportunity I have to brief you in full.'

Here we go, I thought. When things get tough, guardians keep information to themselves for as long as it takes to build bulwarks around their backsides.

'At eleven forty-five this morning I received a call on my personal mobile from a number that cannot be traced. The voice was muffled and I could not make out any accent, or even if it was male or female.'

I sat down on the chair that had belatedly been brought for me. I was going to let the guardian talk herself into a hole until I made any comment. That way she'd be desperate for help, and desperate guardians can be useful. Then again, they can also bite your head off.

'The caller said, "Tynecastle, the centre circle, there's a gift for you. Be discreet. I'm watching."'

'Is there a recording of the call?' the recreation guardian asked. Peter Stewart had been a fine athlete in his youth and was popular among citizens because he'd brought football back. His face was unusually pale and his hands were trembling.

Guardian Doris looked sheepish. 'I'm afraid not. It was over before I could react. But I sent Guard personnel disguised as ground staff immediately and the heart was found. The medical guardian visited and advised that the organ should be covered until the citizen here saw it. As subsequently happened.'

'One moment,' said the education guardian, a desiccated man in his fifties who was notorious for nitpicking. 'As I understand, the citizen didn't arrive at the football ground until after five p.m. What happened in the intervening period?'

Now the public order guardian looked bilious. 'I was in meetings with the senior guardian and the finance guardian,' she said. 'We had to make various decisions.'

'What decisions?' asked the education guardian, barely disguising his anger. 'An emergency Council meeting should have been called.'

'Calm down, Brian,' said the finance guardian, giving up on titles. He was wearing a grey suit that had definitely not been made in Edinburgh and a silk version of the black-and-white tie that only Council members are entitled to.

'Don't take that tone with me, Jack MacLean,' the education guardian barked.

'Colleagues,' the senior guardian said. 'There's an ordinary citizen present.'

I wondered how heated the debate would have got if I hadn't been there. MacLean was the thrusting type who brooked no opposition. He fancied himself as a captain of industry rather than a bureaucrat, which must have been frustrating for him considering how little industry there was in Edinburgh. Coal mines to keep the population warm, farms to feed the citizens and foreigners, tourism's great rewards – they were all controlled by other directorates. He was just a number-cruncher. Then again, frustration can be a hell of a motivator.

'Initial investigations in certain areas had to be instigated,' Guardian Doris said, speaking the stilted language her rank has always favoured.

'We checked the infirmary and all the city's clinics for the donor corpse,' Sophia put in.

The public order guardian gave her a grateful look. 'And the Guard has been put on full alert.'

'Discreetly,' said Jack MacLean.

'Indeed.'

'And has any such body been located?' said the education guardian, sticking to his guns.

'No.'

'I still don't understand why the finance guardian was involved.'

'Brian,' said the senior guardian, 'leave it, please. Anything that might affect the city's income is within Jack's purview. A human heart in the middle of a football pitch is unlikely to do the city's image much good, not least since, as of the season that's about to begin, tourists will be able to attend matches.' He caught Sophia's eye. 'The medical guardian has the floor.'

She ran through what the pathologists had found, then sat down.

The senior guardian's eyes were on me. 'Well, citizen, you've heard the whole story now. What have you to say?'

I leaned back in the chair and crossed my legs. 'It's the biggest cock-up I've come across in years, Fergus. The call wasn't recorded, I wasn't told about it till now and I wasn't involved with the case from the start. Plus it's been decided that potential witnesses aren't to be located.'

'Discretion, citizen,' Jack MacLean said.

'Sticking your heads in the sand, more like. So what if the bastard or bastards finds out there were witnesses? Are their hearts going to be cut out too?'

'Anything's possible,' said the senior guardian. 'We'll have to risk that.'

'Uh-huh. It's all about the city's image, eh?'

'Do you have anything positive to contribute?'

'How about this? Are you checking for missing persons? I've got several on my books we can start with.'

The public order guardian grabbed that like a drowning woman. 'We'll get on to that with you, citizen.'

'Any reports of unusual activities, particularly in the suburbs?' I asked.

'There are always plenty of those,' Guardian Doris said.

'Are you checking any premises where screams were heard or people seen being dragged in unconscious or struggling? I know the gangs do that all the time, but whoever's behind this could be using gang activity as cover. Or could even be in a gang.'

There was general shock and horror. Gangs were one of the city's enduring problems, but they'd never done anything as extreme as this.

The finance guardian gave me a disparaging look. 'Gang members are drunk or stoned most of the time. They couldn't cut a heart out without damaging it, never mind get it to Tynecastle unobserved.'

I smiled. 'Who said they were unobserved? And if you think gangs aren't capable of cutting out people's internal organs, ask your colleague Doris.'

'There was a wave of that about a year back,' she confirmed. 'We caught the citizens involved.'

'Eventually,' I said. 'Are they still locked up or have they been given a pat on the head and told to behave themselves?'

'Two are still in the castle dungeons.'

'Good. I'll be talking to them.'

'Anything you need, citizen?' the senior guardian asked.

'A mobile phone.' Only guardians and senior auxiliaries were provided with those. 'With all your and senior auxiliaries' numbers pre-loaded.'

'Of course.'

'A Council authorization giving me authority to question anyone, including guardians, and access to all premises in the city.'

He didn't look happy but he nodded.

'I also want City Guard Commander Bell 03, a.k.a. Davie Oliphant, to be seconded to me for the duration of the investigation.'

Guardian Doris gave that one the nod, though there was a second or two of reluctance.

'One last thing,' I said, looking at Jack MacLean. 'You're in charge of negotiating with representatives from other Scottish states and cities, aren't you?'

He looked anxious briefly, then rallied. 'That's correct, citizen.'

'I want access to them when they're in the city if I deem that necessary. Kindly provide me with a full list of scheduled visits.'

MacLean glanced at Fergus Calder. 'Very well.'

'Send it to the public order guardian.' I stood up.

'One moment, citizen,' the senior guardian said. 'The authorization we give you does not mean you can operate outside the City Regulations.'

'Of course not,' I replied dutifully.

If they believed that, they were fully paid up members of the Loch Ness Monster Is Alive and Well Society. Then again, maybe Nessie had made an appearance in the last three decades. How would we have known?

THREE

To my surprise, Davie was still in the 4×4 outside.

'Nothing to keep you busy, guardsman?'

'I knew you'd ask for me to be your sidekick.'

'My sidekick? What do you think this is? A mystery novel?'

'It's certainly a mystery.'

'That's true.' I told him about the call that had been made to his boss.

'I thought there was something going on,' he grumbled. 'Hang on, how did they get through to her? Guardians' numbers are restricted.'

'Good point. What a surprise – there's someone on the inside.'

'Oh aye,' he said, turning on to the Canongate. 'No doubt the heart-taker's an auxiliary.'

'Could well be.'

'Give it a rest, ya pillock. There are plenty devoted people in the barracks.'

'I know. It only takes a few rotten ones, though.'

He couldn't argue with that. We'd uncovered plenty of bent guardians and auxiliaries over the years. Which made me think of someone. Later.

Davie parked on the esplanade and we walked into the castle between the statues of Bruce and Wallace. It was a surprise they were still there. Brian Cowan, the education guardian, had gone even further than previous education guardians – the first of whom was my mother – in skewering what he regarded as the pernicious myths bedevilling Scottish history. Admittedly, Edinburgh's children were mainly taught the city's history but, with the referendum looming, Guardian Brian had initiated a policy to demolish ancient heroes. Wallace was a bandit, Bruce a thief and a murderer, the Stuarts were wasters, James VI and I a misogynist, the Covenanters religious fundamentalists, even the intellectual superstars of the eighteenth-century Enlightenment were bigots (especially those from outside Edinburgh), etc., etc. No one else on the Council seemed bothered by his actions – David Hume was still a hero to many of them – but maybe they were going to vote 'no' anyway. It might be that most of them would lose out if Scotland became a nation again.

'Are you with us, Quint?' Davie said, nudging me harder than was necessary.

'What? Just thinking. What are you going to vote in the referendum?'

He gave me a questioning look. 'What business is that of yours?'

I laughed. 'None, but I can still be nosy.'

'I suppose you're a nailed-down no.'

'Actually, I'm not. I haven't liked a lot of what the Council's done in the last twenty years, but people have generally benefited.'

'By still being alive and well.'

The cobblestones were slippery and I grabbed his arm. 'That was true about the early years. Without independence, the securing of the borders and the wiping out of the drugs gangs, people would have been massacred as happened in plenty of other cities. But austerity went on too long. Weekly sex sessions, thank God they've got rid of them. Then again, life-long education was a good thing. Not many people bother now it's voluntary.'

'Plus there's the big bad wolf factor.'

'What?'

'We haven't a clue what's waiting for us outside the city-line. OK, Glasgow seems to be a functioning democracy.'

'Is a functioning democracy,' I corrected. 'The ward representative idea came from there.'

'Aye, but remember the shenanigans their leader got up to in New Oxford.'

'True. We'll have to wait and see. There's oil in the north-west and that might change everything.'

'Makes you wonder why they're interested in our little tourist attraction.'

'The Bangkok of the North. It does make a lot of money.'

'It does, most of it tainted.' Davie always had a Calvinist streak about him, not that he ever attended church. He was a hard-line guardsman and probably would have been quite happy still on border patrol. Guard commanders don't get out much.

We reached the Public Order Directorate command centre in what had been the Great Hall. Guard personnel were looking at screens, hammering away on keyboards and talking into mouthpieces. The equipment was the most high-tech in the city, though it had been in operation for several years. There wasn't much technical surveillance of citizens. Instead, the twenty guard barracks across Edinburgh kept order in a hands-on fashion despite the recent loosening of regulations.

'Citizen.'

I turned to find that Guardian Doris had crept up behind me. Davie had gone to lean over an attractive red-haired guardswoman, as was his wont.

'I have your authorization and mobile phone. Perhaps you'd come to my office.'

'The commander's invited too,' I said, beckoning to Davie. 'There'll be no secrets in this team.'

She looked dubious, but let it go.

In her quarters in what was once the Governor's House, I got my goodies. The rain had started again and the view barely included Princes Street to the north.

'So, citizen, where do we go from here?' the guardian asked.

'Good question. Have you got your people checking out reports of screaming and the like?'

'Yes. There were several, and squads are on the way to check.'

'Discreetly.'

Spots of red appeared on her high-boned cheeks. 'The Council wants to follow the caller's instruction.'

'Why don't you tell Davie here about the call?' I was putting the squeeze on her, always a good idea with guardians.

Davie took the news with studied nonchalance, but I knew he was pissed off that he hadn't been told earlier.

'Right,' I said, 'I'll be talking to the gang bosses you've got under lock and key.' I fixed her with an iron stare. 'They are still under lock and key?'

'Yes, citizen,' the guardian said wearily.

'Good. Tell me what happened in the Council meeting after I left.'

'I can't—'

'I'm not interested in the bureaucratic bollocks you people sign off on every day. I'd like to know what was suggested about the symbolism of the heart.'

'How do you know . . .?' Guardian Doris broke off and sighed. 'I suppose it's obvious. Although not many of us are professors these days, we're still intellectual enough to debate ideas.' She went into a daydream.

'Who said what about the heart?' I prompted.

She came back to herself with a jerk. 'Oh, Brian Cowan gave us a lecture about William Wallace's heart having been burned in London when he was executed and Robert the Bruce's being taken on a crusade but ending up at Melrose Abbey.'

'Highly evocative,' I said, 'but what was his point?'

'I'm not sure. He went on about the people who were hung, drawn and quartered at the Old Tolbooth in Edinburgh too, and how their hearts were usually burned.'

'Everyone in the city and thousands of tourists know about that,' Davie said. 'Ever since the replica of the old jail was opened, there have been fake executions and mutilations staged every day.' He shook his head. 'It's disgusting.'

He had a point, but he'd also made a useful connection. The New Tolbooth was one of the most popular attractions in the city. Was the heart-remover making a reference to it? If so, it was pretty obscure. Or maybe not. The original Old Tolbooth stood on the

Royal Mile. When it was demolished in the early nineteenth century, a heart-shaped memorial of cobbles was left, traditionally spat on by Edinburgh folk. Sir Walter Scott's interminable novel *The Heart of Midlothian* had many scenes set in the prison, while the football club took its name from it. Was it a coincidence that the heart had been left on the centre spot at Tynecastle?

'The medical guardian spoke about the heart as being seen as the centre of the body and the seat of will in many cultures, while Plato said the mind was located in the heart as well as the emotions.'

'I wondered when Plato was going to appear.'

'Whereas the Roman physician Galen saw reason as being located in the brain and the emotions in the heart.'

'There's also a lot of religious iconography about the sacred heart,' Davie said, to my astonishment. 'There was a lecture about it in barracks a few weeks ago,' he said, by way of explanation. 'I found it quite interesting.'

'You're not a closet Christian, are you, commander?' the guardian said in an attempt at humour.

'No,' he replied gruffly. 'Though I could be if I wanted to.'

He was right. Earlier in the year, auxiliaries had been given the same freedom as ordinary citizens to join religious groups. In a city that had been officially atheist for three decades, very few of its servants did.

'Of course, the heart-remover might just be a psycho and we're reading too much into the symbolism,' I said, unconvinced. It's not exactly an easy organ to extract and care had been taken. Could there really be religious or symbolical dimensions?

'Right,' I said, changing the subject, 'what about the call you received? Why do you think you were given warning?'

Guardian Doris returned my gaze. 'So that we found the heart quickly.'

'I agree. Why would that be desirable?'

'So there wouldn't be a delay and—'

'Ordinary citizens wouldn't come across it,' interrupted Davie.

'Correct and correct,' I said. 'But there still remains the underlying motivation. The perpetrators – I doubt it's a one-man or woman show – want to make the Council jumpy, but not bring the city and its business to a standstill.'

The guardian looked at me. 'I tried to move quicker, but Fergus wouldn't let me.'

'He had to meet with the finance guardian. You think they know more about this than they're admitting?'

'I doubt they'd have acceded to my request to put you on the case if they had anything to hide.'

'Quint Dalrymple always gets his man,' said Davie.

'And woman,' I added, not amused by his ironic tone. I stood up. 'It's time I got to work. You monitor the squads in the field, guardian. We'll compare their lists of missing persons with mine.'

If Doris Barclay was unimpressed by my taking charge of the case, she didn't show it. What was etched on her thin face looked more like relief.

'See you later,' I said to Davie, as we exited the guardian's hang-out.

'What? Where are you going?'

I tapped the side of my nose. 'Somewhere your presence isn't required.'

'I'll give you a lift,' he offered, trying unsuccessfully to disguise his curiosity.

'No, thanks.' I headed off down the slope. 'Come to my place first thing in the morning.'

'Please.'

'That was an order.' I kept my eyes front and my lips pursed. Winding up Davie was risky but worth it – as long as you didn't laugh.

I turned on to Bank Street at the Deacon Brodie Visitor Centre and hailed one of the Council's recent innovations – a taxi. The vehicle was large, luxurious and meant only for tourists, though a flash of my Council authorization persuaded the driver. I told him to take me to Haymarket. On the way I wondered what deal the Finance Directorate had done with the Sri Lankan manufacturers. Free accommodation and hookers for life? I didn't know if the Sri Lankans' religion would permit that. In fact, all I knew about the island was that it had prospered after India went back to the collection of small states it had been before the British took over, apart from some which had gone Communist. Numerous civil wars had resulted.

'At least the rain's keeping off,' the driver said.

'Aye, but for how long?'

'Ah'd gie it five minutes,' he said and laughed.

He was wrong. The cats and dogs didn't start landing until I was a few minutes' walk from Tynecastle stadium. I decided to try the highest tenement first. The people on the top storey could definitely see over the top of the west stand. I pushed open the street door and felt a heavy hand on my shoulder. I looked round so quickly I almost ricked my neck.

'Fuck, Davie! Don't do that!'

He grinned. 'Thought you could get round me, eh? I'm not as thick as you think.'

'That would be difficult. And you even thought to change into civilian clothes. The moustache is a step too far, though.'

He twirled the ends of the stick-on. 'What was the name of that Belgian detective?'

'Poirot, Hercule, given plenty of help by his creator.'

'Aye, that's the one. "Zee little grey cells".'

'How little only you know. All right, since you're here, how do you want to do this?'

'I'll kick the doors in and you do the talking.'

'Remember what the caller said. Be discreet.'

'Never heard of it.'

'No, seriously. Knock lightly and keep your mouth shut.'

He nodded.

We went up the stairs to the top floor. There were four doors, one of them freshly painted and the others waiting for the Maintenance Department to appear. Given the financial limitations of the citizen-friendly policy, they might be there in five years.

There was no answer at two of the unpainted doors. The other was opened by a scared teenage girl who said her parents were on the night shift and she'd been at school all day. I told her not to open the door to strange men with moustaches and then went to the pristine pale blue one across the landing.

This time an elderly woman with her hair in a maroon-and-white scarf appeared, security chain on. I took a chance and said we worked for the football club.

'Come away in,' she said, taking off the chain and beaming as she ushered us in. 'Ma Tam was a great fan o' the Hairts. Ah wish he was here tae see them playin' again.' She shook her head. 'The cancer took him. What is it Ah can dae fir ye?'

'We're having a bit of a problem with the staff,' I lied, not feeling proud of myself. 'Some of them aren't coming in when they should and we wondered if you could help us.'

'Sit doon,' our hostess said, taking a bottle of Supply Directorate whisky from the dresser and filling three glasses. 'Here's tae Tam.'

It would have been churlish not to drink, even though citizen-issue whisky was not for the faint of throat, especially undiluted.

'Ahm Morag Oswald,' she said, sitting back in her chair.

I gave her a couple of names I'd made up on the spot and got to the point.

'What it is, one of our people says he was working on the pitch this morning but we have reason to believe he was at the Edlott stall in Haymarket.' Despite being implicated in a major case some years back, the Council's lottery is still in operation, though it's no longer compulsory.

'Och, we cannae be havin' that at Tynecastle,' Morag said. 'Ma Tam wid be horrified. He was doon the mines, ye ken. Voluntary, nae punishment details. Loved his work, ma Tam.' The original Council was strict about language, seeing the Edinburgh tongue as socially divisive. That policy has been softened now, but I had the feeling the old woman had never observed it much. Good for her. And good for her Tam. A lot of people had been so grateful to the Enlightenment for saving the city that they did the dirty jobs without being coerced.

I parted the thin curtains and looked out. The centre circle was visible, despite the rain and the dull evening light. Morag Oswald's chair was half turned towards the window.

'Whit time did ye say?'

'Late morning,' Davie said, then rapidly put his finger on his moustache to stabilize it.

'Say, after eleven,' I said, glaring at him.

'Aye, Ah wis here. Let me see . . .' The old woman took another slug of whisky. 'Ah remember. There wis someone oot on the pitch, even though it was raining fit tae drown a body.'

'And what was he doing?'

'That wis the strange thing aboot it. Carries a box oot there, puts it on the centre spot and then comes back.'

'One person.'

'Oh aye.'

'Did you see his face?'

'Ah did.' Morag smiled triumphantly. 'It wisnae a man, it wis a wummin. A young one, tae. Long blonde hair under her rain jacket and a fine pair o' lungs on her.'

I asked a few more questions but the answers didn't get us any further. There had been no sign of the woman outside the ground, which made me wonder how she'd made her getaway.

We left Morag Oswald to her whisky and memories of her Tam. She'd been a useful witness, but the idea that a young woman had deposited the heart didn't make me want to dance in the sodden street.

'Get some better glue for that lip slug,' I said as we got into the 4×4.

'I don't think I'll be using it again. Here, you're the master of disguise. You have it.'

I opened my window and threw the sticky object out. Davie didn't arrest me for wasting Public Order Directorate resources or littering. Maybe my luck was finally turning.

FOUR

'Why can't I come?' Davie demanded as we turned on to Heriot Row, still one of the most exclusive streets in the New Town.

'You know he doesn't like you.'

'And he likes you? How many times has he tried to terminate you with plenty of prejudice.'

'Just the once.'

'You're being generous.'

'Look, I've known him since we were kids. That still means something.'

'I hope so. Do you want me to wait?'

'No, go back to the castle and see if anything's turned up.'

'Shall I put out an all-barracks alert for a young blonde with a – quote – "fine pair of lungs"?'

I thought about that. With Edinburgh full of tourists from rich states around the world, several of them well populated by blondes, that would be the opposite of discreet. And with the locals now allowed to dye their hair, there was no shortage of unnatural blondes.

'No, it isn't enough to go on.'

'All right, Quint. You know best.'

'Irony doesn't become you, guardsman.'

'Your irony's too ironic for me.'

'Good night, idiot.' I got out of the vehicle and walked down the street. The trees in the park on the right blocked out most of the noise from the bars and clubs on North Castle Street. The dark stone of the well-kept houses on my left was grim, a reminder that the New Town had always been full of disquieting secrets. The man I was about to visit was privy to most of the contemporary ones, I was sure.

I rang the bell and mugged at the camera above the door. Only guardians and the most senior auxiliaries merit that level of security. There was a buzz and the door swung open.

'Well, well, the great Quintilian Dalrymple,' said the crumpled figure in the wheelchair a few yards away in the ornate entrance hall. 'I had a feeling you might turn up tonight. Though you might have rung ahead.'

'Though you might have not been at home, Billy.'

His laugh was a cackle the weird sisters would have been proud of.

'You do me an injustice.' His eyes narrowed. 'Not for the first time.'

I shook my head. 'Everything that happened to you was caused by your own actions.'

'You think?' Billy Geddes, former deputy finance guardian and demoted auxiliary – the latter a distinction we had in common – studied me for longer than I was comfortable with, then spun round and rolled away across the tiled floor. I followed him into a large, well-appointed room. The paintings on the walls were from the City Gallery, one of them a Degas that I've always been fond of.

'I heard you'd wormed your way back into favour, but I didn't realize how much. Even guardians only get the loan of a work of art.'

'Everything's changing, Quint, and for the better.'

I looked at his wizened face, the thin beard he favoured doing little to obscure the results of the injuries he'd sustained in 2020.

'And guess who's got a finger in every pie.'

More cackling. 'What's good for the city is good for me, Quint. Do you want a drink?' He was already pouring a large measure of a dark malt. I took it, but didn't drink – the bouquet was glorious but, as ever with anything to do with Billy, there was an underlying hint of corruption.

'What did you do to get this? Sell off the museum?'

'Come on,' he scoffed. 'You're an ignoramus when it comes to the modern world. Let me educate you.'

I leaned back in the red leather armchair. Billy's lectures were informative but there was more to them than that. It was only after giving them that he would open up. Sometimes.

'So, you know that Europe isn't in as much chaos as it has been?'

I shrugged. 'There are tourists from Provence and Aquitaine.'

'Well done,' he said with a mocking grin. 'They're examples of states that have finally done what we did – beaten off the drugs gangs. Of course, they also had the Muslim fundamentalists to deal with. Now their borders are secure and they've started trading again – wine, mainly, but they've got heavy industry going, even shipbuilding.'

'Who buys ships these days?'

'Good question. For decades world trade has been shafted by well-equipped raiders, thanks to what used to be the Russian Federation and is now back to Serf Central. Don't you just love oligarchs?'

'Not the ones who're in charge here.'

'The guardians aren't that kind of oligarch, you moron. They're a benevolent dictatorship.'

'Benevolent to you, maybe.'

Billy glared at me. 'You helped set the Council up, Quint. You like to play at being an ordinary citizen working for your peers, but you're still at the guardians' beck and call.'

I didn't rise to that. 'So who buys ships?' I repeated.

'People who want to move goods around the world. You see, there's one thing that survives nuclear and any other kind of meltdown.'

'Cockroaches?'

'I'm talking about trade, buying and selling—'

'Turning a profit.'

'You're not as dumb as you look, Quint.'

'But unregulated capitalism and feral banking were what landed us in the shit at the beginning of the century, weren't they?'

'Those and a large number of major criminals and ruthless religious lunatics. But my point is, trade still went on. It wasn't long after the last election that the Council realized the city needed tourist income to survive.'

'And now things are better around the world?'

'In some parts. States are still a lot smaller than they were – the last count I saw had fifty-seven of them in what used to be Canada, while the former USA has over a hundred, many of them hermetically sealed against outsiders for religious reasons. I heard that southern Florida and Cuba merged last year – main products, orange-flavoured rum and teenage-thigh-rolled cigars, choose your gender.'

'But with China and Russia in ruins, where are the big markets?'

'Australia, for a start. Or rather, ex-Australia. There are twenty-three states now, four of them for Aborigines only; Indonesia, finally rid of fundamentalists and very keen on exporting its natural resources; Japan, though the northern islands have been occupied by Russians escaping from the remains of their homeland. And South America – Brazil, Argentina and Chile are flying high, while Venezuela's still making the most of its oil.'

'Speaking of black gold, what about the Middle East? You don't see many Arab tourists these days.'

'Gone up in flames, mostly. The jihadists were only recently eradicated. Turkey's the regional superpower, though it's smaller than it used to be thanks to the Kurds setting up their own state.' He leaned forward, unable to contain his excitement. 'The potential is huge and we can be in at the start. Not just as a tourist attraction, but as the capital of a reunited Scotland. You wouldn't believe the resources this country has.'

'Oil in the Hebrides,' I said, hoping to take the wind from his sails.

'That, but there's been amazing progress in wave and wind-power technology in Inverness and Aberdeen. Those cities have taken over a lot of the neighbouring territories and erected ultra-efficient wind turbines on the high ground. They're ready to start exporting energy to Denmark and the German Federation. And that's not all. There's fishing, minerals, agriculture . . . this country is a gold mine.'

'We were always taught Scotland was a harsh land, that there was nothing without heavy industry. Except sheep.'

'That's bullshit now. For a start, we're decades ahead of most other countries, plus we've got some of the best-trained people in the world.'

'In Aberdeen and Inverness.'

'And Glasgow. Since the original Silicon Valley in California was carpet-bombed by Christian fundamentalists five years ago, the west of Scotland has become a world leader in digital processing and programming. Of course, Dundee is still an anarcho-syndicalist state and Stirling is run by ultra-feminists, but we can live without them.'

'I take it you'll be voting "yes" in the referendum.'

'Anyone with a brain cell will be doing that.' He groaned. 'Don't tell me, Quint. You're still loyal to the Enlightenment ideal of an independent Edinburgh after all you've been through. You're a DM, remember?'

I looked at the faded stamp on my right hand. Demoted citizens were rehabilitated a year ago, but there's still a stigma, at least among auxiliaries. That had made me want to get the letters re-inked in one of the many parlours that have opened since the Council made tattoos legal – thirty per cent of profits going to the Finance Directorate, of course. In the end I hadn't, partly because the Council's actions have been less objectionable recently.

'All right,' I said. 'Global capitalism is starting up again and everything's wonderful. Where's the catch?'

Billy looked puzzled. 'There is no catch.'

'You know what I'm investigating.'

'So?'

'Why are the senior guardian and the finance guardian so spooked by it, and don't tell me they're worried about the city's image. It goes deeper than that.'

'Why do you think I know?'

'Because you know everything that goes on in Edinburgh, Billy. What's your title now? Éminence Grise of the Finance Directorate? Extremely Private and Highly Rewarded Secretary to Jack MacLean? The Power Behind the Throne?'

'I'm a SPADE – Special Advisor, Executive. The only throne I know is the one I drag myself on to when I need to shit.'

'At least the great global leap forward doesn't seem to involve hereditary monarchies.'

He raised a twisted hand. 'Not in what used to be the UK, no. The Windsors who survived the break-up run a llama farm some-where in South America. But some of the successful African states have got kings again. The ones that had in effect been colonized by the Chinese for their minerals are now home free, selling to the highest bidder. Haven't you noticed black tourists in the city? A lot of them are businessmen.'

I waited for him to continue, but he didn't. Time to play hard football.

'You were there, weren't you?'

He glared at me. 'Talk sense, man.'

'This afternoon, when the senior and finance guardians met.'

He looked away, suddenly fascinated by the Degas nude.

'Billy, you need to be straight with me.' I knew that was a hope too far, but even tricky people are open to appeals for honesty – usually because it gives them the opportunity to be even trickier. But that's the kind of thing I can spot.

'All right. Yes, I was there.' He took a pull of whisky. 'In fact, it was on my insistence that you were assigned the case.'

'Am I supposed to say "thanks"?'

'Only if you feel like it.'

I didn't.

'You knew I'd come here, didn't you? Tell me what's going on.' I put my glass down on the Georgian side table with a thud. 'Or I'm hitting the road.'

'No . . . no, stay where you are, Quint.' He smiled, never a pretty sight. 'What's going on? That's what you're supposed to discover.'

I stood up.

'No . . . oh, for fuck's sake, sit down. I'll tell you what I know.'

'That'll make me swoon with joy'

'Arsehole. This human heart stunt. It isn't the first time it's happened.'

'What? In Edinburgh?'

'No, in Glasgow. And Inverness.'

'Wonderful. When?'

'A week ago at Celtic Park and three days ago at wherever Inverness Caley Thistle play – any idea?'

'Search me. When was I going to be told?'

'I just told you, didn't I? Jack and Fergus decided they wouldn't inform the rest of the Council. If you hadn't agreed to the public order guardian's summons, I'd have called you.'

'Why the hyper-secrecy? Besides, decisions to call up non-auxiliaries are supposed to be taken with full Council agreement.'

'You were at the meeting, weren't you? The guardians know you've been taken on.'

'But they don't know the full background. Is even Guardian Doris up to speed?'

'No, and you're not to tell her. Or your oversized guardsman friend.'

I let him think I agreed.

'What did the authorities in the other cities discover?'

'Nothing. No leads, no evidence – apart from healthy young male hearts – and no witnesses.'

'No one saw someone deposit a heart on the centre circle of the cities' main football clubs?'

'That's the same here, isn't it?'

I wasn't going to correct his assumption.

'Have they got any idea about motive?'

'Apparently not. And they haven't found anyone missing a heart either.'

I took out my mobile and called Davie.

'Get undercover surveillance teams into Easter Road and all the other football grounds in the city.'

'You think there could be more hearts?' he asked, the background noise of the command centre audible.

'No point in taking the chance.'

I cut the connection.

'Good move, Quint,' Billy said with a grin. 'You've still got it.'

'I could have done that nearly twelve hours ago if your bosses had bothered to tell me immediately.' I had a thought. 'How did they know about the hearts in the other cities?'

'How do you think? Jack and Fergus talk to their counterparts all the time.'

That was the second time he'd prioritized his boss's name over the senior guardian's name. Departmental loyalty or something more?

'How cosy. Shame it's against City Regulations about contact with the outside world.'

'I told you, Quint. Everything's changing.'

'To the extent that your guardian pals spend hours on the phone to non-locals before talking to their colleagues – and then not telling them the whole story? There are bound to be guardians who are against reunification.'

'Not for long.'

I gave him a heavy stare. 'What else do you know, Billy?'

'Nothing that's germane to this. Oh, and you're forbidden to make contact with the Glasgow and Inverness investigators.'

'How would I do that?'

'Carrier pigeon? In case you're interested, Hel Hyslop's in charge of the Glasgow police now.'

Another specimen I couldn't trust further than I could throw her, though that wouldn't be far.

'One more thing,' I said. 'Why's the heart business so important?'

He made the best of raising his shoulders. 'Someone's putting the screws on three of Scotland's major cities in the lead up to the referendum.'

'Hang on, are they voting on re-unification too?'

'Yes. There are different concepts of democracy, of course. I don't think the Lord of the Isles will be accepting "no" votes.'

'So this isn't just about Edinburgh.'

'No. Everything's connected now, Quint.'

That was all I got.

I left the house and walked home through a heavy drizzle, hoping to make some sense of what I'd learned. Waste of time.

I put together my files of missing people. There were only five, though two were young men whose hearts could have fitted the specification. I eventually got to sleep after listening to the blues on my decrepit headphones. The last song was the Reverend Gary Davis's 'Death Don't Have No Mercy', which may have been why my dreams weren't exactly sweet. I was haunted by the women I'd loved, their faces and bodies tantalizingly close, but disappearing as soon as I stretched out my arms. Caro, my first love, her eyes wide and unseeing as the rope tightened round her neck and squeezed her life away – she was killed on a drugs-gang raid I planned and led in 2015, and I got there just as she kicked out for the last time. Caro. Later I killed the bastard who throttled her and gave up on the Enlightenment. She wouldn't have liked that – we'd been strong supporters of the party since it started – but I hope that remembering her, even in my dreams, meant something to her soul, wherever it was wandering. Then Katharine, her green eyes and full lips almost taunting me. We'd been together, on and off, for ten years, but she never fully opened up. She'd suffered terribly at the hands of drugs-gang members outside the city and coped with that by being even more spiky and contrarian than I was. She had secrets, the last of which were the preparations she'd made to cross the city line. It wasn't the first time she'd done that – her feelings for the Council were antagonistic, and more recently she'd been working with people she thought had been let down by the system. Something had obviously driven her to desert them as well as me. We'd been distant for months before, but we still spent the night together occasionally. It wasn't enough and I knew it, but Katharine wouldn't let me closer. Maybe she thought Caro still meant more to me. She'd been angry about my original dalliance with Sophia, though it had started when Katharine was out of the city and hadn't picked up again till after she left, whatever she might have imagined.

Then another figure came out of the mist – a younger woman. Her hair was long and blonde, and in her hands she was carrying a human heart covered in blood. As she got closer, I saw it was still beating . . .

The pounding on the door was a welcome release.

FIVE

'Croissant, coffee and . . . no banana.' Davie tried to look apologetic. 'Bananas are off today. But I got you a nice pear.'

I had slumped on the sofa.

'What's the matter with you?' he demanded. 'Big case, no clues, only you can solve it . . . the city's your mussel.'

'Dreamed about my women,' I mumbled.

'You don't want to do that,' he said, putting my breakfast on the table.

'Besides, plenty more citizens in the, well, not in the sea obviously . . .'

I gave him the Katharine Kirkwood memorial glare. She and Davie used to get on worse than Mary, Queen of Scots and the English cousin who chopped her head off.

'By "no clues" I take it you mean the Guard sweep squads haven't picked up anything.'

'Correct.'

'What are you looking so happy about?'

'At least there weren't any more hearts at the city's football grounds. We've even checked all the schools.'

I sipped my coffee without screwing up my face. I still hadn't got used to that. 'I suppose that's something. Get your Herculean brain round this.' I told him about the hearts in Glasgow and Inverness.

'I don't understand,' he said.

'Join the club.'

'No, I mean how does the former Heriot 07 know about the other cities?' Davie had never forgiven Billy for his egregious scheming and avoided using his name.

'It seems that Fergus Calder and Jack MacLean are in frequent touch with them.'

'Does the Council know about that?'

'I don't know. Let's keep it that way for the time being.'

'Who am I going to tell?'

'The public order guardian? Speaking of Doris, I think we'd better not tell her about the blonde woman at Tynecastle either. It'll just complicate things.'

Davie looked at me suspiciously. 'I'm only seconded to you, Quint. My loyalties are still with the directorate.'

I bit into the pear. It was surprisingly juicy, which made me wonder where it came from. One of Billy's deals with some foreign state? As far as I knew, the Agriculture Directorate didn't run to fruit trees. Then again, where did the bananas come from? Had global warming turned Aquitaine into a banana republic?

'Your loyalties lie with me, my friend, and have done for thirteen years. Think how much I've taught you. I remember how keen you were to learn from the master when you first ran up those stairs.'

That shut him up for a few moments.

'What are we doing today?' he asked, making a move for my croissant.

'Leave that alone. How many have you already had?'

He muttered something.

'What?'

'Seven.'

'Right, I'm reporting you to your boss.'

'Like she'd care.'

'Well, let's cheer her up. Answer your own question.'

'Those scumbag drugs-gang bosses in the dungeons.'

'Bullseye.'

When we got to the castle, we compared my list of missing people with the Guard's, the latter being considerably larger. Only one of mine – not the young men – was repeated. Davie got squads sent to the young men's houses. There wasn't time for my velvet-glove approach.

A quarter of an hour later we were going down the slippery steps that led to Edinburgh's only remaining prison. It was packed, though there were only twenty cells. The Guard personnel assigned to the dungeons were volunteers who had substantial experience on the city line or the border – the only places where firearms were issued. Here they had to make do with truncheons, although they also had their standard-issue auxiliary knives.

'Citizen Dalrymple,' said the burly guardsman at the bottom of the steps. 'You'll have to share a cell, I'm afraid.'

'Very funny, Rab.' I knew him of old. He was one of many Guard members who thought I was an insult to the Enlightenment. Which, to be fair, much of the time I was. I turned to Davie. 'What are the guys we want to see called?'

'Jackson "Swallow Ma Pish" Greig and "Muckle" Anthony Robertson.'

'Yellow Jacko and Muckle Tony,' put in Guardsman Rab.

I smiled. 'That'll be a help. We don't want to antagonize them by getting their names wrong.'

'Yes, we do,' said Davie.

'This way.' Rab – Raeburn 97 – led us down a long passage with iron doors on either side. 'We keep them away from each other.'

'So they don't plot and scheme?' I asked.

He laughed. 'No chance. They hate each other.'

That could be useful.

'Right,' said Rab. 'This is Yellow Jacko's abode.' He inserted and turned a key that looked like it dated from the eighteenth-century Enlightenment. 'Visitors, you piece of piss!' He turned to Davie. 'Keep a hand on your knife. He's a serious head-banger.'

'I've read his file.'

'Have you?' I said. 'Thanks for the briefing.'

'Guard Eyes Only.'

I jabbed my elbow into his midriff, where it encountered firm layers of muscle.

'Sit down, Citizen Greig,' I said.

'Fuck you.'

Davie went over quickly and hit him in the abdomen. The prisoner obviously didn't work out like he did. When he'd caught his breath, we started again.

'What's he in for?' I asked Davie.

'Seven counts of murder, one of running a drugs gang, three of crossing the city line, seventeen of grievous bodily harm and one of possession of firearms.'

'Ya fuckers, where are ma Uzis?' the skinny, bald figure on the bed said hoarsely.

'Don't worry,' Davie said, 'the Guard's making good use of them. Baltic Barracks in Leith has got them. That's your old territory, isn't it, shitebag?'

'Drink ma pish.'

'No today, thanks,' I said, obviously having been allocated the role of good interrogator. 'Citizen Greig, we'd like to ask you some questions.'

'Drink ma—'

'Boring,' Davie said, going over to the covered bucket in the corner. 'Fancy consuming the contents of this?'

'Ye cannae dae that!'

'I think you'll find he can,' I said emolliently. 'How about a few answers? It won't take long. Or it'll take all day and you'll have the taste of your own urine in your mouth.'

'That's not all that's in here,' Davie said.

'Splendid. So what do you say, Jacko.'

'Yous fuckers dinnae get tae call me that.'

'I'm sorry – Yellow.'

'Fu—' The prisoner broke off as Davie stepped towards him. 'Whit is it ye want?'

'Have you ever cut someone's heart out?'

'Nuh.'

'He cut a thirteen-year-old boy's hands off,' Davie supplied.

I swallowed the wave of bile that rose in my throat. 'Do you know of anyone else in the gangs who cut out a heart?'

'Aye. That cunt Muckle Tony.'

Davie nodded. 'After Pish here sent a young woman to infiltrate Robertson's gang, the Leith Lancers.'

'Cut off her airms and legs tae, the bastard,' Grieg said, shaking his head so his long greasy hair obscured his face.

I glanced at Davie. 'Are we in the right place?'

'Possibly not.'

We got up and headed for the door.

'Hey, whit aboot me? I want a favour for talkin'.'

Davie put the bucket down as Rab opened up. 'The favour is you aren't sitting with your own turds for headwear.'

'That was short and sweet,' Guardsman Rab said as he led us further down the poorly lit passage.

'Long enough for me,' I said. 'How do you live with the stench down here?'

'Fuckers like these killed guardsmen and women, citizen. Smelling them rot is a privilege.'

'Uh-huh.' I was glad Rab wasn't on the streets, but he was right. The drugs gangs that had grown in strength after the Council's relaxing of the regulations were vicious, though less than their earlier counterparts. So far.

He stopped at the last cell on the right and hit the door with his truncheon.

'Guess what, psycho, you've got visitors.'

There was no reply.

Rab looked through the spyhole. 'Fuck!' He fumbled with the key and got the door open.

Before us a gargantuan flabby man was slumped to the floor under the window, a strip of material round his neck. He had managed to break the glass and loop the ligature round one of the external bars. The ripped remains of a shirt lay on the floor beside his bare feet. He must have bent his knees and pulled downwards, which suggested determination.

'That glass is supposed to be unbreakable,' Rab said, his eyes wide.

Davie touched the hanged man's neck. 'No pulse and he's cold. He did this some hours ago, I'd guess.'

'When did you last check on him?' I asked the guardsman.

'They don't get breakfast, so it would have been the night warden at midnight. I saw the log when I came in.'

'All right, Rab. Go and call it in.'

After he'd left, I turned to Davie. 'Search the body. I'll take the cell.'

'What are we looking for?'

'Anything that might explain why he did this, now of all times.'

We looked everywhere, which didn't take long. There was a concrete bed built into the wall, a latrine bucket – empty – and a pile of books on the floor. It seemed that the Education Directorate had sway even in the dungeons. Apart from the *City Regulations*, the tomes ranged from *Free City – The History of Edinburgh*, *Why Scotland Failed*, *The Enlightenment: How Edinburgh Survived the Global Crisis* to the collected stories of Robert Louis Stevenson. I took them all to look at later.

'Nothing in his pockets?'

Davie shook his head.

'How about his rectum?'

'He crapped himself. No suicide note or anything else that I can see.'

'Thanks for checking.'

Davie grimaced. 'I can't get into his mouth. Rigor's set in.'

'Sophia's people can check that. I'll make sure I'm present.'

'Aye,' Davie said. 'What do you think? The only person in the city to have cut out a heart commits suicide the night after the heart was left at Tynecastle. Coincidence?'

'We don't believe in coincidences, do we, guardsman?'

'No, we definitely don't.'

I got out of the way as a team of Guard personnel arrived with a stretcher.

'He's going to the infirmary,' I said, flashing my authorization. 'And I'm coming with you.'

Then I called Sophia and asked her to tell the pathologists we were on our way.

'Well, well,' I said. 'Murder, not suicide.' Davie was already trying to locate the warden who'd been on the night shift at the dungeons.

'Definitely,' said the tall pathologist. 'The bruising above his knees was made by hands that pulled him downwards. You can see the distinct marks of fingertips.'

'How come he didn't resist? He was a gang boss, after all.'

'Good question,' said the short pathologist. 'We'll have to wait for the toxicology report. Maybe he was drugged.'

I shook my head. 'If he was drugged, the murderer wouldn't have needed to pull him. He'd have been suffocated by his own weight.'

'Maybe he – or she – wanted to be sure,' said Sophia.

'Wanted to make sure Muckle Tony didn't survive,' I said.

'That's your department, Quint,' she said.

'Shame there wasn't anything up his nose or down his throat.'

The medical guardian looked at me coolly. 'This was a human being.'

'A multiple murderer who removed a young woman's heart, arms and legs.'

'Oh. Come with me, Quint,' she said, turning on her heel.

I went after her and we ended up in her office with the door closed.

'How can an incarcerated drugs-gang leader's death have anything to do with what was found yesterday?' she asked, from behind her desk.

'I don't know if it has,' I said, sitting down and putting my boots on the desk.

'Off!' she said firmly, as I'd hoped.

'Trousers?'

'Grow up, Quint.'

'Speaking of which, how's Maisie?'

Sophia was the first guardian in office to have had a child, a sweet but precocious six-year-old whose idea of fun was looking at anatomy books.

'Her manners are a lot better than yours.'

'Maybe I could come round and see you both. When this case is over, of course.'

'These cases can take a long time, Quint.'

'Not if I can help it.' I stood up and leaned over to kiss her.

'Finish the case,' she said after our tongues had reconnoitred thoroughly.

'I'm on a promise, right?'

She sighed, but there was a smile on her lips when I left.

Davie picked me up outside the infirmary.

'Hume 481, the night warden, has disappeared.'

'One of your lot. Do you know him?'

'Of course. He's thirty, has a spotless record, and has done five tours on the city line. After the last one ended a month ago he asked to be put on dungeon duty.'

'Interesting. What's his name?'

'Michael Campbell,' he replied. 'I presume we're going to the castle.'

'No, we're going to your barracks.'

'You'd better not stir things up there.'

'No, no, I'll just let the usual complement of dirty auxiliaries get on with ripping off the city.'

The rain came on again, stair rods from heaven.

'We don't have dirty auxiliaries in Hume,' Davie said, his brow furrowed.

'Let's see about that.'

Ten minutes later we were at the barracks, the traffic confined to buses and taxis, and citizens on bikes. It was in St Leonards, to the south-east of the centre, in a block that had housed a police station in pre-Enlightenment times. It was an eyesore, but Hume personnel were renowned for sticking together, as if the lack of a decent barracks made their communal spirit stronger.

Davie led me in, nodding at auxiliaries. He'd been based at the castle for years, but he still turned out to support the Hume rugby team. The barracks commander's office was on the first floor.

'A pleasure, Citizen Quint,' Hume 01 said, getting up from behind his desk. 'I'm a great admirer of your work.'

I glanced at Davie, who must have been aware of that but hadn't bothered to tell me. Senior auxiliaries who approve of what I do are as rare as bedbugs in a tourist hotel.

I nodded to the heavily built commander. The Hume canteen had a reputation for big servings and there was no shortage of large personnel.

'Call me Stew,' he said, touching his badge. His full name was Stewart MacBride.

'Call me Quint,' I replied, 'without the citizen.' No way was I calling him by his first name. There weren't many auxiliaries I was on friendly terms with and I didn't even know this one. Besides, I was about to get up his nose.

'Michael Campbell. Why's he bolted?'

The commander immediately took the huff. 'We don't know he's done any such thing. He could have been in an accident, he could have taken ill, he could have—'

'Used his knowledge of the city line to cross it.'

'That's a highly offensive suggestion.'

I shrugged. 'Call the infirmary and the control centre, Hume 253.'

Davie looked happier being addressed that way. A few minutes later he shook his head. 'No reports of Mike in the system.'

'I need to see his file,' I said to Stew.

That brought about the usual display of reluctance, but he handed it over before I had to flash my authorization. I started turning the pages.

'Excellent physical fitness . . . commendations for bravery . . . no blots on his disciplinary record . . . heterosexual, not in a long-standing relationship . . . intelligence level B2 . . . member of the barracks athletics team, long jump and pole vault. Interesting combination.' I looked up. 'Anything you want to add?'

The commander shook his head.

I kept going, stopping when I reached the Family page. Six months ago the Council decided to allow auxiliaries to have monthly contact with their relatives, something that had been banned before to ensure their primary loyalty was to the city.

'I see he didn't miss a visit to his parents, even when he was on border duty.'

'I believe that's the case.'

'John and Val Campbell, 15 Wardie Road.' I looked at Davie. 'What's the nearest barracks? Scott?'

He nodded.

'Get them to send a patrol round right away.'

'You think he might be there?' the commander asked. 'We checked a couple of hours ago. He wasn't, but they were. Everything was fine.'

'You didn't think to leave anyone with them?'

'No. Frankly, I think the idea of 481 being up to no good is ridiculous.'

'I'll convey that to the Council this evening.'

He looked like a barracuda had attached itself to his backside.

'There's a patrol round the corner,' Davie said. 'They're on their way.'

We waited, not for long.

'No one there,' he said. 'And the front door was open.'

'Any damage, blood?'

He asked.

'No.'

'Any sign of them having packed clothes?' Citizens aren't issued with suitcases because there's nowhere for them to go. 'Hangers on the floor by the wardrobe, that kind of thing?'

Again there was a pause after he asked the question.

'No.'

'Get them to ask the neighbours if they saw the Campbells leave and call you back.' The likelihood of citizens helping the Guard wasn't great, but with the relaxing of regulations you never knew.

I caught the commander's eye. 'Are you a hundred per cent sure there isn't anything you want to tell me about missing Mike? You and I both know that personnel reports don't tell the whole story.' I glanced at Davie. 'How about you?'

He shook his head, but Hume 01 sat stiller than a statue.

'There is one thing,' he said eventually. 'His post commander on the border told me unofficially that 481 crossed the line during his last tour.'

'When was that?'

'Three days before he finished – June the twenty-seventh.'

'Then he had a week off and started his spell in the dungeons.'

'Correct.'

'Why wasn't it noted on his record?'

'He told the commander that he wanted to pick brambles. You know how early they come nowadays.'

'Pick brambles?' I said, astonished. 'And the leader bought it?'

'Apparently he came back with a whole rucksack full.'

And what else, I wondered.

SIX

The Scott patrol called Davie as we arrived on the esplanade. I spoke to them.

'There's no sign of a rushed departure, citizen,' said the guardswoman. 'We've checked the clothing in the wardrobe and chest of drawers. All that's missing is what they'd have been wearing.'

That's one of the few advantages of the Supply Directorate. All citizens are issued with a standard number of shirts, sweaters, trousers etc., so it was possible to see if anything was missing. Of course, there was the black market but it was more directed towards drugs, cigarettes and jewellery, all still banned though not, of course, to tourists.

'What about the neighbours?'

'Nobody saw anything. To be fair, most people are at work. Do you want us to haul some of them in?'

'What, old ladies and the like?'

'Em, yes.'

'Em, no. Get your vehicle picked up and take up positions in the house. You never know, parents and son might just be out for a walk.' I cut the connection and gave the phone back to Davie.

'What now?'

'We need to do some research into Muckle Tony Robertson's gang. If it's still active, we need to nail the lot of them and squeeze their nuts.'

'Rather you than me. The Leith Lancers do what they like, with very sharp instruments.'

'Could Yellow Jacko have had him killed?' The Lancers and the Pish had been sworn enemies for years.

'His people might have got to the night warden – threatened to take a knife to his parents.'

He was right, but it wasn't a pleasant thought.

We walked up to the command centre. I was hoping Guardian Doris wouldn't be around – there was a lot I either had to tell her or keep quiet about. There was no sign of her. Davie sat down in front of a terminal and hammered at the keyboard.

'Shite,' he said after a few minutes.

'As in?'

'As in the fuckers are all either dead or have disappeared, no doubt over the city line.'

'How many were there?'

'That we know of? Seven, including two women.' He called up the relevant mug shots.

'At least neither of them has long blonde hair.'

'Could be a wig.'

He was right about that.

'Let's have a look at Yellow Jacko's crew.'

'The Portobello Pish.'

'They've been around for years.'

'Aye. They're still operating on their home territory. Shall we go and rattle their cages?'

'Maybe later. Let's have a look at their faces.'

Four men with threatening expressions appeared, then one woman with short red hair, a yellow star tattooed on her forehead and a ring through her left nostril.

'Mavis "Maybe Not" Forbes,' Davie said, shaking his head. 'I nailed her once. She nearly had my eyes out – nails like eagle's claws.'

'I think we'd better have another chat with Jacko Greig.'

'I think not, Citizen Quint.'

I turned and there was the public order guardian, her face greyer than a citizen-issue sausage.

'He's in the infirmary. Can you explain that, commander?'

Davie had stood up. 'Yes, guardian. He came at us and I had to use restraining force.'

'His small intestine is ruptured.'

'Ah.' Davie bowed his head.

'Ah, indeed. Citizen, come with me.'

I followed her to a meeting room off the command centre.

'Progress report, please.'

I confirmed that Davie had told the truth about Yellow Jacko – that scumbag deserved everything he got. She already knew about Muckle Tony's supposed suicide and Hume 481's disappearance – there was still no sign of him or his parents, she said.

'There must be more, Quint,' she said, dropping my rank at last.

'There is, Doris,' I said, returning the favour. 'Are you sure you want to know it?'

She smoothed back her lank hair. 'Only if it directly concerns this directorate.'

I could see what she was doing. As a recently elevated guardian, she was still establishing her authority over her own patch. Playing high politics with the likes of Jack MacLean was well beyond her.

'All right. The heart was put on the centre circle at Tynecastle by a young woman with long blonde hair.'

'How did you—?' She broke off, raising a hand. 'I don't want to know, but I hope you were discreet.'

'I think so.'

'We can hardly go through the entire citizen roll compiling a list of young blondes. There must be thousands now.'

'That was my thought.'

'And now you're looking at the gangs.'

'The Portobello Pish are still strutting around on the northern shore. I have a feeling that there'll be Leith Lancers in action too.'

'Do you really think common criminals would carefully cut out a heart?'

'They might have been operating under instructions.'

'From whom?'

I raised my shoulders.

'No one in Edinburgh would do something so calculatedly savage.'

I left that highly contentious assertion unanswered, though the hearts in Glasgow and Inverness suggested she might have been right – was there a single individual behind all three extractions? I wasn't going to tell her about the hearts in the other cities though – not yet. Foreign affairs weren't her concern and besides, I had plans for that information.

'There's something else,' the guardian said. 'Alec Ferries, the Heart of Midlothian manager, has disappeared. The recreation guardian just told me. Apparently he hasn't been seen since last night. He lives alone.'

There was a heavy knock before I could respond and Davie's head appeared.

'Excuse me, guardian. A male body's been found in the Union Canal by the Boroughmuir playing fields.'

'Heart missing?' I asked.

'No,' he said emphatically. 'Head.'

The rain had slackened, but the streets were still treacherous. We were there in ten minutes, lights flashing but no siren – the Council doesn't like to scare the tourists. Davie might have given a few blasts, but Guardian Doris was in the back seat. A couple of Guard vehicles were already on scene, paramedics lifting a sodden corpse on to a tarpaulin. I saw the rubber-covered heads of three divers in the canal. The water level was high and the flow rapid. I heard a quick blast of 'When the Levee Breaks', Bonham's drums thundering and Plant's harp screaming. What Memphis Minnie would have made of it, only the god or devil of blues knows.

This time I managed to grab a Guard-issue rain-jacket. I went over to the body, casting an eye over the surroundings. The grass was sodden and footprints would be hard to pick out.

'Male, citizen-issue clothing, no ID,' said the guardsman in charge. 'And no—'

'We can see that,' I interjected. 'Who found him?'

'Her.' The guardsman pointed at a middle-aged citizen holding an umbrella in one hand and the lead of a small black dog in the other. Pets were another of the Council's recent innovations. In the height of the drugs wars, cats and dogs had been eaten by the starving citizenry. In the years of austerity that followed, nothing could be spared to feed the few animals that had lain low.

I went over and asked her name.

'Ann Muir,' she said, shivering.

'What did you see, Ann?'

'That . . . horror,' she said, pointing at the body, which was now covered by a transparent plastic sheet. 'It was stuck against the side over there.'

I made out a broken wooden prop that was projecting into the flow.

'Did you see anyone else?'

'Anyone alive, you mean?' She glared at me as if I was responsible.

I nodded.

'No, but with the rain like it is . . .'

'Do you often see people here?'

'No. It's usually just me and Bobby.'

The dog was pulling at the lead, showing extreme interest in the corpse.

'Go with the guardswoman and make your report,' I said, patting her on the shoulder. 'Then get out of those wet clothes.'

Her head jerked back as if I was propositioning her. I wondered how she'd coped with the compulsory sex sessions. Not well, I hazarded. Another triumph for the Council.

I went back to the guardsman. 'Was the body fixed to that piece of wood or had it just been caught by it?'

'It wasn't tied on or anything. I'm thinking it floated down and bumped into it.'

'Which means we've no idea where it was dumped.'

'Looks that way, citizen. The divers are looking for the head, but with this current it could be anywhere.'

'Let's get the body to the morgue,' I said to the paramedics.

'I agree,' said Sophia, who had just arrived. 'There's not much we can do here except certify death.'

I went over to Davie. 'Get a squad to comb the playing fields.'

'That's already happening. We might be lucky.'

'Aye,' I said, looking up at the grey heavens. 'And bacon rolls might fly.'

In the morgue Tall and Short were busy, removing clothing, scraping beneath fingernails, taking photos and so on.

I led Sophia to a corner.

'You'll have heard about a prisoner from the dungeons being brought in?'

'The live one, you mean. What was he known as? Yellow—'

'Jacko.'

'Yes. He's out of surgery.'

'And?'

'He had a heart attack when he was in the recovery room. The chief cardiologist says he's unlikely to survive.'

'Fuck.'

'You needed him?'

'It would have been good to have another conversation with him.'

'I'll let you know if there's any change. Oh, and regarding the dead one.'

'Muckle Tony Robertson.'

She nodded. 'There were significant traces of flunitrazepam.'

'What's that?'

'In the old days it was used as a date-rape drug. It was slipped into drinks and people woke up remembering nothing, having been sexually assaulted or robbed. More to the point, it's not available in the city and never has been.'

'So someone brought it over the line.'

Sophia nodded. 'I don't think our drugs gangs are up to manufacturing it.'

'Guardian?' called the tall pathologist.

I followed Sophia over. The body was naked and the neck was a mass of tattered skin and roughly severed muscle, arteries and veins. At least there was no blood.

'As you can see, the head was removed with a jagged instrument.'

'I suggest a wood saw,' put in the short pathologist, getting an irritated look from his colleague.

That conjured up a horrific image. Chopping someone's head off with an axe was bad enough, but sawing would have taken time and caused terrible pain. 'Very different from the blade used to extract the heart,' I said.

Tall and Short nodded, as did Sophia.

'What about the rest of the body?'

'As you can see, the hands have recent abrasions,' said Short. 'Other than that, there is no external damage.'

I looked at the corpse. 'What do you think, around six feet tall?'

'I'd say so,' said Tall, this time beating his colleague to it.

'And I calculate his weight, head attached, at around thirteen stone,' said Short.

'He looks well fed enough,' I observed.

'Yes, there's impressive muscle development on the upper arms and thighs.'

I looked at the hands again. 'I wonder how recent some of these abrasions are. The nails are cracked too. A manual labourer, I'd say.'

'Yes,' concurred Tall and Short.

I went over to the nearest table and examined the clothing. The shirt, underpants and trousers were standard citizen-issue, as were the boots, which were scratched and worn. The dead man took a size ten. His pockets were empty, as the guardsman at the scene had said. I felt round the collar of the donkey jacket, my latex-covered fingers running over the rough material. Nothing. Then I tried the sleeves – nothing. All that was left were the bottom seams. Citizens sometimes sewed valuables in there. Not this one.

I nodded at Sophia, stripped off my gloves and gown and went out of the morgue.

Davie was waiting in the corridor, having sent the dead man's fingerprints to the castle.

'We have his identity,' he said, opening his notebook. 'Grant Brown, 12 Grange Terrace. He worked for the Housing Directorate as a builder. His record's clean.'

'Family?'

'Parents are dead. No record of a long-term relationship. He's hetero.'

'We'd better get over to his home.'

My mobile rang as we reached the infirmary's entrance hall.

'Citizen Dalrymple, this is the senior guardian. Come to my office immediately.'

I groaned. 'Can't it wait till the Council meeting? It's only a couple of hours from now.'

'No.' The connection was cut.

I was tempted to ignore the call, but decided to play along with the guardians – maybe they'd let something drop without realizing. Davie went off to the headless man's place with an attractive guardswoman, so he was happy.

I got a guardsman to drive me down the Royal Mile. The senior guardian's office was in the former Scottish parliament, behind the Council chamber.

'Ah, there you are, Quint,' Fergus Calder said, suddenly my best friend.

Jack MacLean was lounging in an armchair and didn't bother to get up. He gave me a languid wave and a smile he thought was welcoming. Then Billy Geddes rolled forward, his eyes cold and his mouth twisted.

'The three musketeers,' I said, looking around. 'Though you seem to have mislaid your peashooters.'

'And one of our citizens has mislaid his head,' said the finance guardian. 'Report, please.'

I glanced at Calder, trying to work out who was really the head honcho. He seemed unperturbed. I told them the little we'd so far discovered about Grant Brown.

'And as far as you know,' said the senior guardian, 'there's no connection between the heart and head cases.'

I narrowed my eyes. 'That isn't the sort of inference I draw. Obviously there are differences in the modus operandi, but we're still looking at missing body parts.'

'Is there some kind of mind–body question being raised?' Calder asked. 'Are the soul, the mind, the seat of the emotions in the head or the heart?'

There could well have been some such subtext, but I wasn't going to indulge that kind of thinking. For a start, there wasn't any evidence.

'No idea, Fergus,' I said, upping the ante. 'According to your friend Billy here, all that matters is global trade.'

Jack MacLean frowned. 'You have a problem with that?'

'I like a banana first thing in the morning as much as the next citizen, but not if it leads to murder and mutilation.'

'Supply Directorate bananas are sourced from cooperatives in Guatemala.'

'Great. How about the coffee?'

'We're getting off the point here, Quint,' Calder said with a nervous smile. 'I understand a guardsman has gone missing.'

I nodded, but didn't speak. It's always interesting to see how guardians cope with auxiliary misbehaviour.

'Probably had enough and took his parents over to Fife,' said the finance guardian.

Since the warring gangs over the Forth had been brought under control by an organization of landowners and fiery young farmers, citizens – and auxiliaries – had been tempted over. None has ever been heard from again.

'Of course, a senior auxiliary has disappeared too.' It looked like I had the jump on them. 'Alec Ferries, the Hearts manager.'

'Why haven't we heard about that?' the senior guardian said, his fists balling.

'I'm sure the recreation and/or public order guardian are on the point of letting you know.'

He pressed buttons on his mobile and shouted at the person on the other end, demanding to know why he hadn't been informed. I got the impression the recipient of his words was the recreation guardian rather than Guardian Doris.

'Feel better now?' I said when he'd finished. Handbrake turns in the conversation often catch guardians off their guard. 'What do you know about flunitrazepam?'

There was a silence that was eventually broken by Billy.

'Date-rape drug, yes? Can't remember what it used to be called.'

'Rohypnol.'

'That's it.' I grinned at him. 'I don't suppose you ever used it.'

'Fuck off, Quint.'

'What's its relevance?' said Calder.

'It was found in the system of Muckle Tony Robertson, the leader of the Leith Lancers, who supposedly hanged himself last night but didn't.'

'What do you mean?' MacLean demanded, suddenly more alert.

'My thinking is that he was drugged into unconsciousness, then strung up and downward pressure exerted so he suffocated. Whoever did it wanted to make very sure he died.'

'The guardsman?'

'It may have been Hume 481,' I said, smiling loosely. 'Or perhaps he was got at and forced to admit the killer or killers. Either way, he'd have good reason to run.'

The senior guardian held up his right hand. 'I'm confused. What has a dead drugs-gang leader got to do with the heart and the head?'

I raised my shoulders. 'Search me. But Hume 481 also crossed the city line some weeks ago. He may have been in touch with outsiders.' I looked at Billy. 'And, as I was told last night, certain outsiders have got problems with hearts on centre-circles as well.'

'My SPADE was told to brief you,' said MacLean. 'I hope you haven't told anyone else.'

I shook my head. 'I was considering breaking the news to the guardians at this evening's meeting.'

Jack MacLean laughed. 'We thought you might, which is why you're here and won't be attending the meeting.'

Interesting, but I didn't react.

'What do you think about the hearts appearing in Glasgow and Inverness?' Calder asked.

'As I'm not allowed to talk to anyone in those cities, what can I think? It lets you off the hook, of course – you can say the heart was left by an outsider.'

'We're not going public about it,' MacLean said firmly. 'That's been agreed with our counterparts in the other cities.'

'Anyway, you're on less steady ground with the decapitation. Or have heads rolled elsewhere too?'

'No,' Billy said. 'That looks like an Edinburgh special.'

'So far,' said the senior guardian.

'Any more calls to Guardian Doris recommending discretion?' I asked. I wasn't sure that she'd have told me.

'No.' This time MacLean was first with the negative.

'Has the head been found?' Fergus Calder asked.

'Not that I've heard.'

'Shit!' said Jack MacLean. 'This is just what we need with the referendum on the horizon.'

Out of the mouths of babes and guardians. The thought had been floating around my brain all afternoon, but now I had it. When I was a kid, my old man used to listen to the news every morning and evening. I didn't pay much attention, but I remember a Scottish politician back in pre-devolution days – there was something fishy about his name – saying that, like William Wallace, Scots could talk about freedom with 'head and heart'.

I didn't know what to make of that, apart from keep it to myself.

SEVEN

I rang Davie when I was outside the Council building.

'Get over here,' he said. 'Grant Brown's girlfriend's just turned up.'

I waved at a passing Guard 4×4 and showed the driver my authorization.

'Grange Terrace. Pretty wild out there, citizen,' the grizzled guardsman said.

'Call me Quint. Pretty wild all over the city these days.'

'True enough. It was better when citizens knew their place.'

I had a live one. Although younger auxiliaries have, on the whole, accepted the Council's relaxation policy, some of the older ones are fans of Genghis Khan.

'I've never known my place,' I said as we headed up the Pleasance.

The driver laughed. 'I know you, Bell 03 as was. I served under you when we drove those head-bangers out of Fettes. Shame they blew the place sky high.'

'Not a shame that we didn't go up with it.'

'True enough. Here, what's this about a headless man in the canal? You're in on that, aren't you?'

'Remember the no-gossip clause in auxiliary regulations?'

That shut him up. He dropped me off in Grange Terrace and accelerated away as soon as I shut the door. A group of badly dressed kids was standing around Davie's vehicle.

'Hey, mister, d'ye fancy helpin' us nick this?' asked a red-headed lad with pimples.

'Did you see the size of the guardsman that got out of it?'

Davie appeared at the front door of a Georgian townhouse that had been divided into flats like all such buildings outside the centre. The would-be car thieves were away before he could open his mouth.

'Might be an idea to get your colleague to stand guard.'

'She's doing a good job calming down Cecilia.'

'Cecilia. You don't hear that name often in Edinburgh. Patron saint of music, you know.'

'What's a saint?'

'You're looking at one.'

He burst out laughing, then put a hand over his mouth. 'The poor girl's in a hell of a state.'

I followed him in. Grant Brown's flat was on the top floor, what would originally have been the servants' quarters. It had two rooms, both with sloping ceilings and a decent view to the hills in the south. There were the standard sparse pieces of furniture. Cecilia was sitting on the single bed, the guardswoman's arm around her.

I kneeled down in front of her and mumbled words of commiseration, not that they offer much consolation at such times. After a while I nodded at the guardswoman, Nasmyth 436, and she slipped away, probably to be consoled by Davie.

'I can't . . . I can't understand . . . why . . .' Cecilia gasped. 'Grant was . . . a good lad . . . everybody . . . liked him.'

I got up and sat next to her. 'Tell me about him,' I said softly.

'Och, he was funny and . . . and sweet . . . and good at his work . . . and . . . and he loved me . . . we were going to get . . . married.' She sobbed pitifully. 'Not that we'd applied for a licence.' That explained why the dead man's file showed no long-term partner, though in the old days even an unofficial relationship would have been noted.

I gave her a few moments before going on. 'Where was he working, Cecilia?'

'In Slateford – they're building new flats.'

Not far from where the body was found.

'When did you last see him?'

'This morning. I was . . . I was here.'

Citizens were now allowed to spend the night together, as long as no other residents of city accommodation minded.

'And how was he?'

'Happy . . . he kissed me and we . . . we arranged to meet here this afternoon. I'm still with my parents in Corstorphine.'

'That's a few bus journeys away. Where do you work?'

'In the tourist zone – a souvenir shop.' That explained the neat white blouse and black skirt beneath her coat.

'Has he been acting normally recently?'

'Oh aye. Nothing ever got . . . got Grant down.' She wiped her eyes.

'Any problems at work? Enemies?'

'I told you, everyone liked him . . .'

I let her weep again. We'd do the relevant checks, but it was possible the dead man had been randomly chosen.

'Course, he did love his football,' Cecilia said in a small voice.

Or maybe not so random. 'Who did he support?'

'No, he was a player.'

My heart missed a beat.

'For Hibs,' she added.

Another unwelcome coincidence. A heart at Heart of Midlothian and now a head missing from a player of their great rivals, Hibernian.

'And you know . . . you know the worst thing?' Cecilia clutched my hand. 'His nickname was . . . was Ironheid.'

She fainted on to the bed.

'What happened?' Davie said from the door.

'You're not going to believe this,' I replied.

To his credit he did.

The Guard unit at Easter Road, home of Hibs, reported that there was no heart on site.

'You don't think he lost his head because of his nickname?' Davie asked, as he drove us towards the ground.

'Who knows? Ironheid sounds like a drugs-gang handle but his record was clean.'

'He could have escaped notice or been a recent recruit.'

I nodded. 'Whatever, I don't think Cecilia knew about it, poor lass.'

'So what do we do? Interrogate the players?'

'You can get that started. I'll do the management.'

We arrived at the green-girdered stadium soon afterwards, the rain now horizontal thanks to a west wind that had got up. If we were lucky, people would be around for evening training – they were all part-timers.

'Who's in charge?' I asked the Guard commander on site.

'I am, citizen,' the keen young auxiliary said.

'Of the football club.'

'Oh. That's Smail, Derick Smail. His office is on the first floor.'

I heard Davie ordering that the players be assembled. He'd have to delegate some of the interviews, but he would quickly spot anyone with a suspicious look to him.

I went in a half-open door that was painted green and white. A portly, middle-aged citizen in a badly fitting suit was bent over papers on a desk that was of much better quality than those provided by the Supply Directorate.

'Derick Smail?' I said.

He looked up as if I'd caught him with his hand down his pants.

'That's me. Who are you?'

I held out my authorization.

'Oh, Citizen Dalrymple. I'm very glad tae see you. Know all about your successes, of course.'

'Uh-huh. But do you know about Ironheid?'

'What?'

'Your player, Grant Brown.'

'Talented striker, aye. Scored over twenty goals last season. Didnae see him tonight, come tae think ae it.'

I wasn't going to break the news to him gently. The city's football managers are notoriously slippery, especially those in the ten-team Premier League. The Recreation Directorate is supposed to keep them in check, but the citizen managers were much cannier than auxiliaries when it comes to wheeling and dealing. Which reminded me – we hadn't found the Hearts manager.

'How many of Brown's goals were headers?'

'Quite a few. That's where the name came frae.'

'Well, he's not going to be scoring any more of those.'

'Why not?'

'Because his head's gone missing.'

Derick Smail's shock seemed genuine. 'You mean, he was . . .' He wasn't capable of getting an appropriate word out.

'Beheaded? Decapitated? That's it. Any idea why?'

The manager had collapsed in his chair. 'I cannae . . . I cannae believe it.'

I moved closer. 'Why's that?'

'Because he was a good lad. Never turned up late for training, fought hard on the pitch but was sweet as sugar substitute off it, had a nice girlfriend . . .'

'Can I see his file, please?'

Smail hesitated, but not for long. I took the green paper folder and opened it. Grant Brown was twenty-eight, had been with Hibs since football was reinstituted three years ago and had no disciplinary record – not even a yellow card, and the referees were auxiliaries with short fuses.

'So you've no idea why he was the victim of such a horrific crime?'

'None at all, citizen. It mustae bin somethin' to dae wi' his work. He was a builder. Ye ken how sneaky some of them are.'

Nothing compared with the average football manager, but I let that go.

'How about friends here? Did he have any?'

'He was very popular, ye ken?'

'Any particular pals?'

'Em, Allie Swanson and Lachie Vass.'

'Their files, please.'

He handed them over and I took a quick look. Swanson, Alistair, was a midfielder and Vass, Lachlan, the goalkeeper. Then something caught my eye. They were both residents of Portobello, the north-eastern suburb where Yellow Jacko's gang, the Pish, came from.

'I'll get these back to you,' I said, heading for the door.

'Here, hang on.'

I did so, but not because he wanted me to. 'Alec Ferries,' I said.

Smail's expression didn't change. 'What about him? Alec might be the boss of our deadly rivals, but we get on.'

'I'm glad to hear it. When did you last see him?'

He thought about that. 'Coupla weeks ago, maybe. We're playing his lot next month.'

'Would it surprise you to know that he's disappeared?'

'Alec? Never! He's got too many—' He broke off and looked down.

'Too many what?' I demanded, moving closer.

He kept his peace, then raised his head. 'Too many good players to look after.'

That sounded about as convincing as a barracks commander ordering his auxiliaries to smile at citizens. I smelled the excremental odour of illicit activities. Not that Derick Smail was going to admit that.

Davie was in the away team changing rooms, which reeked of embrocation and malfunctioning drains – the latter no doubt deliberate to put the opposition off their game. He was talking to a player with a green-and-white Mohican, while another four with less lunatic haircuts sat on the benches at the far side. They were all looking down and keeping quiet, having obviously been yelled at. Davie questioned citizens as if the Council's relaxation of the regulations had never happened.

'Spoken to these guys?' I asked, showing him the folders.

'This clown is Allie Swanson. The other one's over there.'

'I'll take him,' I said, pointing out their addresses to him.

Davie nodded. 'The showers are in there. I recommend giving him five minutes in a cold one before you start.' He grinned at Swanson. 'You'll get yours after.'

'Lachlan Vass,' I called.

The player who stood up was tall and well built, as befits a goalkeeper. He had a moustache Pancho Villa would have revolted for and his hair looked like an anti-personnel mine had gone off in it. At least it wasn't dyed in the club colours. I led him into the shower room and closed the door.

'Citizen Dalrymple,' I said. 'Call me Quint.'

'Ah ken who ye are,' Vass said, lowering his head.

'You're a friend of Grant Brown's?'

'Aye.'

'I'm sorry to tell you that he's dead.'

That made him look up. 'Whit? Ah saw him at training the day before yesterday.'

'There's more. He was found in the Union Canal. Without his head.'

This time the goalkeeper didn't respond.

'Can you think of any reason for that?'

The eyes were down again. 'Accident? He's a builder, ye ken.'

'I don't think so.' We still had to check the squad he worked on, but if there had been a major accident it would have been reported. 'You and Allie stay in Portobello, eh?'

'So?'

'Grant lived in the Grange. Quite a bike ride.'

'Aye, well, we usually get pished on Sunday nights in the Easter Road pubs. And efter training.'

'Did you not wonder where he was tonight? I hear he never turned up late.'

'Naw, he didnae. Ah thought he mustae got caught up at his work.'

I moved closer, making him back up against the erratically tiled wall.

'Pished. Know what that makes me think of?'

Lachie looked away. 'A sore heid?'

'Don't!' I yelled.

'Whit?' he said in a hurt tone.

'Play games with me, son. What's Porty most famous for? And don't say the beach.'

'Aw, Ah get ye. The Portobello Pish.' He shrugged. 'Ah dinnae ken any ae them. Honest. Ah'm a kitchen porter at the Waverley Hotel. Ah only go home tae sleep.'

'You went to school in Porty,' I said, glancing at the file. 'You must have known some of the gang.'

He was avoiding my eyes again. 'Ah kent Yellow Jacko's wee brother, Pete. He wisnae a friend, though.'

'And he was shot dead in a raid on the bonded warehouse in Leith five years ago.'

'Is it no' longer?'

I shook my head. 'Memory playing up?'

'Naw, it's amazin' how time flies.'

'This is official, Lachie,' I said. 'If you lie to me, you'll spend a year down the mines.'

He gulped. 'Aye, OK.'

'You, Allie and Grant – none of you have anything to do with the Pish?'

Now he was looking at me again. 'Ah dinnae ken aboot the others, but Ahm clean. And that's the truth.'

It was also suggestive. I led him out and took another of Davie's suspects. He lived in the western suburbs and seemed well out of his depth, even when it came to football. When we'd finished, we compared notes.

'I didn't get much out of mine,' Davie said.

I told him about Lachlan.

'What about the manager?'

'He seemed to be genuinely surprised on all counts. All right, let that thrusting young guardsman handle the rest of the questioning. It's time we got an overview at the command centre.'

'I'm pretty keen on getting a five-course meal as well,' Davie said.

I was about to abuse him for prioritizing his gut, then my own rumbled louder than a packed citizen bus going up Leith Walk. Fortunately the canteen at the castle was one of the city's best, though it was still substantially worse than the cheapest tourist restaurant.

I had soup and haggis, neeps and tatties. Davie had three bowls of soup, four rolls, two platefuls of haggis etc., and a bowl of the concrete-like porridge that's on offer round the clock.

'That was more than five courses,' I observed.

'Who's counting?' Davie replied, grabbing an apple from a passing guardswoman's tray. She gave him a smile that suggested they were more than acquaintances.

'No,' I said. 'You're on duty till this case is over.'

'I've got to sleep.'

'On my sofa.'

'I resign.'

'Can't see you as an ordinary citizen, big man.'

'No, I resign from working for you.'

I shrugged. 'Suit yourself. But if we make sense of this, think of your career prospects. If Scotland reunites, you might be top cop.'

'If Scotland reunites, I'll eat my boots.'

'You eat them on a monthly basis anyway. How about going on a diet?'

'A what?'

'Ah, there you are, Quint.' Guardian Doris sat down on my side of the bench. 'Anything to report?'

'I was going to ask you the same question.'

She smiled tightly. 'Except that guardians don't report to citizens, not even special investigators.'

'If you're going to be like that . . .' I started piling my plates and cutlery.

'All right,' the guardian said, her hand on my arm briefly. 'Report, please.'

I told her about Cecilia, and the Hibs manager and players.

'I've spoken to Grant Brown's building team leader,' I went on. 'He swears there was no bad blood or anything else at his work. The Housing Directorate's carrying out further checks.'

I would do my own interviews in time, but the housing guardian was one of the few Council members I respected and his fiefdom had never been involved in any major case. Still, there was always a first time.

'I don't suppose Alec Ferries has made a miraculous reappearance?'

'No, and there's been no sign of Hume 481 or his parents. Oh, I have this for you.' The guardian handed me a folded sheet of paper. 'Upcoming visits by outsiders.'

I had a look. 'Nothing tomorrow, thank Plato. The day after tomorrow, the governors of Orkney and Shetland.'

'They're in some kind of union,' the guardian said.

'Good for them. Friday, the Lord of the Isles.' I looked at Davie. 'I thought he was just here.'

He nodded.

'He controls a lot of financial interests,' Guardian Doris said.

I immediately thought of Jack MacLean and Billy Geddes. Their tongues would be heading straight up the aristocrat's kilt.

'And Saturday, the first minister of Glasgow. I thought it was first secretary.'

'Andrew Duart got himself upgraded.'

'He's still in place, is he?' I said, remembering the hole he'd dug himself into five years ago. 'At least his chief cop isn't on the list.'

'Hel Hyslop?' said the guardian. 'She'll be coming. He never goes anywhere without her.'

'Magic,' I mumbled. Hyslop and I had history, not of the peaceful variety. Her first name was extremely apposite. 'No sign of the missing head?'

'I'm afraid not. At least no more hearts have turned up.'

'Not yet. Anything on those missing citizens?'

She shook her head. 'Those five you gave us have been gone for weeks – they must have crossed the border. As for our list—' She sighed. 'There are dozens of them and I don't have the resources to follow up on the last sightings of them and so on.'

She didn't have the resources or the volition, I thought, frowning at her. 'Come on, guardsman.'

'Where are we going?'

'The Portobello Pish. You know they only come out at night.'

Davie's face lit up. 'Gang-banger banging. My favourite.'

'There's a couple of reports of suspicious behaviour that haven't been checked yet,' said the guardian. 'One in Leith and one in—'

'Porty,' I supplied.

'Correct.'

Davie was already on the way to the command centre to get the details.

'Do you really think this is gang-related, Quint?' Guardian Doris said.

'They're the nastiest criminals we have in the city so it makes sense to look at them.'

She nodded, not convinced. 'Be careful down there. You know what it's like after dark.'

'I do, but I have Davie to cover my front, back and sides.'

'You'll be taking a squad or two as well?'

'I presume so, but the younger Guard personnel don't have the commitment that he has.'

'No one does, Quint,' Doris said, shaking her head. 'The Enlightenment's running out of steam.'

I knew that, but I never expected a Council member to say it. Maybe becoming part of Scotland wasn't such a bad idea. After all, we were few and they were many . . .

EIGHT

One of the abiding irritations concerning the Portobello Pish was that the Guard had never been able to pinpoint the gang's headquarters. It was likely that several premises were used, none for very long. The head-bangers had been communicating by mobile phones smuggled in from Glasgow for years, technicians they knew having adapted the signals so that they could be passed on by the Edinburgh system. The number of competent telecommunications experts the city had was smaller than the members of a football team, substitutes not included. But even when it seemed the Guard had a solid lead, the gangs slipped away before they got close. That was very much not a feather in Guardian Doris's and her predecessors' berets, but no one else could do any better.

'Where to, exactly?' Davie asked, as we took our place at the head of a line of 4×4s.

'Grant Brown was an only child and his parents died when he was young, so let's go and see his footballer friends' families. Get your people to split up and keep their distance.'

'Two hundred yards?'

'That should do. But as always in the northern suburbs, they need to be ready to respond as rapidly as a meteor.'

Davie gave the orders and we moved off. I'd considered sending him to Lachlan Vass's place and handling Allie Swanson myself, but decided we'd better stick together in the badlands. Besides, Davie had a bad feeling about Swanson so we were going there first.

We headed down London Road, past what was now the Meadowbank Rangers ground. Decades before independence it had been an athletics stadium, then the original Meadowbank Thistle played there – that emblem of Scotland wasn't acceptable to the Council, of course. It had been a barracks rugby ground too. I remember seeing Davie take out an opposition guardsman with a shoulder charge that would have got him a straight red card before the rules were changed to make the game more spartan.

'What was it about Allie Swanson?' I asked. 'Apart from the haircut.'

'You'll see. He's hiding something.' Davie turned on full beam. The only other vehicles in the suburbs were Guard patrols, street lights being few and far between. We passed a few citizens on bikes, but what their aged dynamos produced could hardly be classed as light.

We turned on to Portobello High Street. About a hundred yards further on, Davie pulled up.

'It's round the corner. Regent Street, number 14.'

We went on foot, Davie having checked the vicinity. The main road was safe enough, but as soon as you were off it . . . At least we knew there was backup a minute or so away.

I knocked on the door of the two-storey terraced house. It was opened by a bald middle-aged man, who was chewing with his mouth open.

'Sorry to interrupt your meal,' I said. 'Call me Quint. Can I see Allie, please?'

'Fuck off,' my host said, spraying the last of his mouthful towards me.

Davie pushed past and grabbed the man by the throat.

'What was that?' he demanded.

The answer was unintelligible.

'Let him go, Davie. Before he chokes.'

'Oh. Right.'

'So, is Allie here?'

Davie suddenly pounded down the hall and up the stairs. 'Backup to Bath Street and Regent Street!' he shouted into his communications unit before disappearing.

I followed the swearie man into the sitting cum dining room. A thin woman with a short blonde perm and two teenagers were at the table, the remains of a chicken in front of them. The Supply Directorate doesn't run to fowl unless you're a tourist. I heard heavy boots in the hall.

'I'm all right,' I said to the hefty guardsman. 'Just stay there.' He loomed in the door, an effective bogeyman. I looked meaningfully at the chicken and then at the adults.

'What's up with your Allie, then?'

They exchanged worried glances.

'Dinnae ken,' the man said hoarsely.

I directed my gaze at his other half. She didn't favour me with a reply, apparently trying to make their dinner disappear by telekinesis.

Time for the Hume 253 memorial threats.

'He's in the Pish, isn't he?'

Silence.

'Let me rephrase that. He's in the Pish. You're doubtless aware of what happens to gang members' families, but let me spell it out. Children under eighteen are separated and put in Welfare Directorate care homes. Fathers are sent down the mines for a minimum of two years. Mothers work on the city farms for a minimum of two years. Grandparents are removed from care homes and—'

'All right!' Citizen Swanson shouted. 'We dinnae ken what he does efter fitba training. He's twenty-three.'

'Shame he didn't get his own flat. Why was that?'

'Likes it doon here,' said the mother.

'He would, what with this being Porty Pish territory. And chicken for dinner.'

'He's no' a bad laddie,' the woman said, her eyes filling with tears. 'He just disnae listen. He nivver did.'

'Nora,' her husband growled.

Davie called on my mobile. 'The bastard got away. We're combing the streets.'

Now I had to play even harder ball.

'Guardsman, take the children.'

He and his colleagues did so, after a lot of screaming and struggling. The parents were shoved back on to their chairs, their shoulders in the grip of Davie's toughest guardswomen. He claimed they were better than their male counterparts when it came to the crunch, as often happened.

'This situation hasn't quite reached terminal yet, Citizens Swanson. I don't give a shit about the chicken, but it proves you've got contacts in the black market – and around here that's run by the Pish, correct?'

The man nodded once. 'We cannae clipe on them. They'll kill us.'

'Not if we put them behind bars like their leader.'

'Disnae matter,' said the man. 'Skinny Ewan's been running . . .' He broke off, his cheeks reddening.

'And where would we find Skinny Ewan?' I asked.

'Dinnae ken,' they said in unison.

'Take him,' I said to the guardswoman. After the citizen had been manoeuvred out, which involved a heavy blow to his abdomen, I told the remaining guardswoman to leave.

'It's just you and me now, Nora,' I said, sitting beside the sobbing woman. 'Your man resisted arrest, so that'll be another year down the mines. Or everything can be forgotten. It's up to you.'

'Ah cannae . . . Ah cannae . . .'

'Yes, you can.'

She looked at me. 'What'll happen to Allie?'

'I can't make any promises about him, especially if he's a gang member.'

She dropped her gaze.

'But I can put in a good word if you cooperate.'

'Ah dinnae believe ye.'

I shrugged. 'I'm not a member of the Guard, but I have direct contact with guardians.'

'Aye, you're their golden boy,' she said scathingly.

'That would be a stretch. Where are the Pish gathering tonight, Nora? Tell me and your family will be finishing that chicken in two minutes.'

She thought about that and then looked up. 'They change their meeting places a' the time, but I heard Allie mention that old church in Brighton Place taenight. St John's, I think it was called.'

I stood up, got her family back inside and called Davie.

Twenty minutes later we were in position round the former place of worship, which was only a few hundred yards from Regent Street. Davie had Guard personnel on every side of the battered building. I remembered it from pre-independence times: the tower was strange, four shorter rounded turrets surmounted by a taller one with a tall metal cross. The whole thing had collapsed, probably during the drugs wars as there were shell and bullet holes all over the rest of the building.

'How are we going to do this?' I said to Davie, in the 4×4. 'The Pish will have firearms.'

'They will,' he said, sounding sublimely unconcerned.

'And your people don't.'

'Correct.'

'Couldn't you send someone over to the nearest city-line post to borrow some?'

'Unnecessary.'

'Is it Long Live Laconicism Day?'

'No.'

I punched his arm and winced.

'Fear not, citizen. We've been equipped with the perfect weapon for such situations.'

'First I've heard of it.'

'Guardian Doris is not just a pretty . . . Anyway, she got them from Glasgow, apparently.'

'The suspense has already killed me.'

'They're called Hyper-Stuns.' He reached over his seat and presented me with an oversized pistol with two tubes mounted over the barrel. 'Ten shots, maximum range fifty yards, multiple settings ranging from mild to extreme electric shock – extreme equals death usually – night-vision sight and high-intensity light beam. All personnel get them when they're on patrol in the outer suburbs.'

We got out quietly and pushed the doors to. Davie contacted his team leaders on his comms unit, changing the wavelengths to confuse potential listeners with scanners, and ascertained that everyone was in position. The nearest to the old church said there were eleven gang-bangers inside and that guns were visible.

'Set to high shock,' Davie ordered. 'Up and at them!'

I followed him to the main door, where two guardsmen were standing by. One of them smashed a sledgehammer against the ornate but rusty lock. They were almost immediately met by fleeing members of the Pish. Davie dropped one of them with his Hyper-Stun, while the other was tripped and disarmed before he could fire his silver-plated semi-automatic pistol.

Multiple gunshots rang out from the interior, but soon they died away.

'Report!' Davie yelled into his comms unit.

The squads called in. One guardswoman had been shot dead and two guardsmen wounded, neither seriously. We moved inside, the space crisscrossed by beams from the Hyper-Stuns.

'Well, well,' Davie said. 'There must be at least five pounds of cocaine here.'

'And a large greenhouse's production of grass,' I added.

'Commander,' said a middle-aged guardswoman, 'we think one of them might have got away.'

'Not Allie Swanson?' I asked.

'No, he's unconscious over there.'

I had a frightening thought. 'They would have known we were chasing Allie. Get his family into protective custody, Davie.'

He sent two 4×4s round, but it was too late.

'Fuck!'

We were in Davie's office off the command centre in the castle.

'It wasn't your fault, Quint.'

'Yes, it was. I should have thought of it from the start. It would have been obvious to the bastard who slipped past us that Allie's people had talked.'

All four of them had been shot in the head by a large-calibre pistol.

'At least we got Skinny Ewan and the rest of the Pish.'

'They're gang members, Davie. They'll never talk.'

'Oh, yes they will.'

I didn't like his expression. It expressed homicidal determination.

The public order guardian appeared. 'Congratulations, commander. And you, Quint.'

I scowled at her. 'Unacceptable citizen casualties.'

'One of my people was killed too, citizen,' she said coldly.

'In the line of duty, not while eating dinner.'

'An illicitly obtained chicken, I gather.'

'Who gives a fuck?'

Davie raised an eyebrow.

'Sorry, guardian,' I said. 'Not your fault either.'

'I suppose it was mine since we let the shit-sucker get away,' Davie said, looking away.

'These things happen,' said the guardian. 'Nobody's to blame.'

I could have debated that at length, not least because the Council was responsible for letting the drugs gangs start up again in the city, but I let it go.

'Where have you put the Pish?' I asked her.

'In a secure ward in the infirmary. They need to be monitored as they come round from high stuns. That can take up to twelve hours. And before you ask, there are two squads on guard.'

I failed to stifle a yawn.

'You need to sleep,' Guardian Doris said. 'Both of you. Bed down here.'

'After a late-night repast,' Davie said.

I shook my head. 'No food for me.' I hadn't seen the Swansons' bodies, but my imagination was working triple time. 'I don't suppose Grant Brown's head has turned up.'

'I'm afraid not,' said the guardian. 'Oh, Yellow Jacko died while you were in the field. He and Muckle Tony are being cremated tomorrow. You might want to attend.'

'They're not scheduled in succession, are they?' I asked. 'There'll be mayhem.'

'No, there won't,' Davie said. 'We caught all the Pish, remember?'

'Bar one very savage scumbag. Anyway, their relatives will still have a go at each other.'

'Robertson's at eleven in the morning and Greig's at three in the afternoon,' said Guardian Doris. 'Guard personnel will be there in force.'

'What about Hume 481 and his parents?' I said.

'No reports.'

I went to the senior guardsmen's bunk room and collapsed. I was exhausted, but sleep was a long time coming. The faces of Allie Swanson's siblings kept coming towards me, screaming as their skulls exploded in blasts of scarlet.

'Wakey, wakey.'

The smell of barracks coffee – better than what I got every morning – dragged me to the surface. I'd been in a deep hole, wrestling with ghosts recent and from further in the past – then my father appeared. That made me sit up.

'Watch it!' Davie exclaimed, getting the mug of steaming liquid out of the way in time.

'I've got to check on the old man.' I looked at my watch. 'Five past six? What the hell?'

'Sorry. Skinny Ewan's conscious. I thought you'd want to squeeze his nuts as soon as possible.'

I groaned, then drank the coffee and ate the cheese roll he handed me.

'Where is he?' I asked as I came out of the bog.

'The medical guardian's waiting for you at the infirmary.'

I felt a mild twinge of erotic interest, then thought of the Swansons.

'What's her interest?'

'Search me.' He grinned. 'Your nether regions?'

I treated that with hypocritical scorn.

The rain was doing its usual highly accurate impression of a waterfall. We ran to the esplanade, slipping and sliding like a pair of cack-footed skaters.

The infirmary looked like it had been doused in black paint, so sodden were its walls. I headed for Sophia's office, but met her in the corridor leading to it. Her hair was tied back and she looked like she meant business.

'Good morning, Quint,' she said with a minimalist smile. 'Commander. Follow me.'

We did as we were told, exchanging glances. What was she up to? We reached a door that had a key pad on the frame, a rare sight in Edinburgh. Once we were in, Sophia turned to us.

'I'm going to experiment on Ewan Gow, a.k.a. Skinny Ewan.'

'You're going to experiment on the leader of one of the city's most wanted gangs?' I said, surprised.

'I've obtained a recently developed drug from Inverness. It's over ninety per cent guaranteed to break down resistance to questioning.'

'A truth drug?' I said.

'In layman's terms.' Sophia gave me a dismissive look. 'I've cleared this with the public order guardian.'

'Why don't you try it on Allie Swanson or one of the others first?' Davie asked.

'Because this citizen is awake, commander. This is a high-priority case. We need answers.'

She led us through another door. A medical auxiliary in a white coat was inserting a needle into the forearm of a man who had been gagged and bound to a chair like those used by dentists. I looked around for the pliers.

'All ready, guardian.'

Sophia dismissed him with a haughty wave. 'Look and learn,' she said to us, depressing the plunger of the syringe that the needle was attached to.

She looked at her watch, counting the seconds silently, and then undid the gag. Skinny Ewan's eyes were fluttering and his breathing was regular. Very regular.

'He's ready,' Sophia said. 'Start with some basic questions so we can establish that the compound is working.' She handed me the citizen's file.

'What's your name?'

'Ewan Gow.'

'Date of birth?'

'Fifth of January, 1997.'

'Address?'

'25 Woodside Terrace, Joppa.' That's the suburb adjacent to Portobello on the east.

'All right?' Sophia asked.

I nodded.

'Try some more obscure questions.'

I looked through the handwritten sheets.

'Where were you working in 2024?'

'Ah was aff sick all year. Glandular fever.'

I tried something more emotive. 'How did your sister Kelly die?'

There was no pause or change in his tone. 'Food poisoning – a bad batch of Supply Directorate beef.'

'What age was she?'

'Seventeen.'

'Where do you work?'

'In the Zig Zag Casino on George Street. Ahm a barman.'

That was interesting. Citizens with access to tourist businesses had to be cleared by the Public Order Directorate. He'd obviously kept himself clean, at least on the surface.

'Everything as it should be, Quint?' Sophia asked.

'Yes.'

'Go for it, then,' she said, unusually excited.

I moved closer to Skinny Ewan. His face was pockmarked and his nose had been broken several times.

'Are you the leader of the Portobello Pish?'

'Yes,' he said without hesitation.

I looked at Davie, who was watching intently. 'Name your associates.'

He did so, Davie taking notes. There were plenty more than eleven gang members, including both Nora and Dirk Swanson. But Allie's brother and sister hadn't been involved.

'What do you traffic?'

'Cigarettes, drugs, jewellery and malt whisky.'

'Who supplies you?'

'The Dead Men from Glasgow give us the booze and fags. The drugs come from . . .'

I waited, but he didn't speak any more.

'Where do you get the drugs?' I said after a minute.

Nothing.

Sophia stepped forward and pressed the syringe plunger further in.

I repeated the question.

Skinny Ewan's eyes blinked rapidly, then he answered.

'The Supply Directorate,' he said.

Then he died.

NINE

We were in Sophia's office. She was trying unsuccessfully to hide her shock.

'How sure are you that the drug is reliable?' I asked.

'I told you.'

'Yes, but that could be salesman's bullshit.'

Her eyes flashed. 'I don't deal with salesmen, Quint,' she said. 'If you must know, I attended a three-day seminar about the compound in Inverness last month.'

I wasn't sure if Davie was more amazed than I was. If so, he must have been as stunned as the Pish had been by our attack last night. Guardians crossing the border? It had happened once before, but the disastrous end to that trip had led to the ban being reinforced even more strongly. I had a flash of Jack MacLean and wondered if he'd been travelling too. Maybe Billy had accompanied him to advise on deals.

Sophia raised a hand. 'No questions. I had Council authorization.'

'Oh, that's all right then,' I said. 'Shame about the City Regulations being overridden.'

She didn't respond to that. Besides, there was a large pachyderm in the room.

'So they got their drugs from the Supply Directorate,' I said. 'Which is run by the current senior guardian, Fergus Calder.' Who, I remembered, had gone into conference with the finance guardian and his SPADE as soon as the heart was discovered at Tyneside.

'That's ridiculous,' Sophia said.

'Either you trust the drug or you don't.'

Davie was looking at me dubiously. He had experience of guardians going off the rails, but he was still loyal to the regime and didn't like to question it, unlike me.

'There's no reason the senior guardian should be involved, Quint,' he said. 'It could easily be delivery men.'

'Or even a less senior auxiliary,' I said snidely. He was right, but the directorate would have to be investigated and we had enough to be getting on with. I turned to Sophia. 'Since you've got so much faith in the truth drug, do you fancy trying it on another guinea pig?'

'Not the full dose, though.'

'You're the expert,' I said. 'After all, you've been to a seminar.'

She ignored that. Shortly afterwards we had Allie Swanson wheeled in. He was only half-awake, his Mohican almost horizontal like he'd just headed the ball. In five minutes we had something to go on. The missing gang member who had killed his parents and siblings was called Tom Lamont, a.k.a. 'Madman'. I sent Davie off to find the psycho, not that we expected him to be at his registered address. Fortunately, Allie supplied us with a list of Pish hideouts, as well as the names of Madman's friends and associates – not all of them had been captured last night.

'Ask him about Grant Brown,' I said, wondering what more might be divulged about the headless man.

He confirmed things we already knew – about Cecilia, who wasn't involved with the gang; about the dead man's work, which had no connection with the Pish's activities; and about what Grant got up to in his spare time. Bingo. Because he lived not far from the city line, he acted as a freelance contact with the Dead Men and other Glasgow smuggling outfits – arranging where cigarettes and other goods were to be dropped off, handling payments and so on. Now I could see a reason for his decapitation. Outsider gangs were savage when they were crossed. Is that what had happened? I thought of Michael Campbell, the missing guardsman from Davie's barracks. He had worked on the city line in the general vicinity of Grant's workplace. Could he have been another contact, one who had landed Grant neck-high in the canal?

'I have to go.'

'The story of my life,' Sophia said with a crooked smile.

I returned it with interest. 'I'll tell Guardian Doris about this –

omitting the unexpected death. She'll no doubt want more questions to be asked.'

'Oh joy. That woman's a pain in the rectum.'

'Is she now? Why's that?'

Sophia gave me an infuriated look. 'She's only been in her job for weeks and already she thinks she's the knees of a queen bee.'

I laughed. 'She doesn't give me that impression. Calder, MacLean and Cowan are much fuller of themselves.'

'Ah, but she's cunning. Give her a few months and she'll be telling us all what to do.'

I found that hard to believe, not least because the senior guardian could fire her whenever he wanted. Then again, you can't fire someone who's put together a file on your questionable activities. Was that Doris Barclay's game? If so, I would be next in line for the Maiden, the medieval guillotine that removed dummies' heads every day at the New Tolbooth.

'No doubt I'll see you at the Council meeting,' Sophia said.

'Some doubt. I was kept away yesterday.

'I wondered what had happened to you. I assumed you were undertaking essential crime-solving.'

'Maybe we could meet up later in the evening,' I said, taking a step closer.

'Maybe,' she said, tossing her head. 'Or maybe not.'

I was close to the esplanade, having arranged for a Guard squad to come with me to Muckle Tony Robertson's funeral, when my phone rang.

'Public order guardian. Drop whatever you're doing and meet me on the esplanade.'

The connection was cut before I could open my mouth. I kept going down the cobbled slope and met the squad that was waiting for me.

'Any of you gang specialists?'

'I am, citizen,' replied Raeburn 362, a short and sturdy guardswoman.

I asked her to take note of who was present and might be of interest. A few seconds later Guardian Doris appeared, two massive guardsmen at her heels.

'Want to tell me what this is about?' I said after following her into the back seat of her armour-plated 4×4.

'We'll be there in a few minutes.'

I rewarded her lack of loquacity by keeping Sophia's truth drug and the Pish revelations to myself. She'd find out soon enough and would be irritated that I hadn't told her. A small victory against Council highhandedness, but they all count.

We were driven down the Royal Mile, then right at George IV Bridge – who knows how that name redolent of the hereditary monarchy survived? – and then right down Victoria Street – same again. As we swung on to the Grassmarket, the mass of the Tolbooth filled the windscreen. Crowds of tourists surrounded it. No doubt an execution was about to take place. The recent reconstruction was the most popular attraction in the city, which tells you something about the Tourism Directorate, the Council and our esteemed visitors. The original building had been on the Royal Mile and had been a meeting place for the city's office bearers as well as a rat-ridden prison. Many a criminal of all classes had been put to death in its environs.

'We need to be discreet,' the guardian said as the vehicle passed the left side of the building and stopped about fifty yards further on.

A fresh-faced guardswoman came up. She must only recently have completed the year on the border that's mandatory for auxiliary trainees, but she still looked pale.

'Where is it, Cullen 538?' Guardian Doris asked.

'On the second storey, first left.'

We all looked, the guardian through a pair of binoculars, which she passed to me. I swallowed back bile. There were four heads on spikes on that level – and another four above and below. The difference was that the other eleven were made of painted plastic and horsehair. The one I had zoomed in on was real – and I was almost certain it was Grant Brown's. I turned to the guardswoman.

'You saw the barracks notification?'

'Yes, citizen. There doesn't seem to be any damage to his features.'

'Fortunately it looks less lifelike than the fake heads and there's no blood,' Doris said. 'I take it no one's given it undue attention.'

'No, guardian. As you say, they seem to be more interested in the other ones. And the executions. There's a hanging, drawing and quartering in quarter of an hour.'

'Lovely,' I muttered. 'We can't get it down until late evening, I suppose.'

'No,' said the guardian. 'Not without drawing attention, which we definitely don't want.'

'Discretion being the rule,' I said.

She glared at me and dismissed the guardswoman. 'You're playing with fire, citizen.'

I got a blast of the early Rolling Stones' hit. That only spurred me on.

'So when are you going to go public about the heart and head?' I saw the ears of the guardsmen in the front seat prick up. As the guardian's elite detail they probably knew about everything, but they didn't like me putting the screw on their chief.

Guardian Doris looked out the window. 'That's a matter for the Council, as you well know.'

'All right, I'll raise it tonight.' I looked at the head again. 'Any thoughts on why Grant Brown's head is up there?'

'Back to the castle,' she ordered. 'I imagine it has something to do with the citizen's dealings with Glasgow gangs such as the Dead Men.' Now her eyes were on mine. 'The medical guardian called me as soon as you left her.'

So she'd known all along about the truth drug. Thanks, Sophia.

'I presume you're making use of the remaining Pish members.'

'My experts are drawing up questions, yes. Just who do you think you're working for, citizen?'

'The citizen body of Edinburgh.'

'No!' she shouted. She had spirit after all. 'You're working for me and the Council, got that? No more secrets.'

I shrugged. 'I'll tell you mine if you tell me yours.'

The guardsman who wasn't driving whipped round and grabbed my throat. 'Show respect, you piece of shit,' he growled.

His barracks name and number burned into my memory as my vision began to break up. Ferguson 249. I'd have him one way or another.

'Enough,' the guardian ordered. 'I repeat, citizen, no secrets.'

I concentrated on sucking air through my windpipe. I knew how easily the hard man could have crushed it. I could hardly croak, let alone speak, which was good. It meant I couldn't agree to Guardian Doris's demand. In Enlightenment Edinburgh secrets are the only reliable currency, especially if you're as poor as I am.

We went back to the esplanade, which was being drenched by the contents of numerous low clouds. I opened my door reluctantly.

'What do you intend to do now?' the guardian asked as a black-and-white striped umbrella was opened above her.

'I thought I'd keep dry here.'

'Not an option.'

'In that case I'll go up to the command centre and see how Davie's getting on.'

'Hume 253,' she corrected, then marched away with her minders. There wasn't another umbrella.

I found a towel in the castle changing rooms and dried my hair and face before going to the command centre. As I'd heard nothing from Davie, I suspected he hadn't tracked down Madman Lamont. There had been no sightings of Hume 481 or his parents, never mind any of the other missing people, including the Hearts boss. I called Raeburn 362, the guardswoman at Muckle Tony Robertson's funeral.

'There was a bit of heckling – of us – but nothing physical, citizen,' she responded. 'Plenty of known faces, but none from the Porty Pish. They're keeping their heads down, at least till the afternoon.'

'Are you staying there?'

She was. I told her I'd be down before 3 p.m. and then set off for a rendezvous I'd put off too long. I took a Guard umbrella but the rain had stopped. I still managed to slip on the cobbles and land on my arse. Wonderful. I said nothing to the guardsman who drove me down to Trinity apart from giving him the address. He was lucky.

'Hello, Citizen Dalrymple,' said the cheery nursing auxiliary as I pushed open the door. 'Haven't seen you for a while.'

'Don't rub it in, Alison,' I said, depositing the umbrella in an antique stand. The home was for retired senior auxiliaries and the building had once been a wealthy merchant's house. The view from the top floor took in the firth, but I didn't need to go up there any more. The familiar smell of old men, cabbage and drains filled my nostrils.

'He's in his room,' she said. 'It's hard to get him to mix with the others these days.'

'He's the oldest here,' I replied. 'Not that he was ever the life and soul.'

She smiled. 'He's my favourite, whatever you say.'

'Mine too.'

I went down the corridor and knocked on the door, eliciting something incomprehensible.

'Hello, old man.'

'Hello, failure.' My father was wrapped in a tartan blanket in his armchair. There were at least ten books in a tottering pile on the small table next to him and he had a large tome open on his lap. 'Where the bloody hell have you been?'

'Keeping the city safe for honest citizens.'

'Pah, there aren't many of them these days.'

'And how would you know? You never walk further than the end of the street.'

'I haven't even done that for weeks.'

'The Big Wet.'

'Yes. Too slippery for me.'

I exhibited my damp backside, which made him laugh. His face was like parchment and there were more liver spots on it every month. The nightcap he was wearing made him look like Marley's ghost, not that I was going to tell him. He was a classicist and regarded authors later than Decimus Magnus Ausonius as substandard, with an honourable exception made for Shakespeare.

'You're working for the Council again,' he said, eyeing me dubiously.

'How did you know?'

'You've got that holier than everyone else in the city look about you.'

'Like you had when you were a guardian?'

'I was university professor of rhetoric before the Enlightenment. I *was* holier than everyone, at least in the intellectual sense.'

'Even Mother?'

'Watch yourself, laddie.'

My parents were academics and early supporters of the Enlightenment and both ended up as guardians, my mother even serving as senior guardian. But Hector, as the old man always insisted I call him, had lost faith with the Council when it had got too tough on ordinary citizens and had resigned. We hadn't talked about my mother for a long time.

'What hole do they want you to dig them out of this time?'

I gave him a rundown of the case, or cases.

'A heart and a head,' he said ruminatively. 'That sounds too symbolic to be a coincidence.'

'My thought exactly. I think it's something to do with the referendum.'

Hector almost choked. I managed to get some water down his throat.

'Referendum?' he said, still coughing. 'What a farce. The reason we gave up elections of all kinds was because they're unrepresentative of what people really want.'

'While the Council knew best.'

'It did,' he said, raising his overgrown eyebrows at me. 'But it hasn't for a long time. Plato never envisaged under-forties in charge of the state.'

There were plenty of things the ancient philosopher hadn't thought of, many of them subsequently identified by Machiavelli.

'Besides, who's to say that a reunified Scotland will work?' Hector said. 'Remember how chaotic things were in every traditional state in Europe.'

'And across the world still. Apparently China's gone to hell in a dim-sum trolley.'

'Ach, Chinese food. What I would give for one of those carry-outs we used to get when you were a lad.'

My tastebuds were tingling. There was no shortage of Chinese restaurants in the central zone, but they were for tourists only. Davie and I had once pulled rank and had a feed in one. Heaven, even for an atheist.

'The guardians have been crossing the border to visit their opposite numbers in Glasgow and Inverness.'

The old man scowled. 'No good will come of that. They were right to loosen the regulations, but standards have got to be maintained. We did the best we could for the citizens during the crisis. You can be sure this'll be about making money, and not only for the city.'

I refrained from telling him that Billy Geddes was back in the frame, though he'd have enjoyed the idea of my school friend as a SPADE. He'd always thought the former deputy finance guardian would use any implement to boost his personal wealth.

'They let the leaders of outsider states into Edinburgh too,' I said.

He looked like he was about to throw up. 'Scum, the lot of them,' he muttered.

'To be fair, some of the cities are doing well – or so I'm told. Oil's been found off the north-west coast. That's brought the Lord of the Isles back.'

'What?'

I thought he was going to have another fit, but he managed to get a grip.

'It's never the same thieving bastard who ransacked the islands before the crisis and then ran away when things got tough?'

I nodded. 'Back from some American state that liked the cut of his kilt.'

'Angus Macdonald,' Hector said. 'He came to us begging for help, which meant money, of course. He had several properties in the city. The public order guardian took him down to Pilton and left him alone for ten minutes. They had the tweed off his back and tore his kilt into strips for Molotov cocktails.'

'I remember. They were nothing if not resourceful, the old gangs.'

'Angus Macdonald,' the old man repeated, shaking his head. 'Whatever he's up to, you can be sure it's rotten to the pips.'

That was useful. At least I knew to be prepared when the Lord of the Isles showed up. I looked at my watch and got up.

'Funeral,' I explained. 'We've finally wiped out the Portobello Pish.'

'Not before time, Quintilian.'

He used the full name of the Roman rhetorician he'd given me at least once in every conversation. It was a power play.

I laughed. 'Don't worry, there are plenty more gangs to keep me busy.'

'There's only one gang you need to worry about in this city,' the old man said as he clutched my hand with what was more like a claw.

'I know,' I said. 'And it begins with a capital "C".'

'Make sure you come back soon, failure,' Hector said, his voice suddenly weak.

'Soon as I can, old man,' I said, worried about how frail he'd become.

I passed those fears on to Alison, as well as asking her to cut his fingernails. His lust for Chinese food made him look like Fu Manchu, though at least he'd omitted the moustache.

TEN

'Quint? Where are you?'

'On the way to Yellow Jacko's barbecue, Davie. You?'

'I'll see you there.' He cut the connection, which

irritated me. Then again, he might have had Madman Lamont in proximity.

The guardsman dropped me at the gates of Warriston crematorium. The low brick building was in better condition than I remembered. The Council must have decided that allowing citizens to see off their relatives and friends in civilized surroundings was a good way to gain support. Shame about the decades of grot that were stamped on older people's memories.

The short guardswoman I'd seen in the morning came up. I could see a couple of 4×4s in the background, far enough away not to annoy the grieving mass but still a solid statement of intent – anyone wanting a fight, we're ready.

'Raeburn 362,' I said. 'Or rather, Catriona. Call me Quint.'

'I'd rather not,' she said abruptly.

'Fair enough. Anything to report?'

'I sent vehicles after some of the faces at Muckle Tony's funeral that we haven't seen before.' She gave a tight smile. 'Now we've got the Pish, we need to take the Leith Lancers down too.'

'How come there wasn't any trouble?'

'The Lancers have got smart in the past year or so. Muckle Tony realized that keeping a low profile was a good idea. Plus, now he's dead, there'll be fighting over who takes his place. They'll do that in private.'

A Guard 4×4 drove swiftly through the gate and pulled up on the asphalt beside us. I looked in the back window – nobody cuffed and gagged.

Davie got out. 'The bastard got away. My people are still after him, but he's in the Leith back streets now.'

'Really?' I said. 'The Pish and the Lancers hate each other's guts, hearts and heads.'

'Aye,' said Davie, grinning at the guardswoman, who was nodding at him. 'Hiya, Cat. How are you doing?'

I suspected they'd have inserted their tongues into each other's mouths if I hadn't been there. Davie has more partners than I have blues cassettes.

'Why did you come?' I said, tugging him away. 'I mean, catching Madman is more important than the funeral.'

'Not necessarily. I got a message from the guardian. She told me that Madman's girlfriend, Lucy MacGill, will be here – she's Yellow Jacko's niece. She wants her brought in after the service.'

So that's how Doris wanted to play – deal with my sidekick rather than me. Bad move.

People were beginning to arrive, most of them by bike. The older and younger ones would have walked from the bus stop on Ferry Road.

A thin, bald man with yellow skin hurried up to me. 'Good afternoon, Citizen Dalrymple,' he said, looking around anxiously.

'Douglas Haigh.' The creepy caretaker didn't get to call me Quint. 'Aren't you past retirement age?'

'Oh, yes.' He smiled in a way that made my skin crawl. 'But you know how much I love my work.'

I did, having had more contact with him than I wanted over the years.

'Would it be possible for that Guard vehicle to be moved from the forecourt?' he asked, rubbing his hands together. They rasped like an unbandaged mummy's.

Davie was already back in the driver's seat. He moved slowly through the burgeoning crowd and behind the crematorium.

Catriona and I stepped back to let the people past. We got plenty of harsh looks.

'Don't worry,' the guardswoman said in a low voice. 'My photographer's up the tree behind us. Don't look.'

'I wasn't born yesterday.'

'No, you're almost as old as the ghoul.'

'Thanks.'

We watched as Haigh skilfully shepherded the crowd inside. His wide smile was about as inviting as an evening with the head of Prostitution Services, who's as old as he is.

'The rest of my people are stationed around the place,' Catriona said. 'Bet you can't spot them.'

'I don't bet.'

'Yes, you do,' Davie protested, having returned.

'Only with suckers – I mean, you.'

'All right,' he said, 'I bet you a bottle of outsider whisky that you can't see any Guard personnel.'

'Apart from the one up the tree behind us,' Catriona added.

I looked around as the last of the mourners arrived.

'Never mind,' she said, taking a photo from a sheaf. 'This is Lucy MacGill. We'll pick her up afterwards.

'Wait a minute.' Davie moved forward quickly. 'That woman over there is Madman Lamont.'

I took in a figure in a long brown dress and a distinctly not matching hat. There was a large bag over the right shoulder.

'Halt!' Davie yelled.

The figure broke into a run.

Davie raised his Hyper-Stun and fired.

The man-woman collapsed to the asphalt. Then there was a blinding flash and a blast that threw us to the ground. I rolled quickly on to my front. Shrapnel and pieces of asphalt rained down on us.

My ears were ringing, but I could still hear something – muted screaming from inside the building, frantic gasps from Catriona by my side, the clatter of Guard boots breaking cover . . . I sat up, wiping my eyes on my sleeve and saw – a splatter of blood and flesh on and around the crematorium doors . . . and a body further back . . . Davie. I got to my feet and staggered over. By the time I got there, I saw movement, his legs kicking. I remembered Caro's last frantic struggle for life.

'Davie!' I yelled, my voice sounding distant. I kneeled by him. He was at least five yards to the rear of where he'd been when the explosion happened, his head away from the building. Had he done a somersault when the wave of displaced air hit him? Or two? What would that have done to his internal and external organs?

I heard a gaggle of voices and looked up to see citizens rushing out of the shattered doors, trying to avoid the spattered remains of Madman Lamont. Some were clutching wounds, but most seemed unhurt, at least physically. Davie had stunned the head-banger before he got close enough to wipe out the families inside. Maybe he really was crazy – if there was to be no Portobello Pish, then nobody was to survive.

'Wha—' Davie sat up.

'Jesus, you're alive.'

'Wha—'

'Can . . . you . . . hear . . . me?' I shouted.

'Yes!' he shouted back, then shook his head. 'Sort of.' There was blood all over his face and a piece of asphalt was embedded above his left eye. He looked around.

'Cat!' He got to his feet and stumbled over to the guardswoman, pushing past the fleeing citizens.

I went after him. By the time I got there, he was kneeling over the motionless body. When he moved back I saw a short shaft of metal protruding from her chest. I was pretty sure it had pierced her heart.

Paramedics were soon on the scene, uniformed personnel swarming around the walking wounded. Douglas Haigh, untouched, was wandering around rubbing his hands – no doubt lamenting the lack of even more customers. A young medical auxiliary had led Davie to an ambulance and was working on his face and the backs of his hands. The public order and medical guardians weren't long in making their appearances.

'What was it, Quint?' Sophia asked.

I could hear pretty well now. 'Some kind of grenade. I think the crazy bastard was planning to throw it into the packed crematorium and take as many of the former gang families out as he could. Including his girlfriend.'

'Let me see that hand,' Sophia said. There were dots of blood all over my fading DM stamp. She pulled on surgical gloves and swabbed the skin, making me wince.

'There are bits of foreign matter in here,' she said. 'You need to come to the infirmary.'

'Not yet.'

'Suit yourself,' she said brusquely. 'But if they get infected . . .'

Guardian Doris came up.

'Sorry about the guardswoman,' I said. 'But Davie deserves a medal.'

'There'll be time for that later,' she said, looking at the sparse remains of Madman, now covered with a blanket. 'Will this spark off a gang war?'

'Not with the Portobello Pish in ruins. I wouldn't recommend a clamp-down on the Lancers for the time being.'

She frowned. 'That hadn't crossed my mind. Does this get us any further with the . . . other incidents?'

I blinked, my eyes still gritty. 'It doesn't answer any questions definitively, does it? Brown may have had links with the smugglers who supplied the Pish and, yes, the Lancers may have killed him. But it doesn't have anything obvious to do with the Tyneside organ.'

She understood that reference to the heart at the Hearts ground immediately, but it took Sophia a few seconds longer.

'Could the whole thing be tied to the football clubs?' Guardian Doris asked. 'Their managers aren't exactly as pure as the driven—'

'Cliché. No, they're not. They're also deadly rivals, especially the ones in charge of Hearts and Hibs. Why don't you haul them all in for a cup of coffee and a beating? Apart from the missing Alec Ferries, of course.'

She frowned at me, then turned away and walked quickly to her 4×4, apparently energized by my suggestion.

Davie walked slowly towards us, staples on his face and a dressing where the asphalt asteroid had hit his forehead.

'Bastard,' he grunted. 'I never thought he'd be carrying a bomb.'

'Me neither,' I said. 'I'm sorry about Catriona.'

He scowled. 'She was a good Guard. Someone's going to pay.'

'Her killer's in small pieces,' Sophia said.

Davie turned his head, favouring his right ear. 'I want to know who the Pish were working for.'

I nodded. 'Me too. But don't you think you should lie down for a few hours?'

'Yes,' said Sophia. 'You should. That's an order.' She looked at me. 'You too, Quint. In fact, you're both coming to the infirmary. I want to run checks on your hearing and get you cleaned up properly.'

'I'm coming to the Council meeting,' I said firmly.

She sighed. 'If I give you the all-clear. And, commander? You're not driving. Both of you in the back of my vehicle. Now!'

Suddenly weary, we did as we were told.

The feeling of the experts was that both my and Davie's hearing wasn't permanently damaged and would return to normal soon. Our wounds were given a proper seeing to and then we were taken to a double-bedded doctors' room and locked in. Sophia's a great one for trust, like all her rank.

We gave up trying to converse because it got boring saying 'What?' all the time. My sleep was deep and surprisingly undisturbed – until Sophia shook me awake.

'Come on, Quint,' she said with a rare smile. 'The Council's slavering to see you.'

'That'll be right.' I looked across to the other bed. Davie was fast asleep. 'Let's leave the commander. Locked in?'

'Why not?'

Sophia drove us to the Council chamber herself. I guessed that meant she had something private to impart, but she was silent until we were halfway down the Royal Mile.

'Come to my place tonight, Quint.'

I only just heard the words. They weren't unwelcome.

'Maisie wants to see you.'

I felt like a bucket of sea water had been thrown over me, even though I liked the wee girl a lot. Then I realized she was laughing.

'The look on your face. Like a child that's had a sweetie taken from its open mouth.'

'I'll give you open mouth,' I said, moving towards her.

'No!' she squealed. 'I'll run a tourist down and then where will we be?'

She had a point. I let her alone on condition that she let me stay after Maisie was asleep.

We arrived at the former – and maybe future – Scottish parliament building shaken and fairly stirred. Then I remembered the stern faces waiting for me.

'Citizen Dalrymple,' the education guardian said after I'd told them most of what I'd discovered, 'you seem to be chasing this investigation rather than applying order to it.'

I looked at the desiccated old professor, then at Guardian Doris.

Eventually she rose to the occasion. 'To be fair, this is a complex set of incidents. There's any number of tangents. For instance, the city's premier-league football managers have been brought in for questioning.'

'Why's that?' Jack MacLean asked, glancing at the recreation guardian. The latter looked uncomfortable.

'Because, finance guardian, the gang known as the Portobello Pish had at least two players who were members.'

'That hardly seems reason to bring in all the other team bosses,' the senior guardian said.

I smelled a rodent with large yellow teeth. Both slick Jack, Billy Geddes's boss, and Fergus Calder, head of the Supply Directorate that had supposedly been providing the Pish with drugs, had evinced support for the other EPL managers. That needed looking into. As did Peter Stewart's failure to object.

'They'll be released when they satisfy my investigators,' the public order guardian said, eyeing them both with what looked like distrust. Nice one, Doris.

'What about this head on the New Tolbooth?' asked the tourism guardian, a middle-aged woman who declined to do anything about her grey hair. I admired her for that, if little else.

'It'll be taken down tonight,' Doris said.

'We'll confirm if it's Grant Brown's,' Sophia put in.

'You realize the historical significance of the head on the spike?' the education guardian said.

'No,' said Calder, 'but do enlighten us.' He sat back, cupping his chin in his hands and closing his eyes.

'Only the heads of criminals were exposed in that way,' Cowan said. 'Criminals under the laws in force at the time, of course.' He looked at me and then the public order guardian. 'Have you considered that this Grant Brown was punished by people who wish to see the City Regulations upheld? He was, after all, a drug-trafficker, not that you did anything to stop him, Doris.'

That was a smart thought, and he was quickly paid back in kind.

'You wouldn't be familiar with a vigilante group, would you, Brian?'

He smiled, a little too easily, I thought. 'Me? I run the city's schools and colleges. What do I know of such things?'

'Indeed,' said the senior guardian. 'Citizen Dalrymple, what do you recommend we do now? Wait for another heart or head to appear?'

I delayed my answer, not least because I was undecided. If in doubt, put the fear of extinction up them.

'I gather the governors of Orkney and Shetland are arriving tomorrow,' I said, my eyes on Fergus Calder.

Suddenly he looked like there was a two-eyed snake in his underwear.

'They are. Why is that of interest to you?'

'You mean apart from the fact that regulations explicitly state that outsiders are not allowed access to the city?'

Jack MacLean gave a hollow laugh. 'Don't be absurd, Quint. The regulations have been amended. With the referendum coming up, we need to see our counterparts regularly.'

'My copy doesn't contain any such amendment.'

There was a pause while they all – even Sophia – gave me the evil eye.

'Citizen,' the senior guardian said, 'not all amendments are made available to people of your rank.'

'Oh, I see. You can do what you like while ordinary citizens are left to believe that their rulers abide by the published regulations.'

'That's enough. What is your interest in our guests?'

I'd made my point. 'Are they arriving at the City Airport?'

MacLean nodded.

'I suggest you do a careful sweep of the buildings there and station more Guard personnel than usual on the road into the city.'

'You have evidence that there's a threat?' said Calder, aghast.

I shook my head. 'We have a heart and a head. The owner of the latter had connections with outsiders. That makes me think that outsiders may be the key to this.' I ran my eyes around the semi-circle of faces above me. 'Because no cases of heart removal or decapitation have been recorded in the perfect city for over ten years, have they? While who knows what they get up to in the wild north and west?'

That got them chattering nervously. I had no reason to suspect the governors of Orkney and Shetland, but the Lord of the Isles, due the day after tomorrow, was another kettle of herring altogether; as was Andrew Duart of Glasgow, arriving on Saturday – Glasgow, where a heart had been found at Celtic Park. There was no harm in rousing the guardians before kick-off.

Then I had another thought, one I didn't intend to share. After the meeting, I arranged with Sophia that I'd come to her quarters at 10 p.m. That gave me plenty of time to have a chat with Cecilia of Corstorphine, Grant Brown's grieving other half.

ELEVEN

Cecilia's surname turned out to be Colquhoun. The file I accessed in the command centre helpfully informed me that the name was pronounced 'Ca-hoon'. I knew that, but auxiliaries who'd never been out of the city and had no experience of the weirder clan names didn't. No doubt Brian 'Know-All' Cowan had provided a helping hand.

Davie was walking up the cobbles as I was heading down.

'You all right, big man?'

'I'll survive. At least I can hear better.'

So could I. We'd been luckier than the nightly tourist winners of the All the Way Club on Rose Street's 'Feel Up Mary Queen of Scots or David Rizzio' competition.

I told him where I was going.

'I'll drive you.'

I took in the state of his face. The stapled wounds had turned into a rainbow of pain. 'All right, but you stay in the 4×4. The poor girl's been shocked enough.'

He wasn't impressed, taking it out on the kerb stones and setts of the Old Town. He'd calmed down by the time we reached Haymarket.

'This is where it all started,' he said, taking the road next to the one that leads to Tynecastle.

I was looking at the file on Cecilia's parents in the evening light. For once the sky wasn't depositing felines and canines by the truck-load on us. 'Mother, Ailsa, a hairdresser, father, Eric, a . . . hang on, we might need backup.'

Davie perked up. 'Oh aye? What is he?'

'A . . . bad man. Two years on Cramond Island back in the drugs wars for—'

'Drugs-gang activity.'

'Genius. Then seven separate years down the mines for acts of civil disobedience.' That was the Guard's phrase for getting up their collective nose. 'Stealing from a shop, then from a coal depot, bartering illicitly obtained Supply Directorate whisky – two terms for that – bartering stolen water during the Big Heat – another two terms – and, get this – crossing the city line. He was sent home a month ago from his last stint.'

'Think he might have gone back to his old ways?'

'There's no shortage of city-line crossing in this investigation.'

Davie drove past the rust-reddened steel supports of Murrayfield Stadium.

When I was young I saw the Scotland rugby team win rarely and lose frequently there. More recently it's been used for barracks rugby, but citizens pay little attention to that now football is back.

'Here we go. Among Eck's close friends, going all the way back to school, is one Derick Smail.'

'The Hibs manager.'

'Correct.'

'That's definitely suggestive. But why do you want backup?'

'Eric Colquhoun is nineteen stone and a certified fight fan, two of the fists in action being his own.'

Davie glanced at the latest photo. 'Just a fat lump. I can take him easily.'

'Except you're staying in the vehicle.'

'I'll sneak round the back and rescue you if things get nasty.'

He turned up Clermiston Road and parked about fifty yards from the Colquhoun house. I took my life in my hands and walked to the front door, while Davie disappeared into the drizzle.

I was let in by a woman whose spectacular coiffure did little to deflect attention from the wrinkles on her face. I said I was a private investigator – no lie – and that I needed to see Cecilia. She might have believed me, but Eric had my number the second he lumbered into the hall.

'Fuckin' Citizen fuckin' Dalrymple,' he roared. 'I ken exactly what kind ae Council-lickin' shitebag yous are.'

I saw Cecilia stop halfway down the stairs. 'Eric, surely you don't want to upset your daughter. She's had a terrible loss.'

'No' as terrible as the yin you're aboot tae get, pal.'

Then he raised his arms like a cartoon monster and twitched all over, before crashing to the floor. Davie came from the rear of the house and removed the Hyper-Stun's prongs from the now motionless heavy's back. He cuffed his hands and ankles, then stood up. What was bothering him was the same thing I was struggling with – neither Ailsa Colquhoun nor her daughter had emitted a sound. Maybe this was par for the course with Eck. Then I wondered how he knew who I was. I'd been in the *Edinburgh Guardian* often enough over the years, but I had the feeling this was more recent. His daughter might have told him about me. Then again, so might Derick Smail.

'Come away in,' said Ailsa, leading us into a tidy sitting room. The furniture was standard issue, but she'd made an effort to smarten it up with brightly coloured rugs and throws. 'Would ye like some tea?'

I declined. 'I'm sorry about that, but your man was about to make mincemeat out of me.'

'Aye, he's terrible. That'll be him back to the mines fir another year, Ah suppose.' She sounded hopeful.

'It depends on how much he cooperates.'

'He was never much for cooperation.'

'I noticed. Listen, I need to speak to you, Cecilia. Alone.'

'That's fine,' her mother said to my surprise. 'Tak him up to yer room, lass.'

Cecilia smiled and inclined her head at me. I motioned to Davie to stay where he was – if he'd fully recovered his wits, he would charm Ailsa into giving away the family secrets.

'In here,' Cecilia said.

Her room was very unlike the sitting room. It was more spartan than the Supply Directorate norm, the walls bare and the bed covered by a thin blanket that must have been woven before the crash of 2003. Everything was spotless, though.

'Sit down, citizen,' she said, pointing to the chair by the small table. She sat primly on the bed. Now that her face wasn't red and wrought by initial stress, I saw that she was an attractive young woman. But her eyes, grey and unwavering, were disconcerting and her manner dispassionate.

'Have you found out anything about what happened to Grant?' she said.

I wasn't going to tell her about his head and where it had turned up – at least, not yet.

'Cecilia, I want you to be straight with me. Do you know what Grant did in his free time?'

Her head dropped, her chin resting on her alabaster neck.

'You do,' I surmised.

'I'm sorry I didn't tell you,' she said, eyes still down but voice steady.

'Tell me now.'

She hesitated before speaking. 'He was smuggling. He went to the city line beyond Colinton at night. Cigarettes mainly, I think.' She shook her head. 'I don't smoke.'

'Who did he sell them to?'

She looked up and caught my gaze. 'The Pish. He played football with Allie Swanson. I didn't like him.'

I nodded. She didn't seem to be concealing anything now.

'I think he sold them at his work too.'

The Housing Directorate foreman needed to be hauled in.

'And he was into betting as well.'

I disguised my interest. Apart from Edlott, gambling was only for tourists – the regulations were still clear about that. There weren't many illicit schemes because the Guard nailed citizens who indulged.

'Who did he bet with and what on?' I said when she stopped being so forthcoming.

'All the Hibs players bet on the games, their own as well as the other clubs'.'

That was interesting. Derick Smail must have known about that – and the bosses of the other EPL teams. No doubt that was why

Alec Ferries had gone to ground. Fortunately Guardian Doris already had the others in the castle. I sent her a text to make sure they stayed there. Then I remembered Jack MacLean's concern about the managers being questioned, as well as the senior guardian's. Council scandal number 247 coming right up . . .

'How are you doing?' I asked Cecilia.

'I'm empty,' she said with a brave smile. 'I loved Grant, whatever he did. Now . . . now I've got nothing.'

I stood up and took her hands.

'You're young, you're pretty and you've got your whole life ahead of you. Grieve for him, then let him go and get on with things.'

I left her on the bed, aware that my words had been nothing more than platitudes. Downstairs, Davie and Ailsa were chattering like primary school kids in break. After a while he got up and shook hands with her, a highly unusual action for a Guard commander to take with a citizen.

'What was all that about?' I said after we'd pushed the still unconscious Eric Colquhoun into the back of the 4×4.

'She knew my mother,' Davie said. 'They went to school together.'

'I don't suppose you picked up any usual snippets of information.'

He shook his head then turned the vehicle round. 'Except maybe this.'

I glared at him in the last of the gloaming.

'The Hearts manager's wife, Eileen Ferries, is a customer of hers. Apparently the club's as rotten as it comes. The shame of it.'

'Don't worry. There's a gambling scheme. Hibs are the same, it seems. And all the other members of the EPL.'

He grinned. 'What a relief.'

There was a groan from the back seat.

'Yous are fuckin' deid,' said Big Eck.

'Not as deid as you're going to be,' countered Davie.

'Leave him alone,' I said. 'Remember Sophia's little helper?'

He laughed. 'That's right. They'll all be spilling their guts.'

Which was true, I thought. But then where would the city be?

So many people had been taken to the castle that there wasn't enough secure space. Eventually the duty commander decided to chain some of them to the weight-lifting apparatus in the gym. She was smart enough to gag them so they couldn't concoct a story that would at least muddy the puddles, if not save their backsides.

'What now?' Davie asked, a file in his hand. 'This is the list. Who do you want to take to the medical guardian first?'

'Let's do it the usual way first. Remember what the truth drug did to Skinny Ewan.' I ran an eye down the names. 'You take Derick Smail.'

'I like it.'

'And I'll take the Morningside Rose manager.'

'Kennie Dove? They won the league last season. I always thought he was a good guy.'

'Another reason why you aren't interviewing him.'

I was given a windowless room beneath the command centre. There were two chairs, one fixed to the concrete floor. As I'd ordered, the Morningside manager was brought in wearing handcuffs and a chain that was then attached to the ring under his seat.

'Call me Quint,' I said with an extravagant smile.

'Right you are,' the thin, short man said. 'Quint.' He was wearing a brown leather jacket and matching corduroys, as well as a loosely fastened black-and-blue striped tie.

I leaned over and undid the knot. 'I'll take that. Wouldn't be the first time that someone's hanged himself in the castle recently. Sort of.'

Dove's eyes opened wide. 'Why would I do that, citizen? I mean, Quint.'

'Because you've been mixing with some very unsavoury people.'

He laughed nervously. 'Aye, well, in this business you need long teeth to survive. See Derick Smail, he—'

'I don't mean your counterparts, though I'm sure they'll be equally complimentary about you. I'm talking about illegal betting.'

'What?' His face was suddenly paler than a December morning when the haar rolls in from the Forth.

'How rife is it?'

The manager looked dazed, even confused. 'How what?'

'Rife – common, prevalent, rampant.'

'Em, citizen . . . Quint, you're making a mistake here.'

'Is that right? So no one's making books, setting odds, taking wagers? No one's fixing games?'

'Em . . .' Kennie Dove's eyes were all over the place, except on mine. 'Can I see your authorization?'

I handed it over.

'You're allowed to question guardians and senior auxiliaries?'
I nodded.

'Talk to the recreation guardian then,' he said, folding his arms.
'I'm not saying another word.'

The door behind me opened.

'Citizen, a word,' said Guardian Doris.

I followed her out.

'I've been listening,' she said.

'I might have known you'd have the place wired for sound.'

She shrugged. 'My domain, my rules.'

'Uh-huh. I take it you'll be calling the recreation guardian up
here for a wee chat.'

The guardian shook her head. 'Peter Stewart isn't involved in
any gambling scheme.'

I considered the tall, white-haired guardian. It was true that he
had a reputation for probity. He'd been a world-class athlete, but
being unable to leave Edinburgh when he was young meant he'd
never competed against his peers. Then again, the last Olympic
Games were in 2000, when he was still a schoolboy. The headquarters of international sports organizations were among the first targets
of enraged mobs in Switzerland.

'So why's Kennie Dove fingering him?' I asked.

'Because Dove is a scheming runt who'll do anything to distract
us from his real bosses.'

'Who are?'

'I'm working on that.'

'But you have suspicions.'

The guardian smoothed back her hair. 'Not that I'm willing to
share. I have no evidence.'

'Except the heart.'

She pursed her lips. 'Which you have singularly failed to explain,
never mind find out who removed it. Or even who it was removed
from.'

'I'm working on that,' I said, repeating her phrase and feeling
the need to change the subject. 'Why don't we take Dove over to
the infirmary and give him a mild dose of the guardian's truth
drug?'

'You're sure he won't talk otherwise?'

'Oh, he'll talk – if you set your heavies loose on him. But that
would be breaking the regulations, wouldn't it?' I tried not to smirk.

'The truth drug is not covered by any regulation,' she said, her eyes flashing.

'There you are, then.'

'That's not what I . . . oh, very well. Go ahead.'

'Given the rivalry between Hearts and Hibs, I think Derick Smail would benefit from the same treatment. Unless Hume 253's already on to the seventh degree.'

She led me to a door down the corridor and opened it. The Hibs manager's expression was that of a man a bus was about to collide with, but he was unmarked.

I took Davie aside and told him the plan. He said that Smail had clammed up too, though he hadn't mentioned the recreation guardian.

We handed them over to a quartet of Guard personnel and went down to the esplanade.

'Do you think Peter Stewart could be dirty?' I asked Davie.

'Never heard the slightest whisper. He's not the most active guardian, but he's strict about the regs.'

I nodded. We got into a 4×4 and went to the infirmary, the prisoners in another vehicle to our rear. I found Sophia in her office, lines of exhaustion on her face.

'I think we'd better postpone our personal rendezvous,' I said, looking at my watch. It was five to ten.

'I was about to call you.'

Although she had the usual icy grip on her emotions, I could tell she was upset.

'What is it?'

She looked up at me and then shook her head. '"Things fall apart, the centre cannot hold."'

'William Butler Yeats, no less.' I went over and put my arm round her shoulders. She was very tense.

'The truth drug,' she said in a low voice. 'It's disappeared.'

That was more bitter than sweet – we'd shaken someone's cage, but he, she or they had managed to jemmy open the door and fly away. The question was, how far?

'It's my fault,' Sophia said, standing by the safe in the supposedly high-security drugs storage room. 'I should have split the consignment. I only found out when I went to check how much was left. I had a feeling you'd be wanting more.'

'How many staff knew the combination?'

'Three. Don't worry, they're all confined to quarters, but they deny involvement.'

'Which isn't to say one of them didn't pass the combination to someone else.'

'Hm.' Sophia looked like she'd been rabbit-punched.

I took her hand. 'It's not your fault. The investigation is making certain people nervous, which is a good thing. Presumably nobody saw any unauthorized personnel down here.'

'No. Pity we don't have security cameras.'

'I'll get a scene-of-crime team to attend.' I checked the floor. The surface was tracked with footprints, all of them similar.

'How many people have a key to this room?'

'Fifty-seven,' Sophia replied hopelessly.

I called the Guard command centre and arranged for a forensics team. They'd do their job, but I wasn't optimistic about the results.

'Never mind,' I said. 'Get the lock changed and reset the combination. For the time being, keep the latter to yourself.'

'That's totally impractical, Quint,' she said, her voice rising.

'All right. Give it to the chief chemist. You trust him, don't you?'

'He's a she. I don't know who to trust any more.'

I nodded. 'That's the way of things when, as you said, the centre cannot hold.'

She gave me an exasperated look. Fortunately my phone rang. It was Davie.

'Quint, meet me at the 4×4. A body's been found and guess what?'

'Surprise me.'

'The heart's been removed.'

It had only been a matter of time.

TWELVE

'Where is it?' I asked as Davie started the engine. Sophia had wanted to come, but I told her to get some rest. Astonishingly she went along with that.

'Granton, near the remains of the last gasometer.'

'Interesting. Only a mile or so to the west of Leith Lancers' territory and close to the Forth.'

'Aye, people who want to leave the city are picked up by the Fife boats around there. Maybe outsiders really are doing this.'

Once we were out of the tourist zone, Davie put on the lights and siren and we were at the shore in ten minutes. At least the rain wasn't horizontal, but the wind was blowing it around enough to soak every inch of you in seconds. I was glad to see that a smart guardsman or woman had erected a Guard tent over the body and set up lights. To the side the remains of the gasometer's skeletal structure loomed. Over the water I could see the glow of towns and farms. For decades Fife had been dark at night, but now it was on its way back to civilization. The random streetlights in the housing schemes on our side suggested the reverse was happening in Edinburgh.

'Who's in charge?' I asked.

'Cramond 127,' said a heavy-faced guardsman with short white hair.

'Bruce!' said Davie, punching him on the upper arm. 'Did you call in this horror?'

'I did, Davie. My team was patrolling the front – you know what goes on here at night – when we came across – well, you'll see.' Cramond 127 gave me a disparaging look. 'Citizen Dalrymple. Wherever you go, someone dies.' He was one of the old Guard who hadn't forgiven me for quitting the directorate.

I smiled. 'It was you who found this dead one, wasn't it?'

He didn't reply. I decided against inviting him to call me by my first name.

We were handed plastic overshoes and rubber gloves by a young guardswoman.

'I was wondering where you'd been, Hume 481,' I said, squatting by the corpse.

'Michael Campbell,' Davie said, taking in his barracks colleague's face. The dead man's mouth and eyes were wide open. He was wearing citizen-issue clothes, but his shirt had been ripped apart and his cracked ribs stood up like miniature replicas of the gasometer's broken spars.

'I wonder where his parents are,' I said.

'I hate to imagine,' said Davie. 'Poor bastard. Whatever he did, he didn't deserve to die like this.'

There were voices at the entrance to the tent and Sophia came in. I might have known.

'Let me have a look,' she said impatiently, hustling Davie out of her way.

She opened her bag and removed various instruments. I stood back, having seen enough of Hume 481's ravaged chest. After about five minutes, Sophia got to her feet.

'Taking into account the ambient temperature and the state of rigor, I'd say the victim died between eight and ten hours ago.'

'No need to ask the cause of death,' I said.

She ignored that. 'The ribs were cut with a modicum of skill and, again, the heart was carefully removed. The lack of blood shows that the victim was already dead when the organ was cut out. There are contusions on his wrists and ankles, suggesting he was tied up and the bonds removed post-mortem. There are also fibre traces in his mouth, showing that at some point he was gagged. It would have been daylight, though it rained most of the time. There may have been witnesses.'

'It's unlikely anyone will come forward,' I said. 'Citizens down here keep their doors and mouths triple-locked. You know what they think of the Council and its works.'

Sophia frowned. 'Of course, this means we potentially have another heart about to make an appearance. The one at Tynecastle was removed while this poor man was still alive.'

'And there are important visitors from Orkney and Shetland arriving in the morning,' I said.

'Indeed,' she said, giving me a quizzical look. 'You think there's a connection.'

'Potentially,' I said, using her term.

'Are you coming to the post-mortem?'

I glanced at Davie. 'The commander will take my place.' That didn't go down well with either of them. 'I've got somewhere else to go.'

Sophia gave a minuscule smile. 'Moray Place, perhaps?'

She wasn't a guardian only because she was a medical genius. She knew which Council members I was going to visit. The idea that I might stop off at her house across the street afterwards maybe afforded her a smidgeon of pleasure.

I commandeered Davie's 4×4 after the Guard squad spoke to the locals. It had been raining heavily, of course, but it could have been a Mediterranean summer's day – which I heard are seriously sweltering now – and no one would have talked. I asked Davie's pal, Cramond 127, to go into Leith with his people and see if he could lay hands on any of the Lancers. The gang-bangers might have located Michael Campbell, but they wouldn't have had the skill to take his heart without making a hell of a mess. Was someone using them as foot soldiers and providing a heart-cutter? Another question for the senior guardian. I considered calling ahead, but decided against it. Surprise was a useful weapon, though he would probably have been told about the body.

Moray Place is in the west of the New Town, a circle broken by four access roads, all of which are blocked by gates manned by elite Guard units. I managed to get to Doune Terrace without stalling the vehicle more than twice. I've never been much of a driver and Davie was reluctant to give me the keys. I got out and went to the gate, authorization in hand.

'The senior guardian is expecting you,' a muscle-bound guardsman said. 'Number 7.'

'I know.' I'd been to most of the guardians' houses over the decades. Each was allocated an entire six-storey house though much of the accommodation was taken up by offices, live-in auxiliaries and Guard personnel.

The door to number 7 opened before I reached it and a female auxiliary in a grey suit and white blouse ushered me in. She tried not to turn her nose up at my soaked donkey jacket and muddy boots, but didn't have the nerve to tell me to take them off. I happily mucked up the carpets. Most guardians don't have enough contact with the real dirty world. Then again, Fergus Calder might well have very soiled hands indeed.

I was taken into a large drawing room on the first floor. The decor was the best the Supply Directorate could provide – Georgian chairs and tables, an Edwardian leather sofa and matching armchairs, and the customary artwork from the city's collection. The senior guardian had chosen El Greco's curious *Fábula*, with two men, one wearing a bright yellow cloak, and a monkey gathered around a light. I've never had a clue what the painting means, but I suspected the senior guardian liked its air of mystery. Or perhaps he thought it was enlightening and thus a link to the Council's founding fathers and mothers.

There was a creak and Billy Geddes rolled forward in his chair.

Then Jack MacLean and Fergus Calder got up from the armchairs. A veritable welcoming committee.

'Gentlemen,' I said.

'Citizen . . . Quint,' said the senior guardian, no doubt thinking he was putting me in my place. 'I'm glad you came.'

'Otherwise you'd have hauled me in.'

He smiled. 'Yes. Tell us about the heartless corpse.'

I thought that was a pretty heartless way of putting it, but I filled them in. Then I hit back. 'Is there anything you want to tell me?'

They looked at each other.

'What are you getting at?' MacLean said with less bonhomie than usual.

'Thought not,' I muttered. I decided against asking them if they were using the Leith Lancers as auxiliary auxiliaries. I had no proof. 'I was wondering if your visitors tomorrow have had any heart or head issues.'

'Orkney and Shetland?' Billy said. 'Not that we've heard of.'

Which showed how close he was to the centre of things.

'You might want to keep security after them tight since you've got the Lord of the Isles and Glasgow's boss arriving in quick succession.'

Fergus Calder looked dubious. 'I still don't understand why. The public order guardian hasn't reported any signs of civil disobedience.'

'Remember the bomb at the crematorium?'

That took the wind from his spanker.

'Surely that was just a bit of extreme inter-gang violence,' Billy said, moving further into the light.

'If we're lucky.' I prepared to knife them. 'Do any of you know about betting on Edinburgh Premier League matches?'

Silence, long and golden.

'Yes? No? Maybe?' I prompted.

'Explain,' Calder ordered.

I told them what Cecilia had told me – which was dismissed as a justifiably hysterical female citizen's fantasy – and that the Morningside Rose manager had fingered the recreation guardian.

'Peter Stewart would never sanction anything that breaks City Regulations,' the senior guardian scoffed.

'Who would, then?' I asked.

They got my drift.

'You're suggesting that one – or more – of us is involved?' the finance guardian said, getting to his feet.

I shrugged. 'Do I get an answer?'

'No!' Billy yelled. 'You do not get an answer. You have no right to make accusations like that!'

Fergus Calder turned to him. 'All right, Billy. I appreciate your concern, but the citizen is authorized to ask any questions, even of guardians.'

'And SPADEs,' I added.

'What would betting on EPL matches have to do with the removal of two hearts and a head?' MacLean asked, standing over me.

'You tell me.'

He didn't like that but, after balling his fists, he turned and went back to his chair.

'Are you sure you aren't allowing yourself to get distracted, citizen?' the senior guardian said.

I met his gaze. 'Do you know about betting on the football or not?'

He didn't look away. 'No, of course not. Jack?'

'Me neither,' the finance guardian said, looking like he wanted to spit in my face.

Interestingly, Billy wasn't given the chance to answer.

'Can we get back to the heart business?' MacLean asked.

'Right. We have one heart, now dissected, and one donor, but they don't match. So, somewhere in the city, are another body without a heart and another heart without a body.'

'Could the second heart have been taken for transplantation?' Billy said.

'I suppose so,' I said, 'but the ruined gasometer at Granton isn't exactly a sterile location.'

'Besides, the first one appeared at Tynecastle,' Calder said.

'Which gives you a link to the EPL,' I said, smiling. 'Along with the Hibs players who were members of the Portobello Pish.'

'So you think this new heart is bound for the centre circle at Easter Road?' said MacLean.

'No,' I replied. 'Security's tight, as it is at all football grounds in the city.'

'And the hearts in Glasgow and Inverness lead you to the conclusion that visitors to the city might be targeted?'

'Or be made to witness the horror beneath the gleaming surface here?' I got up. 'Make sure the haggis is checked before it's served.'

They let me go. I was pretty sure they knew about the betting, but the guardians had learned plausible denial. Billy hadn't, though.

Sophia's house was on the other side of the gardens in the centre of Moray Place, but Peter Stewart's was third to the left of the senior guardian's. This was a good opportunity to ask him about the football betting. I rang the bell and mugged to the security camera.

The grey-suited male auxiliary who opened the door knew who I was, but he wasn't keen on letting me in.

'The guardian has retired,' he said, nose in the air as if I stank – which I did.

'It's urgent,' I said, holding up my authorization.

'Very well, I'll advise him.'

'No, you won't. Tell me where he is.'

The auxiliary's resistance was broken only when I grabbed his balls.

'Second . . . floor,' he gasped. 'Second . . . door . . . left.'

I let him go after telling him not to call the Guard members on the premises, then ran up the stairs. The red carpet was new, which was unusual for austere guardians like Stewart. It wasn't as if the recreation guardian received guests from other cities. Or was it? Maybe a national football league was on the cards. That had been a real success before the 2003 crisis – referees bribed, running battles between fans, a completely corrupt organizing body.

I knocked on the door. Nothing. I knocked harder. Same again. I turned the handle, but the door was locked. I pounded, not least because I could hear Guard boots thundering up the stairs – I should have pulled the auxiliary's balls off. Then I put my shoulder to the door. On the second attempt, the Georgian hinges splintered. I stumbled in.

Too late.

The recreation guardian was hanging from the light fitting, a small table on its side beneath his feet. Around his neck was a thin cord that had cut deep into the skin. His eyes were bulging and his tongue protruding.

A guardsman pushed past me, heading for his boss's body.

I ordered him back, then called Sophia.

It didn't look like either of us was going to get any sleep tonight, never mind carnal action.

I had a job keeping the scene uncontaminated before the forensics team arrived. Guardians clustered at the door, Fergus Calder to the fore. I explained to them that Sophia had taken personal charge and that I needed to speak to everyone who had been in the house, without the presence of Council members. They moved away, muttering about the disgrace. Suicide is still an offence and surviving family members are severely punished, as well as the self-murderer's name being removed from all city records. No guardian or auxiliary had ever committed suicide. As far as I knew.

Davie came up the stairs when they were clear.

'This is a turn up for the books,' he said, rubbing his eyes.

'Hm.' I let him in and closed the door. The scene-of-crime experts were working the room, while Sophia and her team were looking at the body, which had recently been cut down.

'Bloody hell,' Davie said, taking in the guardian's swollen face.

'Quite. Can you handle the interviews with the house staff? I want to know who saw him last, how he was, you know the drill.'

He nodded and left. Then Guardian Doris came in, surprisingly late. She looked as shocked as the rest of her rank.

'I was interrogating football-club managers,' she explained. 'I told my people not to interrupt me.' She looked at her colleague's body. 'This is awful.'

She was right about that.

Sophia stood up and motioned us over.

'There's no doubt he was asphyxiated. The p-m will show if any of the cervical vertebrae were fractured too. Rigor hasn't yet set in, so he died in the last two hours.'

The scene-of-crime team leader came over.

'Excuse me, guardians,' she said. 'This is curious. Apart from residue from the mud on Citizen Dalrymple's boots, the rest of the carpet is extremely clean.'

'As if someone vacuumed it?' I asked.

'Yes. The only fingerprints we've found are the guardian's and those of his staff – I've made comparisons. Oh, and only his are on the table that he stood on and on the ligature. Which, by the way, is standard Guard-issue all-purpose cord. Finally, we've found no handwritten note. There is no sign of his computer.'

That was curious, though he might have left it at the directorate.

I went to the room where Davie was interviewing and told him to ask about the sound of vacuuming. Outside, the auxiliary whose testicles I'd twisted gave me a look that dripped hatred. Davie would soon sort that out.

'Are you coming?' Sophia said as she came down the landing.

'Immediate post-mortem?'

'Actually, no. Remember the gang leader who was asphyxiated in the cells?'

'Muckle Tony? That was no suicide.'

'Exactly. I want to wait and see if any bruises develop on Peter's legs or arms. We'll do the p-m at nine a.m. Plus, the head from the New Tolbooth will have arrived by morning.'

'Right.'

'In the meantime, I'm going to get some sleep. Coming?'

I was, but I didn't. We both dropped into the arms of Morpheus a nanosecond after our heads hit the pillows.

THIRTEEN

I could have done with another twelve hours' sleep, but the breakfast Sophia's staff provided got me going – bacon, scrambled eggs, sausage, wholemeal toast and coffee that would normally only be available in the best tourist hotels. Sophia liked a few luxuries.

Maisie was in her school uniform. Edinburgh kids only get a two-week holiday in what passes for summer and she was still in class.

'Why are you here, funny Quint man?' she asked, as I stole her untouched sausage.

'Well, very odd Maisie girl, your mother and I are working together.'

'Uh-huh,' she said, far too knowing for a six-year-old. 'Are you making a baby?'

Sophia choked on her coffee, while my mouthful of sausage only just stayed where it was.

'No, dear, we're not doing that. Quint's helping me with some problems.'

'But he's not a doctor.'

I smiled. 'No, but I'm very good with my hands.' I grabbed her and tickled her until her laughter turned into squeals.

Sophia gave me a frozen look. 'That'll have put her in the mood for study.'

An auxiliary appeared and took Maisie away. She stuck her tongue out at me, but only because I'd done so first.

'What age are you, Quint?' Sophia demanded.

'Twelve. And next birthday I'll be eleven.'

'Plus thirty-nine.'

'Thanks.'

'Time we went for the p-m's.'

Suddenly breakfast didn't seem like such a joy after all.

Davie called when we were on the way to the infirmary.

'Bet I had a better breakfast than you,' I said.

'Bet you didn't have a bigger breakfast than me.'

'Ha. Find out anything interesting last night?'

'Not really. The guardian went to his room at 21.05 and no one heard anything from him after that. They said he seemed normal enough. Apparently he wasn't much of a talker at the best of times. And – guess what? – no one heard any vacuuming.'

'What do you think?'

'Not sure. I ran the house machine from the room and it wouldn't have been audible except on that floor. Those old houses are pretty solid. By the way, what did you do to Watt 529?'

'Who?'

'You know who.'

'Ah. He was obstructive. I took temporary possession of his nuts.'

Davie laughed. 'We'll get you back in the directorate yet, Quint.'

'Hm. Guess where we're going.'

'I'm not attending another p-m, thank you. Anyway, Guardian Doris wants me to help with the football manager questionings. And they've brought in Madman Lamont's girl.'

'I thought the guardian finished with the managers last night.'

'None of them talked. Then there are the other Porty Pish members. They've come round from their stunnings.'

'Good luck with all that. See you later.'

I turned to Sophia. We were halfway up Lothian Road and the rain was ricocheting off the bonnet.

'What happened at the p-m last night?'

'My preliminary observations were confirmed. Hume 481 was killed in daylight, around midday, cause of death heart failure due to shock. He'd taken a heavy blow to the back of his head. As I said yesterday evening, he was gagged and his wrists and ankles were bound – those bonds subsequently having been taken off – and his heart was removed with some skill.'

I remembered what Billy had said about transplantation and asked the question.

'It's not very likely. You'd want a sterile location to remove the organ, certainly not al fresco. Besides, the first one wasn't transplanted.'

'I wonder where heart number two's going to turn up.'

'Don't,' she said with a shiver.

I put my hand on hers. Even though the driver could probably see that in his mirror, she didn't shake it off. That was progress. She liked to imagine that our liaison was secret. It wasn't.

In the morgue, Tall and Short were waiting for us with eager looks that I didn't take to at all.

'Where do we start?' the former asked Sophia. 'The guardian or the head?'

'The latter,' she replied.

We went over to the table where a small sheet covered a football-shaped lump. Short whipped the cover off with a flourish.

There's something about decapitations that really gets me. To varying degrees all dead bodies are obscene, but severed heads are the ultimate desecration of the body because they contain what makes us what we are – the brain and all its layers of sense processing and thought, emotion and personality. No wonder the ancient Celts used to set their enemies' heads in gates and walls to exploit their spiritual power.

Though I wasn't sure how much spiritual power had been abstracted from Grant Brown's head. It was a sorry specimen, the hair plastered about the slack face, the eyes closed and the lips badly damaged. As for the neck, it was lacerated but clean, the arteries and veins like electrical wires rather than once living capillaries.

'It's Brown,' I said, comparing the face with the one in the file on a nearby table.

Sophia nodded. 'And I think a saw was used.'

Tall was bent over the table. 'Yes, the spine was severed between the C4 and C5 vertebrae by what I'd hazard was a hacksaw with a low number of tpi.'

'Teeth per inch,' I said. 'So fourteen or thereabouts?'

The pathologist raised his eyebrows. 'That would seem about right, citizen. We'll know more after further tests.'

'Leave it for now,' Sophia said, turning back to the recreation guardian and pulling off the larger sheet that was covering him. 'Och, Peter, how did it come to this?'

I was surprised even by that small display of emotion. The two guardians had never struck me as being close.

'Look here, Quint,' she said, pointing at bruises that had blackened on his lower thighs.

The pathologists craned forward, but I didn't need to. It was obvious that Peter Stewart had been pulled downwards like Muckle Tony Anderson. The question was, who had got to him? Had he been in bed with the gambling bosses or had he been about to spill the pulses? He couldn't tell us now.

I called Davie.

'Meet me outside the infirmary. Tell the guardian I need you.'

'Yes, darling.'

I took Sophia out of the morgue. 'What's happening with your investigation into the truth drug?'

'Good question.' She took off her elbow-length gloves and made a call.

'Nothing?' I said when she'd finished.

'None of the suspects will talk. My head of security says they're shit-scared, to use his words.'

'Keep them under several locks and keys.'

'Where are you going?'

'Better you don't know.'

'Charming,' she said, but she was smiling. 'Maybe we can meet in the late evening.'

'Guardian, I must warn you that such behaviour can be habit-forming.'

'Citizen, I already know that.' She turned back to the tables in the morgue.

I left her to death's realm. I had football on my mind.

The Recreation Directorate had moved to a recently completed building in the Market District. Davie turned left off Lothian Road and parked in front of the block of glass and steel. The conference hall was only a hundred yards away. A lot of Guard personnel and vehicles were stationed around the circular building.

'The governors of Orkney and Shetland are being taken there,' Davie said. 'There are extra units all along the road from the airport.'

Interesting: the senior guardian and his sidekicks had done what I suggested.

'Maybe we'll take a walk over there later,' I said. 'Find out anything from your interrogations?'

'Aye, Lucy MacGill's just a scared wee lassie. I think she's glad Madman's gone. She wasn't in the Pish.'

'Fair enough. What about Eck Colquhoun?'

'Still doing a decent imitation of an angry elephant seal. I threw a bucket of pig swill over him and left him to marinate.'

'Didn't know you were so well up on cooking terminology.'

'I'm a gourmet.'

'Gourmand, you mean.'

'It's possible to be both.'

I raised an eyebrow. 'What about the football managers?'

'I had one Alan Mowat of St Bernard's Rangers. A right loud-mouth, you know the kind.'

'Who said nothing useful. Did he mention Peter Stewart?'

'No.'

'Any other managers? Any other guardians or senior auxiliaries?'

He glared at me and shook his head.

'All right. I want you to put the fear of any deity you fancy up Peter Stewart's people.'

He grinned. 'My kind of job.'

I let him march ahead with a look on his face that would have made Godzilla turn tail. Not that I had more than a vague memory of who or what Godzilla was.

By the time I got to the spacious entrance hall, which was hung with banners bearing the insignia of the ten EPL teams, there was a distinct atmosphere of fear about the place. Auxiliaries were scurrying about like ants that had just been hit with anti-ant spray.

'Where's the guardian's office?' I asked when I got to Davie.

'Top floor,' he replied, leading me to the lift. 'Eight.'

We were conveyed upwards quickly enough to make me regret breakfast yet again. At least it didn't reappear.

There was more scuttling about in the open-plan office in front of us.

'Stay where you are!' Davie yelled. He'd never needed a

loudspeaker indoors. 'This is Citizen Dalrymple, the Council's special investigator. You do what he says or you answer to me.'

That did the trick. We were in the ex-guardian's office under a minute later, followed by his personal assistant, an elderly female auxiliary whose eyes were red and watery. Apparently the deputy guardian had been called to a meeting with Fergus Calder.

I looked at the desk.

'Where's his computer?'

'He had two desktops. The towers were gone when we came into work this morning, citizen.'

'No sign of his laptop?'

'No.'

'Who took them?'

'There's no record in the security log.'

'Get the night Guard unit,' I said to Davie, going over to the desk. It was mahogany and looked new. I opened the drawers. They were all empty, as were the file cabinets on the walls.

'I presume you kept records, Wilkie 88.'

'Yes, citizen,' she said, looking down. 'But the directorate main-frame was down when we came in this morning. The technicians are still trying to restart it.'

- 'Whatever happened to good old paper archives?'

The auxiliary looked at me as if I'd grown an extra nose. 'We gave them up a year ago.'

'Unlike some other directorates.'

'The Finance Directorate's fully digital now. And the Supply Directorate's heading that way.'

Oddly, Fergus Calder, Jack MacLean and Billy Geddes hadn't bothered to mention that. Why were their directorates and the late Peter Stewart's at the frontline of the city's technological revolution? I mean finance, yes; supply, obviously; but recreation? And what about the Council's bulwark against chaos, the Public Order Directorate? Why hadn't it been given priority?

'Sit down,' I said, beckoning her to an armchair and taking the one opposite. I checked her name panel. 'Listen, Christine, I can see you're upset about the guardian's death.'

She stifled a sob. 'We . . . we were friends before the last election.'

And more after it, I was sure.

'I'm very sorry. Can you cast any light on what happened? Why would Peter kill himself?'

She shook her head repeatedly. 'He wouldn't . . . he wouldn't.'

'Was there something in the directorate that was troubling him?'

Wilkie 88 was an experienced auxiliary. She wasn't going to break easily.

'Something about football, maybe?' I continued, assuming she was party to high-security matters. 'The heart at Tynecastle must have been quite a blow to him.' I thought back to the Council meetings. The recreation guardian hadn't seemed overly concerned. Then again, it was strange that he hadn't asked me about the investigation. After all, he was honorary president of all the EPL clubs and the managers reported to him.

'Football,' she repeated faintly, her gaze still directed at the carpet.

'Look at me, Christine,' I said softly. Eventually she complied. 'Peter didn't kill himself. He was murdered.'

'What?' She dropped her phone and electronic notepad. 'He . . . what?'

I wasn't going to spare her. 'A rope was put round his neck and attached to the light fitting. Then somebody pulled on his legs until he choked to death. His tongue came out of his mouth and his eyes almost popped out of their—'

'Stop it,' the grey-haired auxiliary moaned. 'Please . . . stop it . . .'

I gave her a few moments, not proud of myself.

'The EPL,' she said, wiping her eyes. 'He . . . he didn't like what was happening.'

I caught her eye. 'What was happening?'

She looked around. The glass door was closed and her fellow auxiliaries were at their desks, pretending to be hard at work.

'Last season there was illicit betting,' she said, her voice so low I could hardly hear it. 'Organized gambling. But it wasn't Peter's idea. He hated it. He tried . . . he tried to stop it.'

Which was probably why he was killed.

'Whose idea was the gambling?' I said.

Wilkie 88 shook her head violently. 'I don't . . . I don't know . . .'

'Yes, you do. You realize the people who had him killed were most likely pro-gambling?'

She thought about that. 'All right . . . but you didn't hear it from me.'

'Of course. I'll protect you.'

She didn't look sure of that, but she spoke again: two words making a proper name that didn't surprise me at all.

'Billy Geddes.'

Shortly afterwards, Davie called and asked me to meet him in the directorate conference room on the seventh floor. As I walked down, I thought about what I'd heard. That Billy was involved in the betting made sense. He was the buffer between his boss, Jack MacLean, and the dirty work. I was sure that Fergus Calder knew about it too, but they could easily disown Billy as a renegade operator – he certainly had form. But what was I to do? Confronting the senior and finance guardians would probably lead to me being taken off the case – if not strung up from a light fitting. On the other hand, the senior guardian had agreed that I head the initial investigation and, despite the face-off in his quarters last night, I was still in place. The death of Peter Stewart made Calder's life more difficult – only one serving guardian had been killed in office. Kicking me into the long grass would hardly strengthen his position. No, I was sure the senior and finance guardians were worried about the heart business, which meant they weren't directly involved. So who was?

Davie was waiting outside a glass-enclosed room which contained four shell-shocked guardsmen.

'I've put the boot in,' he said. 'Last night they were playing cards in a room behind the reception desk. They claimed they were keeping an eye open but that's a load of shite. They were drinking too. One of them still reeks of it.'

'Do you think they were told to turn a blind eye?'

'If so, they've got some balls keeping that to themselves.' Davie grinned. 'Certain threats were made.'

'Demotion, five years down the mines . . .'

'That kind of thing.'

'Any point in me playing soft cop?'

'Too late for that. Besides, the head of computing is looking for you.'

I looked over my shoulder. A male auxiliary who couldn't have been more than twenty-five was leaning against a desk, looking sicker than a dog.

'Well, then, Watt 475,' I said, looking at his ID panels. 'Or rather, Douglas.'

'Doogie.' There were spots on his nose and his eyes were twitchy behind thick-rimmed spectacles.

'Call me Quint. So, what's the damage?'

'We've got the mainframe up and running,' he said. 'As far as we've been able to ascertain, no files have been corrupted.'

'What's the catch?'

Doogie the Pluke looked like he was about to throw up. I took a step back.

'Peter – the guardian's – personal archive . . .'

'I thought you said nothing had been corrupted.'

He took a deep breath. 'Well, technically it hasn't. It's . . . been wiped.'

'So why were his computers taken?'

'To make sure he hadn't hidden an encrypted file, I'd say.'

I went up to him and caught his gaze. 'You called the guardian Peter. That means you were close.'

The auxiliary swallowed a sob. 'He was like a . . . like a father to me.'

'I'm sorry. The best thing you can do is work with Christine to find any of those encrypted files. Maybe he hid a – what are they called?'

'Diskette?'

'Yeah, those.' I had very little idea about computers, not least because the Public Order Directorate made sure I never got my hands on even a superannuated one. 'Maybe he secreted one somewhere in his office.'

'I'll get on to it right away.'

'Just a minute.' I grabbed his forearm. 'Have you heard anything about betting in the EPL?'

His eyes shot open. 'What? No, never.'

I half-believed him. 'OK, keep that to yourself.'

He nodded nervously.

I watched him walk off. His suit looked like it had been slept in for several nights.

'Any luck?' Davie said, arriving at my side.

'Not a lot.' I could see activity at the conference centre. The Council's only luxury vehicle – a pre-crisis Rolls Royce Phantom that had somehow survived the years of disorder – had drawn up. An honour guard saluted and I saw two men in suits walk into the building. Orkney and Shetland. Did they use to wear kilts in the old days? I thought not. It was very windy up there.

'What's next?' Davie asked.

'Not much more we can do here. Did Guardian Doris tell you anything about her chats with the other football managers?'

'Only that three of them referred her to the recreation guardian. They haven't been told he's dead yet.'

I started walking to the stairs. Given the power cuts that bedevil the city, I avoided elevators, at least on the way down.

'Curious that – considering he seems to have been implacably opposed to gambling.'

'Almost like they knew he was going to be killed.'

I stopped and looked at him. 'Premeditation. That's a nasty and very credible thought, guardsman. What did the night Guard at Peter Stewart's quarters say?'

'That no one entered before you. That feeble auxiliary said the same. I sent them all to the castle. Shall we go and pull their chains?'

'Stop licking your lips. All right, you can have another go at them. And at the night guard from the New Tolbooth – how did Grant Brown's head get there without anyone noticing? Meanwhile, I've got other fish to fillet.'

'Namely?'

'There's a drugs angle too, remember? According to Skinny Ewan, the Porty Pish got their dope from the Supply Directorate. Now, who knows everything that goes on in each directorate?'

'The deputy guardian.'

'Correct. I'm going to pay a call on that individual.'

Before I did so, I rang Doris and asked her to send a forensics team back to the recreation guardian's house in Moray Place. In case he'd left any documentation or diskettes referring to gambling, they were to tear the place apart. Unfortunately, in my haste, I forgot to check out Peter Stewart's deputy, who would now have taken his or her place unless the Council had something against him or her.

FOURTEEN

T he Supply Directorate was located in what had been Waverley Station before rail links with the rest of the country were cut by the first Council after independence was declared.

The city's stores of everything from food to toilet paper (hard, thin and scratchy) and carpets to light bulbs (notoriously short-lived) were arranged in vast rows and tiers on the concrete base that had been laid over the rail tracks and platforms. The directorate's headquarters were in a grimy grey block just to the south of the stores. It had been some joker of an architect's take on brutalism, even though it was originally a hotel. Welcome to Ugly Town. The auxiliaries who worked in the Supply Directorate had a reputation for sticky fingers. A few of the most egregious thieves were demoted every year and sent to clean toilets in the worst of the tourist bars. The rest just got on with lining the pockets of their grey suits, depot overalls and Guard uniforms. The fact was citizens would have revolted in under a week if they weren't able to obtain food and other essential supplies. The Council knew that and let the staff do what they wanted, within reason, as long as the directorate functioned. Plato, the Enlightenment's presiding philosopher, had been a great one for reason, to the extent of kicking poets out of his ideal state. There aren't many poets in contemporary Edinburgh.

I took out my authorization and went past the guards at the entrance. 'Where's the deputy guardian?' I asked the pretty auxiliary on the front desk.

'I . . .'

'Actually, who's the deputy guardian?'

'Adam 159, citizen.'

'And where is he?'

'I'll have to call his secretary.'

'Don't call anyone,' I ordered. 'Unless you want a year on the pig farms.'

She quivered more than her rank is supposed to. 'Yes, citizen. I mean, no, citizen.'

'Where's his office?'

'Sixth floor. The lift's over there.'

'Don't tell him I'm coming,' I threatened.

I went to the lift, speed being of the essence. I was unsure whether my imminent arrival would be communicated. It would have been a disgrace to intimidate the young woman for nothing.

Fortunately there was no power cut, accidental or otherwise; stopping the lift would have been a good way of buying the deputy guardian time. It would be the stairs for me next time, even going up.

The doors opened and I walked into a warren of small offices.

There were few signs, directorates being deliberately organized to confuse visitors. I saw a tea lady, a middle-aged citizen in pale blue overalls, and went over to her.

'Hullo, dearie,' she said with a smile. My lack of uniform didn't seem to bother her.

'Hullo yourself.'

I leant closer. 'It's the deputy guardian's birthday and I've got a surprise from the Council for him. Do you know where he is?'

The original Council banned birthday celebrations on the grounds that they were excessively self-indulgent. That's been relaxed for ordinary citizens, but not for auxiliaries, at least officially.

'Oh, that's nice,' she said. 'I gave him his tea a few minutes ago. He's in with the head of personnel. Second corridor, fifth office on the left.'

'Thanks, Evie,' I said, having taken in her name panel.

'That's aw right. Here, haven't I seen you before?'

I left before she remembered my face from stories in the *Edinburgh Guardian* about successful cases – the credit mainly being given to the Public Order Directorate. The corridor was stuffy, the smell a combination of over-boiled root vegetables, the flatulence they produce and sweat. Even barracks-issue soap is underpowered, the best ingredients being kept for the tourist variety.

I found the office. The sign said 'Moray 402 – Head of Personnel'. Underneath it a wooden slide shouted 'DO NOT DISTURB' in red ink.

I disturbed.

The tableau could have come from one of the porn magazines that I'd frequently come across before independence and afterwards were smuggled in from Scandinavian states. The deputy guardian was kneeling on the floor with his back to me, his trousers and pants down. Moray 402, naked from the waist down, was lying on her desk, legs spread as her boss lapped away. Her moaning turned to a shriek, but Adam 159 stayed on the job, only pulling away when she closed her thighs on the sides of his head. She'd seen me.

'Wha—?' he gasped, rolling away and pulling at his trousers.

'Wha indeed, deputy guardian,' I said, closing the door.

The head of personnel had got off the desk and disappeared behind it, fumbling with her clothes.

'What's the meaning of this?' the deputy guardian roared after he'd buttoned himself up. He frowned. 'I know you.'

'Citizen Dalrymple. Call me Quint.'

'I fucking well won't. What the hell are you doing here?'

I held up my authorization, though he should have known about it as all senior auxiliaries receive a daily update from the Council. He blustered incomprehensibly, eyes off his subordinate. I showed her the authorization too. She was a handsome woman, her bright red cheeks a minor and temporary flaw.

'Right then,' I said, picking up a condom wrapper and sitting in front of the desk. 'I think Yolanda'– it was the first time I'd met an Edinburgh native with that name – 'had better go and solve her personnel problems elsewhere.'

The auxiliary left at speed, her shoes unlaced.

'I suppose you think that was clever, Dalrymple,' Adam 159 said. He was an unusually corpulent auxiliary in his fifties, his face pitted with either acne or shrapnel scars.

'I could say the same to you, Joseph Sutherland. Don't tell me – your nickname is Uncle Joe.'

He didn't favour that with an answer, rather fishing out the condom from his pants. He tossed it in my direction. That got him both barrels.

'Someone in this directorate is trafficking drugs, you fuck!'

The air went out of him like a pricked balloon. 'What?' he said faintly.

'Drugs!' I yelled. 'Tell me what's going on *now* or answer to the Council tonight.'

'But I don't know anything about drugs,' he said, dropping into Moray 402's chair. 'What kind of drugs?'

'Narcotic, not pharmaceutical.'

'Where did you hear that?'

'From a confidential but one hundred per cent credible source.' Pity Skinny Ewan was dead. Maybe the truth drug was unreliable in other ways too – he might have told us whatever came into his mind. I kept that idea to myself.

'You can't walk into my directorate and make accusations like that.'

'Yes, I can. But you can't expect me to believe that you know nothing about drug supplies emanating from the depot across the road.'

He wiped the sweat from his brow with a grey tissue.

'You've been keeping this from your guardian, haven't you?' I said.

'I . . . the guardian has much on his mind, especially considering his role as the city's leader.'

'You do remember that anything related to illicit drugs is graded by the Public Order Directorate as a class-one crime.'

He nodded rapidly. 'I tell you, I don't know anything.'

I stood up. 'All right, you've had your chance. We're going to the castle.'

'Wait,' the auxiliary said, scrambling to his feet. 'If I put you in touch with my drugs squad leader, would that be any help?'

I played hard to get. 'You have a drugs squad?'

'Of course. We can't have Guard personnel from the castle stamping around the warehouse and causing chaos any time they get a tip off.'

'And when did this elite team last catch a trafficker?'

He blanched. 'Well, it acts more as a deterrent than an apprehension unit.'

'Uh-huh.'

'But my man, Knox 31, has his finger on what's happening.'

'Knox 31?'

'You know him?'

'Once upon a time. Where is he?'

'The team's office is on the left as you enter the warehouse from this side. I'll tell him you're coming.' Suddenly the deputy guardian was as compliant as a child being offered sweeties.

'Don't,' I commanded. I love taking that tone with senior auxiliaries. 'And Joe? You aren't off the hook, but I'll hold back on telling Fergus about your illicit sex session for the time being.' Although auxiliaries were encouraged to engage in sexual liaisons with members of their rank, making whoopee in the workplace was strictly forbidden. What kind of example would that set Evie the tea lady?

'Quite a lunch, Jimmy Taggart.'

The white-haired auxiliary at the table in the mess room looked up from a spread that included caviar, a large crab and a loaf of whiter-than-snow tourist bread.

There was also a small round of a creamy cheese that I hadn't seen since a family holiday in France when I was thirteen.

'Is that you, son?' he said, getting to his feet with difficulty. He had the kind of belly that normally contains twins.

'You used to call me "sir".'

'True enough,' he said, wiping his hands and shaking mine. 'Bell 03, as was. Long time no see.'

He'd been in the Tactical Operations Squad that I'd run before I got myself demoted. So had my lover Caro. Old Jimmy had been there when she died. He had the kindness not to mention that.

'Call me Quint. You on your own?'

He nodded. 'My people are checking a shipment of turnips from a farm near Soutra. Get stuck in.'

I did. Rich foods didn't often feature in my diet.

'What were you after, sir? I mean, citizen. I'm sorry, I can't bring myself to call you by your first name. You were my commander.'

'Long time ago, Jimmy.' I took in the ragged two-inch scar above his right eye. He'd fought hard for the Enlightenment. I wondered if he still had it in him. 'Adam 159 told me about your drugs squad.'

'Did he now? That fat shite only knows one thing – how to lick his way to the top.'

I considered telling what the deputy guardian had been up to with the head of personnel, but decided that could wait.

'Do you find a lot of drugs?' I asked.

Taggart gave me a weary look. 'What do you think, sir? I've got four auxiliaries and hundreds of deliveries a week.'

I told him what Skinny Ewan had said.

'The Portobello Pish? They've got contacts in the warehouse, there's no doubt about that. Nailing them isn't easy, though. There are over five thousand citizen workers here.'

'How many auxiliaries?'

He grinned. 'You always had a thing for corruption in the ranks, even when you were in them yourself.'

'Unfortunately the subsequent years have only made me more sceptical.'

'We're all Hume's children.'

'True. So have you got anything for me?'

'There are over five hundred auxiliaries in the Supply Directorate. Take your pick.' Which was his way of saying he'd like to keep his current sinecure.

Jimmy Taggart packed up the remains of his lunch and stuck them in a surprisingly ancient fridge, given where we were.

'Couldn't you get a replacement?'

He laughed. 'This one actually works. The new ones from some breakaway island in the Philippines last one summer, if you're lucky.'

I caught his gaze. 'The beans. Spill them.'

The old guardsman got up and closed the door. 'Right, sir. Since we're old comrades and I think it's about time this directorate got cleaned up, I'll give you a hand. It's like this. Every week the fools in command send me a printout of deliveries, some from the city farms, some from the airport and some from the docks at Leith.'

'Which fools across the road?'

Taggart laughed harshly. 'Good question. Here, look.' He went to a filing cabinet, took out a folder and handed it to me.

I opened it and ran my eyes over it. 'Everything from vegetables to tourist delicacies, hotel wallpaper to traffic lights, souvenirs to fabrics.'

'Aye, and here's the best bit. We aren't meant to check those shipments. We're to leave them alone.'

I stared at him. 'It doesn't say that here.'

'No, but when the system started about five years back, I was told I'd end my life down the mines if I or any of my squad so much as breathed on the listed deliveries.'

For the first time ever I saw fear on Taggart's face.

'You were told by who? Presumably not the deputy guardian or he wouldn't have sent me to you.'

'Like I say, that shite doesn't get his hands dirty. Or rather, his bosses don't trust him.'

'Come on, Jimmy, who was it?'

He looked away. 'I can't say, sir. I'm almost past it. I wouldn't last six months underground.'

I nodded. 'How about we do it this way? I say a name and you nod or shake your head.'

There was sweat on his rutted forehead, but he went along with it.

'Fergus Calder.'

No dice.

'Billy Geddes.'

Same again.

'Jack MacLean?'

Zero from three. I was getting desperate. Then I had it. Although he was seconded to the Supply Directorate, Taggart was still a guardsman and all Guard personnel ultimately answered to the Public Order Directorate. Five years ago that was . . .

'The late, not even minimally lamented Hamish Buchanan.'

This time my old comrade gave a single nod.

'Why are you worried about him?' Buchanan had been one of the most useless guardians in Council history, his incompetence matched only by his arrogance and spitefulness. I'd never heard that he'd been corrupt, but it didn't exactly come as a surprise.

Taggart took the file from me and put it back in the cabinet.

'When the current guardian took over, I sent her office a message asking if the order should be revoked. She wrote back that it was to stand.'

That *was* interesting. Guardian Doris had been deputy guardian for most of Horrible Hamish's reign. She would have known more than him about the Public Order Directorate's secrets. Then it struck me that she hadn't appointed a deputy. Davie told me she hadn't had time, but I wondered about that. Did she want a finger in every pie her directorate was baking? Ten would hardly be enough. Not even adding her toes would suffice. She was trading directorate efficiency for personally controlling as much as she could.

'Right, Jimmy,' I said. 'Get that file out again.'

He looked at me in horror.

'That's right, you, me and your squad are going to check this week's shipments.'

'You're fucking joking.'

For once in my life I wasn't.

We were in luck. In the second delivery, one of fine wine from Provence, we found a box of straw containing over five pounds of cocaine.

'Put it back,' I said, 'and seal the consignment.' I turned to Taggart. 'Who's the recipient?'

'The Tourist Services Department,' he read from the manifest.

It supplied restaurants, bars and so on in the central zone, but narcotics for the tourists were imported by a unit in the Public Order Directorate. What the hell was going on?

'Let's see who comes to pick it up,' I said, looking over his shoulder. 'Delivery's to take place by four o'clock this afternoon.'

I sent the squad about other business and waited with Jimmy Taggart behind a heap of potatoes across the aisle. Half an hour later a Korean truck backed up and two warehousemen loaded the consignment into its cargo space. After it set off towards the east gate, Taggart and I got into the battered Land Rover he had parked nearby – no new 4×4 for him – and went after it.

'Tourist Services have a depot down in Stockbridge,' Jimmy said, wrestling with the elderly vehicle's wheel. 'Where that school used to be.'

'The Academy. I remember playing rugby against them. The bastards always won.'

He grinned. 'You'd have been upset when it was blown up during the drugs wars, then.'

'I cried for weeks. Hold on, where's he going?'

The truck hadn't taken the turn to Waterloo Place and the north, but headed south after a zigzag on the Canongate. It stopped about half a mile down the Pleasance, outside what had once been a church and was now a disused carpet warehouse. The high windows were blocked with boards and the door was chained and padlocked. There was no sign identifying the building's purpose or affiliation. The driver had the key. A minute after he'd opened up, a new-looking white van arrived and a citizen in standard-issue grey overalls helped the driver to unload the crates.

'Prima facie case of thieving,' Taggart said.

'We need backup,' I said, hitting buttons on my phone.

'Davie?' I said, giving him our location. 'Get down here, but don't tell the command centre or anyone else where you're going.'

Fortunately the driver and his helper took a break after they'd emptied the back of the truck. We were parked beyond them and they paid no attention to the elderly Land Rover. Its lack of directorate markings helped. I asked Taggart about that.

'No one cares what I do – obviously because I don't do anything that counts. There was an order to stencil on the Supply Directorate logo a few months back, but I binned it.' He smiled sadly. 'I like to pretend I'm still in the Tactical Operations Squad. We really mattered then.'

I nodded, then watched as a Guard 4×4 pulled up outside the former church. Jimmy Taggart got us down there at speed.

Davie had the situation under control, the driver and his helper on the ground with their hands on their heads.

'What's this then, Quint?' he asked, smacking his nightstick against his palm. 'Thieving bastards?'

'Got it in one. IDs please, citizens. No rapid movements.'

'I already took those from them,' Davie said, pointing to a pair of flick-knives on the pavement by the 4×4.

I looked at the cards that had been taken from the men's pockets.

'Means, Gerald,' I read. 'Supply Directorate driver. Date of birth 13/5/2004, eyes blue, hair blond, height five feet nine, weight eleven stone three, address 17 Lochend Avenue.' I broke off and looked at Davie. 'In between Leith and Portobello. Which do you think he is? A Lancer or a Pish?'

'Fuck the Pish!' said Means, earning a kick in the gut.

'You weren't invited to speak,' Davie said, leaning over the writhing man.

'How about number two. Yule, George—'

'D'yer pals call you Log?' Davie asked.

'Fuck—' The citizen doubled up, gasping for air.

'Can I have a go?' Taggart asked.

'Sure, next time they screw up,' said Davie, with a grin.

'Barman, Kenilworth Casino, Rose Street.' I remembered that Skinny Ewan, deceased leader of the Pish, had worked in a George Street establishment. Had the two gangs split up the central zone? 'Date of Birth 26/12/2002, eyes and hair brown, height five-eleven, weight, twelve-one, address 4 East Hermitage Place.'

'A Lancer, obviously,' Davie said.

'Lancers rule!'

Jimmy Taggart gave the shouter the boot.

'So,' I said, 'two Leith Lancers, a load of expensive wine and five pounds plus of coke.'

'Is that right?' Davie said.

'See if you can find it, Jimmy,' I said.

After he'd gone inside, I told Davie about the old guardsman's squad and Guardian Doris's reconfirmation of the order not to search specific shipments.

'I don't like the sound of that,' he said, shaking his head.

'Me neither. Then again, this place is a few hundred yards down the road from your barracks. How could it not have been noticed? They unloaded in broad daylight and it isn't even raining.'

'Michael Campbell,' he said.

Hume 481, last seen in the morgue with his heart missing.

'Time we went to talk to Hume 01,' I said.

Jimmy Taggart came out, the package of coke under his arm. 'You've got to see this,' pointing to the old church's door.

Davie cuffed the prisoners' wrists and ankles, then followed us in.

A lot more than forty thieves had put together this treasure trove.

FIFTEEN

'You'd better get back, Jimmy,' I said.

'What about the shipment? My squad will have been seen checking it.'

'I'll cover for you. If anyone asks, say I flashed my authorization.'

'Right you are, sir.' He stuck out his hand. 'It's been a pleasure working with you again. And if you need any backup apart from Thunder Boots here, don't forget me.'

I shook his hand and watched him drive off.

'One of the old breed,' Davie said. 'Or else I'd have used my thunder boots on him.' He looked at me. 'What?'

'I'm trying to make sense of this. Guardian Doris has Taggart avoiding certain shipments specified by the Supply Directorate every week. Those shipments contain drugs' – I motioned to the cocaine now lying on the floor of the 4×4 – 'and plenty of other luxury goods, as in the church. Members of the Leith Lancers pick them up.'

Davie looked over his shoulder to the pair of gang members in the back seat.

'Are you sure we should be having this conversation in front of them?'

'You reckon they don't know who they're working for?'

Davie grimaced. 'Steady, Quint.'

'Let's ask them.' I turned round. 'Who's in charge of the treasure trove?'

Silence.

'Davie, have you got those knives? There's a certain poetic justice about cutting their throats with their own weapons.'

'Whit kindae justice?' said George. 'Gerry, whit's he sayin'?'

'Whit's justice in this shitehole?' said Gerry, ignoring him.

'Cut off their noses,' I ordered.

'Now you're talking,' Davie said, opening one of the blades. 'Vertically or—'

'Naw!' squealed George.

'Dinnae tell them anythin', Jaw!'

'Unconscious, please.'

Davie obliged with a booming left hook.

'Right then, Jaw,' I said. 'Horizontally, I think.'

Davie made a move and the Lancer moved back as far as he could.

'Stop! I'll tell ye everythin'.'

'Been in the Lancers long?' Davie asked. 'Only, you're not very well endowed testicle-wise.'

'Whit?'

'He means you're not the average Lancer nutter,' I said.

'Naw, Ahm just a driver.'

'Uh-huh. Who tells you what to do?'

'Ah cannae . . .'

Davie slashed at him with the blade, drawing blood from the tip of his nose.

The shriek could have been heard at the airport.

'Bloody hell,' said Davie. 'He's pissed himself for a minor flesh wound.'

'Who tells you what to do?' I repeated.

'Ah . . . oh, Christ . . . he's a fitba manager . . .'

I glanced at Davie. This was getting interesting.

'Is that right?' I said. 'A fine, upstanding body of men.' I paused. 'Which one?'

'Derick . . . Derick Smail.'

Davie laughed. 'The Hibee whose team is – or was – home to Pish members. I love it.'

I scowled at him. 'What's the betting Alec Ferries has got his own heap of treasure somewhere else?'

Davie shrugged.

'Whit happens now?' said Jaw.

'We're off to the castle.'

This time he only managed a squeak.

I hadn't forgotten Hume 01 – he had to know about the contents of the church – but I wanted to turn the spotlight on the Hibs manager first. Then there was the guardian. While her predecessor had been a waste of space, I didn't think she was – nor had she given the slightest impression of being corrupt. A frank conversation was required.

The rain started again as we turned on to the Royal Mile. Fortunately the 4×4 was equipped with an umbrella. Davie and I made it to the command centre reasonably dry, while Jaw and Gerry got very soggy. At least the former's trousers looked less of a disgrace. They were handed over to Guard personnel with orders to separate them.

'And now?' Davie asked.

'Go and stuff your face. I've got something to do. Meet me at Smail's cell in half an hour.'

He gave me a quizzical look, then let the needs of his stomach prevail.

I looked into the command centre but the guardian wasn't there, so I headed to her office. Her gatekeeper ushered me straight in.

'Quint,' Guardian Doris said from behind a pile of folders. 'Where have you been?'

I didn't sit down – I wouldn't have been able to see her because of the paper barricade.

'Knox 31,' I said.

'Fine old soldier,' she said, looking up.

She'd been his barracks commander. I'd forgotten that.

'What about him?'

'You confirmed an order Hamish Buchanan issued to Jimmy Taggart.'

Her eyes stayed on me. 'Did I?'

'He's at the Supply Directorate.'

'Oh, I remember. Something about checking certain deliveries.'

I was watching her carefully. I couldn't see any sign of dissembling.

'Actually, it was about *not* checking certain deliveries.'

'Really? That I don't recall.' She stood up. 'Tell me about it.'

So I did, including the treasure trove on the Pleasance and ending with the package of coke, which I put on top of the pile of files.

'You tested it?'

'See the taped-over section? Yes, I tested it. I'm not a chemist but I think it would blow the minds of many tourists.' I paused for a couple of seconds. 'Or citizens.'

'What?'

'The Leith Lancers, even though some of them work in the tourist zone, don't supply drugs to outsiders. They don't have to, since the Tourism Directorate does that, using the stocks kept in the castle. They supply to ordinary citizens. The point is, who controls the Lancers?'

'I have the feeling you know.' The guardian was irritated by the way I was playing her, but she still didn't seem to be hiding anything.

'Derick Smail. I think he was facilitating the Porty Pish's drug pushing too. It's a shame the medical guardian's truth drug went missing.' I caught her gaze. 'You wouldn't know anything about that, would you?'

Her face flushed, but her eyes didn't leave mine.

'No, citizen, I wouldn't. Nor do I know anything about Derick Smail's activities.'

I turned to the door. 'Fine. Let's put the squeeze on him.'

I was taking a risk presenting my back to her. To my relief, her Guard-issue knife remained in its sheath.

Davie was outside Derick Smail's cell. When he saw us approach, he stood to attention but his eyes were restless. I nodded to him to calm him down.

'Put him in interview room two, please,' I said. That was the one I knew was wired for sound. 'Then get Eric Colquhoun and stick him in there too.'

I led the guardian away, but then she took me to the listening station.

'This Colquhoun is the father of the beheaded man's girlfriend?' she said.

I nodded. 'He's been a friend of Smail's since school – and he's got a record as long as my leg.'

'You think they're involved.'

'Certain of it. I just don't know how. If this doesn't work they're both getting the twelfth degree.'

The guardian raised her eyebrows. 'Torture was banned after the end of the drugs wars.'

'The Leith Lancers taking delivery of five pounds of coke doesn't strike you as movement towards new drugs wars?'

She rubbed her forehead. 'Let's see what happens.'

'I've got another idea before you get out the thumbscrews and pliers.'

'I'm so glad.'

We stopped talking when we heard the interview-room door open and close. The two men were now together. For over a minute nothing was said. I began to wonder if they knew sign language. It was typical of the austerity of the original Council that a two-way mirror hadn't been provided. Then again, the original Council didn't question drugs-gang members, it just killed or – rarely – imprisoned them.

'What the fuck's goin' on?' Derick Smail asked in a low voice. The guardian twiddled knobs.

'You fuckin' tell me, big man,' Colquhoun replied. The title was honorary, considering that Smail was about half the size of his interlocutor.

'D'ye think they've found the shipments?'

'Naw. We'd be in chains.'

'We are locked up. Here, d'ye think they're listening?'

Guardian Doris and I exchanged frozen looks.

'Who cares?' said Colquhoun. 'They're wurse than we are.'

'Have we got enough?'

'Nearly. Another week should dae it.'

'Wheesht. I dinnae trust these cunts.'

And that was it. Audition over.

After two minutes the guardian asked, 'Enough what?'

I shrugged. 'Search me. Remember what I said about not going after the Leith Lancers? I think you should do now. Maybe they're not only talking about dope.'

She looked at me uneasily. 'What else?'

'With all these outsider leaders visiting the city, don't you think they might be talking about weapons or explosives?'

That turned her whiter than a boiled codfish.

'What was your other idea concerning Smail?' she said after a long gap.

'Stay here and you'll hear it.'

I called Davie as I was walking out. 'Want to act the heavy, Thunder Boots?'

'Act?'

'Ha. Get down to the interview room. We're going to put on a performance for the guardian.'

'Hold me back.'

'Try not to kill the subject this time.' Thinking of Yellow Jacko stirred something in the depths of my memory, but it remained stubbornly out of reach.

We'd only just started on Derick Smail – no application of fists or boots – when the door burst open and Guardian Doris ordered us out. 'Follow me!' she yelled, setting off down the corridor at a run.

'What is it?' I called after her.

'Male body missing a heart at the Salutation.'

By the time we made it to the esplanade – only mildly damp from the drizzle that had set in – she had lost her breath. Davie, fitter than almost every member of the Guard, had been in touch with the command centre.

'The governors of Orkney and Shetland were having high tea with the senior and finance guardians when the corpse made its appearance. In a wheelchair, would you believe?' He followed Guardian Doris's 4×4 down Castle Hill, turning left at Bank Street.

'What the hell were they doing in the Saly?' I asked. 'It's the most old-fashioned place in the city.'

'Maybe the islanders don't like naked waitresses.'

We roared down the Mound and were at the tea rooms on Princes Street in a couple of minutes. There were several Guard vehicles outside, a tape barrier having been erected. The tourists were walking round it without interest, their minds fixed on gambling, sex, shopping or simulated death – the New Tolbooth had executions till well into the evening.

A tall Guard commander led us into the building, which had been refitted as a Victorian establishment, full of cast iron, aspidistras and lace. The smells of fried food and fresh baking made my mouth water. Then I remembered why we were there.

'The senior guardian and his guests were in a private room on the third floor,' he said.

Guardian Doris and her gorillas took the lift, while Davie and I stuck to the stairs. We got there last, even though I'd paid only passing attention to the hunting prints on the walls. To think the cream of society used to saddle up to chase foxes. The Lord of the Isles has probably reinstituted the practice, though his ancestors preferred persecuting crofters.

'Citizen!'

I came back to myself to find the guardian glaring at me.

'Sorry. Where's the body?'

We were taken into a large room with a single round table in the centre. It was piled high with silver serving dishes, cake towers and teapots. All the chairs had been pushed on to their backs. The reason why was in a wheelchair, head flung back. The smell here was of rotting flesh, despite the feast.

Sophia looked round at me. 'Come and see, Quint.'

I joined Guardian Doris and looked down at the naked male body. The arms and legs had been tied to the frame with cord. There was a gaping hole in the dead man's chest. It was crawling with maggots.

'Fuck,' I said.

Sophia looked at me dubiously.

'Is this the donor of the first heart?'

'Probably. He's been dead for at least three days, I'd estimate.'

I took in the swollen abdomen and blue-veined flesh. 'Not an auxiliary.'

'Obviously not,' Guardian Doris said waspishly. 'The shoulder-length hair and moustache make that crystal clear.'

'As does the state of his teeth.' They were stained, cracked and worn, despite the fact that the dead man didn't look over thirty. Citizens do have access to dentists, but the waiting lists are long and anaesthetics are rarely used.

Davie came in. 'I've been checking how he got here. There's a service lift. They – two people dressed as waitresses – came up that way and pushed the others aside before rolling him in here. In the chaos they got away down the back stairs.'

'What about the guardians' bodyguards?'

'They'd been told by their bosses to make themselves scarce. Apparently they made the governors nervous. They were down in the kitchen filling their bellies.'

'No Guard personnel in Rose Street?' I asked. It was behind the building and was a pedestrian precinct.

'Yes. Two male citizens in standard-issue overalls and caps were seen getting into a Supply Directorate van, registration number not recorded. Their faces weren't visible, but I know they were clean-shaven because the waitresses said so. Presumably they'd left a change of clothes somewhere in the building.'

A slim guardswoman appeared at his side and spoke to him.

'Right. The waitress uniforms have been found inside the back door. The forensics team has them.'

There was a creak to my left.

'What do you think then, great detective?'

I looked down at Billy Geddes. 'Have you been here all the time?'

He smiled crookedly. 'I thought it best to keep out of your way.'

'You were at the tea?'

He nodded. 'Unfortunately I had my back to the doors, so I can't help you with the waitresses' looks.'

'Who else was here?'

'The senior and finance guardians. They've taken the island governors back to their quarters in Ramsay Garden.'

That's the gaggle of luxury flats to the east of the esplanade where the city's honoured guests are housed.

'How were they?'

Billy shrugged. 'Shocked, but not excessively. From what I've gathered, life in the far north has been short and brutish since the oil ran out. Apparently there aren't many fish either.'

'No doubt the Fergus and Jack double act jollied them along.'

'Quint,' Sophia said sharply.

Billy cackled. 'You can't stand them, can you, Quint? But without them, life here would be even worse than it is in the islands.'

Guardian Doris beckoned Davie and me to a corner.

'Why did this happen?' she asked.

'And who did it?' I countered. 'They're both good questions. It looks like a statement of intent to me.'

'What do you mean?'

'They're saying, "Look what we can do – get to the senior guardian and his guests right in the centre of the tourist zone." Meaning, nobody's safe anywhere.'

I went to Billy and wheeled him over. I knew that would annoy him intensely – he always insisted on getting himself around – and that was the point. I wanted him fiery and loose-tongued.

'Any reason why these particular leaders should have been given this show?'

'Fuck off, Quint.'

'Answer the question, please,' Guardian Doris said, giving him the eye.

'No . . . not that I can think of.'

'Come on, Billy,' I said. 'Why are they in Edinburgh? What do we want from them and vice versa?'

'That's confidential.'

'Take him to the cells,' the guardian said curtly.

Billy laughed. 'I'll be out before you can do fifty press-ups.'

'Very well, we'll break your bones here. Commander?'

Davie stepped up and took a hold of Billy's twisted left arm.

'No!' Billy shrieked.

'So talk,' said Guardian Doris.

'We . . . we want their support with the referendum,' Billy said, whimpering.

'What?' I said. 'How can they support us? And who's "we"?'

'The Council, of course.'

The guardian stared at him. 'That's news to me.'

Billy looked at us like we were nursery school kids. 'The referendum isn't only taking place in Edinburgh. It's happening all over Scotland.' He shook his head. 'Apart from Commie Dundee and the mad women in Stirling.'

'I'm aware of that,' Doris said. 'But each referendum is separate. How can Orkney and Shetland support us?'

Billy groaned. 'Where do they find you people? The referendums are just the start. It's what happens after that really matters.'

'What happens if Scotland is reconstituted,' I said.

'Which it will be, you can be sure of that.'

Could I, or even he? How did he know which way the citizens of Edinburgh would vote?

'So the senior guardian is getting other states on his side to bolster his bargaining position.'

'Bravo, Quint! Of course he fucking is. We want Edinburgh to be the capital again, don't we?'

I looked at Guardian Doris. She seemed all at sea in a pea-green boat. 'That doesn't explain why the heartless body was wheeled in here,' I said.

'No, it doesn't,' Billy said. 'Over to you, Sherlock.' He rolled himself over to the window.

'The implication is that some people in the city don't want Edinburgh to become capital of Scotland,' the guardian said.

'Or they don't want Edinburgh even to be part of the new nation.' I thought about the head and heart symbolism. Was the idea that a no longer independent Edinburgh had no heart? Or head? Or were the two things unconnected?

'The Supply Directorate van,' Davie said.

'Quite.' I looked at Guardian Doris. 'Tonight's Council meeting would be a good opportunity to ask the senior guardian what's going on in his fiefdom.'

'It would,' she said, her eyes wide. 'If I want to end up on a farm.'

I knew it. Any shit storm would have to be raised by me. Oh well.

SIXTEEN

As it turned out, there was no Council meeting that night. It was rare but not unprecedented. Fergus Calder advised that he had to tend to the city's guests after their shock. Given what Billy said, I wondered if the senior guardian was running scared.

I didn't fancy another post-mortem, so I left it to Sophia and the Tall and Short pathologists. Back in the castle, Davie and I went back to Derick Smail's cell. Only to find it was empty. A quick check of the other football managers showed they had all gone too.

I stormed over to the guardian's office.

'I'm sorry, Quint, it was out of my hands.'

'The senior guardian.'

She nodded. 'He said it was essential not to cause citizen unrest with the new season about to begin.'

'But they're all as bent as a Rose Street exotic dancer.'

'That may be, but with the referendum coming up, no risk can be taken.'

'Fantastic. So illegal betting's been given the green light.'

She frowned. 'You haven't actually proved that any such thing's been going on. The forensics team in the recreation guardian's accommodation has found no hidden documents or diskettes.'

'What about the coke and the treasure trove in the Pleasance?'

'That's a Leith Lancers operation. You haven't established a firm link to Derick Smail.'

I groaned. 'You heard him talking to Colquhoun. What else are they smuggling?'

'Circumstantial at best. Oh, and by the way, the senior guardian vetoed any action against the Lancers. He doesn't want chaos in the northern suburbs while there are guests in the city tomorrow and the day after.'

'So we're just going to sit back and wait for the Lord of the Isles, the Glaswegians and the missing heart to appear, are we? Or more heads to be detached? This isn't exactly the Public Order Directorate's finest hour.'

Guardian Doris gave me a sharp look. 'There's no shortage of leads to be followed up, citizen. Kindly do so.'

I almost told her to kindly stick her head in the toilet bowl, but managed to restrain myself. The thing was, she was right. I went out of her office at speed and called Davie to a meet in the canteen. He was already there.

'Fill a few holes?' I said, taking in the pile of plates.

'Getting there.' Davie was taking bites from a banana.

I ate some soup and a pork chop. At least heart wasn't on the menu.

'All right, chief,' he said, 'what do we do?'

'Go back to basics.'

'Meaning?'

'Nail the outstanding leads.'

'Oh, that kind of basics.' He looked disappointed. 'I thought you meant we'd go to Easter Road and pick up where we left off with that shite Smail.'

'It's a thought, but we need more proof. You saw how he and the others clammed up.'

'All right, what's outstanding?' He looked across the room. 'Apart from that guardswoman's—'

'Mind on the job, please.'

He grinned. 'It was.'

'I'm serious, guardsman. Take notes.'

'Yes, sir.'

I glared at him ineffectually. 'Hume 481.'

'Michael Campbell, poor sod. There's not much we can do for him now. Or his parents.'

'Wherever they are. No, but we think he was in contact with outsider gangs, as was the late, decapitated Grant Brown.' I paused. 'I wonder what Campbell knew about the old church that's full of treasure. Anyway, we need to get out to the city line and see what's going on.'

'That should be fun. We'll need reinforcements.'

I shook my head. 'Just you and me. I don't trust anyone else.'

'Let's hope I know some of the personnel on the line then.' His face brightened. 'They've got firearms.'

'What do you need them for? You've got your trusty Hyper-Stun. Next, Grant Brown's foreman in the Housing Directorate. We need to talk to him – he might know what the dead man got up to.'

'Before he was dead.'

I sighed. 'There are plenty of ghosts in Enlightenment Edinburgh.' Immediately Caro's face loomed up, followed by a succession of others who'd died on my watch, some worthy of death, others definitely not.

'Of course,' Davie said, looking down.

'Then there's Grant Brown's head. How did it get on the spike at the Tolbooth?'

'The Guard squad claimed they didn't see anything.'

'Let's go and scare the shit out of them.'

He got up.

'Hang on. There are also the Porty Pish members. At least they haven't been let loose.'

Davie's head dropped. 'Not exactly.'

'What?'

'The males are down the mines and the females on the farms. The guardian signed the order this afternoon.'

'And omitted to mention it to me.' I thought about that. 'They probably wouldn't have talked much anyway and it's the Lancers who are still running free. And not to be disturbed, though we'll see about that.'

'Anything else?'

'Yes. Who vacuumed the recreation guardian's room before I got there? Who shut down his directorate's mainframe and stole his personal computers? Who took the truth drug from the Medical Directorate store? And where did George Yule, that Lancer, get his unmarked van?' I looked up. 'I suppose he's still in custody.'

'Yes, as is his pal, Gerald Means.'

'Looks like they're our first port of call.' I laughed. 'Get it? First "porty" call.'

'But they're Leith Lancers,' Davie said, playing dumb.

I punched his arm and swallowed a squeal. He was one who should have been called Stalin.

'You never learn,' he said, heading to the holding cells.

The two tossers were still in separate residence. We took George Yule first, not least because he'd wet himself yesterday. He didn't look much more courageous now.

'Tell me, Jaw,' I said after I'd sat next to him on the rickety bed, 'how did you get to be a Lancer? Don't they have a tough initiation process?' Tough as in setting fire to potential members' trousers, making them drink a bottle of whisky in one and getting them to lead an attack on the Pish.

'Aye,' he said proudly. 'I passed it nae problem.'

Davie leaned over him. 'Did you fuck.'

Jaw swallowed frequently.

'Muckle Tony was your uncle.'

Nice one, Davie. I hadn't noticed that in the file.

'Aye, well . . .'

'Aye, well, here's a question for you,' I said. 'Where did you get that van? The report on it says the plates are false, the engine number's been filed off and the serial number's from a decommissioned Land Rover.'

'I dinnae ken anythin' about that.'

'Uh-huh. Where did you pick it up? And don't tell me you dinnae ken. I saw you driving it.'

'Em, well—'

'Answer the man right now or I'll cut your bollocks off!' Davie roared.

I watched to see if Jaw's trousers got damp again. They didn't but it must have been close.

'It was . . . it was in Cables Wynd.'

'In Leith,' Davie supplied.

'The key was in the . . . in the ignition. I was to take it tae the Pleasance and help . . . and help Ger.'

'Who told you to do that?'

'Ger.'

I looked up at Davie.

'Are you pulling our cocks, sonny?' he yelled.

'I . . . I widnae . . .'

This time there was evidence of bladder emptying.

'I believe him,' I said, getting up quickly.

'Something else. You work in the Kenilworth Casino, tourists only, yes?'

He nodded, his expression sullen.

'As a barman, you must have plenty of opportunities to steal booze, cigarettes and so on.'

'I dinnae dae that. Too dangerous. There's auxiliaries all over the place.'

'Any of them take what they shouldn't?'

Jaw gave Davie a nervous look. 'Naw,' he said. 'They're all straight as a snooker cue.'

I believed that too. Despite Davie's louring presence, Jaw Yule would have taken any opportunity to dump on auxiliaries. Unless he was even more scared of them . . .

Outside, I said to Davie, 'I don't think that technique's going to work with hard man Ger.'

'Want me to get the pliers?'

'Might be a good touch.' As I waited for him, I thought about what we were doing. The Leith Lancers were scumbags who didn't give a shit for the Council or its regulations. Worse, they didn't care about their fellow citizens except as sources of income. That didn't mean torture was right. Then again, neither was dope-trafficking, stealing people's ration cards, running protection rackets and so on. I wasn't comfortable that Davie's blow had led to Yellow Jacko's death, even though he deserved it for his past misdeeds. Certainly Davie hadn't lost any sleep over it. That was the difference between him and me.

Davie returned with a pair of pliers that tapered to narrow points. I hoped they would only be a prop.

'Right, Ger,' I said as we stormed in. 'Up against the wall.'

'Fuck you, Citizen Cocksuck—'

Davie punched him in the midriff. He hit the floor, gasping and retching.

I put a hand on Davie's arm.

'As I was saying, right, Ger. This can go like it's started or it can go easy.'

He was still mouthing abuse, but his voice had gone on holiday.

'Who are your contacts in the Supply Directorate?'

Davie hauled him up and dumped him on the bed.

'You heard, you piece of shite. Answer the man or I'll pull your fingernails out.' He leaned forward, brandishing the pliers.

Ger tried to laugh, but managed only a smile. Then, quicker than a crow going for a dead lamb's eye, he pulled Davie's service knife out of its sheath and cut his own throat.

We both leaped back from the pumping spray.

'Fuck,' said Davie.

As we walked away, Jaw Yule called his friend's name plaintively from down the corridor.

I felt worse than I had for a long time.

'Jesus, Quint, I never thought he'd do that.'

'I know, Davie.' We were on the path outside the guardian's

quarters. 'Was he so scared by the people he worked with in the Supply Directorate?'

'Maybe. Or he was just a head-banger who preferred death to years in the mines. He wouldn't be the first one.'

I nodded and called Guardian Doris. She wasn't happy but there wasn't anything she or we could do about it. She asked what we were following up next and I mumbled something about Grant Brown's fiancée. For some reason I couldn't explain I didn't want her to know that we were going after the Housing Directorate foreman.

'Do you think he'll still be on site?' I asked Davie as we headed away.

'Should be. According to the file, they're working double shifts. You know how keen the Council is to improve citizen housing.'

There were referendum votes in it – people would vote whichever way the Council recommended if they were in decent flats. That wasn't a bad plan. Pity they hadn't thought of it twenty years before.

Slateford is to the south-west of the centre. The flats that were being rebuilt were on Allan Park Crescent, only a few minutes' walk from the Union Canal. Grant Brown's headless body could easily have been dumped in the water there. I swore to myself. We should have checked the place out days ago, but the rush of events had distracted me.

'Is that Hyper-Stun fully charged?' I asked as we turned into the crescent. I had a bad feeling about this trip. Maybe we should have brought a squad along.

'Of course,' Davie said, giving me a disparaging look.

'Sorry I asked.' I got out after checking the file. It was still drizzling, which was mild for the Big Wet.

I lifted the safety tape outside the building site and was immediately confronted by a big man in a helmet.

'Who the hell are you?'

I held up my authorization. 'Where's the foreman?'

'On the second floor.'

I followed Davie, who had his service torch switched on.

Banging, thumping and laughter came from above. We went up the ladders between each floor. The rungs were covered in damp concrete. I wished I'd brought gloves.

'John Lecky?' I called.

'Who's that?' came a voice from the far end of the area, where lights glowed and men were at work.

I identified myself. The noise stopped immediately. I picked my way across the planks that had been laid over uncovered beams. Davie's boots clumped along behind me.

'I need to talk to you about Grant Brown,' I said as a short, thin man came towards me. He was wearing a high-visibility jacket and a safety helmet, and carrying a torch.

'Oh aye? The Guard's already taken ma statement.'

'I read it. Brown finished the early shift on the day before his body was found. You saw him leave as you clocked on.'

'That's almost right.'

'What?'

'My mate Johnnie MacMurdo had to leave early – his kid was sick – so I actually came on at two in the afternoon.'

That hadn't been noted in the report, suggesting it was either a rush job or a cover-up. I felt the hairs on the back of my neck rise.

'So you saw Brown for the last two hours of his shift.'

'Aye.'

I became aware that dim figures were gathering around us.

'Keep your distance,' Davie said.

'Fuck you!' Lecky said as his men came at us, jumping from beam to beam with hammers in their hands.

'Behind me, Quint,' Davie said, pulling out his Hyper-Stun and aiming it at our nearest assailant. Lecky had taken a few steps back.

There was a dull *phut* from the weapon.

'Shit,' said Davie, pulling the trigger again. Phut number two.

The workmen started to laugh as they came closer. I realized that Lecky was now holding a hacksaw.

'Follow me!' I said to Davie, then jumped through the ceiling between the beams. And the floor of the storey below. I landed with a crash on the ground floor in a cloud of dust, having bent my knees. By the sound of it, Davie made a bigger impression.

'Get out!' I yelled, heading for where I thought the door was and thudding into a wall. A hand grabbed my arm and I was dragged out. I jerked my head back and caught the big guy who'd been outside on his chin. He hit the deck.

A body thudded on to the floor in the hall, the man screaming. The torch he'd dropped showed that he was clutching his left leg. Davie had pulled the ladder away.

'Nice one, big man. Let's move!'

The dull glow of a streetlight lit our way towards the 4×4. We got in and Davie reversed away, then called for backup.

'They can get away,' I said. There were both right and left turns at the end of the road.

'Not if I disable their van. Hang on!' Davie drove forward at speed and rammed the Housing Directorate vehicle against the garden wall. The front wheel sustained major damage.

Then there was a crack, a spider web with a white centre appearing on the windscreen.

'Shit!' he said, going backwards as fast as he could. 'Are you all right?'

'What was that?'

'Rifle shot, I think, but I'm not sticking my head out to make sure.'

Rounds hit the bonnet and ricocheted off the frame of the windscreen.

Davie reversed further away.

'Get down!' he shouted. 'Who knows how good that laminated glass is?'

We sank down, me making a better job of it than him. The shots gradually tailed off, then stopped altogether.

'Fuck this,' Davie said, opening his door. He got out and rolled away from the 4×4. No shot was fired.

A Guard vehicle appeared behind us, lights flashing and siren screaming.

'Get down there!' Davie yelled, pointing to the end of the road. He followed them on foot.

I hitched a ride with the second guard 4×4. By the time we got there, Davie and his subordinates were standing by the side of the canal.

'I've sent squads over there,' he said, 'but they'll have to be quick.'

I looked down. There were tools all over the bank, as well as abandoned work belts, but of the hacksaw and the rifle there were no signs at all.

Wouldn't you know it? The rain came on hard again and what few tracks there were on the other side of the canal were soon obscured. It looked like the builders were heading south, which made sense.

They had no future in the city after attacking a Guard commander with a firearm. Shooting at an ordinary citizen like me – Council's official investigator or not – would only have got them a few years in the mines. Or a pat on the back.

'I've alerted the city-line guards,' Davie said.

'We need to get out there anyway,' I said. 'Where was it Hume 481 served his stint?'

'Bonaly Tower.'

'Which is only about a mile away.'

'Correct.' Davie exchanged the keys for his 4×4 for those of another and we headed to the far end of the street.

'What do you think those bastards were up to?' I asked as he set off through the southern suburbs, the street lighting becoming sparser as we got further from the centre.

'I'd say the whole lot of them were in contact with outsiders, maybe the Glasgow Dead Men we heard about.'

I turned over pages in the file that had been provided by the Housing Directorate. 'None of them were named by Skinny Ewan or Allie Swanson, so we can presume they weren't linked to the Porty Pish. And none of them lives in the north.'

Davie swerved to avoid a fox that stood motionless in the middle of the potholed road. 'That doesn't mean they weren't working with the Leith Lancers. There aren't many gangs in the south.' He laughed. 'Apart from the Oxgangs Guys.'

'Not all of whom are male, but they're all in rehabilitation.'

'True. But others will have taken their places.'

Oxgangs was only about a mile to the east of where we were heading. Maybe the builders were going there.

Davie had already thought of that, directing a couple of squads to the rundown suburb. Three high-rise blocks of flats had been the centre point of drugs-gang activity after the crisis. Eventually the Public Order Directorate had used the last of its heavy artillery shells against them, leaving only heaps of rubble and dust. The Council wasn't popular around here, but it had done what it could to relocate citizens. The only people who lived close to the city line now had some reason for doing so. With some it was probably just nostalgia.

Davie pulled up at the headquarters of the Bonaly Guard post. It was in what had been a primary school before the last election. Now it was surrounded in razor wire, with a fifty-foot steel tower

at its southern perimeter. The city line had been built on the north
side of the old city bypass, which was only passable in very few
places, having seen numerous pitched battles in the early years of
the Enlightenment. The border of independent Edinburgh was
between fifteen and twenty miles further south, encompassing the
mines and farms the city depended on, but the guard's control of
that area was much less tight. Smugglers and the like had the run
of it if they were careful to avoid the fortified parts.

'Come on,' Davie said. 'I know the commander.'

As it turned out, so did I. What surprised me was that she hadn't
been demoted.

SEVENTEEN

Raeburn 124 had been known during her short time at the top
of the Public Order Directorate as 'the Mist', though she
was far too heavy to be suspended in air even after losing a
fair amount of her previous heft. Life on the city line will do that.

'Citizen Dalrymple,' she said with a mixture of surprise and
distaste. She must have been in her late fifties by now, her mousy
hair thinning and the skin slack on her face.

I nodded to her, tempted to use the old nickname. It had come
about because she'd appeared out of the blue in the senior echelons
of the directorate – as I later discovered, because she was a supporter
of a disgraced senior guardian – and because she put a major damp-
ener on things within seconds of entering a room. She had probably
appealed to the former guardian's sense of rectitude – inasmuch as
he had one – though I had no idea why Guardian Doris had recon-
firmed her posting, as all new guardians had to with senior personnel.
Maybe, as with Jimmy Taggart's order, she'd signed it without
paying attention. She really should have got a deputy guardian in
place by now.

'How long have you been here, commander?' I asked as she led
us into her office. The Guard combat tunic and trousers didn't do
her any favours from any direction.

'Five years in October,' she said, looking over her shoulder.
'Though why that should concern you . . .'

I smiled. 'Just making polite conversation. Fill her in, Davie.'

He told her about the builders who might have been heading her way and then asked about Hume 481. I listened as she spouted the standard line about regretting his death and that he had been a valuable member of her team.

'He crossed the line on his own,' I said, 'without authorization.'

The Mist looked like I'd thrown a bucket of fish guts in her face.

'It's in his service record,' Davie said, 'which you signed off on. He said he'd gone to pick brambles.'

Raeburn 124 twitched her head. 'Ah, yes, I remember. He came back with a huge load. We all partook.'

I eyed her dubiously. 'Was he searched?'

'I imagine so.'

'He wasn't,' Davie said, showing remarkable recall of the records. Then again, the guardsman without a heart had been a member of his barracks and that made him even more conscientious. 'Which, of course, is also contrary to regulations.'

The Mist sat down and looked at the files on her desk.

I stepped closer. 'Are you familiar with a group of Glaswegian smugglers who call themselves the Dead Men?'

Her eyes were on mine immediately. 'Of course, citizen. My people often chase them off towards the border. We've caught some of their Edinburgh contacts, but the Glaswegians always manage to elude us.'

'Unfortunate.' I stuck out my hand. 'The names of the Edinburgh citizens, please?'

She produced a list with remarkable speed. Davie and I looked at it. None of the names were familiar and the dates of arrest weren't recent.

'The last of these was sent to the castle over a year ago.'

'That's right.'

'And he'll be long out of rehab by now. What's been going on? Have the Dead Men given up and gone home?'

'I doubt it,' the commander said, her voice low.

'Grant Brown.'

'What? Who?'

I repeated the name.

'Oh, the citizen whose headless body was found in the canal?'

'Glad to see you're keeping up with directorate reports.'

She glared at me.

'Ever see him around here?'

'I think not.' She turned on a decrepit computer. After a few minutes she said, 'No, we never apprehended him.'

'Not officially.'

She looked puzzled, but also curious. 'What do you mean?'

'I was wondering if he and Hume 481 were friends.'

Raeburn 124 stood up, her face twisted. 'You know very well that friendship between auxiliaries and ordinary citizens is prohibited.'

I glanced at Davie. 'Oh, dear.'

He took the baton skilfully. 'So if we go round all your personnel and ask if Hume 481 knew Grant Brown, they'll say no?'

The Mist was silent – even damp.

I gave her a flash of my authorization to gee her up. 'I answer to the Council. Any untruth or misdirection will be reported to that body.' Dropping into the bureaucratic language favoured by senior auxiliaries seemed to get to her.

'I . . . I did hear that Hume 481 was meeting a male citizen. You know how it is out here. Guard personnel serve for a month without break. It's common practice to allow them contact with . . . citizens offering services.'

I glanced at Davie.

'Amateur hookers who're paid with Guard rations and alcohol,' he said brusquely. 'I know. But there are two things wrong with your story.'

Raeburn 124 sat down again.

'First, such contacts must be reported to the command centre on a weekly basis. I've seen none from this location. And second, Hume 481 was registered hetero.'

'Maybe . . . maybe he was experimenting . . .' the Mist said lamely.

'And Grant Brown was engaged.'

I didn't hear the sound of deflation but I could see that was happening to the commander.

'You're lucky the guardian hasn't had you demoted already,' Davie continued. 'Don't worry, it won't be long.'

'Wait,' she said, waving a finger about wildly. 'There was talk of Hume 481 and Brown being in contact with outsiders. I . . . I was monitoring the situation in advance of laying an ambush.'

I laughed. 'Is that the best you can do?'

'I . . . I can tell you where they went,' the Mist said desperately.

'How do you know where they went?' I demanded.

'Because I . . . I asked Hume 481. I saw them once with my binoculars on their way out.'

Davie loomed over her desk. 'Did you keep any record of this? Did you tell any of your subordinates?'

'I . . . no.' Raeburn 124 seemed to have shrunk.

I sat in a chair that almost gave way, secure in the knowledge that we'd got her. I didn't think she was involved in smuggling – she would never have opened herself up to such a serious charge – but she was just the kind of slippery operator who would have tried to improve her standing by pulling off a coup catching Glaswegian or other outsider smugglers. Still, there was no harm in setting the hook deeper.

'Did you ask Hume 481 and his friend what they came back with?'

The Mist was now fading fast, her mouth opening and closing emitting a sound.

'You did, didn't you?' said Davie.

'I . . . yes, I did. It was . . . cigarettes and tobacco.'

'Are you sure?'

'That's what he said.'

'You didn't see the goods?'

She shook her head.

'Never mind,' I said cheerfully. 'The solution's at hand.'

'What?' she said faintly.

'Well, it's obvious that you'll have sent out another guardsman or woman with Grant Brown before he lost his head. Barracks number, please. And what have you got on him or her?'

Raeburn 124 looked like she was going to be sick. I handed her the waste-paper bin, but she managed to keep her lunch down. 'Wilkie 455,' she said, lowering her head. 'I told . . . I told him he'd be here for five years if he didn't obey my orders and keep them to himself.'

Davie was shaking his head. 'You're supposed to look after your subordinates, not threaten them to further your pathetic career. Jesus!'

'Disgraceful,' I agreed, enjoying every second of the scene. 'Don't worry, a solution is in sight. You set up the ambush you've no doubt got carefully planned and we take the credit. You get to stay out here till you retire. How's that?'

'No good, citizen,' the Mist said, her voice faint. 'The guardsman's been missing since yesterday midday.'

Davie and I left the commander's office, locking her in. She'd admitted that no search party had been dispatched.

'We can't send a squad out in the dark,' I said. 'Smugglers are always armed.'

'First light tomorrow,' he said. 'I'll supervise the watch for the builders and catch whatever sleep I can. You go back to the centre.'

I thought about that. It was after nine o'clock. The main reason to return now would be to meet Sophia. It was tempting, but I managed to hold myself back. I remembered the look on John Lecky's face as he came forward with the hacksaw. I badly wanted to catch that animal, so I stayed at Bonaly watch tower.

Throughout the evening Davie kept in touch with the Guard squads that were combing the southern suburbs. There were no sightings of the runaways, though the pouring rain didn't help. They'd have gone to ground somewhere. Then again, if they wanted to go over the line, night was the time to do it. There's a double layer of twelve-foot-high fencing, topped with razor wire, all the way from the coast north of the airport in the west to Musselburgh in the east. The first Council planned to electrify it, but there was never enough power available. So people cut through it to get in and out, no matter how quickly Guard personnel send in repair teams. The professional line-crossers have even learnt how to replace the wire without making it obvious. There are also tunnels under it – as soon as one is found, another is nearing completion. There's been talk about bringing the city line nearer to the centre, but the Tourism Directorate has resisted, worried that the city's legitimate visitors might be at risk. The fact is, they're in danger from Edinburgh natives if they walk more than half a mile from the central zone. That's why there are so many checkpoints around it.

And that was the problem. Because there were so many Guard personnel in the city centre, there was a shortage for both the city line and the border further out. The latter was originally wired, but now there are gaps all across it and the undermanned posts every mile struggle to maintain even marginally effective patrols. The smugglers have given up attacking them because there's no point. Slipping past in the dark and the rain is easier than opening a can of Supply Directorate vegetable stew.

Davie sent foot patrols out in the Bonaly sector. Not long after eleven, one called in to say that the wire had been cut 400 yards to the west. Soon afterwards, another said that there was a gap 550 yards to the east.

'Standard tactics,' Davie said. 'Organized operators cut the wire in more than one place so we miss where they really go through.' He shook his head. 'There aren't enough people to cover all the wire, even with the majority of them out at night. Not to mention, check for tunnels. That happens during daylight, but Guard personnel have to sleep sometime.'

'Fancy a stroll.'

He gave a hollow laugh. 'Yeah, your authorization will really put the shits up them, Quint. This is the Wild South.'

'So what do we do?'

'You get some sleep.' He raised a finger. 'But go and confiscate the Mist's phone. Her direct line's been cut off.'

Shit. That might have been a bad oversight. I'd assumed Raeburn 124 was working for herself, but she might well have been recruited, either by smugglers or by the people who were leaving bodies and bits of bodies around the city.

I went up to her door quietly and listened. She was snoring. I unlocked it and barged in, bringing her back to consciousness with a bang. She rubbed her eyes as I took the mobile from her desk. The poor quality devices that even senior auxiliaries are supplied with don't register the numbers that have been called, but at least she wouldn't be getting in touch with anyone else. The computer enabled her access to the Guard command centre. If some of the personnel manning it were bent, we were well and truly shafted.

'What's going on, citizen?' she asked.

'Nothing you need know about. Anything you want to tell me?'

'What do you mean?'

'If it transpires that you've been keeping things to yourself, your head will end up on the New Tolbooth.'

She shivered.

'Now get some more sleep. You'll be stretching your legs in the morning.'

I left her to it and went to the male dormitory. There was even more snoring in it, but I dropped into an unoccupied bunk and a deep and dreamless sleep.

I woke to find Davie crashed out in the bunk opposite. It was six in the morning and the rain coming down outside the armoured window wasn't as heavy as it might have been.

I carried out my ablutions in facilities that would have put the old prison on Cramond Island to shame. The Mist ran a very smelly ship. By the time I was finished, Davie was awake.

I waited for him, then we went to the operations room. None of the personnel on duty was bothered by Raeburn 124's absence. Besides, who would stand up to Davie?

'Report,' he ordered.

'Signs of a tunnel having been used two hundred yards to the east.'

'Bastards,' Davie said. 'They go through within screaming distance of the tower.'

'It isn't the first time, commander,' said a tall, thin guardswoman. 'At least we can block that tunnel.'

Davie grunted. 'The line's a rabbit warren. We need proper surveillance gear.'

There was a burst of uncontrolled laughter from his subordinates.

'We could do with more personnel, better weapons, more whisky and better rations,' said a young guardsman with a deep scar on his forehead. 'Oh, and a cleaner.'

'But we aren't going to get them,' said the guardswoman, Adam 392. Out here auxiliaries don't wear name panels.

'Probably not,' Davie said. 'Then again, the citizen here's in direct contact with the Council and he's a particular friend of our guardian.'

Thanks a lot, big man. Several pairs of eyes were trained on me.

'The commander exaggerates,' I said. 'It's a particular talent of his. But I'll pass on your concerns. This facility is a fucking disgrace.'

That got me a round of applause, but I didn't let it go to my head. They were about to receive some less than pleasant orders.

'Right,' said Davie. 'We know people crossed the line last night.'

'In both directions,' said Adam 392. 'But there aren't significant tracks on the sodden grass.'

Davie nodded. 'Any reports from the neighbouring towers?'

'Quieter than here,' she replied, 'but crossings were made.'

'It's like Piccadilly Circus,' I said.

They all looked at me blankly. The Education Directorate's policy of no reference to what had been the UK was obviously bearing fruit.

'Whatever that is, citizen,' Davie said, playing dumb to side with his comrades – or maybe he really didn't know about Eros's erstwhile location. 'Never mind where they went inside the line. What we've got to do is go in the other direction.'

That raised a few eyebrows.

'What?' Davie demanded. 'Don't you make weekly patrols over there?'

'Er, no,' said the scarred guardsman. 'The Mi— Raeburn 124 stopped them about six months ago.'

I looked at Davie.

'Why?' he demanded.

'She didn't give a reason,' said Adam 392, dropping her gaze.

'You're her second in command,' Davie said. 'Why didn't you ask for clarification?'

'I did,' she said. 'According to her, it was an order from the command centre.'

'It bloody was not!' Davie roared.

Now they were all studying the splintered wood floor.

'What do you know about Hume 481's activities?' I said, taking advantage of the awkward silence.

They looked up and then at each other.

'Why don't *you* speak for your colleagues?' I said to the tall guardswoman. Her fair hair was pulled back tightly and her eyes were bloodshot.

'Hume 481?'

'Don't pretend you didn't know him!' Davie thundered.

'I . . . no, I knew him. We all did. Except Ferguson 569 over there, who only joined us last week.'

'Go on,' I said, before Davie could fire another broadside.

'Well, he used to go over the line frequently.'

That was more than we'd heard, not least from the Mist.

'Brambles?'

She smiled tightly. 'That was his cover, at least the last couple of times.'

'They were good,' said a sturdy guardsman, only to be given a stony look by Davie.

'What was he doing on these frequent trips?'

'You'd have to ask Raeburn 124,' said Adam 392.

'Oh, we will,' Davie put in. 'But what did you think?'

'I . . . I presumed he had a girlfriend on one of the farms.'

'Did you fuck!' yelled Davie.

The guardswoman looked down again. 'I didn't like to think anything, commander.'

'Well, that's pretty spineless.' Davie grinned malevolently. 'Never mind, you can make up for that now.' He turned to me. 'Time the Mist came down.'

That raised some sniggers. I went to get her.

'I've discovered that Hume 481 crossed the line frequently. Last chance to tell me what he was doing.'

'Carrying out orders,' Raeburn 124 said defiantly.

'Whose?'

'Mine.'

'Ah, of course. He was laying the ground for that ambush you were planning so carefully.'

'That's right.' A night of slumber had obviously restored her spirits. I saw the remains of fruit and sandwiches in her rubbish bin.

'I see you've already had breakfast. That's good, because you're going to need all the energy you've got.'

'But . . .'

'That word isn't permitted in the City Guard,' I said.

Which is why I use it as much as I can.

EIGHTEEN

H alf an hour later we were pushing our way through the tall grass beyond the fifty-yard area immediately behind the fence that's mowed every week, though the rain had put paid to that recently. Amazingly, the drizzle was only light, but I knew that wouldn't last. There were no city farms in the vicinity because shots were often fired both by outsiders and by Guard personnel. Davie had arranged for a five-man squad, which included two women, under the command of Adam 392. The squad members were all carrying reconditioned Lee-Enfield .303 rifles, while the guardswoman had a sub-machine gun that could have come from the Second World War. Davie had picked up a rifle too, while the Mist and I were unarmed. I don't like guns.

'Where was it you saw Hume 481 go?' I asked her.

'Up there,' she pointed, already struggling for breath. 'The trees to the left of the burn.'

I followed her arm and made out a body of water that was more like a torrent than a humble burn. Then she slipped and went her not exactly great length in the damp grass. I helped her up.

'Thank you, citizen,' she said, panting.

I hoped she didn't think I was her new best friend. The way things were going, she was going to need one of those and I didn't fancy the job.

The squad was in inverted V-formation, the new boy Ferguson 569 leading. That was the Guard way – throw them in the deep end. His comrades were swinging their eyes and rifles from left to right. It wasn't likely that outsiders, or even rebel citizens, would attack in daylight, but it had been known to happen. The Mist and I were at the rear, in the centre, while Davie and Adam 392 were in front of us. To my amazement, he wasn't chatting her up. Maybe he'd seen that she was homo in her file, though I wasn't getting that vibe.

It took us nearly an hour to make the target location, mainly because Raeburn 124 was so out of condition. That would have got her busted down the ranks on its own, but she'd have more serious charges to face. Then someone took a shot at us.

'Down!' Davie yelled, though we'd all hit the grass already.

'Rifle,' Adam 392 said. 'Maybe a sniper. Anyone hit?'

Everyone called in healthy.

'Ferguson 569!' the guardswoman called. 'Move forward on all fours.'

That was standard tactics to avoid a squad getting pinned down. It wasn't much fun for the leading man or woman, but it was tried and tested. The casualty figures for those in front weren't published.

There was another shot.

'Unhit,' called the guardsman. The moving grass had given him away, but he was lucky.

'Fuck this,' Davie said. 'Give me covering fire!' He waited a few seconds then moved forward on two legs, his upper body horizontal as shots cracked out around us.

I hardly dared to watch, but he made it to a small rise in the ground that offered cover. From there he waited for the gunman to fire again before letting off five shots in rapid succession.

'Got the bastard,' he called. 'But he may have friends. Come forward in a crawl.'

That got us completely soaked, but we made it without further incoming.

'What was . . . that about?' I said, trying to catch my breath.

'Don't know. Could have been trying to scare us off or might just have been a trigger-happy head-banger.' Davie's face was red but his breathing was under control. He was completely in his element.

Unlike the Mist, who looked like she was crying.

'That didn't happen when Hume 481 went out, did it?' I said.

She wiped her eyes. Maybe they were drops of water from the grass.

'No,' she said in a low voice.

'Why was that, do you think?'

'I couldn't tell you, citizen,' she said, turning her liquid eyes on me. 'Honestly.'

I believed her.

'Time to move out,' Davie said.

'I'll lead, commander,' said Adam 392, without hesitating.

I was impressed. Though I'd led more than my fair share of raids when I was in the Guard, I'd never enjoyed it. Or got used to it.

As it turned out, there were no more shots. We followed the guardswoman, backs bent at first, but upright soon enough. The trees by the surge of water were close. In front of them stood the bramble bushes that Hume 481 had plundered. There were only unripe fruit on them now.

We reached the trees and stopped to catch our breath. The Guard squad and Davie soon recovered, but Raeburn 124 and I needed longer. I was embarrassed, but not too much. I survived on citizen rations, not what the Guard got – even though the poor sods on the city line seemed to have been forgotten about. Or maybe the Mist was running a scam with the suppliers – recompense of some sort for her, shit food and drink for her people. I wouldn't have put it past her.

My thoughts were interrupted by the sound of retching. Davie moved quickly forward to where Ferguson 569 had gone, about twenty yards to the front.

'Quint,' he called. 'Get up here. The rest of you stay where you are.'

I could tell by the tone of his voice that there was something bad ahead, but curiosity got the better of me and I almost broke into a run. I soon wished I hadn't.

There was a small clearing in the pines and the smell that hit my nostrils was much worse than the contents of the young guardsman's stomach.

'What the—?'

'Fucking, bastarding, bleeding hell?' Davie suggested.

'Something like that.' I walked forwards and took in the contents of the natural circle. There were two bodies, each of them without a head.

'That's . . . that's Wilkie 455,' the guardsman said, on his knees.

I checked the panel on the blood-soaked combat jacket. He was right.

'I'd say the other is a male citizen,' Davie said. He'd pulled on latex gloves and was going through the corpse's pockets. 'No ID, but the clothes and footwear are Supply Directorate finest.'

I agreed with him. No outsider would be seen alive or dead in the ill-fitting, faded and poorly stitched garb that covered the citizen's body.

'No defence wounds on either of them,' Davie said in full forensic mode now. 'Or rope abrasions. I'd say they were held down before a jagged blade was taken to their necks.'

I took a look. The wounds were ragged, even more than Hume 481's had been. If a hacksaw had been used, it wasn't the one carried by John Lecky. Besides, apart from the missing guardsman, the bodies were at least two days old, judging by the swelling and lack of rigor mortis. They had pine needles on them, but there were fewer on Wilkie 455. There were also marks on their necks and hands that suggested crows had been at them.

'Plenty of footprints,' said Davie, 'but the ground's been soaked since they were made.'

'The last ones would be the guardsman's,' I said.

'And his executioner's.'

I nodded, then became aware that the Mist was standing behind me. This time she was definitely crying, but she wouldn't speak. In her position I'd have held my tongue as well.

It was a bit of an operation to get the bodies back across the line. Guard squads from neighbouring posts were deployed on the higher ground in case of further attack, then 4×4s got as far up the slope as they could. The bodies were put in bags and carried down to the vehicles by Guard personnel.

Davie and Adam 392 helped, while I oversaw a forensics team at the clearing.

They found nothing obvious, suggesting that the killers – more than one had been involved if the victims were held down – had been careful. That smacked more of auxiliary activity than it did of outsiders'.

'Why?' said Raeburn 124, before she was taken off to the castle.

'I was going to ask you that,' I said.

She shook her head, her eyes squeezed shut. 'I wish I knew. I would never have sent Wilkie 455 out if I'd known . . .'

I watched her walk slowly down the hill between a pair of guardsmen. Guardian Doris appeared in their wake.

'Oh, great,' I muttered.

'What on earth?' she said, visibly shocked.

I told her what we knew as Davie and Adam 392 took a squad up the hill to find the shooter he had taken out.

'Where do you think the heads are?' the guardian asked.

'In the city,' I replied. 'Where else? I haven't heard of a functioning group of headshrinkers, though you never know in Glasgow.'

She gave a sharp look. 'Why do you say Glasgow?'

I shrugged. 'It was the Council's bugbear for decades. And is the source of most smugglers.'

'Groups like the Dead Men.'

'Has anything happened in the city?'

'No. The missing heart hasn't turned up and there have been no more bodies without the said organ. I'm afraid there's been no sign of the men who attacked you last night. On the wider front, the governors of Orkney and Shetland are staying on to meet the Lord of the Isles.'

I pointed up the slope. 'Let's see what Hume 253's got.'

Davie and three Guard personnel were carrying a corpse towards us, while Adam 392 was holding a rifle with a telescopic sight. The body was lowered to the ground in front of us. It was a young woman with long blonde hair. My stomach somersaulted. Could she have been the one who left the heart at Tynecastle?

'Some shot, Davie,' I said. There was a hole in the shooter's throat and, as he turned the body on its side, a much larger and messier exit wound to the rear.

'That's why I practise at the range every week. Morning, guardian.'

'Commander. So who is she?'

Davie was going through the dead woman's pockets with gloved hands. He produced a packet of Glasgow Green cigarettes and a plastic lighter with a logo saying 'Top City'; a soiled handkerchief – the Supply Directorate didn't run to those, soiled or otherwise; a silver-plated semi-automatic pistol and two clips of ammunition, and two clips for the rifle, which looked new and highly sophisticated to my less than expert eye.

'No identification,' Davie said, 'not that outsiders carry any.' He undid the woman's green-and-yellow camouflage jacket. 'A bullet-proof vest. She was unlucky.' She was also not well endowed on the mammary front.

'Look at these boots,' I said. They were eighteen-hole lace-ups, the dark brown leather in good condition. I checked the soles. They were heavy tread, with a distinctive pattern. I wondered if we might find any prints in Tynecastle and mentioned that to Guardian Doris.

She dropped to a squat. 'Made in Casablanca,' she read. 'Where's that?'

I raised my eyes to the darkening sky. 'Haven't you seen the film?'

She gave me a blank look.

'It was in Morocco, but it's probably an independent city-state now.' Billy Geddes would know that, which reminded me: I needed to have a serious talk with him about gambling in the EPL.

'All right,' said the guardian, standing up. 'Leave her to the forensics team and the pathologists.'

'Tall and Short are going to be busy,' I observed, suddenly struck by the absence of Sophia. She'd made a bee-line for every other crime scene. Maybe she was sticking needles into those of her people who had the combination to the safe that had contained the truth drug.

'She's very pretty,' Guardian Doris said.

I looked at the corpse's freckled face. Her eyes were wide open, a pale shade of brown, and her open mouth displayed teeth that were in good condition.

'She'd have been prettier alive,' I said, taken aback by the guardian's words. I couldn't remember whether she was hetero or homo, but the observation seemed misplaced.

Davie stripped off his gloves. 'I suppose you'd have preferred her to have gone on shooting at us.'

'Of course not, but she'd have made a good interview subject.'

'I'm so sorry I didn't manage to wing her,' said Davie, his chest swelling. 'You know these people don't talk anyway, Quint.' He walked away, Adam 392 following him with the rifle.

'Oops,' I said.

'Haven't you learnt to keep your nose out of operational matters,' the guardian said. 'You can't shoot to wound at that range.'

'I bow to your superior experience,' I said, giving her heavies the eye and heading down the slope.

As I got to the 4×4s I overheard Davie arranging a date with Adam 392 on her next leave.

It was early afternoon by the time we got back to the castle. The Mist was taken off for interrogation by Guardian Doris. Davie, looking pleased with himself, led me down to the command centre. There was nothing out of the ordinary to report, which was a relief. We still had a backlog to clear.

'Where's that auxiliary from the recreation guardian's house?' I opened my notebook. 'Watt 529. I want to put the squeeze on him.'

'I'll get him up here.' Davie made the call.

'Next, have we got an ID for the heartless man in the Saly?'

He made another call, this one more protracted.

'A drawing of his face as it would have been under normal conditions was circulated to all barracks this morning. No word back yet.'

'Hm. Derick Smail and Fat Eric Colquhoun?'

'"Have we got enough?"'

'Exactly. I think we should put tails on them.'

'I thought we'd been warned off EPL managers.'

I looked at him.

'Right, I'll put people I trust on them.' This time he made several calls.

'And now, a refuelling break.'

I had one late lunch, while Davie put away three.

My mobile rang as we were on the way to rip the crap out of the recreation guardian's auxiliary.

'Quint, it's Doris. Those boots the dead shooter was wearing. We've found several prints at Tynecastle.'

'Whereabouts?'

'At the rear entrance. There's a small area that's sheltered from the elements. She must have gone out there.'

'How come the prints weren't found before?'

'I'm trying to get to the bottom of that. You can be sure someone will soon be cleaning tourist toilets. But it's good news, isn't it? We know who put the heart on the centre spot.'

'So it seems,' I said, suppressing my doubt about the dead woman's lack of 'lungs'. 'See if forensics can get any blood stains from her clothing. We still don't know who the donor was.'

'I'd say the body was buried.'

'Maybe. But don't get too confident, Doris. She wasn't working alone, you can be sure of that. And now there are two more heads that might appear anywhere any time in the city.'

There was a short silence. 'Quite,' she said, deflated. 'Any other news?'

'I'll be in touch,' I replied.

'Oh, I almost forgot. Your presence isn't required at this evening's Council meeting.' She cut the connection.

I thought about that. She could pass on everything I'd told her, but was there a reason I was persona non grata? Was I getting too close to comfort to something under the senior guardian's purview? Only he could have given Doris the order to exclude me.

'He's in there,' Davie said, his thumb indicating a door down the corridor.

I led him in. Watt 529 was standing in the far corner, rubbing his hands together like Uriah Heep. He wasn't at all happy to see us.

'Why did you vacuum the floor in the recreation guardian's room?' I asked mildly.

'I . . . I didn't, citizen.'

'You did.'

Davie stepped forward, his fist raised. 'If you contradict him one more time, your nose is going to be flatter than a flounder.'

I managed not to laugh. Davie's threats had become more imaginative. He was getting plenty of practice.

'I . . . yes, it was me,' the auxiliary said, slumping to the floor.

I motioned to Davie to keep his distance and went over.

'William,' I said, taking in the name panel.

'Will,' he sobbed.

'Will. All you have to do is tell me what happened. I promise you'll feel much better.'

The auxiliary let loose a torrent of tears. I gave him all the time he needed.

'I . . . I loved Peter,' he said, his head in his hands. 'I loved him.'

I glanced at Davie.

'Wasn't the guardian hetero?'

'Yes, he was . . . but he understood me. He accepted my . . . devotion.'

I thought about that and the bruises on Peter Stewart's lower thighs.

'You tried to save him, didn't you, Will?'

He looked at me and then smiled sadly. 'That's . . . that's right. I went in to see . . . if he needed anything . . . and I found him . . .'

Hanging.

'So you tried to get him down?'

'Yes . . . I stood on the chair and I lifted him as much as I could . . . I tried to unhook the rope . . . but . . . but it was too late. There was no . . . no pulse. So I . . . I gave up.' He wept again.

I waited and then whispered, 'He committed suicide, didn't he, Will?'

'He . . . he was so ashamed . . . he wouldn't tell me . . . but I know it had something to do with the directorate . . .'

'And you cleaned up – why?'

'I . . . I wanted the place to be the way he would have liked it.'

'You didn't consider telling me what had happened when I arrived?'

The auxiliary tried to speak without success. I suspected he was still in shock.

'Now, did you see any documents about the Edinburgh Premier League?'

'Stupid football. Yes, lots, of course. It was the big thing.'

I caught his eye. 'Anything that you should have reported?' Auxiliaries are expected to be loyal to their guardians, but also to advise the Council of any misconduct.

He buried his face in his hands.

'There was . . . there was gambling. Contacts to syndicates in other cities.'

That was an away win.

'Such as?'

'Glasgow, Inverness, Oban, Stornoway. Oh, and Orkney and Shetland. I can't remember the names of the capitals.'

Neither could I, but no matter.

'Who took the computer from his residence?'

'I don't know. Honestly. It was gone when I went in.'

'Do you know where the guardian . . . Peter . . . might have hidden any documents or diskettes?'

He shook his head. 'I looked in all the places I know. There's nothing.'

'Do you know who else was involved in the gambling?'

'No, citizen. Peter . . . Peter didn't trust me with that.' He sobbed again.

'All right,' I said. 'I'll send in some tea. Well done, Will. You've been a great help.'

Davie turned to me when we were outside.

'You believe that snivelling disgrace to his rank?'

I looked at him. 'Yes, I do. So it was suicide and Peter Stewart was dirty – so dirty that he couldn't live with himself. But someone else was pulling the strings and I know exactly who to ask about that.'

'Billy demoted-piece-of-shit Geddes.'

'Right in one. See if you can locate him.'

A couple of calls later, he turned back to me. 'He's with the senior and finance guardians at a dinner for the Orkney and Shetland governors and the Lord of the Isles.'

'I couldn't eat another thing, but I know you can always find a space.'

He grinned.

'Let's go and gatecrash. Where are they?'

'At the Walter Scott Rooms.'

I set off down the corridor. 'Saddle up, Ivanhoe. It's time you got your lance out.'

'If I'm the knight, are you my second?'

'If you're the knight, I'm King Richard.'

He laughed. 'Right you are, Dick.'

NINETEEN

The Walter Scott Rooms – no Sir for the old novelist in Enlightenment Edinburgh – were in a neo-classical former bank at the east end of George Street. I remembered going there occasionally with my parents. The large glass-domed lobby where the tellers used to work had been turned into a trendy bar and restaurant before the last election. The building survived the drugs wars and is now used by the Council to impress its most honoured guests. When there weren't any of those around – which was usually the case until recently – the wealthiest tourists were encouraged to empty their wallets in the ornate building.

I held my authorization up as we approached the guards at the door, though they were more impressed by Davie's glower. I glanced at the bar on the left, but it was closed. The dulcet tones of the Recreation Directorate's string quartet came from the restaurant ahead. There were enough flowers and ferns to make you think you'd wandered into a magic garden. But there was a snake in the grass.

'What are you doing here?' said the deputy guardian of the Supply Directorate, getting up from a table in front of the circular bar. Other senior auxiliaries gave me hostile looks.

'Uncle Joe,' I said, giving him a big grin. 'How are your personnel problems?'

That made his complexion more florid. I took his arm and led him back towards the entrance hall.

'I've got a couple of questions for you,' I said, nodding to Davie. He took up position half an inch behind Adam 159.

The auxiliary gulped but didn't dare make a fuss.

'What do you know about a former church on the Pleasance?'

Uncle Joe held my gaze with difficulty. 'Nothing, citizen,' he said, apparently surprised by the question.

'A Supply Directorate truck made a delivery there yesterday afternoon.'

He shrugged. 'So? Have you any idea how many deliveries are made in the city every day? You can't expect me—'

'There were five pounds of cocaine in this one.'

His face fell as rapidly as the House of Windsor.

'Commander, correct me if I'm wrong, but don't recreational drugs for tourist use have to be registered with the Guard and kept in a high-security lock-up?'

'You aren't wrong, citizen,' Davie said loudly, making Adam 159 jump.

'You shouldn't . . . you shouldn't be speaking to me. I told you, Knox 31's in charge of drugs in the warehouse.'

I smiled. 'Knox 31 and his team found the cocaine. I'm on my way to tell the senior guardian about it now.'

'No . . .' The auxiliary gasped as Davie's service knife appeared at his throat.

'I think you mean, "Yes, I'll tell you all about it, citizen".'

Uncle Joe's face was a bath of sweat.

'Um . . . yes . . . I . . . the . . .' He broke off, unable to speak from what looked very like terror.

I moved my head and Davie's knife disappeared.

'Nothing to be frightened about now,' I said.

'If . . . if only you knew.' Adam 159 was still as nervy as a drugs-gang member in front of a Guard firing squad in the old days.

'Tell me, Joe,' I said, taking his arm. 'It'll be a relief.'

He looked around and then leaned close. 'I'm only following orders.'

The excuse of every spineless bureaucrat in history. I managed to restrain myself from kneeing him in the balls, but only just. He realized that.

'It's true. Every week a list of consignments not to be checked by the drugs unit is sent to the directorate.'

'We know.'

'You . . . how?'

I tapped the side of my nose. 'The question is who sends the list?'

'I . . . I don't know.'

Davie stepped closer again, his knife scraping across the back of the auxiliary's hand.

'The Public Order Directorate. Or at least they arrive in a POD envelope.'

'It wouldn't be the first time that gangs had used stolen stationery,' I said. That had just occurred to me.

'Does your boss know?'

'I . . . I'm not sure.' Adam 159 suddenly looked like he was going to throw up.

I took a step to the side. 'You haven't shown him any of the lists?'

'He . . . doesn't like to be bothered by detail.'

'Detail? Five pounds of coke isn't a fucking detail.'

The auxiliary hung his head. 'They . . . threatened my mother.'

'What? Who did?'

'The . . . the Lancers.' He gave me a crazed look. 'They'll track her down, whichever home I have her transferred to.'

'How are these threats delivered?'

'By phone.'

I scoffed. 'Someone phones up saying they're from the Leith Lancers and you believe them?'

'They sent me . . . a photo in the post.' Now he really did look like he was going to empty his stomach. I led him swiftly to the toilets and let him get on with it.

'What did the photo show?' I said when he'd finished swallowing water from the tap.

'The . . . the severed head of an old woman.' He retched again.

'And, of course, they told you not to show it to anyone,' I said, cutting him some slack.

'They told me to destroy it, which I did.'

That was a great help. I left him at the sink and went out to the hall.

'Do you believe that fat shite?' Davie said.

'Yes.' I told him about the photo.

'What is it about heads?'

'Seems to be the Lancers' new modus operandi.'

'You think they cut the heads off the guardsman and the citizen beyond the line?'

'They or someone they're working with. Or for.'

'What about the hearts?'

'They may be another story altogether.'

He looked confused. I didn't blame him.

'Right, come on,' I said.

'Billy Geddes?' Davie said.

'Yes. I saw him in the private dining area with the senior guardian and the guests.'

'Is this a good idea?' It was one of the few occasions when Davie showed reluctance.

'Probably not. You stay here if you like.'

He thought about it. 'No, where would you be without your knight in muddy combat gear. Lead on, Dick.'

I led.

There was a pair of tunic-bursting guardsmen at the partition that marked off the private dining room. They couldn't say no to my authorization, but that didn't mean they were happy. One of them went to consult the senior guardian. I skipped in after him while Davie restrained his colleague, I wasn't sure how. Testicles, probably.

The diners were sitting around an oval table, halfway through their main course. A huge rib roast of beef sat on a smaller table to the rear and I almost started drooling. Apart from Fergus Calder, Jack MacLean and Billy Geddes there were the two island governors, who looked out of their depth in ill-fitting suits and garish ties. Then there was the Lord of the Isles. He was resplendent in full highland evening dress. His silver-studded black jacket set off his puffy red face and his primarily red kilt. I could see the latter because he'd stood up.

'What's the meaning of this?' he demanded, in a high voice that was a strange mixture of the Queen's English that was still hanging on during my youth and an American twang. 'Who is this scarecrow?'

At least he didn't call me a tattie-bogle.

'Citizen,' the senior guardian said, a smile on his lips but not in his eyes, 'this is hardly the time or the place. Guards.'

The gorilla to my rear was still in Davie's grip, but the other one came at me.

'Heads or hearts?' I said rapidly.

'What?' The Lord of the Isles was less interested in my clothes now. 'What is this, Fergus?'

I'd been grabbed by the scruff of my neck and lifted from the ground.

'Tell your guests,' I said. 'Tell them about the heads that have joined the hearts in popping up.'

I'd been hauled beyond the partition when the senior guardian called his man back. I was deposited at his end of the table. From the middle, Billy was staring at me and shaking his head.

'What is he saying?' the Lord of the Isles asked, still on his feet. 'Fergus? Jack?'

The two guardians exchanged looks and then nodded at each other.

'Very well,' Calder said. 'Please sit down, Angus. And you, citizen.'

I was pushed into a chair by the guardsman, who stood within skull-crushing range behind me.

The senior guardian gave me a long-suffering look. 'What's this about, Dalrymple?'

'Dalrymple?' said the Lord of the Isles, emptying his wine glass. 'Is this the famous Quintilian of that ilk?' His hair was pure white, cut en brosse. He was a cross between a tourist attraction and a retired Marine Corps general. Not that there'd been a Marine Corps since the USA disunited.

'The same.'

'My lord,' said the finance guardian.

I ignored that. So did the lord.

'Clan Dalrymple,' the man in the kilt said. 'Ayrshire origins, I believe. Do you know what the clan crest is?'

'Em, no.' The original Council had banned clan societies and removed books about the ancient families of Scotland from the city's libraries in its drive to root out all remnants of the class system and potentially nationalist material. Neither of my parents was interested in genealogy before the crisis, while I was keener on the roots of blues music.

'A rock proper.' The aristocrat gave me a pitying smile. 'Which means in its natural colouring. How about the clan motto?'

'Never unprepared?' I suggested.

'No, no, that belongs to Clan Johnston – "Nunquam non paratus". Clan Dalrymple's motto is "Firm".'

There was a faint laugh from Davie and a guffaw from Billy.

'I've no doubt you're aware of your own clan's characteristics, Mr Geddes,' the Lord of the Isles said caustically.

'Actually, no.'

'Sadly the Clan Ged is without a chief and has no legal standing. Its crest is the head of a pike and its motto is "Durat ditat placet".'

Billy had to ask for a translation.

'"It sustains, it enriches, it pleases".'

This time I was the one who laughed.

The Lord of the Isles turned to the guardians, who turned out to be never unprepared.

'Calder – a hart's head caboched sable, attired gules,' said the senior guardian. 'Motto, "Be mindful".'

'Again, how appropriate,' I muttered.

Jack MacLean stood up. 'A tower embattled argent. "Virtue mine honour".'

I almost swallowed my tongue.

'And you, my lord?' Calder asked.

'On a castle triple towered, an arm in armour, embowed, holding a sword, proper. "My hope is constant in thee".' The aristocrat smiled tightly. 'Thee referring to God, not you, Fergus. It's such a shame you did away with religion in your city. Not to mention the traditional great families.'

'Well, things are changing,' the senior guardian said, giving me a sharp look.

'What about Oliphant?' I asked, determined that Davie shouldn't escape torture by surname.

'Ah, a fine old family, supporters of Mary, Queen of Scots and Bonnie Prince Charlie, the latter at the cost of banishment. Let me see . . . unicorn coupled argent, crined and armed, or. Motto, "Tout pourvoir", or "Provide for all".' The Lord of the Isles looked at me curiously.

I pointed to Davie, who now had the gorilla in a headlock.

The Lord gave a high-pitched laugh. 'Wrong kind of provision, I think. At least he isn't using a unicorn horn.'

The others round the table smiled at the witticism.

'Let him go, commander,' Calder ordered.

Davie looked at me and then complied. The guardsman gave him a blacker-than-the-devil look.

'After that pleasant diversion, back to heads and hearts.' Angus MacDonald's small blue eyes fixed on me. 'What were you referring to, Dalrymple?'

'I don't know if you've been informed,' I said, ignoring the guardians and Billy, 'but Edinburgh's having a bit of a problem with those parts of the anatomy.'

'I—' The Lord of the Isles broke off, glancing at his distinctly non-aristocratic counterparts from the northern islands. 'I am aware of the heart issue.'

'Having had similar organs placed in the centre spots of your own football fields.'

That got to them in a big way. Variants of 'How do you know?' and 'Who told him?' flew at me, while the Orkney and Shetland representatives exchanged puzzled looks.

'Don't worry, I haven't told anyone,' I said. 'Oh, apart from the Oliphant.'

All eyes were on me. I love a keen audience.

'I take it you have no idea who left the hearts?' I said, looking at the Lord of the Isles. 'Two, was it?'

'Three. And no, I have no idea.'

'Did anyone caution discretion?'

He glared at me and then nodded.

'Who were the victims?'

Apparently no heartless bodies had been found.

'Seditionists,' Angus MacDonald said. 'I'm sure of it. They'll be found and hanged.'

'Why would seditionists – I take it you mean members of your citizen body – cut out human hearts?'

My question went unanswered.

'Betting on the football,' I said, tossing in the phrase like a hand-grenade whose pin had been removed.

There was another volley of 'What?', 'Pardon?' and the like.

'Is there betting on the football in your states?' I clarified.

'Certainly not,' said the Lord of the Isles. 'Gambling is not the behaviour of good Christians.'

The men from Orkney and Shetland also confirmed the absence of gambling in their islands, though without the religious element. It was too windy for football in the winter, I also learned. Their season ran from April to October.

'What are you getting at, citizen?' the senior guardian said in a low voice.

'Let him continue, Fergus,' commanded Angus MacDonald.

'Whereas here, there is gambling,' I said. 'Illegal, of course –

apart from the tourists – but organized by the clubs in the Edinburgh Premier League.' I stared at the guardians. 'The strange thing is no one in the city hierarchy seems to be aware of it.' I turned to Billy. 'Unless it's being run under his nose by the finance guardian's special adviser, executive – it, or rather he, who sustains, enriches and pleases.'

Billy's mouth was open as if he was lost for words – an unusual state of affairs.

Jack MacLean glared at him. 'What is this, Geddes?'

'Take him to the castle, citizen,' the senior guardian said.

'One moment,' said the Lord of the Isles. 'Dalrymple, you mentioned heads as well as hearts. Explain.' He raised a hand. 'No, Fergus, let the man speak. After all, he is your Sherlock Holmes.'

My Doctor Watson grinned.

'Two days ago, a severed head was found among the fake ones on the New Tolbooth. In addition—'

There was a loud crash as the window behind the table was smashed by a large rock, pieces of glass landing on the men around it. I ducked and got a shard in my scalp for my pains. Fortunately it didn't go in deep. I had just finished pulling it out when something else came through the hole in the window and landed on the table, knocking over a silver candle-holder.

There were shouts of horror, the Lord of the Isle's being particularly shrill.

Propped upright against a bowl of roast potatoes and looking at him with eyes wide open was the limp-haired head of a middle-aged man.

In the chaos that followed, I managed to keep hold of Billy's wheelchair, much to his irritation. The guardians took their guests away, surrounded by Guard personnel, while Davie organized the search in Rose Street, behind the Walter Scott Rooms. There was no shortage of guardsmen and women in what was one of the tourist zone's most frequented streets, lined by bars, restaurants, clubs and casinos. It quickly became clear that two men in Maintenance Department overalls and helmets had been seen entering and leaving the area behind the Rooms. Behind a screen, put there to provide security and privacy for diners, was a low scaffold beneath the window. From there the men were invisible to passers-by and carousers and in the noise from the bands playing in the pubs, no one had noticed either the crash from the rock or the subsequent throwing of the head.

I wheeled Billy round.

'I don't suppose you know anything about this?' I said.

'Of course not, you wanker.'

I laughed. 'Like you don't know anything about gambling in the EPL.'

'No comment.'

'Uh-huh.' I watched as an auxiliary in a ludicrously short skirt and a blouse that left nothing to the imagination led a group of African men in brightly coloured robes into a club called Toss Your Caber. Traditional Scottish objects were blithely used by the Tourism Directorate, no matter what the Council laid down for ordinary citizens.

'I don't believe it,' Davie said when he came back from ordering his subordinates about. 'No one saw a thing.'

'What about the men in overalls?' I asked.

'Gone.'

'Vanished into the crowds like mist on the morning hills,' Billy said with a cackle.

'Listen, my friend,' I said, 'we're going to the castle and you're going to talk.'

Billy gave Davie a dismissive look. 'What, the big lump's going to torture me?'

'That can be arranged.'

Davie grinned malevolently, but Billy was a tough little bastard.

'We could always use the medical guardian's truth drug,' I said, watching his twisted face.

That made his eyes shoot open. 'What truth drug?' he demanded.

'Haven't you heard of it?' I said, more interested in the fact that he didn't know the compound had been stolen. 'The leader of the Porty Pish spilled his guts in under five minutes.'

Davie laughed. 'Course, it didn't end too well for him.'

'What happened?' Billy said, his face white.

'He croaked,' I said.

The drive to the castle was uninterrupted by conversation.

TWENTY

'Stick him in an interrogation room,' I said to Davie. 'I've got to see Guardian Doris.'

I found her in the command centre.

'I can't understand how those men in overalls could just disappear on Rose Street,' she said after greeting me. 'We've got an alert out, but they'll be long gone.'

'Any news on the head?'

'It's been taken to the infirmary. We'll get a photograph and circulate it to all barracks.'

'You could always try to match him to the list of those who've gone missing.'

She gave a hollow laugh. Updated daily, that list is long. 'We're working on it. The senior guardian wants answers.'

I nodded. 'What did you get from the Mist?'

'Raeburn 124 still has senior auxiliary rank,' she said, not very convincingly.

'Until?'

'The disciplinary board tomorrow.'

'After which she'll be mopping vomit in a tourist dive?'

'I don't think so, Quint. She's a former holder of my office.'

'Not for long she wasn't. If Hamish Buchanan hadn't looked after her, she'd have been demoted years ago.'

She gave me the look that guardians use when lower ranks get uppity.

I paid no attention. 'Did she tell you anything useful?'

'Nothing you hadn't already reported.'

'You don't think she was in with the outsiders, like Hume 481 was.'

The guardian thought about that. 'I can't be sure, but I'm inclined not to believe so.'

'She's good at keeping things to herself. I'd postpone that board and put her in the cells.'

'Very well. What are you doing?'

I told her about Billy and the gambling.

'Are you sure there's anything in that?'

'That's what I'm going to find out.'

'Quint,' she said over her shoulder as she walked away. 'No nail removal.'

'He was my school and university friend.'

'I'd keep that to yourself.'

I thought about that as I went to the interrogation room. Was Billy's star finally about to fall into the deepest of wormholes or did she just feel the standard disgust auxiliaries have for those demoted from their rank? Such as me. One thing I was sure of – if Jack MacLean really needed Billy, it wouldn't be long till he got him out of the castle. All the more reason to get stuck into him without delay.

Davie burst into the interrogation room like a bull with a thistle up its arse. I strolled in, examining my nails.

Billy burst out laughing. 'Good cop, bad cop. Remember those movies we used to sneak off from school to see, Quint?'

I did, but I was going to be bad too.

'Right, Billy, here's where we are. Several people have identified you as being behind the gambling in the EPL. You can either own up or take your chances with Thunder Boots here.'

He rolled his chair back. 'You don't scare me, Quint. And as for your boot boy, do you really think he can inflict worse pain on me than the racehorses did back in the day?'

'Actually, I do.'

'You won't go along with that.'

'Watch me.'

Billy looked unsure of himself for a split-second. Progress.

I held up my authorization. 'You know this means I can keep even guardians off your back.'

He laughed like a hyena. 'Listen to yourself, Quint. You know how easy it is for people like me to disappear.' He grinned. 'Not that there's anyone else like me.'

'That's your blessing and your curse, isn't it, Billy? People take you on because of your expertise then drop you in the shit when you take advantage. That's what you've been doing with the gambling.'

'I don't know what you're talking about.'

I slammed my fist on the table – bad idea, I should have left the hard-man stuff to Davie, who was looking at me in amusement from behind Billy.

'All right, let's take this from the start. Do you know who put the heart on the centre circle at Tynecastle?'

'No.'

'Do you know anything about Peter Stewart's activities?'

'Of course not. I've never had anything to do with the Recreation Directorate.'

'Because it only deals with Edinburgh citizens and you don't give a fuck about them.'

'Something like that.'

'Do you know Derick Smail?'

'The Hibs manager? I think I met him once at an Independence Day drinks party.'

October 11th had been established as the sole annual holiday. The first Council meeting had taken place on that date in 2003.

'Do you know any of the other EPL managers?'

'I don't . . . hang on, the Hearts manager was at the same function. What's his name? Ferguson?'

'Ferries, Alec Ferries. When was this?'

'Last year. They're all jumped-up citizens scheming to make their fortune. It doesn't surprise me at all that they're running a betting scam.'

'You still claim you know nothing about it.'

He looked me in the eye. 'I don't claim, Quint. It's the truth. No matter how much your pet psycho makes me scream, the answer won't be any different.'

Davie laid a paw on Billy's shoulder, but he still didn't show fear. The little bastard had always been like that, even when he was eight. He really did seem to be telling the truth.

'All right, answer this. Why did Fergus Calder get the EPL managers out of here before we finished questioning them?'

Billy groaned. 'Come on, you know the answer to that. The season starts next week – as long as the rain lets up a bit. If games are postponed because the managers are in the castle, there could be serious civil unrest.'

'And who wants that with the referendum ahead?'

He gave me a condescending look. 'Clever lad, Quint.'

Davie's fingers squeezed Billy's shoulder.

'Get off me!' Billy shouted. 'I'll have you sent down the mines.'

That only made Davie tighten his grip.

This time Billy suffered in silence and I shook my head at Thunder Boots. He let go, unimpressed.

'There's a former church on the Pleasance,' I said.

'So?'

'It's a Leith Lancers' warehouse, stocked directly from the Supply Directorate.'

'I'll tell Fergus.'

'You think he doesn't know already?'

He raised one shoulder. 'Why should he?'

Why indeed?

'Five pounds of cocaine was in a consignment from the main depot. It ended up there. Well, it ended up in my hands, actually.'

'Bravo, Quint,' he said with a twisted smile. 'Another victory for demoted citizens.'

I brought my fist down again, this time not so hard.

'So you know nothing about illicit drug trafficking.'

'I'm pure as the driven . . . snow.' He giggled manically.

'Shut your face!' Davie yelled.

Billy raised a finger to his ear. 'Is that it, then?'

'Got an important deal to close?' I asked.

'Something like that.'

I grinned. 'Well, no, it isn't it. Stay here and stew for a while. You've taken his mobile, Davie?'

'Oh, yes.'

We left the SPADE in the interrogation room.

'The twisted little fucker's lying,' Davie said.

'I don't think he is, but he can stay there while we follow up loose ends.'

'Such as?'

I lowered my voice. 'The tails you put on Smail and Colquhoun.'

He nodded. 'I'll go and find a quiet place to make the calls.'

'Right. I'll see you in the canteen.'

'Don't clean it out.'

'That's your job.'

On the way to the refuelling station I took a detour to the command centre.

'Any luck?' said the Guardian Doris from her chair on a dais in the centre of the room.

I told her about Billy's denials.

'I've had both the senior and the finance guardians on my back. They're insistent he be released.'

'Let's keep him here for a while. He knows things they don't want him to tell us.'

'Like what, if he doesn't know about the EPL gambling?'

I looked at the bank of less-than-up-to-date monitors and terminals on the wall. 'Like I don't have the faintest idea. But you can be sure he's involved in things you and the rest of the Council – apart from Calder and MacLean – aren't aware of.'

'Proof, please.'

'I'm working on it. Have you managed to identify the headless citizen?'

'Not yet.'

'How about the heartless man in the Saly?'

'No.'

'Any sign of Hume 481's parents?'

'No.'

'Anything positive to report?'

'I could ask you the same thing, Quint.'

'I'm doing my best. By the way, who's the new recreation guardian?'

She gave me a sharp look. 'There nothing "by the way" in your world.'

I refrained from comment.

'Alice Scobie, the former deputy guardian.'

'Don't know her.'

'She's very good.'

I smiled. 'Of course.'

'No, really. She's been All-Edinburgh curling champion for the last four years.' The guardian puffed out her chest. 'Meaning she's better than all the men as well as the women.'

'Good for her. Does she know anything about football?'

She got up and walked away. I caught her up.

'You really have no respect, have you, citizen?' Doris said, her cheeks red.

'What do you mean?' I said disingenuously.

She wasn't buying it. 'Alice is completely honourable and fully committed to Enlightenment principles. As deputy guardian, she would have plenty of contact with the managers, but that doesn't mean she's guilty of wrongdoing.'

I began to wonder if the guardian held a flame for the newest addition to her rank. I'd just remembered that Doris was homo.

'Honestly, you're a disgrace, Quint,' she said, turning on me.

I shrugged. 'I do my job. By the . . . out of interest, when's Peter Stewart's funeral?'

'Tomorrow at eleven a.m. Are you planning on being there?'

'I didn't know him,' I said.

Which didn't mean I wouldn't be paying my respects before the ceremony.

Davie was already in the canteen, a turkey drumstick in one hand. I turned up my nose at that – the city farms' fowl are fed fishmeal and reek like kippers before and after death. I took a hunk of bread, a lump of cheese – at least the cows eat grass – and a couple of apples.

'Stomach upset?' Davie said.

'No, just a normal appetite.'

'I do the heavy lifting, remember?'

I smiled. 'Yes, guardsman, you do. In fact, you'll be doing some of that shortly. What about the tails?'

'Smail's been at Easter Road all day. He was driven to a house in the Grange an hour ago and hasn't emerged. No visitors at the latter location and no one who stuck out at the former.'

'There are plenty of entrances to the stadium.'

'I've only got so many people I can trust.'

'I know. And Fat Eric?'

Davie extracted a bone from his mouth, making me close my eyes.

'Said individual's in the Citizen's Rest on Corstorphine Road. He's been there since eleven in the morning.'

'What about his work?'

'He called in sick.'

I thought about that. 'He'll probably be sick soon if he's been boozing all this time.'

'I think Citizen Colquhoun has a high tolerance.'

'Yes, but how will he be paying for more than the daily limit?' Which is three pints and three whiskies. Then you've blown half your weekly allowance.

Davie laughed. 'You know how it works. Barter. Stolen vouchers. There are plenty of ways to get round the regs.'

'Get a man inside. We need to know who he's talking to.'
He made a call. 'All done.'

When we'd finished eating, I stood up. 'Are you coming?'

'Where to?'

'Magical mystery tour.'

'What?'

The Beatles weren't banned any more, but that didn't mean people knew who they were.

Davie pulled up in front of Warriston Crematorium.

'Let me handle this. Scowl when appropriate.'

Douglas Haigh appeared at the refurbished entrance to the building. Even the hole in the asphalt had been filled in. Nothing was too good for a guardian's exit. The story in the *Edinburgh Guardian* and on Radio Free City was that Peter Stewart had died of a heart condition. Which was kind of true, in that his heart had stopped beating. Any mention of suicide would have been catastrophic for the Council, whose members were expected to set perfect examples to the citizen body.

'Is there something wrong, Citizen Dalrymple?' asked the parchment-faced old ghoul.

'That's why we're here.' I went up close to him. 'This visit is unofficial, you understand? If you mention it to anyone, I'll let drop what you get up to with the corpses.'

Haigh froze. That was proof of the suspicion I'd had for years that he was a necrophile. I managed not to knock him down.

'How can I help?' he said with a smile that was supposed to be ingratiating but was simply vile.

'Is the recreation guardian's body here?' I asked.

'Indeed. He's resting in state.'

'Any Guard personnel?'

Haigh looked at Davie with a mixture of interest and fear.

'Only your . . . friend. The honour guard will arrive at 6 a.m.'

I looked around the building. There was only a low light on in the main chamber. I stopped Haigh turning on any more.

'Lock the door,' I ordered, then moved towards the light.

The late recreation guardian's coffin was on a stand in the middle of the room. The box was substantially higher quality than those for ordinary citizens, though unlike theirs it wouldn't be consigned to the flames. Recycling of high-value materials was one of the original Council's by-words. I wondered if my mother had been in the same casket. At least I could be sure of one thing. There was no way Haigh would have dared to open it when she was inside. I'd put the fear of an excruciating death up him before she died back in 2021.

'Right,' I said to him. 'We've done this before. Screwdrivers.'

Douglas Haigh feigned horror. 'But this . . . this is a guardian.'

I had switched on the torch I'd taken from the 4×4 and was examining the screw-heads. They were new and didn't bear many marks.

'This is a lump of flesh,' I said over my shoulder. 'Would you like to join it? I'm sure there's room.'

He looked tempted for a couple of seconds, then went off to get the tools.

'Er, what are we doing?' Davie said, looking around dubiously.

'What does it look like? We're going to open this up and see if Peter Stewart's taking anything with him to the fire.'

'But . . .'

'But what?'

'It's . . . what's the word? Sacrilege.'

'Sacrilege is disrespect of holy things. The Council is an atheist body.'

'Come on, Quint. We're disrespecting a guardian's body.'

'Which will tomorrow be turned into smoke and ashes. Besides, we're doing our job.'

Davie gave me a dubious look as Haigh came back with the screwdrivers.

'You were gone a long time,' I said. 'I hope you didn't make any calls. My colleague is particularly fond of tearing disobedient citizens' arms off.'

The old man was trembling, but I suspected it was more from excitement than terror.

'No calls, citizen.' He licked his dry lips. 'Shall we get on?'

'Before that, who accompanied the coffin?'

'A young auxiliary. Watt 5—' He scratched his liver-spotted scalp.

'529?' I said.

'That's it. Poor lad, he was very upset.'

I wasn't. Will, Peter Stewart's devoted auxiliary, might have had the opportunity to slip something into his clothing.

I took one screwdriver while Haigh kept the other. Davie wasn't having that and removed it from him.

'Stand back,' he said with a glare Genghis Khan would have been proud of. 'You dirty old man.'

We had the screws out in less than five minutes, taking care not to leave any marks. Haigh was hovering around like a blowfly and I was surprised Davie didn't swat him.

'Heavy lifting, please,' I said.

Davie got the coffin lid off easily and stood it against the wall. The smell that flooded out wasn't pleasant, at least, not to normal people. Haigh looked like he was in seventy-seventh heaven.

'Bloody hell,' Davie said, looking down at Peter Stewart's swollen face.

'Gloves,' I said.

Haigh provided long-sleeved, thick rubber versions. There was no embalming in 'the perfect city', but I had the distinct impression that he spent some of his spare time up to his elbows in entrails.

The former guardian had been dressed in a tracksuit. No doubt his lounge suits would be distributed among guardians or senior auxiliaries. Then again, maybe Will the grieving angel had provided the tracksuit in honour of his boss's prowess as an athlete. That thought touched me. Then I got back to feeling the distended limbs.

'What exactly are you looking for, citizen?'

I looked round at Haigh. 'That's classified,' I said, as if I had a clue. There was no sign of files or folders.

'We're going to have to turn him over,' I said to Davie.

'I can assist,' volunteered Haigh with far too much enthusiasm.

Davie floored him with a punch to the chest. I wouldn't have wept if he'd gone the way of Yellow Jacko.

We lifted the guardian up gently and then got him face down. His head and limbs flopped alarmingly and the smell got worse.

'I fucking hate this, Quint,' Davie said, stepping back.

'Don't worry, I'll finish the search.' I ran my hands down Stewart's shoulders and back, then over his swollen buttocks. I might have known. There was something between them.

'Jesus,' I said under my breath, breathing through my mouth only.

Then I slipped my hand under the tracksuit bottoms. The diskette I removed was covered in thick but still transparent plastic. I put it on the floor and searched the lower part of the body. There was nothing else.

'Come on, guardsman,' I said.

We managed to get the guardian on his back again and arranged his clothing as best we could before putting the lid on the coffin and screwing it down.

I heard a sound behind me. Haigh had got his breath back and stood up.

'What's this?' he said, leaning over and picking up the diskette.

This time I was the one who deposited him on his backside. Maybe he had some corpse make-up he could apply to his face for the service.

'That was utterly disgusting,' Davie said as he drove the 4×4 away from the crematorium. 'I'm not doing any more heavy lifting.'

'Sorry, Davie. But, as you saw, it was worth it.'

'That diskette might be full of mumbo-jumbo.'

'I doubt it.'

'To the castle?'

'I think not. Moray Place.'

He glanced at me as we headed west down Ferry Road. 'You're not going to go after the new recreation guardian at this time of night?'

'No. I want to see what's on this first.'

'So why not the castle?'

'Because Sophia's got a high-powered computer in her place.'

He laughed. 'Oh aye? Needing a kiss and a cuddle, are we?'

'Might be,' I replied. 'Keep your eyes on the road, please.'

A Guard vehicle went past on the other side, missing us by inches.

'I had it under control,' said Davie touchily.

'Of course you did.'

'There is one thing, though.'

'What's that?'

'We reek like undertakers. How do you think the medical guardian will like that?'

'What do you think she smells like all day in the infirmary?'

Davie grunted. 'She's got a kid. Do you think she goes home stinking like a charnel house?'

He had a point. I directed him to my flat. He could listen to music while I showered and changed clothes.

But I'd forgotten what was waiting for me there.

TWENTY-ONE

The books were in a couple of piles on my coffee table. I'd had them delivered after Muckle Tony Robertson's murder-disguised-as-suicide in his cell at the castle. It had struck me as odd at the time that a gang leader would be into reading, though that was fatuous considering the Council's life-long education programme. Then again, hard men tended to take science courses so they could learn how to make weapons and bombs. Edinburgh writing was the only compulsory literature subject.

Davie had put on Miles Davis's *Bitches Brew*, which gave me a bit of a headache. When I asked for something softer, he responded with some awful seventies pop. The Bay City Rockers, was it? How the hell were they in my collection? We ended up in silence.

'What was the boss of the Leith Lancers doing with the City Regulations?' I said, picking up the tattered black book. 'Trying to work as many ways to get round them as possible, I suppose.'

'There's a copy in every cell,' Davie said. 'As if they'll see the enlight.'

I laughed. 'That wasn't bad for you.'

'Piss off.'

I flicked through pages, looking for notes or messages. 'Do they get writing equipment?'

'No chance. You know how dangerous pens and pencils can be in skilled hands.'

That explained the unmarked pages. I checked all the books carefully. Nothing of interest, not even pages with the corners turned. Then I came to *Free City: The History of Edinburgh*. Brian Cowan, the education guardian, had written most of it and introduced it into the city's senior schools a couple of years back. There was widespread hysteria amongst citizens who'd lived through the drugs wars and subsequent years, and many parents made sure their kids heard the real story as opposed to the rose-red narrative the guardian had imagined.

'Hang on,' I said. 'What's this?'

Davie looked at the small holes in the paper under certain letters, starting on page three, continuing on page six and on every third page until page 126. 'How did he make the holes?' he asked.

'Assuming he did. The book's in good nick, so he probably was the first reader.'

'Only everything sharp is taken from them.'

I thought about that. 'Could he have grown his nails and bitten off the tops of the larger ones?'

'As far as I recall, prisoners have their finger- and toenails cut short every week – they can be dangerous weapons too.'

'Whatever. Let's assume Muckle Tony made the marks. There are about thirty on every page, times forty-two pages equals 1260 letters.'

'Yes, but do they make sense?'

Davie had me there. They didn't, certainly not as sequences that could be broken down into words.

'It's a code,' I said.

'Brilliant,' Davie said, leaning back gingerly in my couch. 'You work it out while I pass out.'

I wrote out all the marked letters and tried to assemble them into something coherent. At some point I remember falling back against my armchair, my head swimming with no known stroke.

'Wakey, wakey!' came Davie's unnecessarily loud voice. 'Coffee, croissants and . . . wait for it . . . a banana. Plus, it isn't raining.'

I looked down at the papers on the table and brushed them aside.

'There are cryptologists in the command centre,' Davie said, handing me my coffee.

'All right, we'll give it to them on the way to the funeral.'

'Aw, shit, the recreation guardian. I'd forgotten. Do I have to come?'

'No, I don't see why – unless someone else has a go with a grenade.'

'There'll be plenty of Guard personnel down there. I'll need to make sure we're not leaving the rest of the city undefended.'

'That may be too late,' I muttered. 'That bastard Lecky with his handsaw might have stayed in the city and joined up with the Dead Men. Think of it – outsider criminals hand in hand with our own.'

Davie crumpled up the paper his croissants had been in. 'Get your glad rags on.'

I had one suit, over twenty years old, but at least it was black. I found a clean white shirt but dispensed with a tie. They don't make one for demoted auxiliaries – though Billy Geddes has got a fine collection of silk ones from outside the city.

Davie dropped me at the esplanade and I got a Guard driver to take me down to the crematorium. As we went, I was thinking about Billy. Was it really possible he didn't know about the football gambling? If he wasn't behind it, who was?

The sides of the road to the crematorium were hung with black and white flags, the longstanding colours of the city that the Enlightenment had maintained. Guard personnel flanked the 4×4 for the last hundred yards. There was a queue of more luxurious vehicles disgorging people a lot more important than me, so I got out and walked to the entrance. The guardians were all in dark suits, male and female versions. Sophia looked very fetching, ice-blonde hair drawn back. I was glad to see that Maisie wasn't with her. Douglas Haigh was doing his 'welcome to my crypt' act at the open doors, oblivious to the disgust he inspired in people.

Then I saw Fergus Calder and Jack MacLean. That was bad enough, but the people talking to them made me swear under my breath.

'What was that, failure?'

I looked round to find my father, leaning on a stick and wrapped up in an ancient raincoat.

'That one of Juvenal's togas, old man?'

'Ha! The old satirist would have a field day here.'

He was right about that.

'Look at that woman,' he continued, his voice high. 'She should have her hair up at a funeral.'

I took in the tall woman with blonde hair down to the upper curve of her backside, which was enclosed in guardian-issue trousers. She must have been the dead man's replacement, Alice Scobie. She turned in our direction, her eyes resting on me for less than an instant. She had the build of a high-jumper, lithe and small-breasted. Then I saw Sophia giving me a chilly glare.

My father had hooked up with another liver-spotted specimen, so I went over to the senior guardian's little party. 'Well, what the hell?' I said.

Hel Hyslop, heavier than she'd been the last time I saw her, shook her head. 'I might have known you'd turn up, Quint.' She glanced at Calder. 'You don't still employ this buffoon, do you?'

'We find him useful,' MacLean said smoothly. 'As have you in the past.'

That wasn't the full story – Hel and Glasgow's leader had put their fingers in several sewage and corpse pies and I'd both saved their skins and nailed their repulsive activities. I was amazed that the finance guardian was supporting me, though he was playing his own game by showing that he knew exactly how dirty they had been – and perhaps still were.

Andrew Duart extended his hand. He'd put on weight too. Maybe he and Hel were not on a diet together. I wondered if they were still lovers.

'Good to see you, Quint.' He drew me closer. 'How are you getting on with the hearts at football grounds thing?'

'Thing?' I said, only just controlling my anger. 'People are being killed and mutilated. This is much more than a "thing".'

Duart took that in his stride. 'You know what I mean. Never mind. I'm sure we'll talk later.'

Not if I can help it, I said to myself, stepping back as the Lord of the Isles appeared in full Highland regalia, some of which I was sure he'd invented himself – such as the crown-like headgear.

I held back as the guests filled the chamber that contained Peter Stewart's coffin. Haigh gave me a smile as I joined him at the rear. I shivered and moved to the side. The Council lament was played by a piper and then Fergus Calder gave a eulogy that was surprisingly sensitive – there was no way he'd written it himself. He referred to the dead man's prowess on the athletics track and then his loyal service in the Recreation Directorate. I didn't know that Stewart had set up athletics clubs across the city personally, producing several athletes who, in other circumstances, might have represented their country. Trust the senior guardian to get a reference to Scotland in. The new recreation guardian stood by Calder, her head lowered. Blonde hair. Could she have put the heart on the centre circle at Tynecastle? No, we'd already put that down to the woman Davie had shot, despite her small chest.

Haigh had disappeared. I next saw him by the coffin, folding the Council flag that covered the coffin and handing it to Alice Scobie. Then he waited for the nod from Fergus Calder. Enlightenment Edinburgh had given up on words of committal, considering its atheist beliefs. I could have done with a bit more humanism, but I don't think like the people who run the city.

There was a surge to get out of the chamber after the coffin had disappeared. It was stuffy and there was a faint smell of decomposition, probably emanating from Haigh. I was among the first out and waited for my father. He was helped out by Guardian Doris, which was a surprise. I'm not sure if he knew who she was. I nodded thanks to her and took his arm.

'Are you being picked up?'

'Yes. There's a do for former guardians – though there are only two of us – and senior auxiliaries at some place on George Street.'

'Mind you don't get seduced by the charms of the tourist zone, old man.'

'Mind you don't get this stick up your arse, failure.'

I squeezed his bony arm and let him go to his former colleague. There were nursing staff in formal uniform in the vicinity.

Some loudmouth – male – was holding forth at the other side of the forecourt.

'. . . while Edinburgh has seen remarkable levels of economic growth.' It was Brian Cowan, the education guardian. 'This city has also improved the lot of its citizens in every possible way, as our departed colleague showed. What possible reason do we have for joining with less successful cities and districts to re-form Scotland? It's absurd.'

'It's certainly absurd the way he puts it,' Hel Hyslop said. 'I'm betting he's never left the perfect city.'

I shrugged. 'Of course, everything's going great in Glasgow. Apart from the heart thing.'

I used Duart's phrase and wasn't surprised to see it evince no surprise from Hyslop. She was a good cop, but she was hard – more like an Edinburgh guardswoman than the native of a free city. Then again, Glasgow citizens were permitted to carry small arms and the murder rate was a lot higher than ours. Too much drink, Council members said, forgetting that they'd been using rot-bladder whisky to keep the people of Edinburgh quiet for decades.

I watched as Jack MacLean went over to Cowan and speak in his ear. The education guardian's face reddened and he moved quickly away. Then the new recreation guardian went up to Guardian Doris. They laughed like a pair of schoolgirls before remembering where they were. I was on the point of going to eavesdrop when I remembered the diskette that we'd found in Peter Stewart's coffin.

It was in my pocket and needed to be run through a high-powered computer.

I went over to Sophia and asked her for a lift. 'I've a reception to attend, Quint,' she said.

'So attend. I just need your computer.'

She raised an eyebrow. 'That makes a change. And by the way, eyes off the recreation guardian. She only likes other women.'

As did Guardian Doris, I thought, as we got into Sophia's 4x4.

I'm no computer expert and I fully expected to be stumped within seconds of inserting the diskette. To my amazement, I wasn't asked for a password. A page of text in the form of an index came up. Why would there be no encryption? Then it came to me. This was Peter Stewart's personal record. He didn't want it to be kept secret. He wanted people to know. There were lists of staff in each club who were in on the betting scheme, names of citizens who acted as bookies and the amounts earned from each match. The odds were set by a panel of no doubt wholly unbiased former players, all over fifty, and three of the five auxiliaries. But there was no reference to the person who sanctioned the betting. Presumably it was Peter Stewart himself, whence his suicide. But the evidence was that he was against gambling, so why would he have allowed it?

I wondered if Stewart's devoted assistant, Watt 529, had opened the files on the diskette before putting it in the guardian's coffin. It was only a few minutes' walk to the recreation guardian's residence. The front door was open and furniture was being moved out. I asked the auxiliary who was overseeing if Watt 529 was inside.

He smiled sourly. 'You won't see him round here any more. The new guardian's had him reassigned. I don't know where.'

There usually was a change of staff when new guardians came in. As I walked up to Queen Street, my mobile rang.

'We've got a match,' said Sophia. 'The head that went through the window at the Walter Scott Rooms came from the male body you found across the city line.'

'That must have made Tall and Short very happy. But we still don't know who he is.'

'Hardly my department, Quint. I've let the public order guardian know. I must get back to charming the city's guests.' She sounded underwhelmed by the prospect.

'Fergus Calder's command, eh? Watch out for the Glaswegians. They're poisonous.'

'You should hear what they're saying about you.' The call was terminated.

Like I gave a flying fruit bat what Duart and Hyslop spouted.

I stopped a Guard vehicle and got the driver to take me to the esplanade. I found Davie in the command centre.

'You hear they matched the head and body?' he said.

'I did. Any ID?'

'Not yet. I've got people going through citizens' photos but you know how long that could take. Besides, the poor sod might have been an outsider.'

I shook my head. 'He wouldn't have been decapitated like the guardsman.'

'Unless they thought he was a rat.'

I smiled. 'Could be. You're finally losing that touching trust in human nature that was such a feature of your character.'

He gave me a sour look.

'Can you find out where Watt 529's been posted?'

'The weed from the recreation directorate? He didn't last long under Alice S.' He called over a male auxiliary, who came back under a minute later.

'He must have really pissed her off. He's been seconded to the Agriculture Directorate, in command of a farm between the city line and the border.'

'Get him on the phone, will you?' I had no desire to go out to the badlands.

After a delay, Watt 529 was reached. He sounded suicidal.

'Listen,' I said, 'I'll do what I can for you, but I need to know if you looked at the contents of the diskette that you stashed in Peter Stewart's coffin – and don't bother claiming you didn't.'

'I . . . no, I didn't open it. I was . . . frightened what might be on it.'

'All right. I'll get you brought back. Out.'

I turned to Davie. 'He won't last a week out there. Find him a job in the city.'

'Yes, sir, yes, sir, three bags of tourist-zone garbage full, sir.'

Five minutes later, Watt 529 had a job in the Public Order Directorate archive and an order went out to recall him. I felt sorry for the auxiliary. He hadn't recovered from the guardian's suicide and hadn't been able to attend the funeral. Alice Scobie clearly wanted him as far away as possible. Maybe she thought he'd read the contents of the diskette. Or did she even know about it?

An elderly stooped guardsman shuffled into the command centre and headed towards us. 'Bell 03,' he said, his wrinkled face cracking apart with a smile. 'I'm a great admirer of your work.'

'Call me Quint,' I said, looking at his badge. 'Raeburn 37.' The low number showed he was amongst the longest serving of auxiliaries.

'They call him Brains,' Davie supplied.

The old man laughed. 'Better than Reginald.'

I could only nod in agreement.

'I have something for you,' he said, holding out a sheaf of papers.

I looked at the top one. It was covered in letters and numbers.

'Ah, sorry,' said Brains, 'you'd better look at the last two pages. It wasn't a particularly clever code. I applied my normal methods and quickly realized that he was using an increasing numerical base.'

'The marked letter corresponding to one that was one, two, three letters or whatever further down the alphabet,' said Davie. I was impressed, even though I'd understood the old guardsman myself.

'Yes,' Raeburn 37 said drily. 'The "or whatever" being the difficult part.'

'Because he could be using a base that would take a long time to work out, for instance his ID number increasing in some complex way,' I said.

'Or decreasing,' said Brains impatiently. 'I checked his personal number, of course, and other obvious sequences like the birthdays of his family and so on. Then it struck me that Muckle Tony was the boss of the Leith Lancers. So I assigned one to "l", two to "e" and so on, the missing letters in alphabetical order. Halfway through he thought he got clever and reversed the order. That took me under ten seconds to spot.'

I was looking at the text on the last two pages. It covered the same material as Peter Stewart's diskette, apart from a small piece of gold: 'Dead Men have last shipments, approved by H.'

My face obviously gave me away.

'H means something to you, Bell 03?' said the code-breaker.

'In terms of Glasgow, yes.' I turned to Davie. 'Let's go and shake up Scotland's movers and shakers.'

'Can I come too?' Raeburn 37 asked forlornly.

'You wouldn't like it, Brains,' I said over my shoulder. 'They make Muckle Tony look like a citizen care worker.'

Davie caught up with me. The bull in a china shop was one of his favourite acts.

TWENTY-TWO

We were halfway to the conference hall in the Market District, where the reception for the outsiders was taking place, when Davie answered his phone and immediately pulled into the side of the road. He listened intently, then told the caller to wait for our imminent arrival.

'What is it?' I said.

He had turned on the lights and siren and was overtaking buses on Princes Street. 'A head. At the Enlightenment Monument. Male and fair-haired.'

I looked ahead to the tower that had been old Edinburgh's tribute to Walter Scott, but renamed after independence. The top had fallen off years ago and the Council had patched it up only partially. The smoke-darkened tower now looked like a rocket whose warhead had been stolen. As we ground to a halt, I saw a crowd of tourists being gently pushed back by a line of Guard personnel. The great Gothic monument had four legs and in the middle of them sat Sir Walter, though now he was covered by a tarpaulin.

Davie led me though the Guard cordon and over to a middle-aged, bald commander I'd met before.

'What have you got, Lachie?' I said.

Moray 279 was notorious for his dyspeptic temperament and he certainly looked like he'd eaten something that disagreed with him.

'The big lump told you, didn't he, Quint?' he replied. 'I'll leave you to it.'

'Hang on. Who was the first person to spot the head?'

'Japanese tourist,' Lachie said, nodding at a grinning specimen who had obviously just had the biggest thrill of his life. 'The Tourism Directorate is looking after him.'

'Perhaps they could look after him somewhere else,' I said acidly.

'Right. I'll get on with crowd control.'

There was a rumble of thunder and the rain began to come down.

'Excellent,' said Moray 279. Although there were the usual maroon shelters around the monument, the crowd was beyond them. People started to drift away.

Davie and I went under the tarpaulin. He shone his torch and, sure enough, there was Sir Walter with another head to keep him company.

'How did someone get that up there in daylight?' Davie said. 'Fuck. It's the young guardsman from Bonaly Tower. I remember the photo in his file.'

I looked up at the blank eyes and open mouth. The skin on his neck had been fixed to the statue's head with black tape.

'So much for discretion,' I said. 'The head people can't be the same as the ones taking hearts.'

'That's rather a random assumption,' said Sophia from behind me. She was still wearing formal dress.

'Any excuse to get out of the reception?' I said. 'I suppose you're right. They might be hard baddie, soft baddie.'

She gave me a puzzled look as she clambered up the statue. I put my hands on her buttocks so she didn't fall. She didn't seem to notice. Sophia in full professional mode is still the Ice Queen.

A pair of paramedics with brighter torches joined us.

'The senior guardian has ordered that the head be taken down as soon as possible,' Sophia said. 'The tourists . . .'

She directed the taking of photos, then unwrapped the tape and handed the head down, fingers in its nostrils. It was put in a plastic box and the lid closed.

'I'll take this back to the infirmary, Quint.'

'How was Fergus when he heard?'

'He went white. I don't think he knew anything about it, if that's what you're asking.'

'It was,' I confirmed. 'I'll see you at the Council meeting.'

'Yes, that should be interesting.'

'Mm.'

After she'd gone, Davie let the crime-scene technicians in. After a few minutes, we decided to take off the tarpaulin. For all most tourists would know, they were doing maintenance. The chances of them finding any suggestive traces in the damp were minimal, I thought, but the job had to be done.

'Where are you off to?' Davie called.

'Back in a minute.'

I went through the gate and crossed Princes Street, getting splashed all the way up to the left arm by a tourist bus. That meant I entered the kilt shop swearing. The tourists who spoke English gave me sharp looks. I smiled but that didn't seem to help, so I took the citizen in charge by the arm and led her to the office at the back.

'Right, Karen,' I said, looking at the badge on her blouse then flashing my authorization. 'What did you see across the road?'

'Someone . . . someone told me it was a man's head.' She was in her thirties. Her hair was pulled tightly back, which brought out fine features.

'Some idiot's idea of a joke,' I said. 'It wasn't real. But you'll understand we have to catch the fool. Can't have the tourists being scared.'

'No, indeed we can't, citizen,' she said, her tone ironic.

I smiled. 'Did you see anything?'

'Aye. The laugh's on the Council, if you ask me. A Housing Directorate van pulled up about an hour ago and a couple of guys started doing something to the statue – cleaning it, I assumed. Then I saw the head. I looked away to take a customer's cash and the screaming started. The van and the men had disappeared.'

'Any of the rest of your people see anything?'

She shook her head. 'They were all busy. Besides, there was heavy drizzle at the time. It let off afterwards.'

'And now it's coming down again like an overflowing bath.'

'If you say so, citizen,' Karen said with a pretty smile.

I left her to her work. It's amazing how many people from across the world want to buy kilts. Apparently Lamont's one of the most popular, the green, blue and white being less retina-burning than the multiple red ones. Hardly any of them have Scottish roots, of course. That doesn't bother me. I've never worn the kilt in my life, partly because the Council banned clan affiliations. The Lord of the Isles would see me as an apostate. Then again, I saw him as something much worse.

Tall and Short were standing by the head and body in the morgue, looking pleased with themselves. There was no question, the parts constituted the young guardsman Ferguson 569.

'Looks like a similar blade was used,' I said, examining the ragged skin that had been covered by tape.

'Exactly the same,' the pathologist confirmed.

I thought of the hacksaw-wielding John Lecky and the builders who had attacked us. They would also have been able to get their hands on a Housing Directorate van – perhaps they had one stashed in case they were uncovered – and they might well have given Sir Walter his second head. They were deeply involved in what was going on in the city, but I was certain they were taking rather than giving orders.

'Anything else the head can tell us?' I asked.

Tall shook his head. 'I think it was kept in a sealed plastic bag.'

'Yes, there's no trace evidence apart from grass and earth, obviously from where he was found.'

'No wounds?'

They glanced at each other and shook their heads.

'So your fellow auxiliary was alive when he was decapitated.'

That got to them for a couple of seconds. Then they turned their fish eyes back to the naked corpse again, the doctors of death.

Ten minutes later I was in Guardian Doris's office. I gave her copies of Peter Stewart's files and of Muckle Tony's records as decoded by Brains.

'These are large sums of money,' she said, 'whether in voucher form or in outsider denominations. Where's it all going?'

'You tell me.'

She gave me a nonplussed look. 'I haven't the faintest idea, Quint. Do you?'

'How about this? The referendum's not many months away. The pro- and anti-campaigns will need funding.'

The guardian screwed up her eyes. 'Really? It's still early days. I've always assumed the Council will allocate funds equally.'

I left her to that naive belief.

There was a knock on the door and Davie appeared.

'Guardian, Quint, we're checking Housing Directorate vans, but all are accounted for so far. We've also picked up a lot of the people on the former recreation guardian's files. What shall we do with them?'

I let Doris take command.

She did so, but with little sign of enthusiasm. 'I need to take this information to the Council. How many are they?'

'Thirty-two,' said Davie, 'all citizens, twenty-seven male.'

'Right, secure and gag them for the time being.'

Davie made his exit.

Shortly afterwards, so did we. The Council meeting beckoned.

Fergus Calder had decided to show off the workings of Edinburgh's government to the outsiders. I was ushered to the side of the hall as the Lord of the Isles, the governors of Orkney and Shetland and the pair from Glasgow was given places of honour in the row above the Council members.

The senior guardian opened the session by asking the tourism guardian for an update on the case of Walter Scott's dicephaly. She said that the Japanese tourist had been unable to give descriptions of the men in Housing Directorate overalls because they'd been wearing goggles and helmets. And because all Westerners doubtless look alike . . . He had been upgraded to the city's top hotel, the Waverley, and given free chips for several casinos. Some members of the Prostitution Services Department would also be drafted in to make sure he kept his mouth shut. Other tourists present had been persuaded that the whole thing was a reconstruction of a notorious – and non-existent – student prank carried out by Sir Arthur Conan Doyle. The affair, the guardian completed, was in hand.

I watched Hel Hyslop whispering to Andrew Duart. I was pretty certain she knew something about what was going on. I considered asking her in front of the Council, but decided against it – no evidence. We needed to find a member of the Glasgow Dead Men. The best way to do that was to track down John Lecky's mob. I was sure they were in contact with outsiders.

Some dry as the Sahara sermons from various guardians followed, in which everything in their purview was seen in the rosiest of colours. Then it was Guardian Doris's turn. Fergus Calder gave her a stern look and demanded what was going on in her directorate. I reckoned he was playing to the gallery behind him, but turning the spotlight on a guardian in front of outsiders, even leading ones, was a first as far as I was aware.

'As regards the head on the statue of—'

'How is it that no Guard personnel were in the vicinity?' the senior guardian demanded. 'In the middle of the tourist zone.'

'They patrol, they don't stay in one place. Besides,' she said, turning to the tourism guardian, 'why didn't the ticket staff at the monument see anything?'

'I've asked that question,' her colleague replied. 'They thought it was routine maintenance and didn't see the head being . . . stuck on.'

Hel Hyslop caught sight of me in the shadows and shook *her* head. It was obvious what she meant – in Glasgow this kind of shambles would never be allowed. She was probably right.

'Proceed,' Calder said to Doris.

She told them about the head being matched to the dead guardsman.

'Have you any idea why such an outrageous thing should happen?' asked Brian Cowan, the education guardian. 'What was that guardsman doing over the city line?'

The senior guardian raised a hand. 'We've already discussed that,' he said firmly. That was news to me, but maybe they'd started having secret meetings. 'Public order guardian, what more do you have?'

It was obvious she didn't want to share Peter Stewart's files or Muckle Tony's supplementary evidence with outsiders in the chamber.

'I—'

'The guardian and I have been liaising about the city's football grounds and have agreed that my directorate will take over some of the patrolling,' said Alice Scobie, clearly out to make an impression. And save her friend's bacon?

Fergus Calder and Jack MacLean exchanged glances, their expressions unreadable.

'Very well,' Calder said. 'The medical guardian will now report on the measles outbreak in Craigmillar.'

No wonder Sophia had been looking ground down, even though she'd still found time to arrive at every head or heart scene. She quickly confirmed that all cases had been isolated and were being treated.

'How is it that there was an outbreak?' asked MacLean. 'Citizens are vaccinated, aren't they?'

Sophia nodded. 'Craigmillar is a . . . problematic area, as you know. There's contact with outsiders given the proximity to the city line, plus some citizens deliberately avoid vaccination.'

'Why is that?' asked the tourism guardian.

'Because they don't like being told what to do,' I said, stepping into the light. I was there, so I might as well give them my one-Edinburgh-pound voucher's worth.

'Citizen Dalrymple,' the senior guardian said. 'I might have known you wouldn't wait for an invitation to speak.'

I shrugged. 'You brought me here, so you must want me to report.'

Fergus Calder gave me the eye, then relented. 'Very well. Have you actually discovered anything relevant to these cases?'

Irony always brings out the worse in me. 'As a matter of fact, I have.' I glanced at Doris and decided to go for it. 'It's clearly no coincidence that the human hearts left in football stadiums in Edinburgh and around what used to be Scotland' – I ran my eye along the outsiders – 'have some connection with that sport.' I took out a copy of Peter Stewart's diskette – the original was hidden where no one would find it – and held it up.

Guardian Doris stood up. 'Quint, I don't think—'

'Let him speak, woman,' said the Lord of the Isles, his high voice piping out.

There was a shocked silence. Not even other guardians addressed each other so coarsely – at least not in meetings.

'No doubt the senior guardian will ensure everyone gets copies. The point is that there's a well-organized illicit gambling scheme in operation in the Edinburgh Premier League.' I looked at Andrew Duart. 'And, I suspect, in outsider locations.'

The First Minister of Glasgow laughed. 'Gambling is legal in my city.'

'Doesn't mean there can't be illegal gambling as well,' I pointed out.

The governors of Orkney and Shetland said there was no gambling where they came from except on catches of fish, and that was regulated.

As for the Lord of the Isles, he let out a whinnying laugh. 'Even if people do gamble, who cares?'

I wasn't buying that.

'How many football teams are there in the territory you control?' I demanded.

'I'm not sure,' he came back. 'About forty. Equally divided between the islands and the mainland. Colonsay won the first division last year, though I had to give the manager a stern warning about poaching players from other clubs.'

'Forty clubs?' I said. 'Even with a small fan base, that could produce a fair amount of profit.'

The Lord twitched his head. 'I think you're talking tosh.'

That was the first time I'd heard the word since I was a kid.

'Does this material name names?' Jack MacLean asked.

'Plenty, but only Edinburgh citizens. Reading between the lines, I'd hazard they're being controlled by people of higher rank.'

The recreation guardian got to her feet, her cheeks reddening. 'Are you implying that these people are in my directorate, citizen?'

'Call me Quint.'

'Because I can assure you that no one in the Recreation Directorate is involved. My predecessor was solely responsible for this gross breach in regulations.'

I didn't think much of her rubbishing the man who had earlier been cremated. 'We'll see if the citizens who have been detained will confirm that.' I smiled coldly. 'It's amazing what a trained interrogator can get people to admit.'

Alice Scobie opened her mouth but didn't say anything more.

'By the way,' I said, 'why isn't there anyone from Inverness at this merry gathering? They've had heart problems too.'

The Lord of the Isles looked at Andrew Duart. 'They're having problems,' he said. 'Of a social unrest nature.'

That was interesting. Had the fans found out the odds were rigged and started to riot? That would explain how worried the high heid yins were about the EPL and other leagues.

'How about Aberdeen? It's flourishing, I hear.'

'Oddly, football's been replaced by lacrosse,' said Jack MacLean. 'The Chief of Chiefs used to play when he was in Canada. No hearts have been reported.'

Whence the absence of Aberdonians.

'I think we'll let you get back to your valuable work, citizen,' Fergus Calder said.

I was still hyped up. 'Could I ask Glasgow Police Commander Hel Hyslop a question, please?'

'I hardly think—' began Calder.

'Fire away,' Hel said, reminding me that she was well versed in the use of guns.

'I gather the Dead Men have the last shipments. What exactly is it that you've approved?' I looked at the senior guardian. 'The murdered leader of the Leith Lancers kept a record.'

Hel Hyslop was a hard woman and she could handle herself. 'You think I was in contact with an Edinburgh gang boss?'

'Via the Dead Men, it would appear. Who exactly are they?'

Andrew Duart's eyes were on me, but he nudged his colleague in what he thought was a subtle fashion. I'd been expecting something of the sort.

'That is confidential Glasgow information and how many people have the initial "H"?' Hel said. 'All right, I can tell you that the Dead Men are criminals we forced out of the city – those we didn't kill. I've never had any personal contact with them.' She gave a twisted smile. 'Apart from one I stabbed in the heart.'

I saw Duart's eyes spring wide open. It looked like his sidekick had let her iron grip loosen for a moment. I couldn't waste the opportunity.

'Did you remove the said heart with your knife?'

I turned on my heel before I was thrown out.

TWENTY-THREE

Davie was waiting for me, as I'd asked.

'You look like a kid who's chucked a live rat at a tourist.'

I told him what had gone down.

'We'd better get a move on,' was his response. 'Your Council authorization might soon be withdrawn.'

'Maybe, maybe not. Amazing though it seems, the senior and finance guardians are in the dark about the gambling racket. And because it's linked to the hearts – and probably the heads – they still want me to solve the case. I hope.'

'Me too,' said Davie, as he accelerated up the Canongate. 'What's next?'

'Obviously we have to talk to the citizens named by Peter Stewart and Muckle Tony. The problem is there are . . . how many?'

'The number's up to forty-one, thirty-five males.'

I sat back in my seat. 'We need to narrow things down. Get your people to check if any of the forty-one have family, personal or work connections with that fucker John Lecky.'

Davie passed the order on. By the time we got to the command centre, a guardswoman had already turned up a link.

'This citizen, Gary Weaver,' she said, holding out a cardboard file. 'He lives two doors down from John Lecky, in West Pilton. The place is in his wife's name.'

'Good work,' I said. 'Keep at it.' We'd sent a squad down to Lecky's registered abode, but the place was deserted and hadn't been lived in for months.

Davie arranged for Weaver to be taken to the interview room. As we were heading there, Guardian Doris turned up, her brow furrowed.

'Thanks a lot,' she said, waving Davie on. 'Could you have made this directorate look any more useless to my colleagues, never mind the outsiders?'

'What do you mean? They're running scared now.'

'Who?'

'The people behind the gambling and, very likely, the heads and hearts.'

'You wouldn't care to share their names with me?'

I raised my shoulders. 'I don't know them. Yet. By the way, are you close to Alice Scobie?'

The guardian looked away. 'We've known each other for some time, yes.'

'I recommend distancing yourself from her at speed,' I said. 'I haven't got the proof yet, but I think she's into this up to her oxters.'

'That's ridiculous.'

'Is it? Maybe we should look into her whereabouts when the heart was left at Tyneside.'

Doris laughed. 'You're letting your imagination run away with you.'

'It's imagination that solves difficult cases. Now, if you'll excuse me, I'm about to interrogate one of the gambling guys. Feel free to listen in.'

She got the hint – 'don't think you're asking any questions your-self'. It wasn't that I didn't trust her, it was that Davie and I had developed techniques that almost always bore fruit. We had a quick chat about how to proceed.

Davie led me into the confined room. The citizen chained to the chair on the other side of the table was middle-aged, overweight and bald. He also looked like he didn't give a shit. That was about to change.

I looked at the Guard file and then smiled as beatifically as I could. 'Gary Dale Weaver, address 22b West Pilton Park, married to Jean, children Duncan, fourteen, and Jessie, twelve. Occupation, Supply Directorate clerk, level 3c.'

'Aye,' said the citizen. 'Whit d'ye want?'

As arranged, Davie rammed his service knife into the table an inch from Weaver's hands, making the prisoner jerk backwards.

'Cooperation,' I said. 'And answers.'

'Or your bollocks,' Davie added.

'Ye cannae . . .'

Davie pulled his knife out and held it against the citizen's crotch. 'We fucking can,' he growled. 'Now talk. And no hesitating.'

'Question one – where's John Lecky?'

'Ah . . . Ah havnae seen him for mo—'

Davie pushed the point through Weaver's trousers. As they were citizen issue, that didn't take much effort. The skill was in not drawing blood. At least, only a little.

'Where's John Lecky?'

'I heard he wus in Liberton, near the old school.' Which had been a victim of the drugs wars. It was also only a few hundred yards from the city line.

'Address?'

'Em . . . 357 Gilmerton Road.'

'Question three – who's your boss in the EPL gambling scheme?'

'The whit?' Then the prisoner screamed. This time Davie's knife had cut skin.

'You heard me,' I said.

'Aaah . . . Luke . . . Luke Lawrie. He works in the Supply too. Ah dinnae ken who he answers tae, honest, Ah dinnae.'

We went out of the door, to be met by Guardian Doris, file in hand.

'Luke Lawrie's not in custody.'

'Typical,' I said. 'Still, at least we got a fix on Lecky.'

'If you can trust it.'

'I think we can,' I said, looking at Davie as he finished cleaning his knife.

'That was rather extreme, commander,' the guardian said. 'But, given the circumstances, permissible.'

'And effective,' Davie added.

'So, what about Lecky?' Doris asked me.

'We get after him now.'

'Even though it's dark and there are very few lights in the far south?'

'We can't risk him getting away. Besides, he and his men are probably out on business. If we neutralize anyone left behind, we'll have the advantage of surprise.'

'I leave it to you,' the guardian said. 'I've plenty of other things to be getting on with.'

I asked her the question that had been nagging at me for days. 'Why haven't you appointed a deputy guardian to help out?'

She flushed and then raised her shoulders. 'Haven't got round to it. Delegation's never been my strong point.'

We watched her walk down the corridor.

'She just delegated Lecky to us,' Davie observed.

'True, but maybe she wants to wash her hands of a potential disaster. Those head-bangers won't give in without a fight.'

'Bring it on,' Davie said ebulliently.

'Make sure you take a backup Hyper-Stun, will you?'

That got me a good guardsman's glower.

An hour later we were in position about a hundred yards from the house in the south of the city. There were three guardsmen in the back of our 4×4, and another to the rear of the building in the backstreets of Moredun. The rain was coming down in sheets and the place was dark, apart from the dim glow from the curtained windows of the few residents who'd remained. Most of them would be involved in illicit activities. No one else would volunteer to live in Sioux Central, as it was known.

'You know what the danger is?' Davie said in a low voice.

'Apart from getting our heads sawn off?'

'Well, yes. That they've left a sentry with a phone to warn them if anything goes bosoms to the sky.'

'And how do you intend to overcome that problem, commander?' I asked sternly, aware of sniggering in the back.

'Cut his or her head off first, citizen,' suggested one of the heavies.

I looked round. He was young, bull-chested and pimply.

'And what if the sentry has to make a regular call to the others, guardsman?' I asked.

'We get the time and number out of him and then cut his head off,' was the supplementary suggestion.

'Did you train this lot personally?' I said to Davie.

'I did not, but if they don't get a grip they'll be howking tatties first thing tomorrow morning.'

No one liked potato-picking, especially given the state of the fields in the Big Wet. Besides, that would involve demotion to citizen rank.

'I'll do this myself,' Davie said, clearly lacking confidence in his men.

'I'll come with you,' I said.

'Only if you do exactly what I say or signal, right?'

'Right.' Davie was more up to date about field operations than I was, though I'd carried out plenty when he was not much more than a kid.

We got out of the 4×4, closing the doors quietly, and moved into the shadows. Davie took the lead, his bulky frame in what looked like an uncomfortable crouch, but I knew he could keep it up for hours if necessary.

'This must be it,' Davie whispered, stopping outside a two-storey building that was scarcely visible in the gloom. 'I counted from the last place that was numbered. Squat down by the fence while I check it out.'

I did so, my heart pounding after he disappeared round the side. We both had torches with narrow beams and I saw the odd flash of his. I heard what sounded like a sash window being moved. Then everything happened very quickly. The front door opened and a tall figure dashed towards the gate. I waited till it was almost alongside me, then put in the best rugby tackle I could manage, my legs straining. My target went over and I heard what was probably a knife blade clang on the pavement. Then the young guardsman with more spots than brain cells was on the writhing figure. It was a middle-aged man.

'Get him inside,' Davie called, in a low voice.

I let the other two guardsmen help their comrade, while I reached out for the knife and ran my finger along it. The blade was long, unusually thin and well honed, but not serrated.

Inside, the curtains were all drawn so we were able to use our torches. The place was musty and there was little furniture in the front room.

'Give me that,' Davie said, holding his hand out for the knife. 'I'll find out if he has to call in.'

I left him and his subordinates to that and went through the other rooms. The kitchen floor was covered with empty food packets and there was a half-consumed pan of porridge on the hob, but nothing specifically to suggest that the builders-cum-killers had been there. Then I went up the creaking staircase. There were sleeping bags in the front rooms, six in total. I breathed through my mouth as it was obvious the bathroom no longer had running water. It was the back bedrooms that made me gape.

'What the . . .' Davie said from behind me.

'Fuck, don't do that.'

'Sorry. The scumbag doesn't have to call in, or so he says.' He grinned. 'I believe him. He's bound and gagged now and I've got his phone. The guardsmen have taken up defensive positions.'

We played our torch beams over boxes that had been neatly stacked. My heart sank after Davie opened some with his knife. The contents matched the numbers and letters stencilled on the outside.

'Automatic rifles, rocket launchers, grenades, machine-guns and sidearms.'

'Someone's out to start a war,' said Davie.

'You got that right. But there's quite a distance from chopping some heads off to armed insurrection.'

Davie was looking closer. 'The rifles have been oiled recently.'

'This keeps getting better.'

He looked across at me. 'It changes the situation, Quint. We can't risk Lecky and his pals taking us out and getting away with these.' He scratched his chin. 'Then again, we could turn them on the bastards. No, we need to get more people out here. I'm calling the guardian.'

'Wait a minute. This is a big find, I know, but there might be others across the city. If we go in guardian-handed, we could make the situation worse. Apparently there's been rioting in Inverness.'

'It'll be a lot worse than rioting if people start using these beauties.'

I raised an eyebrow. 'Stick to the Hyper-Stun, and on the lowest effective setting. We need these assholes alive.'

We went back downstairs and waited. The sentry wriggled occasionally and got a kick from the greater spotted guardsman for his trouble. He'd been searched and had no identification on him, but there was a packet of Glaswegian cigarettes – St Mungo's Delight

– in his shirt pocket. Without interrogating him, I couldn't be sure if he was an Edinburgh citizen or an outsider. That would have to wait. At least we knew Lecky and his builders were locals.

I had nodded off when Davie nudged me. It was still dark.

'They're coming.' He looked around. 'From all directions. Told you I should have called for backup.'

'How many are there?'

'At least five. The squad at the rear is watching two of them. Here, take this. It's on the setting you wanted.'

I felt the plastic grip of a Hyper-Stun in my right hand and changed it to my left. Pulling a trigger with the stump of a forefinger is hard. Then again, my aim has never been great on the sinister side.

Then a buzz came from Davie's pocket. He took out the sentry's phone.

'What do you say?' he said, pointing his Hyper-Stun at the bound man's groin and pulling down his gag.

'Aye aye,' the captive croaked.

Davie looked unconvinced, but he couldn't get anything else out of the head-banger. He pressed the Answer button and said the words.

'The connection was cut straight away,' he said. 'Prepare for incoming.'

I crouched under the front window, moving the curtain slightly. It was impossible to make anything out in the dark and rain. I let the damp material fall back and then heard a sound near the door. Several sounds, heavy boots on the cracked paving.

Then the key turned in the lock and a figure appeared.

'Skank? Where are ye?'

Davie tried a mumble, but the guy didn't buy it and turned away.

'Ambush!' he yelled, then collapsed halfway down the path after Davie stunned him.

'Where's the rest of them?' the chesty guardsman asked from the kitchen.

'Right behind yeh,' came a reedy voice, then there was a loud blast.

Davie ran out and I heard the Hyper-Stun's characteristic crack. Then it sounded again and again as the remaining guardsmen got in on the act. After about a minute things went quiet.

'Davie!' I yelled.

'Here,' he called.

I went to the kitchen and shone my torch. The little I saw of the over-enthusiastic guardsman's exploded head on the wall was enough. Davie pushed past and asked if the others were all right. They both responded. Then a hail of bullets came in the kitchen and other ground-floor windows. I dropped to the filthy floor, my hands over my head. I heard Davie's boots pound up the stairs, then frequent cracks from his Hyper-Stun. Eventually everything went quiet again. Davie came down, then started swearing loudly.

I got up and went into the hall. The guardsman there was lying in a pool of blood. The other one, in the front room, had taken at least one shot to the region of his heart.

'All three,' Davie said. 'For fuck's sake.' He ran out and opened the back door. 'Mari!' he shouted.

'Nello,' came the response from the Guard personnel to the rear.

Peter Marinello had been a star forward for Hibernian in the late 1960s and eventually played for Hearts too. But had we really got to the stage that the Public Order Directorate was using footballers' names for the daily code word?

Davie didn't care about that. He was incandescent about the loss of his people – a guardswoman from the backup squad had been killed as well.

At least we had John Lecky and three of his builders, all of them unconscious. Lecky had nearly got away, but was hit by a middle-aged guardsman with his truncheon – no modern technology necessary. The question was, had anyone else vanished into the grey and drenching dawn?

The four prisoners were taken to the castle and put in separate cells. By the time they were locked up, they were starting to come round. Davie went off to supervise the transfer of the arms we'd found. Guardian Doris came to look at Lecky and his men. They had been chained to the walls next to the rickety wooden beds.

'Any IDs?' she asked.

'No, but their photos match their Housing Directorate files. I remember them well enough from when they came after us.' I wondered where Lecky's hacksaw was. It hadn't been found at the house, suggesting he might have another base. Shit, maybe he and his pals were all over the place.

Guardsman Rab, the day warden, had just come on duty. He came up to us.

'Such a parcel of rogues, eh, guardian?'

Doris nodded, then I saw the light.

'In here,' I said in a low voice, leading them into an empty cell. The previous occupants had been sent off to a secure facility in Beaverbank on the grounds that we'd be needing the space for new villains.

'I just had a thought,' I said, aiming the Hyper-Stun I still had at the guardsman and relieving him of his knife. 'Secure him, please, guardian.'

'What is this?' the big man said as Doris took his night-stick and got cuffs round his hands and ankles – these were then chained to a ring in the wall.

'You've got some explaining to do, Raeburn 97,' I said.

He played dumb, but not very effectively.

'You were the one who delivered messages to and from Muckle Tony.'

'That's pish!' he shouted, his face red. 'Utter pish!'

'No, Rab, Muckle Tony was a Leith Lancer. Or were you working for the Porty Pish too?'

'I was not. Where's your proof, smartarse?'

I looked at the guardian. 'Proof is not essential in City Guard investigations, as you well know. But in this case, I'm sure we'll find copies or notes of the messages in your quarters or your locker. The thing is, we're in a hurry. Play ball and you'll be treated more favourably. Not the mines, maybe.' I aimed the Hyper-Stun at his face. 'Otherwise, I'll fry you.'

Raeburn 97 lowered his head. 'All right. I've been doing favours for the Lancers for years.'

'For Hume's sake, why, man?' Guardian Doris demanded.

Rab kept his head down. 'It gets to you after years – the discipline. No personal property for auxiliaries, sharing a dormitory even in your sixties. I . . . I wanted my own space.'

'And where's that?' I asked.

He hesitated. 'A two-bedroom flat in Quarryholes. The Lancers arranged it.'

'What will we find there?' the guardian asked.

'Nothing like the tourists get,' he said fiercely. 'Just a decent sofa and a soft bed. And outsider whisky, mainly malt.'

'I think she meant what will we find that's either useful to ongoing investigations or incriminating. Or both.'

'I never gave them anything important. Just Guard dispositions and patrol times, that kind of thing.'

'Not important at all,' I said, shaking my head. 'You helped those gangs make the north coast a no-go area for the Guard after dark *for a soft bed*?'

'Give me the address,' the guardian ordered. After she'd got it, she left to arrange a search of the place.

Shouting started in the cell next door, though the walls were thick enough to muffle it.

'You got this far, Rab, and you turned it all to shite.'

He looked up at me. 'Blast me with that fucking thing, full power. Go on!'

I understood his anguish – after all, auxiliary life got to me nearly twenty years ago – but I wasn't going to give him an easy exit. At least not yet.

'I'll think about it. But I need information from you, names and addresses. Who handled you?'

'There were different contacts over the years.'

'I'll bring you a pad and pencil – no, I won't because you'll ram the latter into your eye.'

'You think you're so fucking smart, citizen.' He pulled at the chains and got precisely nowhere.

'Why did Hume 481 kill Muckle Tony? Did he get on to you?'

'Did he fuck. He was in with the Pish. He got rid of Tony because he was told to – otherwise his parents would be turned to mince.'

That sounded plausible. I hoped the elderly couple had managed to get away.

'I need more, Rab. Did you deal with anyone in the Supply Directorate on behalf of the gangs?'

'Are you going to shoot me?'

'After I've got what I want.'

'All right. The deputy guardian, Adam 159.'

No surprise there. I'd been sure he was dirty.

'The Recreation Directorate?'

'Em, the guardian. The former guardian, I mean.'

'Liar!' I yelled. Peter Stewart was basically clean, I was sure, even if someone had a hold over him that had driven him to suicide.

'All right,' Raeburn 97 said morosely. 'Cullen 366.'

The female barracks ID rang a bell.

'Alice Scobie,' the guardsman said, before it came to me.

'That might well earn you a stunning,' I said, moving to the door. 'But not yet.' A long-drawn-out groan came from behind me.

Davie was waiting in the corridor. It was time to start on Lecky and his men.

TWENTY-FOUR

We decided to let them stew for a while. We grabbed a couple of hours' sleep, then got to it. The builders – and decapitators – were hard to break down. Even Davie's imaginative threats about how he was going to use a screwdriver and a frying pan got us nowhere. These guys were professionals. Then it occurred to me. They were also Edinburgh citizens with families and friends. Some had gone to ground – or perhaps crossed the border – but we managed to find at least one relative and one friend for each of the quartet.

'So what's it to be?' I asked John Lecky, my hand on the shoulder of the pretty, black-haired seventeen-year-old girl who had refused to accompany her mother to Fife six months ago.

'Leave her alone, yeh fuck!' the prisoner yelled. 'Fi, are yeh aw right?'

'Yes, Dad. What have you been up to?'

That was interesting: father had kept daughter out of the circle; also, daughter was speaking the unaccented English that the original Council had insisted on. The only citizens who do that nowadays are keen on raising their social status. Auxiliary training starts at eighteen and I wondered if Fiona Lecky had applied. If so, she might be a useful means of applying pressure. I texted Guardian Doris to check if her name was on the list.

'Nuthin' for yeh tae worry aboot, darlin',' said John Lecky, glaring at me. No doubt he was embarrassed by that display of paternal affection.

'He's been cutting people's heads off,' I said, deciding on shock tactics. 'Among other things.'

'Dinnae believe them,' Lecky said, smiling at his daughter. 'Yeh ken how worked up these eedjits get aboot nuthin'.'

Fi Lecky looked horrified. 'You haven't really been decapitating people?'

Father kept his mouth shut but shook his head.

We hadn't found the hacksaw so I couldn't brandish it in front of her. What I could do was show her the photos.

'You didn't,' she said, her voice high.

'Ah tellt yeh Ah didnae.'

She looked at me. 'Is he lying, citizen?'

'Well, he came after me with a saw. And a rifle. And the house he's been staying in is full of guns and other illegal weaponry. So, yes, he's lying.'

'How could you, Dad?' she moaned, tears blurring her eyes.

While Lecky proclaimed his innocence, I looked at my phone. Doris had replied.

'Right, you,' I said to the prisoner. 'Do you know that Fiona here has applied for auxiliary training?'

'Whit?' The shock on Lecky's face was genuine enough. 'Are yeh oot o' yer mind?'

I moved closer to him. 'You'll be aware of what happens to the family of people convicted of major crimes.'

He hung his head. 'Aye.'

'Do you really want your daughter to spend her life on the city farms? Or cleaning tourist toilets?'

'Ah dinnae care,' he said after a pause. 'If she's dumb enough tae want tae be one o' yeh, she can take what she gets.'

Fi stifled a moan, her face soaked.

I nodded to Davie.

'Remember what I said about the screwdriver and the frying pan?' he said, his mouth close to Lecky's ear. 'Regulations permit us to use persuasive methods on family members.'

'Dae they fuck!' yelled the prisoner.

'It's a recent development,' I said. 'Very recent. Since you've been removing heads, in fact.'

'Shite!'

'All right, commander,' I said. 'Take the girl down to Room 111.'

'With pleasure,' Davie said, pushing Fi ahead of him.

'Yer bluffing, ya cunt.'

I met his gaze. 'The Council's given me full powers to investigate this case. And full means what's going to happen to your daughter

and the relatives of all your pals. You can be sure some of them
will talk.'

'No they willnae.'

I didn't reply, occupying myself by sending texts to Doris and
Davie. The former reported that two of Lecky's group had started
to talk, while I told the latter to take Fi Lecky to the canteen.

I informed her father that his sidekicks were already spilling their
guts and that his daughter was about to be stunned.

'Which is a shame,' I added, 'as she's pretty stunning already.'

'Dinnae!' John Lecky screamed. 'Dinnae dae anythin' tae her.'

I shrugged.

'Aw right, I'll talk,' he said. 'Fuckin' bastards.'

I called Davie and told him to lay off the girl.

'He's opening up?'

'Correct. Out.'

Then John Lecky told his tale.

Four hours later we compared notes.

'I can't believe this,' Doris said. 'Do you think the two other
arms dumps are the only ones in the city?'

'Obviously we can't be sure,' I said, 'but all three of them gave
the same addresses. Have the properties been secured?'

'Fully,' the guardian said.

'Good.'

'It's hard to believe that Lecky's little gang was able to bring so
much over the line,' Davie said.

'According to him, they had help,' I said. 'The Dead Men.'

'Glaswegians,' the guardian said. 'They're supposedly out of the
city now.'

'I don't believe that. Remember "approved by H"?'

Doris stared at me. 'We can hardly arrest the chief of the Glasgow
police.'

I smiled. 'Maybe not yet.'

Davie scratched his stubble. 'So Grant Brown was working for
Lecky both as a builder and as a gangster. Why did they cut his
head off?'

'According to Lecky, Grant had a big mouth,' I replied. 'He talked
to team mates who were in the Pish, so he had to be dealt with. I
think Lecky was wrong, because we never heard anything about it
from them. Besides, they needed a head to put on the Tolbooth.'

'To up the pressure on us,' the guardian said. 'You don't think there's any connection between these scumbags and the people responsible for the hearts?'

'Could be, but I haven't heard anything to support that.' I looked at my notes, which were extensive. 'What we do know is that auxiliaries in the Supply and Housing Directorates were involved, providing transport and properties.'

'I've had Adam 159 and his opposite number at Housing brought in,' Doris said.

I picked up my pen and pointed it at her. 'I think there are rotten apples in the Public Order Directorate too, in addition to Warden Rab and Hume 481.'

The guardian's head snapped back. Davie didn't look too happy either.

'It stands to reason,' I said. 'How did they manage to get the first head on to the spike at the Tolbooth? How did they manage to throw the second head through the Walter Scott Rooms window from one of the most heavily patrolled streets in the city? How did they manage to stick the guardsman's head on the writer's statue on Princes Street? They had to have Guard personnel looking the other way.'

Guardian Doris grabbed the pencil from my hand. 'Those are serious and, as far as I can tell, uncorroborated charges, citizen.'

Quint had obviously been consigned to the dustbin as a form of address. I raised my shoulders. 'It's true, no names or numbers have been mentioned. Maybe you'd like to check the patrol rosters covering the relevant times and places.'

She threw my pencil to the floor and stormed out.

'Nice one,' said Davie dourly.

'I'm only starting – while you have the joy of watching the guardian grill Uncle Joe and making sure she doesn't cut him any senior auxiliary slack.'

'You're only starting what?'

I laughed. 'Wait and see, big man.'

He didn't like that. If he'd known what I was planning to do, his countenance would have been even grimmer.

Late afternoon. Sophia was at home – she always spent an hour with Maisie after school. That suited me. I took a taxi from the Lawnmarket rather than a Guard 4×4 – this was a private visit. On the way down the Mound, the clouds parted for a few moments and a dull sun shone down. Then it disappeared and the rain started again. There was a metaphor in there for contemporary Edinburgh, but I couldn't be bothered to dig it out.

'The guardian is not to be disturbed,' said a pale-faced female auxiliary.

'Tell her who it is.'

When she was on her way back, Maisie pushed past her and ran into me. That hurt.

'Hello, man with the funny name.'

'Hello yourself,' I said, moving her head gently backwards. 'Doing your homework?'

'Finished it already,' she said, smiling proudly. 'Do you know what a quadratic equation is?'

'You're a bit young for those, aren't you?' I said, trying to cover my memory failure. I was sure I hadn't been able to do them.

'That's what Mother said.'

Sophia appeared in the hall.

'Isn't she a bit young to be calling you Mother?'

'It's her idea.' Sophia glanced at the auxiliary. 'At least, I hope it is. That'll be all, Simpson 492.' She watched as the woman went into the office to the left. 'Come on, there's tea.'

'And scones,' put in Maisie.

'Scone,' Sophia corrected. 'Quint can have it.'

'You're too kind.'

After a while Sophia let Maisie go to her room.

'She's crazy about maths. I can't keep up with her.'

'Me neither. Well done with the measles outbreak, by the way. You kept that quiet.'

'It's what guardians do, Quint.' She poured me the last of the tea. 'Right, what do you want?'

'Charming.'

'These are difficult times.'

'I noticed. Alice Scobie.'

Sophia was immediately on her guard. 'What about her?'

'You must have heard talk.'

'I hardly know her.'

'Come on. Guardians and deputy guardians attend briefings and functions. You must have met her often enough.'

'I have, but I never spoke to her beyond the usual greetings. I don't know – she's one of the abrasive ones who eye up their guardian's seat from the day they're appointed to a directorate.'

'I think she's dirty.'

Sophia raised an eyebrow. 'Where are you going with this? Oh, no, you don't . . .'

'I can't ask Guardian Doris. She's a friend of Scobie's and she thinks she's clean.'

'No, I'm not going to let you access her file.'

I took out my authorization and held it up.

'That doesn't apply to guardians' records.'

'Of course it does. Even if it didn't, I'd expect you to give me special consideration.'

She laughed. 'You like taking advantage of me, don't you?'

'Hugely. And I'll be hugely grateful.'

'We'll see about that.' She shook her head. 'All right, come on.'

She led me upstairs to her private office. 'Make yourself at home – as you always do.'

I went over to the large Victorian desk and opened her laptop. 'Password?'

'I'll do that. Look away.'

I buried my face in her midriff. Which was good.

She giggled, a rare occurrence. I was tempted to make the most of it, but time was also pressing.

The Council has its own archive, for which Sophia had to input another password and I did more burying.

'What is it you want to know about her, anyway?' She smiled cattily. 'I wouldn't have thought she was your type.'

'If she's dirty, she's definitely my type.'

'But I'm not dirty.'

I laughed. 'Not in that way.'

She gave me a slap that was probably meant to be playful.

'Right. Cullen 366, Alice Buchanan Scobie, born 23/9/1996, parents members of the original Enlightenment, father former labour guardian – I remember him, he was reliable. Died relatively young – yes, 2014. Alice attended Primary School Number 3 and High School Number 2, then went for auxiliary training. Under-sixteen and under-seventeen city high-jump champion, also achieved honours for netball and weightlifting. Won numerous Education Directorate prizes for academic performance.' I clicked through the pages. 'Guard reports uniformly excellent. Served a year extra on the city line, six bravery awards. Then chose to enter the Recreation Directorate.' Again I ran my eyes down the text. 'Look at this. All her superiors give her glowing reports until Peter Stewart. He calls her "over-zealous", "concerned more with herself than the directorate", even "disobedient". At least that was until two years ago, when she became deputy guardian – which is a surprise, judging by the guardian's comments. Why did he choose her? Suddenly she's "extremely supportive", "the most dedicated auxiliary I've ever had the honour of serving with" and "a credit to the city". No wonder she succeeded him. But why did he change his attitude towards her?' I went back through the file and found no explanation.

'Maybe she was in a relationship with him.'

I went to the first page. 'She's classified as "homo".' Which might explain her friendship with Doris.

'Maybe she just fell for him,' Sophia said, grabbing my head. 'It does happen, you know.'

'But you're not "homo" or "bi". Surely Alice would have identified herself as the latter if she swings both ways.'

Sophia's forehead furrowed. 'What are you getting at?'

'That she had some kind of hold over him, not necessarily sexual.' Guardians and their deputies are strictly forbidden to get involved sexually or romantically – the original Council saw that as dangerous for the smooth running of directorates.

'Like what?' asked Sophia.

I leaned back in her ergonomic chair. 'Peter Stewart killed himself over the football betting scheme. It's a fair bet that his deputy was the one who set it up.'

'On whose authority? There was never anything approved in Council.'

'Good question. I'd better ask her.'

Sophia looked dubious. 'Would she tell you?'

'Probably not, but she must have the records of the scheme somewhere. They were removed from the Recreation Directorate database – or perhaps they were never in it. Peter Stewart would have had access, but Scobie or one of her sidekicks got to his computers.' I decided against telling Sophia that we had Stewart's diskette. In any case, it didn't name anyone in authority.

'She's got powerful backing,' Sophia said.

'Who?'

'Well, no one gets on the Council without the senior guardian's approval.'

I nodded. 'I'm still not clear if Fergus Calder's involved. It wouldn't be very smart of him to let me investigate if he was.'

'He's not the only guardian with a power base. There's Jack MacLean, with his business contacts in outsider states and that worm Geddes at his beck and call. And don't forget Brian Cowan.'

'The education guardian? He's just a raving Edinburgh ideologue, isn't he?'

Sophia opened her hands. 'He's certainly raving, but that doesn't mean he isn't capable of organizing opposition to Council policies.'

'Such as?'

'Such as I don't know, but I don't trust him.'

'Point taken.'

'What's been going on, Quint?'

I told her about the arms dumps and the other developments.

'That's shocking,' she said. 'Does Fergus know?'

'I imagine Doris has told him.'

'Isn't that your job?'

'At the Council meeting. Besides, there may be more to talk about by this evening.'

'I hope not.'

My phone rang and I listened to Davie's agitated voice. In a few seconds I was agitated too.

'All right, the medical guardian will want to see. She'll give me a lift.'

'What is it?' Sophia said.

'Another heart. Guess where.'

'Just tell me!'

I took her hand. 'At the Heart of Midlothian.'

'On the Royal Mile? How many tourists saw it?'

'More to the point, whose is it?'

We set off at speed in her 4×4. I caught a glimpse of Maisie's face in a third-floor window. It was completely impassive, which sent a chill through me.

By the time we got to the High Street, there was a Guard cordon about fifty yards on each side of the cobbles that formed the heart-shaped mosaic, which marked where the Old Tolbooth had been. It was a fitting place for the extracted organ to have been left, not only because of its shape but because many hearts had been removed there when people were hanged, drawn and quartered. And, of course, the football club where the first heart had been left took its name from the mosaic. Then there was Walter Scott's novel *The Heart of Midlothian*. Someone was pulling everything together on several levels.

The tape was raised for Sophia's vehicle and she drove to within ten yards of the sheeting that had been raised around the Heart and the heart.

Davie stepped towards us, followed by Guardian Doris and the tourism guardian. The latter started to complain about the effect on the city's main source of income but Doris told her to keep her distance.

Sophia and I put on overshoes and gloves and went into the sheeted area.

The heart was grey-green, maggots slithering across the slick surface. It had been placed in the centre of the circle that had been picked out between the diagonals of the St Andrew's cross. The red stones were shiny in the drizzle.

'Has the crime-scene squad finished?' I asked.

Davie nodded.

'Let's get this thing to the infirmary, then,' said Sophia.

A plastic box was brought and the organ placed in it.

'Get the rumour going that it's another prank by irresponsible citizens,' I said to Davie. 'And that the heart's not real.'

He nodded dubiously. 'They won't all buy that. I heard some Americans say they were going home a week early.'

'Too bad. The Council will no doubt put out something official. Come to the morgue when you're finished.'

'Oh great,' Davie said, turning away.

It took the pathologists Tall and Short under five minutes to confirm that the heart was Hume 481's.

'His body was in Granton but at least his heart was in the heart of the city,' Tall said, getting an icy stare from Sophia. 'At least we don't have any more bodies missing organs, guardian.'

He was right, but the night was still young.

TWENTY-FIVE

Davie gave me the lowdown on the preliminary Guard investigation of the heart on the High Street – as usual, the area had been crowded, the tourists under the shelters at the sides and only citizens with jobs or homes to get to walking in the road. Several had been traced, but none had noticed anything out of the ordinary – except those who heard the screaming. This time it was a group of Africans from one of the wealthier countries.

Guardian Doris reported all that to the Council, fortunately with no outsiders present.

'This time it wouldn't have been hard to do,' I said. 'The perpetrator could just have slipped the heart from a bag and walked on.'

'There are visitors around the heart all the time,' said the tourism guardian.

'That's why no Guard personnel saw anything,' Doris said.

'The last thing we want to do is start interrogating tourists,' Jack MacLean said. 'Stick with the prank story.'

That was agreed by all.

'A decomposing heart,' said the education guardian. 'One of a guardsman.' Sophia had already confirmed that. 'The symbolism is obvious.'

Fergus Calder sighed. 'Explain.'

Brian Cowan looked at him as if he was a five-year-old. 'Whoever's behind this thinks the city is rotting from the inside. And that the body politic's most important organ, the heart, has failed so badly that it has been torn out.'

'The original Enlightenment Party saw the heart and the brain of the body politic as the guardians,' I said, which got me a lot of hostile looks.

The education guardian nodded enthusiastically. 'And it was right. Heads have been removed, though fortunately not from Council members. That might point to the lack of brains and thought in Edinburgh. And the city is seen as heartless too, meaning we have failed in our sworn duty.' Cowan looked around the gallery of

guardians. 'To protect citizens and give them the best life possible.'
He stared at Alice Scobie. 'And meanwhile, illegal betting has been
fostered by the Recreation Directorate. That only brings out the
worst in people – grasping greed and selfishness.'

He was quite the orator, but something didn't ring true. I tried
and failed to put my finger on it.

'That will do, Brian,' Calder said, looking at me. 'Citizen
Dalrymple, you have a lot to get through.'

Indeed I did, but I made it as brief as I could. I didn't want to
be in the Council chamber all night.

'This is all very well,' the senior guardian said, referring to the
discovery of the arms dumps, 'but we still have no idea who's
behind it.'

'I have some ideas,' I said, 'but they're still provisional.'

'Provisional?' MacLean said with heavy irony. 'How much time
do you need to clear this case?'

I smiled at him. 'How much time do you need to sell the city to
outsiders?'

That got me thrown out, which was the point. I'd had an idea
that needed to be acted on immediately.

'Get a squad of Guard personnel you trust to meet us on the esplanade,' I said to Davie as he pulled away from the Council building.

'Where are we going?'

'The recreation guardian's residence. She'll be tied up in the
meeting for what I hope is long enough for us to locate her computer,
or at least her diskettes.'

He made the call, then glanced at me as he drove up the Royal
Mile. 'You're taking a big risk, Quint. Guardian accommodation is
sacrosanct.'

'Good word for a bunch of confirmed – ha – atheists.'

'This isn't a joke.'

'All right. Give me a vehicle and I'll go down myself.'

'That's not what I mean. I've been your partner for years and no
one's managed to demote me. But Scobie's staff will try to stop us
getting in.'

'They'll also notify her. That's why I'm going to tell them she's
been arrested and her accommodation put under Public Order Directorate
control. Plus, her staff members are to be put in a single room, having
been relieved of their phones. That's why I want your people.'

He laughed bitterly. 'Glad we can be of service.'

'By the way, what do the tails on Derick Smail and Eric Colquhoun say?'

'The latter was carried home by some friends, completely out of it. Smail's still at Easter Road.'

We drove through the damp evening at speed after rendezvousing with two Guard 4×4s. Down on Princes Street the tourists were sampling the delights of the dope cafes and souvenir shops. There wasn't any sign of a mass exodus. Maybe our visitors were as brainless and heartless as the victims whose body parts had been briefly on display.

We were admitted to Moray Place on the strength of my authorization. I told the guardswoman at the checkpoint that I was going to the medical guardian's residence to put her off the track. The trees in the circular gardens would give us some cover because where we were going was on the other side.

The eight guardsmen and women formed up behind me and Davie. When the door opened I pushed past the besuited male auxiliary and let the hounds loose – in under a minute all were back with the staff's mobiles. The auxiliaries were put in the reception room under the eyes of four of Davie's people.

I ran up the stairs to what had been Peter Stewart's private quarters. No laptop. Alice Scobie obviously had it with her. Her desk was covered in papers, none of which at first glance was suspicious. There were no diskettes to be seen. Obviously she was careful – and we didn't have time to take the place to pieces.

'What's all that?' Davie said, pointing at a pile of boxes.

'The guardian hasn't had time to unpack.' I lifted down the top one and opened it. 'Athletics, netball and curling trophies, plus team photos.'

'Similar in this one,' Davie said.

I took down another. This time the contents were books – the usual handbooks issued to deputy guardians, bound annual directorate reports and . . .

'Wait a minute,' I said. '*The History of Scottish Football, 1867–2000.*'

I flicked through the pages of the large tome. There was a brown envelope between pages 224 and 225. It was unsealed. I pulled out three printed pages. The first was a birth certificate dated 4th January 2005 for one Alistair Lyon Stewart, parents Peter and Mavis, unmarried. I handed it to Davie.

'The ex-guardian had a son? How did that happen?'

Auxiliaries were only permitted to have children from 2015, when the drugs wars ended and social disorder ended – they were seen as potential distractions before that.

'The usual way, I expect.'

'Smartarse.' I handed him the second page.

'Confined to Rehabilitation Centre Number 5 on 8th March 2028, heroin addiction. Shit, that must have been embarrassing for the guardian.'

'Check the name.'

'Alistair Stewart Lyon. His names were changed round and a citizen background fabricated. Secretly, his father thought.'

The third page, a photocopy, was handwritten. I read it aloud.

'"Thirtieth of June, 2031. I, Peter MacCraw Stewart, recreation guardian, hereby confirm that I am the father of Alistair Stewart Lyon, permanent inmate of Rehabilitation Centre Number 5 and former heroin addict. I admit that I facilitated the change of my son's name in order to protect my position. Signed, P. M. Stewart."'

'So that's what Alice Scobie had over her predecessor,' I said. Then I had a thought. I called the command centre and got them to put me through to the rehab centre. The female auxiliary who ran the place was initially reluctant to talk, so I read her my authorization.

'What is it you want, citizen?' she said, pronouncing my status as if it tasted of citizen-issue meat paste.

'Alistair Lyon. I need to talk to him.'

There was a pause. 'That isn't possible. Nor would it have been if you'd rung before his death.'

My heart skipped a beat. 'When did he die?' I said, looking up at the light fitting from which Peter Stewart had hung himself.

'Last Wednesday afternoon.'

The former guardian had committed suicide that evening.

'Did Lyon have visitors?'

Again, the auxiliary paused.

'This will go no further but I need confirmation,' I said. 'Did the ex-recreation guardian visit?'

'Once a month, in disguise. We had an . . . arrangement. Not that there was any point. Alistair Lyon had been a vegetable for over a year.'

That stuck in my craw. 'Maybe that made it even more necessary for his father to see him. Be careful I don't go back on your immunity.'

'Sorry, citizen. I didn't mean anything by it.'

'Which is even worse. What was this arrangement you had with Peter Stewart?'

'I . . . he looked after my daughter. She's a clerk in the Recreation Directorate.'

'Right. Notice that I'm not asking for her name. But you'll understand that I can easily find it out if you cross me.'

'Yes, citizen. Thank you, citizen.'

I cut the connection. Some of the staff in the city's welfare services were good, but a lot only thought of themselves – a result of the Council's less than caring attitude towards Edinburgh's neediest. At least that couldn't be said of Peter Stewart. Or could it? Would it have been better if he'd come clean about his son and the EPL betting scheme he'd been manipulated into waving through?

'What the fuck are you doing here?' said Alice Scobie, moving swiftly into the room.

'Nailing you to the wall,' I said, holding up the sheets of paper. 'Davie, relieve the guardian of her phone and service knife. And the pen in her breast pocket. In fact, cuff her. She's no better than a gang boss.' I gave her a tight smile. 'In fact, she *is* a gang boss.'

Alice Scobie struggled, but she had no chance against Davie. As we headed for the door, she spat at me. A confession in saliva.

Doris arrived as we were putting Alice Scobie into an interrogation room at the castle.

'What the hell are you doing?' she said, her face white. 'You can't arrest a guardian!'

I told her what we'd found out. She didn't look convinced, even after she'd read Peter Stewart's declaration.

'What does that prove?'

'That Scobie had leverage over him. When we go through the files in her computer, you can be sure her involvement in the gambling racket will come to light.'

'You won't be going through her files, Quint. That's guardians' work.'

I raised my shoulders. 'Up to you. But be advised that I've called Fergus Calder. He was shocked but he gave me his support.'

The guardian's fists were clenched and I almost thought she was going to attack me. Then she turned and walked away in rapid strides. Off to talk to the senior guardian, I reckoned. That was why I'd told him first. His surprise had seemed genuine.

I went into the interrogation room. Davie had attached Alice Scobie's handcuffs to the chain in the floor.

'I'm not saying anything to you,' she said, her eyes down.

'True, you're entitled to be questioned by your peers,' I said. 'But Fergus Calder's given me the job.'

'You're wasting your time.'

I grinned. 'This is as good as it gets for me, grilling a guardian. Davie, will you bring in the electric heater.'

'You don't scare me, you demoted shit.'

'Maybe not. But the people who put you up to organizing the EPL betting scheme do, don't they?'

She looked away, her expression less assured.

'How about we do it this way? I ask you a question and if you keep quiet, I'll take that as a positive response. Helping will earn you a lighter sentence.'

That wasn't a promise I could realistically make. Still, she didn't say anything, so I went on: 'You set up the football gambling scheme.'

Silence.

'Are Fergus Calder, Jack MacLean or Billy Geddes involved in the gambling?'

She couldn't resist answering. 'All three of them are useless fools.'

'Did you get that bit about "useless" fools, Davie?' He was taking notes, even though the secret tape was running. It's surprising how nervous that makes suspects.

'I did,' he said in his most efficient tone.

'How about Andrew Duart?'

She kept quiet. So the Glaswegians were in on it. I'd thought as much.

'The Lord of the Isles?'

Silence again. Got him.

'The leader of Inverness, whoever he is?'

'It's a she.'

'Whoever she is.'

Silence. This was going surprisingly well.

'Are there any more guardians or senior auxiliaries involved?'
Silence.
'Adam 159?'
Silence. I'd been sure the deputy supply guardian had his finger in the pie.
'Any other guardians?'
'No.'
Her reply was so firm that I immediately knew it was a lie.
'That's enough,' she said. 'I'm not saying anything more and my silence can't be construed as agreement.'
I was surprised she'd admitted as much as she had. That made me suspicious, but giving her the third degree wasn't an option unless the Council approved.
'All right,' I said. 'I'll have some food and drink sent in.'
'I don't want anything from you, Dalrymple. You're a louse.'
We left her.
'If you're a louse, what am I?' Davie pondered.
'A dung beetle,' I suggested.
He punched me on the upper arm and I squealed.

Guardian Doris had been listening. She took me to her office, a sober look on her face.
'Alice admits to setting up the gambling scheme,' she said, shaking her head. 'I can't believe it.'
I wasn't sure that I could either – at least, that Scobie had done it without help. But who in the city would she have got that from? Unless Glaswegians had been sent over the city line. Was that who the Dead Men really were, at least some of them? Gambling experts?
'I've interrogated the deputy supply guardian,' Doris said. 'He didn't say anything about this.'
'He wouldn't volunteer his involvement, would he? You'll have to go back to him. Did he admit anything else?'
'Oh yes,' she said, a steely glint in her eye. 'Knowledge of drug-trafficking and the treasure trove in the Pleasance, and tolerating gang involvement in his directorate. He's for demotion and the mines.'
'Are the outsiders still here?' I asked.
'The Orkney and Shetland governors have left, but the Glaswegians and the Lord of the Isles are in Edinburgh for another two days.'

I thought about that. I had the distinct feeling something bad was about to happen.

'Have your people turned up any more arms dumps?'

'No. We're still checking likely places though.'

'Good.' I got to my feet.

'Where are you going?'

'To eat.'

'All right. I'll see you in the command centre afterwards.'

But I never got to the canteen, let alone Guardian Doris's home base. Neither did she.

Davie and I were on the cobbles leading to the canteen when the first explosion happened. We ran to the ramparts. The rain had stopped and a red glow came from the north-east.

'It's at Easter Road,' Davie said after calling the command centre. 'The Hibernian stadium.'

'Let's get down there,' I said. We were halfway to the esplanade when the second blast went off. This time it was to the west.

Davie made another call and held the line open for a report. Meanwhile, we kept running.

'Tyneside,' he said as we reached the ranks of 4×4s.

'The Hearts ground?'

'Where else?'

'You take Easter Road, I'll go to Tyneside.'

He frowned, but accepted my decision. 'Take some of my people with you.'

'Ditto.'

There was chaos as Guard personnel skidded over the wet asphalt, their hobnailed boots as useful as slippers in a snow storm.

When I had a driver and two guardsmen, I gave the order to set off. Davie immediately called.

'There are reports of machine-gun and small-arms fire. I'm sending more people after you. Wait at Bank Street.'

I didn't pass that on – no time to lose.

The driver used his lights and siren and we made it to the Dalry Road in ten minutes. The traffic was backed up there, so I told the guardsmen to follow me on foot. They had Hyper-Stuns and service knives, while I was unarmed. For some reason, that didn't make me think twice.

As we got nearer to the football ground, we heard screaming between grenade blasts and the rattle of automatic weapons.

'We should wait for backup, citizen,' one of the guardsmen said.

'You wait if you want. People need help up there.' I ran on, the breath rasping in my throat.

The guardsmen overtook me easily, which was a tonic. Then a crowd of citizens came towards us and we had to fight our way through them. Some had their hands to their heads, blood leaking between their fingers, while others were holding children and helping old people.

We were near the road that leads to the stadium when there was another explosion. My ears rang as part of the east stand roof canted over and crashed to the ground. I was pulled down by a guardsman. Flashes of light came from the windows facing us.

'At least six shooters,' another guardsman shouted. 'We need to wait for support.'

I knew that wouldn't make much difference, given that the castle's armoury wasn't well stocked with machine guns or explosives. The Council had preferred to invest in Hyper-Stuns, which are fine for close-quarters fighting but of limited use in full-on combat, which is why almost all the Public Order Directorate's guns are on the city line and border.

So I crawled on, taking cover between vehicles riddled by bullets. I managed to make it to the far right of the car park. Then I saw a black-clad figure smash a window above me and throw a grenade.

It bounced off the roof of the nearest car – an official club vehicle with the emblem of the heart from the Royal Mile on its door – and came straight towards me.

TWENTY-SIX

My experience in the Guard, rusty though it was, kicked in. I caught the cylindrical metal object and threw it back. It exploded outside the window. There was no one there when the smoke cleared. I made a dash for the wall. No one fired at me so I went for the door at the end of the building. It was unlocked, but that was hardly a blessing. I wasn't safer inside than out unless I could do something about the shooters.

I almost wet myself when the door banged open again. Two of

the guardsmen piled in, Hyper-Stuns in their right hands. They shook
their heads when I asked about their comrade.

'What do we do, citizen?' asked one of them, a middle-aged man
with a bald head – he'd lost his beret.

'Well, Geoffrey—'

'Geoff,' he corrected. Diminutives weren't allowed on name badges.

'Right. Were you seen heading here, Geoff?'

'We were,' said the other guardsman, who was younger and called
Rufus.

'They'll be coming for us,' I said.

'Yes, we need to get away from here now,' said Geoff.

We ran down the passage, past changing rooms and equipment stores.

'Stop!' I said, going into a well-equipped gym. 'See anything
we can use?'

Rufus picked up a fork with a long stock. 'How about this?'

'Better than nothing,' I said, taking it.

'These might be handy,' said Geoff, picking up a dumbbell.

'Bloody right.' Rufus took another. 'We've got our knives too.'

'Lucky you,' I muttered, looking round the door and pulling my
head back quickly. 'Two men in black combat gear and balaclavas,
both armed with two machine-pistols.'

'Since they didn't fire, they mustn't have seen you,' whispered
Geoff. 'Stand by.'

The door was open and I had a flashback. A grenade came in
and I managed to catch it, throw it back and crash to the floor with
my hands over my ears. The blast was still shattering.

The guardsmen got to their feet and we moved slowly to the
passage. Blood and other body matter were splattered over the walls.

Rufus picked up one of the machine-pistols. 'Useless,' he said. 'Pity.'

The same went for the other weapons. We didn't bother searching
the ravaged bodies. I did pull off the balaclavas, but couldn't make
much of the facial remains.

'Shit,' said Geoff. 'I know that guy. He's in Hume. Used to serve
on the city line.'

A guardsman. It made sense. Members of the Public Order
Directorate had been turning blind eyes or worse since the first heart
had been put in place.

'What is this?' Rufus said. 'A revolution?'

'Maybe,' I said, calling Davie. He didn't answer, which made
my heart pound. Had he been hit or was he in the heat of battle?

'We need to move on,' Geoff said, leading us down the passage.

It ended at the club's reception hall, team photos old and new all over the walls.

Bullets ricocheted around us as he pulled his head back.

'Fuck!' he said, moving backwards. 'There are at least four of them.'

'What do we do?' Rufus said.

My years in the Guard took over. 'Draw them to us,' I said. 'When they're close, we can deal with them.'

'What about grenades?' Geoff said.

I smiled. 'Leave them to me. Right, get off some blasts with your Hyper-Stuns.'

They did so, provoking a prolonged blast of fire. I opened the door to what looked like a ticket office – there were narrow windows with circular grilles in the centre.

'Grenade!' Rufus yelled.

I turned round and managed to kick it through the doorway. After it exploded, I couldn't hear anything. I signed to the others not to return fire. I watched as a grenade came through the air in front of me and managed to deflect it into the room with my hand. I motioned to the others to stand flat against the wall of the ticket office and nodded at the dumbbells. They got the message.

After a couple of minutes the first shooter came cautiously down the passage. The second he turned towards us, Rufus swung the dumbbell against the side of his head. He went down and was instantly hauled into the room. The guardsmen took his machine-pistols.

'All clear?' another of the shooters yelled. My hearing was muffled but at least I heard it. I nodded to Geoff.

'Clear!' he shouted. It was a standard response – if our attackers were Guard personnel, they might buy it.

'I want them alive,' I said. 'Use your Hyper-Stuns, but not on maximum.'

They nodded.

The next man to appear was more cautious than the first, but Rufus got him the split-second he saw us. How many more were there? The shooting had stopped throughout the stand. Maybe they were making a getaway. I passed that thought on to the others.

'We need to get after them,' Geoff said. 'Let's do it.'

I exchanged the fork for a machine-pistol, while the others put down the dumbbells.

'Use one of them as a shield,' I said.

Rufus picked up the man he had almost brained and moved slowly towards the end of the passage. Then he pushed on, ducking behind the unconscious man. Nothing happened.

'Clear!' he shouted.

I recalled times when the drugs gangs had lured us into advancing. 'No!' I screamed.

There was a blast of fire and Rufus fell back, the shield on top of him. They'd both taken shots to the head and chest.

'Fuck!' Geoff yelled. Then he put his hand round the edge of the wall and loosed off the entire magazine of a machine-pistol. He waited, then did the same with another of the enemy's weapons.

I looked at him, then nodded. We ran into the hall, heading for the staircase. On the way I saw a black-clothed man sprawled over the railing and another at the bottom of the steps.

'Down!' Geoff screamed, taking a round in the shoulder before he managed to fire back.

I saw a man in black run out of the doors to the left, heading for the pitch. I grabbed Geoff's Hyper-Stun and went after him. He wasn't moving too fast – perhaps he'd been hit – and by the time he was on the grass he was struggling. I wasn't in the mood to play games, not least because he had a machine-pistol slung over his shoulder. I couldn't remember what Davie had said about the Hyper-Stun's range, so I waited until I was about ten yards behind the fleeing attacker. Then I let him have it. He flew through the air horizontally, like a footballer going for an outrageous header, and hit the ground hard, his weapon detaching itself and landing several yards away.

I looked around the remaining stands and saw no one through the rain. Either the attackers were all out of action or the survivors had escaped. I pulled off the stunned man's balaclava and got a major shock of my own.

The eyes of Brian Cowan, the education guardian, stared unseeingly up at me.

A few minutes later reinforcements arrived, led by Guardian Doris. I pulled Cowan's balaclava on so Guard personnel wouldn't recognize him and told her to send a squad round to the rear of the stadium, and others to set up roadblocks all around. My phone rang.

'Quint. Are you OK?'

'Yes, Davie.'

'Why are you shouting?'

'Hearing's messed up. What's going on at Easter Road?'

'It's quiet now, but there was a lot of shooting until a few minutes ago. Get this – some of the dead are guardsmen and women.'

'Same here.' I decided to keep quiet about Brian Cowan until I'd spoken to Doris. 'I wonder if the others are Glaswegians.'

'Could be.'

'Have you blocked all the neighbouring roads?'

'What do you think? I'm not sure if any of them got away.'

'Casualties?'

'I lost three good people and two are wounded. I'm going to crucify the fuckers we didn't kill.'

'You didn't have your Hyper-Stuns on maximum?'

'Unfortunately not. We captured some of their weapons.'

'Same here. You are, of course, carrying out a full sweep of the facility.'

'You can, of course, kiss my hairy arse. Out.'

The guardian came up. 'I've got squads going through the entire place,' she said. 'Was that the commander?'

'Yes, he's doing the same at the Hibs ground.' I told her about the casualties, both Davie's and mine.

'Who the hell are these people?' she said angrily.

I beckoned to her to kneel down and removed Cowan's balaclava.

'What?' she said, her eyes wide. 'This was Brian's doing?'

'With the help of his friends in the Guard. And maybe from outsiders as well.'

'I don't believe this,' Doris said.

'I never had the education guardian down as football mad either.'

She gave me a sharp look. 'This isn't funny, Quint.'

'Am I laughing?' The adrenaline rush that had kept me in one piece was now receding and my hands had started to shake.

'I'm finished,' she said. 'The Public Order Directorate will have to be purged.'

'Not to mention the Education and Recreation Directorates. Still, Fergus Calder's good at that kind of thing.' When he'd taken over at the Supply Directorate, the senior guardian had demoted over twenty auxiliaries. Then again, Adam 159 – Uncle Joe – hadn't been nailed. Maybe the entire Council needed to be hauled over the coals.

Doris put the Guard on full watch and a curfew was applied in the citizen suburbs. A story was put round the tourist zone that old buildings had been demolished and the opportunity taken to carry out military exercises. No one in their right mind would have bought that, but the tourists had other priorities and there wasn't any obvious unrest. That made me wonder what it would take to distract Edinburgh's visitors from their fun and games. Then again, Brian Cowan and whoever was working with him had chosen not to stage attacks in the city centre. Yet.

When things were stable at the football grounds, Davie and I went back to the castle. His face was blackened and his hands grimy. Then I saw myself in a mirror. At least my hearing was almost back to normal.

We exchanged combat stories.

'Bloody hell, you were lucky with those grenades,' Davie said.

'Luck had nothing to do with it, my friend. Years fighting the drugs gangs saved my skin.'

'I thought you'd forgotten all that.'

'Tried to forget it, more like. Just as well it remained in my subconscious.'

'Once a guardsman, always a—' He broke off when I raised Cowan's machine-pistol.

'Don't mess around with firearms.'

'Magazine removed, nothing up the spout. Besides, I only lifted it as high as your groin.'

'Gentlemen,' said Guardian Doris, her face the colour of a corpse. 'I've been advised by the medical guardian that Brian Cowan has come round. Let's get over to the infirmary, Quint.'

'Has Sophia informed the senior guardian?' I asked.

'I asked her not to. This directorate's got most to lose in the aftermath of the attacks. Before I report, I want to squeeze everything out of the bastard.'

'That's certainly an enticing prospect.' I turned to Davie. 'You'd better come too. I want the attackers who are Guard personnel identified. Then we'll know which of them are outsiders.'

We went down to the esplanade, the guardian accompanied by her pair of gorillas.

Davie followed her 4×4 off the esplanade.

'What the fuck's this all about?' he said.

'We'll see what we can get from Cowan – pity that truth drug still hasn't turned up. As for the attacks on the football grounds, it's pretty obvious he'd be anti-football, especially with the gambling scheme having been revealed. You know how forceful he is about the virtues of Edinburgh independence.'

'I don't follow.'

'Well, the original Enlightenment banned football. Plus, hearts were left in other cities. He must have seen that as some kind of attempt to tie Edinburgh to the rest of Scotland.'

'In advance of the referendum.'

'Right.'

'So you think he was behind both the hearts and the heads?'

'He's suspect number one. Let's see what Doris can, as she put it, squeeze out of him.'

Davie turned into the infirmary courtyard. 'I'll tell you what I don't understand. Why isn't the senior guardian, let alone Jack MacLean, more involved in getting to the bottom of this?'

'Probably keeping a strategic distance so they aren't soiled by association.'

'If Cowan's dirty – which he obviously is – the present Council's up Excrement Creek without any form of propulsion.'

I laughed. 'You'd think so. But don't forget that Fergus Calder's got the support of Glasgow and other cities and regions.'

'Who gives a shit?' Davie said, his nostrils flaring. 'Fucking outsiders.'

'So you'll be voting against joining a reconstituted Scotland?'

'Won't you?'

'I don't know. Plenty might change before we get to make our crosses.'

We got out of the 4×4 and ran through the rain. There was a heavier Guard presence than usual, which pleased me. I didn't want anything to happen to Sophia.

Then again, if there were dirty Guard personnel, who was safe in the city?

Guardian Doris called me over and said she'd been called to a meeting with the senior guardian. I hoped she wouldn't ask me to go with her. She didn't.

We found Sophia in her office. She looked exhausted, rubbing her eyes.

'You survived,' she said to me, as if it was an accusation. 'What were you doing playing soldiers?'

'Excuse me for trying to save the city.'

'Um, I'll wait outside,' Davie said.

'No, stay here, commander,' Sophia ordered. 'Tell me what happened.'

I let him give her a rundown, interspersing a censored version of my battle.

'I can't believe it,' she said. 'Brian Cowan a revolutionary? Ultra-conservative schemer, maybe, but guerrilla fighter?'

'It was a surprise,' I said. 'Is he conscious?'

She nodded. 'And chained to his bed. I don't know how much sense you'll get out of him, though. The stunning seems to have damaged his synapses. Hold on, I'll come with you. It's not every day a fellow Council member goes haywire.'

I refrained from pointing out that I'd nailed several less than sane guardians over the years, admittedly none in full-scale combat.

Two guardsmen from Simpson Barracks, the one that provides most of the city's medical staff, stood outside a room in the depths of the building. Davie nodded to one of them.

'Is he trustworthy?' I said in a low voice.

'I think so.'

That was the problem – once a few auxiliaries went wrong, you had no idea how many others might have.

The education guardian was lying with the upper half of his body propped up, steel cuffs on his wrists and ankles and chains from them attached to the floor. He turned his head as we came in and smiled wryly.

Sophia slapped his face. 'Don't you dare! You're a disgrace to the Council.'

'Let alone the city in general,' I added.

'Spare me your fatuous outrage,' Brian Cowan said. '*I* have Edinburgh's best interests at heart, not you or the senior guardian.'

'Rather a strange way of showing that,' I said. 'So you don't like football. That doesn't mean you have to storm the grounds.'

He glared at me. 'Football will be the ruination of this city. That weakling Peter Stewart and his ghastly replacement have a lot to answer for.'

'And you, pal,' Davie said, looming over him. 'You're a disgrace to Hume Barracks too.'

Shit, I'd forgotten Cowan had been in Hume before he became a guardian, which was about a decade ago. Davie could have reminded me, but he was no doubt ashamed of Cowan even before the bullets started to fly. I remembered the treasure trove in the Pleasance, within

Hume's patrol area. That was, in effect, Cowan's bank. I had a feeling a fair number of the Guard personnel who'd taken part in the attacks would have been Davie's comrades – not that he'd spent much time there in the last five years. Hume 01 would need to be arrested, though. I took Davie aside and put that to him as diplomatically as I could. He scowled but went off to do the job himself.

'Right,' I said, turning back to the education guardian. 'Would you like to explain what you've been doing or shall Sophia start operating on your groin without anaesthetic?'

She looked as fierce as she could – which was pretty frightening – but I knew she'd never transgress the Medical Directorate's code of ethics.

'I'll talk with pleasure,' said Cowan. He was obviously proud of himself; that turned me right off.

'On second thoughts, we haven't got all night. I ask, you answer, OK?'

'Very well,' he said, looking deflated. 'But I will have my say before the Council.'

Sophia shrugged. It was as likely that he'd be taken out the back and shot.

'You suborned a number of auxiliaries—'

'No, I did not. There are many who disapprove of even the idea of a referendum, let alone actually rejoining Scotland.'

I smiled to soften him up. 'All right. How many?'

'I'm not going to give their identities away.'

'No problem. Some of those we captured will be less reluctant.'

He returned my smile, but his was spiteful. 'They are true Edinburgh patriots, they won't talk.'

'Uh-huh. What was your plan? To get into bed with outsiders, build up arms dumps and overthrow the Council?'

'Get into bed with outsiders?' he said, as if I'd thrown a pig's pizzle at him.

'Come on, Brian. Hume 481 was in contact with the Glaswegian Dead Men, as well as the Portobello Pish. A smart move that, making use of the city's gangs.'

'They're animals, but they served their purpose.'

'I'm sure they look on you as a much higher form of life – the few that are still alive and free. Anyway, John Lecky and his crazy builders were your initial shock troops, no doubt bolstered by the odd Glaswegian.'

Cowan shook his head. 'I know nothing about outsiders. That must have happened on the ground.'

I laughed. 'Who did you think you were buying the arms from? Santa Claus Industries?'

'I didn't care,' he said, glaring at me. 'The end justifies the means.'

'That old get-out clause,' I sighed. 'You had tame Guard personnel put the first head on the New Tolbooth, the second through the window of the Walter Scott Rooms and the third on the top of the old writer's statue. Don't you like his books?'

'He was a buffoon, welcoming George IV to Edinburgh and propagating all sorts of misconceptions about Scottish history and culture. But that's irrelevant. The idea was to spread fear and uncertainty.'

'Well, the Lord of the Isles only just kept his lunch down.'

'Another buffoon. How can Council members seriously want to be involved with a tyrant, let alone the so-called democrats in Glasgow.'

'Last time I looked they were actual democrats.'

'And that's what you want for Edinburgh?' Cowan screamed, spittle flying.

'Can't be worse than what we've currently got.'

'Quint,' Sophia warned.

I looked at her and shook my head, but this wasn't the time for an argument.

I looked back at the education guardian-cum-terrorist. 'Did you expect the disgruntled citizenry to rise up and fight alongside you when the football grounds were attacked? That's not exactly the royal road to many hearts.'

'We . . . you got on to us before we could strike across the city. I decided to go out with a bang rather than a whimper.'

'Thanks for that. But what do you think you've achieved?'

He smiled with the assurance of the deranged. 'People won't fall for the pro-Scotland propaganda any more.'

'You think the Council will let any mention of this appear in print or on radio?'

'No, but plenty of citizens heard and saw our attempts to put pressure on the Council.'

'Moving on,' said Sophia. 'Was it really necessary to remove people's hearts as well?'

Brian Cowan stared at her. 'I know nothing of that, apart from what I heard Dalrymple say in the meetings.'

'I don't believe you,' Sophia said, pointing her finger at him.

'Hume 481's heart was taken, was it not? Why would I sanction the mutilation of one of my own?'

He had a point, though the guardsman could have crossed him or one of his other people.

'You seriously expect us to believe that you had nothing to do with the hearts that were put on the football grounds that you subsequently attacked?' said Sophia.

Cowan smiled crookedly. 'One, I don't care what you believe, and two, the hearts turning up at Tynecastle and Easter Road was perfect for me. They sullied the ethos of city football. I never wanted that fatuous sport to be brought back.'

I beckoned to Sophia and we left the room.

'I don't suppose the truth drug has turned up,' I said.

She shook her head. 'It would be useful now, you're right.'

'Get someone to check if any of the potential thieves had links with Cowan or Hume Barracks.'

'I don't think so, but I'll let you know. What are you going to do?'

'Go to the castle and check that all's well. Then eat, then sleep for a bit.'

She walked past me. 'All right. I'll see you tomorrow.'

Shit. I'd been hoping for an invitation to her bed. Then again, she had wards full of the wounded and the stunned to supervise. As I headed for the courtyard, it suddenly struck me that Sophia could be part of Cowan's lunatic plan. No, they'd seemed genuinely at odds during the questioning. Still, stranger things have happened in this city of lies.

TWENTY-SEVEN

Davie was at the castle, in the command centre.

'How are things?'

'Pretty quiet,' he replied. 'There are some head-bangers having a go at the patrols in Leith and Portobello, and some Hearts fans have had to be taken in hand. They assumed Hibees had occupied Tynecastle and set off to burn Easter Road down. They're cooling their heels in Raeburn.' That was the barracks with the biggest holding area.

I told him what the education guardian had admitted.

'Fucking shit,' he said, eyes bulging.

'What about Hume?' I asked gently.

'I've arrested the commander. Speaking to him in the 4×4, I didn't get the impression that he knows much. Maybe Cowan manipulated him.'

'That's not going to save his career.'

'No. I took in some other Hume personnel, most of them people I don't like. I'll be seeing if they're dirty overnight.'

'Have fun,' I said. 'Any sign of Guardian Doris?'

'She's in her quarters. Told the duty commander that she wasn't to be disturbed until seven a.m.'

'Fergus Calder probably tore her to pieces.'

Davie nodded. 'Food?'

'In moderation.'

As it turned out, I ate nearly as much as he did. Fighting for your life gives you a hell of an appetite. Afterwards, we split up. I got a lift back to my flat and listened to the blues. Sister Rosetta Tharpe's 'That's All' hit the spot. In fact, it got me thinking that we hadn't got it all at all, as regards the hearts and heads cases.

I didn't get much sleep that night, but at least I had a plan when the rain became visible in the grey light of dawn.

I was outside the senior guardian's house in Moray Place half an hour later, having had a shower and changed into my only remaining clean trousers. My donkey jacket had taken a beating the previous evening, so I put on the flash black leather jacket I'd been given when I went to Glasgow in 2026. It still fitted, just.

The auxiliary on the door told me to wait while she called up, then told me to follow her upstairs. I tried to avoid looking at her shapely behind, but my genes countermanded that. I hate myself for a macho swine.

'Citizen,' Fergus Calder said as I was let into the dining room.

'What, no Quint?' I said with a sad smile.

'Let's keep it formal,' he said, angling his head towards the people further down the table: the Lord of the Isles, Andrew Duart and Hel Hyslop from outside the city, and Jack MacLean and Billy Geddes from inside.

'Am I interrupting?' I asked.

'Yes, but take a seat,' said the finance guardian. 'Have you eaten?'

The gorging with Davie still lay heavy on my gut, so I stuck to scrambled eggs and toast. There was fruit, but I was about to play the hard man and grapes didn't really cut it.

I gave the company a general good morning.

'You're lucky to be alive,' said Billy, a trace of concern in his voice.

I grinned. 'It takes more than an uprising with weapons from Glasgow to do for me.' I hadn't intended to get after Duart and Hyslop so early in the day, but why waste the opportunity?

'What are you talking about, Quint?' Duart said. Across the table from him, Hel was doing her best not to lunge at me.

'I'm sure the guardians have briefed you about the activities of Brian Cowan.'

Fergus Calder narrowed his eyes and then nodded.

'To some extent,' the Lord of the Isles said, skewering a devilled kidney.

Duart raised his shoulders. 'We wouldn't expect our hosts to tell us all their secrets.' He turned to me. 'What's this about weapons from Glasgow?'

I laughed. 'As if you don't know.' I looked at Hel. 'You approved at least one shipment. All of them, I'd hazard.'

The senior and finance guardians looked as if weasels had got up their trouser-legs.

'What's the matter?' I asked. 'Worried your pro-Scotland supporters are subverting the city? I would be.'

'You're talking rubbish, Quint,' Duart said. 'Show me physical evidence that the arms came from my city. You haven't got any, have you?'

'There are different forms of evidence, First Minister,' I said. 'Including your police commissioner's complexion.' It was redder than a raspberry.

Billy rolled over to MacLean and whispered in his ear.

'I quite agree,' said the finance guardian. 'Shouldn't you be concentrating on who put the hearts on the centre circles, Dalrymple? I gather that Brian – I mean, Cowan – denied involvement.'

'He did. And I *am* concentrating on it. That's why I'm here.'

Fergus Calder's eyebrows shot up. 'What do you mean?' he said, his voice breaking.

I looked around the table. 'There were hearts left in Glasgow and in your region, Angus.' No way was I going to address him by his self-awarded title.

They all returned my gaze, their lips sealed.

'Have you no idea who was responsible?' I continued.

They all shook their heads, Hyslop sheepishly.

'No idea at all?'

'No,' said Andrew Duart. 'What are you getting at?'

I played my ace. 'Maybe someone from Edinburgh was behind it.'

There were several sharp intakes of breath. Even Billy was taken aback and he's the biggest cynic I've ever come across.

'Have you got any proof of that?' demanded the senior guardian.

'Have you?' I shot back.

He twitched his head. 'What do you mean?'

'It's the case that several guardians have been out of the city, isn't it?'

Calder glanced at MacLean and then nodded. 'What of it? We're trying to secure Edinburgh's fut—'

'Yes, yes, but is there a list?'

'A list of what?'

'Of all guardians – and other individuals – who have crossed the city's borders.'

There was a pause. 'Well, not exactly,' said the senior guardian.

I raised an eyebrow.

'Permission is granted on an individual basis.'

'And those are kept in a file.'

Fergus Calder nodded.

'I need to see it.'

The senior and finance guardians conferred with Billy.

'Very well,' said Jack MacLean. 'Come with me.'

I followed him to the door and then upstairs to Calder's study. MacLean took out a thin silver laptop and tapped away on the keys.

'Here,' he said, holding out the device.

I took out my notebook and wrote down the names. There weren't many, rather the same individuals – the senior and finance guardians plus Billy Geddes – appeared as many as twelve times, mostly visiting Glasgow. Sophia's visit to Inverness was also there.

'What's going on in Inverness?' I asked.

'Full civil disorder,' MacLean said.

'What we escaped last night.'

He nodded. 'Brian Cowan. I can't believe it.'

'At least he never left the city.'

'That's a good thing, true enough.'

I continued to write down names.

'All right?' said jingling Jack in his Glasgow suit.

'Very far from it,' I said. 'But enough to work on.' I turned and headed for the door.

'Are you not coming back to breakfast?' he called.

I managed to stop myself telling him where to stick the sausages.

I called Davie and asked him to pick me up in Charlotte Square – I didn't fancy being called back by the jittery guardians. The rain was off, giving the betting tents and marijuana cafes in the centre of the square an almost carnival appearance. Unless you considered how demeaning they were for the citizens who had to work there.

A 4×4 pulled up beside me. 'Morning, citizen.'

'Commander. I just had breakfast with the senior guardian and his party.'

'Lucky bastard. Were the sausages as good as is rumoured?'

'I had other things on my mind.'

'Such as?'

'The possibility that we're about to be detained.' I looked around. 'Turn round and head for my old man's.'

'It's hardly the time to go visiting.'

'We're not. We're rescuing him.'

Davie racked the wheel and headed towards Queen Street. 'That nurse of his is quite presentable.'

'Fool.' I took out my notebook. 'Here's a list of guardians and senior auxiliaries who've been granted permission to leave the city.' I pointed to a name that appeared several times.

'What the fuck?' he gasped.

'Exactly. Now drive like the wind.'

He got us to Trinity in ten minutes. I ran into the old merchant's house.

'Oh, citizen,' said Alison, the nursing auxiliary, 'your father's being given his wash.'

I went to his room and found a pair of young nurses wielding facecloths and soap.

'Failure!' he said, his eyes lighting up.

'Morning, old man. It's your lucky day. We're off on an excursion. Dry him as quickly as you can, please.'

'Do as he says,' said their supervisor, from behind me. 'Can I help?'

'If they come, tell them you couldn't stop me taking him.'

'They? What do you mean?'

I shook my head and handed my father his trousers. 'Probably auxiliaries, maybe armed citizens, or even outsiders.'

'Should I bolt the door?'

'It's pretty solid, isn't it? Yes, do that. And get everyone away from the windows.'

'Will do.'

That was the good side of auxiliary training and service – people did what they were told without panicking.

Five minutes later we were in the 4×4, my father in his coat and Enlightenment tartan beret.

'Morning, guardian,' said Davie, as he pulled away.

'It's a long time since anyone's called me that,' said the old man. 'Not sure if I like it. What's going on, Quintilian? Have you made some new enemies?'

'Quite possibly.'

'What the hell does that mean? Express yourself clearly.'

I raised my eyes. 'Yes, if you must know. Davie, these vehicles don't have digital positioning units, do they?'

'Not that I know of.'

'And you probably would know. All right, head for that safe house in Stockbridge.'

We got to the inner suburb by the Water of Leith, about a quarter of a mile north of the central zone, in just over six minutes. The house – or rather first-floor flat – was in a narrow street in a maze of similar ones. It wasn't registered to any directorate, but I'd kept the key after the owner did a bunk to Fife. He'd helped us in a major case and I'd managed to doctor his record to show that his family was still in the place, although they'd left with him. If you control the data you can do anything in Edinburgh.

'OK,' I said when we stopped on Raeburn Place. 'Take the 4×4 into the Colonies.' That area nearby has plenty of narrow streets too. 'Give us half an hour and then join us. Try not to get picked up.'

'I'll set my Hyper-Stun to er . . . stun.'

'Come on, old man,' I said, helping him out. 'It's just a couple of minutes' walk. Or ten minutes' stagger in your case.'

'Very funny, failure. You know, this is rather exciting.'

'Rather,' I muttered, locating the keys in my wallet.

I opened the street door and pushed my father up the stairs. The second key turned and I pushed the door open.

I knew instantly from the smell of sweat that someone was in residence.

'Who are you, son?' an elderly woman asked, coming in from a room to the rear.

'I could ask you that question,' I said, getting the old man into a tattered armchair.

'Ahm Val Campbell,' she said, smiling sweetly.

'And Ahm her husband John,' said a broad-chested man, who must have been in his seventies.

I identified myself and Hector, my heart sinking.

'The investigator who works for the Cooncil?' the woman said. 'We've read lots aboot you over the years.'

'Em, thanks. How did you find this place?' I asked.

'Oor son, Michael – Hume 481 – told us aboot it. He kens a lot ae useful things, being in the Guard.'

Shit. I couldn't bring myself to tell them that their son's heart had been removed. So this is where they'd been. No wonder they'd disappeared off the radar. Both their faces were drawn.

'Can ye get us something tae eat, son?' Val said. 'Only, Michael tellt us tae wait here and no go oot, and he hasnae come back.'

I thought about that, then called Davie and told him to pick up some bread, milk and cheese. Then I had an idea.

'Go to Raeburn. You'll soon know if there's an alarm out for us. Bring a couple of reliable Guard personnel back with you after you ransack the canteen.' The barracks was only a few minutes' drive away.

'D'ye ken aboot oor son, Citizen Dalrymple?' John said. 'Is he to dae wi' one o' yer big cases?'

'No,' I lied. 'But I'll check when I go to the castle.'

'That's great,' Val said, smiling broadly.

I felt like a bastard, but I couldn't have people weeping and wailing till things were sorted out.

We chatted, my father even chipping in with dry comments. He'd

never had a problem talking to ordinary citizens, whereas my mother
used to look down on them.

'What do you think about the football being brought back, John?'
I asked.

'Och, it's brilliant, it is. Ahm a Hibee and Ah went tae Easter
Road a good few times last season.'

'I'm a Hibee too,' I said, hoping he didn't ask me about their
performance. I hadn't a clue where they'd ended up in the EPL.

'Great!' John said, sticking out his hand.

I shook it, then went for broke. 'You ever gambled on matches?'
He looked down. 'That's illegal.'

I laughed. 'Aye, technically, but who do you think organizes it?
The Recreation Directorate, of course.'

John's head stayed low. 'Ah wouldnae ken aboot that. Ah just
enjoy the fitba, even if it's shite compared wi' the old days.'

It was obvious that he had laid bets – perhaps he was embarrassed
to admit it in front of his wife. Citizens had to use food and clothing
vouchers to pay, meaning they went hungry and cold if, or rather
when, they lost.

There was a faint knock on the door. I went down and opened
it an inch, then further to admit Davie and two of his comrades.
One, Raeburn 302, was an experienced-looking guardswoman and
the other, Raeburn 499, was young and built like an old-fashioned
police box. They were both carrying boxes of provisions.

I took Davie aside. 'You trust this pair?'

'I saved their lives, not at the same time. They'll walk through
fire for me.'

'Excellent.' I went over to Val. 'Do you think you could look
after my father for a few hours? The guards will help, but I think
you've a more homely hand.'

'Course Ah will, dearie.' She bent over the old man's chair. 'Ah'll
get a nice cup of tea for you in a minute.'

I went into the bedroom and opened the wardrobe doors. I would
stick out like a gigolo in my leather jacket, so I was glad to see an
old donkey jacket on a hanger.

'Is this yours?' I said to John.

'Naw, it wus here when we arrived.'

'Ah'll look after that, son,' Val said, taking my leather jacket.
'Nice cut. Maybe it'll fit your father.'

I left them to it and told the Guard personnel to contact us the minute anything suspicious happened – and to barricade the door after we left.

Davie and I moved slowly down the back street. I hadn't said goodbye to my father. There was a chance I wouldn't be coming back, but I didn't want to worry him.

'What's the plan?' Davie asked.

'I'm working on it,' I said as we headed towards the 4×4.

In truth, I was all at sea. I needed to set a trap, but being unsure who I could trust made that difficult. Then it came to me.

'Where to?' Davie said after we got into the vehicle.

'The Supply Directorate depot.'

He gave me a dubious look. 'You trust the senior guardian?'

'Of course not, but if he's got dirty hands, his stronghold will be the last place he'll expect us to attack.'

'Is that what we're going to do?'

'What, are you scared?'

'Fuck off. But we'll be heavily outnumbered.'

'No, we won't. Trust me.'

He shook his head. 'I've done that plenty of times and nearly lost my head.'

'In this case, it would be your heart. Set your Hyper-Stun to maximum and pray to the ghost of Plato.'

'That'll be all right, then,' he said.

Davie dropped me at the Fruitmarket entrance to the Supply Directorate depot at the old railway station.

'Are you sure you can tell who to trust in Hume?' I said.

'Don't worry, I've kept up with the good ones.'

'Get back here as fast as you can and look for me in the security section on the left as you go in.'

'Here,' he said, handing me his Hyper-Stun. 'I can get a replacement at barracks.'

I took the bulky weapon and held it under my jacket. The guards on the gate inspected my Council authorization. If they were in league with the opposition, my arrival would be passed on. I was hoping for that. If they turned out to be clean, I'd find another way of attracting attention.

I banged on the door and went in. To my relief Jimmy Taggart was there, tucking into what looked like Parma ham and polenta.

'Hullo, sir,' he said, getting to his feet.

'Jimmy. Where's your team?'

'Out in the stacks.'

'Have you got today's list of shipments not to be inspected?'

He nodded to a printout at the far end of the table.

'Right, if you can tear yourself away from pork and corn products, let's go and tear these incoming loads apart.'

He grinned. 'Are we going up against the bad guys?'

'You could say that. Your people, are they dependable?'

'I weeded out the thieves and informers, aye.'

'Good. Hume 253's bringing backup.'

'Crazy Davie? He should liven things up.'

I'd never heard my friend called that. If we survived, there would be major mockery potential. Along with Thunder Boots.

'Here,' I said, handing him the Hyper-Stun.

'You keep that, sir,' Taggart said, going over to a steel cabinet and unlocking the door. There was a row of combat rifles, and boxes of sidearms, ammunition and grenades. 'For use only in extreme situations. I take it this is one.'

'It will be.'

The old guardsman grinned. 'I miss being out on the border with real weapons. Now I can die happy.'

That was inspirational but also deeply worrying.

TWENTY-EIGHT

Davie called when Jimmy and I were going through the first shipment. Inside school desks from a woodworking company in East Kilbride were ten blocks of plastic explosive and another package of cocaine.

'Quint, the pillocks at the gate won't let us in. Do I throw the book or my fist at them?'

'The latter. We're in Stack 12b. Stun anyone who has a go at you.'

The connection was cut.

A couple of minutes later, Davie and a band of about twenty guardsmen and women arrived, Hyper-Stuns raised.

'Any trouble?' I asked.

'A few idiots who'll wake up with their heads buzzing. I told them we had Council authorization.'

'Interesting. Do you think anyone else saw you?'

At that moment a siren began to wind up to full blare.

'Yes,' Davie mouthed.

'Where's the nearest shipment on the list?' I said in Taggart's hairy ear.

He checked. 'Next stack.'

We all moved round the corner, Davie putting down a Guard commander who came at him. I bowed my head as wires began to whip around me. The Guard personnel on site definitely weren't friendly, but they stood little chance against more hardened comrades. The Supply Directorate was notorious for inducing laziness and a lack of sharpness in Public Order Directorate personnel, despite the importance of the posting.

There were at least fifteen prone guardsmen and women in the passage way, while none of the Hume group had been hit.

'That crate there,' Jimmy Taggart shouted, pointing.

We levered open the top and hit serious pay dirt.

'Is that gold?' Davie said.

'Ingots,' I confirmed. 'The shipment's supposed to be tins of water chestnuts and bamboo shoots from Malaysia.'

The noise around us increased, shouted orders and the tramp of Guard-issue boots getting closer.

'Time to make a call,' I said, kneeling down behind the gold. I passed on my message. It seemed to be taken seriously.

Guard vehicles came closer, 4×4s and armoured personnel carriers that the Public Order Directorate had recently bought from Glasgow. They had our range and they also had machine-pistols. We took some hits, none of them fatal.

'Pull over the crates and barrels on both sides,' I yelled. 'We need a fortress.'

A few minutes later we had one.

'This isn't going to last long,' Davie yelled, stunning a guardsman who had climbed up the neighbouring stack. 'Shouldn't you call—' He broke off to take down another intruder. At least there was no need to make any more calls.

Suddenly the enemy fire stopped. APCs blocked both ends of the stack.

I gave Davie instructions, my hand on his arm. 'Watch my back,' I said, handing him the Hyper-Stun.

'Are you out of your—'

I was over our makeshift wall before he finished the sentence. I probably was taking too big a chance but I didn't want unnecessary casualties.

I walked towards the vehicle on the right because I could see the person I wanted in the front seat. I raised my hand.

Guardian Doris opened the front door and stood behind it for a few moments before moving into the open. Her two gorillas flanked her. Numerous muzzles, including all three of theirs, were aimed at me and I felt sweat run down my arms.

'What on earth are you doing, citizen?' she shouted, playing the injured party.

I laughed, though not too disrespectfully. I wanted my body to come out of the encounter unstunned and without entry, never mind exit, wounds.

'What on earth have *you* been doing, guardian?' I found it hard to use her first name now.

'I've no idea what you mean,' she replied, her jaw jutting.

'Tell your people to lower their weapons.' I pointed to the heap of crates behind me. 'It's not as if we're going to fight our way out.'

I heard a growl from Davie, but he must have understood that I was right.

She gave the order, but the semi-automatic pistol remained in her hand, pointing at my feet.

'Why did you do it?' I asked, hoping Davie had one of his team relaying the conversation to Radio Free City and elsewhere, as I'd asked.

The guardian frowned. 'What do you mean?'

'Put on a blonde wig, pad out your chest and place the first heart on the centre circle at Tynecastle.'

'What?' She looked as if I'd kicked her in the belly.

'I saw strands from the wig the last time I was in your office.'

'Rubbish,' she said. 'You're imagining things.'

'Uh-huh. You invented the call to your mobile advising discretion, didn't you?'

'You're rambling, man.'

'Guardian numbers are classified. How did the supposed caller obtain it? In any case you realized it was risky, so you didn't pretend there was one after the murder of Hume 481.'

She took a step back, presumably shocked by the accuracy of what I was saying.

'I . . .'

'You arranged for those boot prints to be found at Tynecastle after we took out the blonde shooter over the line.'

'I . . .' The guardian was struggling to concoct a story. My problem was that she didn't have to. If I wasn't able to keep surprising her, she could simply shoot me.

'Did you know about Brian Cowan's activities?'

'I . . . I knew he was planning something.' She shook her head. 'But he's a madman. I preferred my own approach.'

'After all, the castle is the heart of the city.'

Her nostrils flared and she raised her weapon. 'Don't try to belittle me, Dalrymple. I love Edinburgh and I know it'll be irreparably damaged if there's a vote to rejoin Scotland.'

'You know that how?' I said, playing for time.

'I know that an independent Edinburgh has been and will continue to be a success. It'll be a disaster if Glasgow and the other states take over. We'll become a backwater.'

'You knew about the football gambling scheme, didn't you?'

She looked at me as if I was the class clown. 'Of course.'

'Your friend – and, I guess, lover – Alice Scobie told you.'

She shrugged. 'I don't approve of it, but I was able to use it for my own ends.'

'What were you going to do with the plastic explosive and gold we found?'

She laughed, almost light-headedly. 'What do you think? Bring pro-Scotland supporters to their knees by the threat of serious violence and buy votes.'

'But despite your huge workload, you didn't appoint a deputy. Couldn't you find one you could trust?'

The guardian pursed her lips. 'There are protocols and procedures, as you well know. Next in line for deputy is Hume 253 and I was hardly going to use him.'

I smiled. 'Davie would have been a liability.'

'Bloody right,' came a shout from the fort.

'Whose idea was it that you put hearts on the pitches in Glasgow, Inverness and the Lord of the Isles' region?'

'You ask a lot of questions, Dalrymple – not that I care. I'm proud of what I've achieved. I was in contact with anti-Scotland campaigners in those places. It was decided that I was best qualified to leave the hearts.'

'Did you cut them out yourself?'

Her eyes opened wide. 'Of course not. I have a butcher on my staff.'

'Lovely. And he used a serrated knife to conceal his expertise.'

The guardian's pistol was now aimed at my heart and I'd run out of stalling questions.

'Where's your father, Dalrymple?' she said. 'I'll find out and it'll go badly for him.'

'I knew you'd go after an old and defenceless man.'

'Hector Dalrymple could be a dangerous opposition figurehead. I'll terminate anyone who endangers my mission.'

I was obviously a dead man in her eyes. 'Your mission is to protect this city and its citizens, according to the regulations and the decisions of the Council.'

She looked round.

I took the opportunity to leap back over the crates. No one fired.

Another APC appeared behind the guardian's, blocking it. Fergus Calder's voice came from a megaphone mounted on its roof, demanding that all weapons be dropped.

'Quite the little hero, aren't we?' said Davie.

Jimmy Taggart grinned. 'Like back in the day.'

I raised my hand and peered out between two crates.

'Citizen Dalrymple did us the courtesy of relaying your conversation,' the senior guardian continued. 'Public order guardian, you'll receive a fair trial.'

Inasmuch as Edinburgh had trials. A quick hearing in Council and a cell in her former fiefdom was the best she could hope for. Execution was more likely.

I heard the sound of more approaching APCs.

'You're outnumbered,' the senior guardian said. 'Anyone who complies will only undergo rehabilitative auxiliary training.'

'Like hell,' Davie whispered. He was probably right. There would be a purge of the Public Order Directorate, indeed of all the directorates. The city's mines and farms would have plenty of new recruits.

I looked around the stacks. Weapons had indeed moved in the direction of the holders' feet. The only people resisting were Guardian Doris and her bodyguards.

'Screw the traitors!' Davie said, standing up and stunning the big men.

The guardian seemed to be in a world of her own, maybe a vision of what Edinburgh could have been with her as leader. Then she snapped out of it.

'For the last time, Doris, drop your weapon!' Calder shouted.

His fellow Council member shook her head, raised the pistol to her chest and shot herself in the heart. The bullet passed through her and ricocheted off the APC. It made Fergus Calder duck.

It turned out that the vast majority of the Guard were loyal, though some of them were no doubt putting on an act. Whoever succeeded Doris Barclay would have to do a thorough check. Or maybe just forget about the whole thing and keep a close eye on future developments.

I was called over to the senior guardian, who was wearing a suit of body armour that made him look like a robot – and he hadn't even poked the end of a finger out of the APC.

'Meet me at Moray Place in half an hour, Quint,' he said.

So first names were back in favour. That didn't fill me with joy.

Davie was dealing with his wounded – there had been no deaths.

'I'll see you later,' I said. 'Can you check with the Raeburn personnel that everything's all right with my old man and the Campbells?'

He nodded.

'I'll tell them about their son later.'

'Right. Hey, Quint, what do we do with the gold and the rest of the smuggled goods?'

'I'm sure Calder's people will come for the precious metal. Make sure the plastic explosive and cocaine go to the castle.'

Jimmy Taggart stuck out his hand. 'Pleasure working with you again, sir.'

'Glad you got through it in one piece. Your team?'

'Two wounded, one seriously.'

'I'm sorry.'

'Ach, it was in a good cause.'

I suppose he was right, though it was hard to tell what was good and what was bad in the 'perfect' city. No doubt Fergus Calder would put me straight.

I got a lift down to Moray Place in a Guard 4×4. The driver was effusive about my role in what had gone down at the depot, but I shut him up. For all the horror she'd been involved in, I'd liked Guardian Doris. She was a genuine servant of Edinburgh and its people but, as had happened in the past with guardians, she'd let power run away with her.

I was let into the senior guardian's house and directed to the reception room on the ground floor. Calder, Jack MacLean, Billy and the outsiders – Andrew Duart, Hel Hyslop and Angus Macdonald – started clapping and even cheering. I lowered my head, not from modesty but because I didn't like being fêted by barracudas.

'Have a drink, man,' MacLean said, forcing a glass of dark malt into my hand. 'You saved us from not one but two armed uprisings.'

'Very well done, Dalrymple,' piped the Lord of the Isles.

'Absolutely,' said Glasgow's first minister.

Even Hel Hyslop raised her glass at me, but it was Billy Geddes's mocking smile that pushed me over the edge.

'Shite!' I said, my voice louder than all of theirs put together.

'I beg your pardon,' said the Lord of the Isles.

'So you fucking should. How many of you knew about the gambling scheme in Edinburgh before I told you about it?'

That shut them up.

'All of you, eh?' I glared at Billy. 'Even those who swore they didn't.'

The senior guardian stepped forward. 'We were evaluating its potential without officially approving it.' He looked around for support.

'We've got something similar in Glasgow,' said Duart, 'though it's run privately.'

'My office runs our scheme,' said the Lord of the Isles.

'You're very quiet, Billy,' I said, moving towards him. 'It wasn't by any chance your idea?'

He laughed. 'You could say that.'

I looked at Calder and MacLean. 'Why didn't anyone tell me?'

'We had full confidence in you,' said the finance guardian. 'And we were right. You've solved everything perfectly.'

'What?' I yelled. 'I did your dirty work by uncovering the actions of two dissident guardians. Meanwhile, you allowed Peter Stewart, one of your colleagues and a decent man, to get so distraught that he killed himself. Fuck your full confidence.'

Calder came over and took my arm. I shook it free. 'This is no way to behave in front of the city's guests, Dalrymple.'

'Licking their arses is pretty demeaning, don't you think, Fergus?' He might have dropped my first name, but I used his to show maximum disrespect. 'You're undoing all the work of earlier Councils to establish Edinburgh as a functioning independent state.'

He shook his head. 'You of all people should know how close to collapse the Council's been in the past because of human weakness.'

'And that's going to go away when you get into bed with Duart and Macdonald? The public order guardian was right. This place will become a backwater.'

'Rubbish. If you can't control yourself, leave.'

He wasn't getting off so easily.

'Have you asked yourself why Glasgow sanctioned arms shipments to Edinburgh?'

'We didn't,' said Duart, putting his hand on an incandescent Hel Hyslop's arm.

I ignored that. 'Well, have you?' I said to the senior guardian. 'Could it be that your supposed allies want to take over Edinburgh?' Then I had another thought. 'Or perhaps you knew about it and were stockpiling arms in case the citizen body gets uppity before the referendum.'

Calder shook his head and looked at MacLean. They kept quiet, which suggested I'd got to them one way or another.

I kept going. 'Who gave the order for the football managers to be released from the castle? I know it wasn't Doris Barclay. She was opposed to the gambling.'

'Does it really matter?' Jack MacLean said wearily.

'It does to me.'

'Very well,' said Fergus Calder. 'I had them let go. They make money for us.'

'They're in league with the city's gangs, you fucking idiot.'

I turned on my heel. If I'd been able to throw up on demand, I'd have done so. But the occupants of the opulent room were so used to muck that they wouldn't have noticed.

TWENTY-NINE

Davie and I went down to Stockbridge and the safe house. The guardswoman behind the door demanded a password, which Davie gave.

I found my father playing cards with John and Val Campbell. To my horror he was wearing my leather jacket.

'What happened, failure?' he said, looking round. 'Did you save the city?'

'This city's beyond saving, old man.'

He stared at me. 'You don't really mean that.' For all his disgust at the dilution of the Enlightenment Party's ideals, he still had some faith in the system.

'No, I probably don't,' I said, suddenly very tired. 'What are you playing?'

'Three-card brag. I'm winning.'

'You're not betting for real, I hope.'

'Val found a box of matches.'

'Uh-huh.' I went closer. 'I need to talk to you,' I said to the Campbells.

They knew immediately what it was about.

'Michael . . .' Val said, clutching her husband's arm.

'I'm very sorry,' I said. 'He was killed fighting against a drugs gang. He took a bullet to the chest and died instantly.'

John Campbell caught his wife, who hadn't lost consciousness but was gasping for breath, tears flooding her face.

'Are ye sure, son?' he asked.

I nodded. 'He did his duty.' I would make sure Hume 481's record showed that. He had already paid in full for his crimes.

John took Val into the bedroom. I wondered if their son had told them anything about what he was doing. After all, he'd taken them into hiding. On balance, I reckoned they were clean. And if they weren't, I didn't care.

'Poor people,' my father said. 'Ordinary citizens are the ones who suffer most.'

He was right about that. The first Council had believed in equality, with guardians and senior auxiliaries living austere lives, devoted to their work. Fergus Calder and Jack MacLean were far from that template, though Peter Stewart probably wasn't.

'Come on,' I said. 'We'll take you and the Campbells home.'

'I rather like it here.'

'Of course you do.'

'I like this jacket too.'

'Well, you can't have it.' I took off the worn donkey jacket. 'Come on, hand it over.'

He huffed and he puffed, but eventually took the leather magnificence off.

After we'd dropped the Campbells off at Wardie Road, Davie headed for Trinity.

'Was their son really a hero?' the old man asked.

'You can read me like a Juvenalian satire. No, he wasn't, but they don't need to know that.'

'You're soft, Quintilian. No wonder you were demoted.'

I thought of the combat zones I'd been through in recent days.

'Very soft,' Davie said. 'I blame the parents.'

By the time we got to the retirement home, the quality of banter was heading for the abyss.

'You stole that jacket,' was the old man's parting shot.

'You were cheating at cards,' was mine.

Davie had given up, but he was laughing loudly. At least we still had humour – not even the Council had been able to do away with that. If anything, thirty years of supposedly benevolent totalitarianism had turned us all into Aristophanes fans. That at least was worth celebrating.

On the way up to the centre, I turned to Davie.

'You didn't tell me you're next in line for deputy guardian.'

'I didn't know. They changed the protocol a few years ago and stopped telling us the rankings – so the guardians could choose whoever they wanted, of course.'

'Why did Doris Barclay say you were next, then?'

'I don't know. Maybe she was having a go at you. After I was made your official sidekick at the beginning of this case – or rather cases – she couldn't have made me her deputy anyway.'

'Hm. I think she was probably raising a finger at Fergus Calder for appointing me.'

'That too.'

'Did you ever think she was dirty?'

He shook his head. 'It's like she said. She really loved the city and she gave everything she had for it.'

'Including using a butcher on two people – one of whose identity we don't and probably won't ever know.'

'I'm not defending her, Quint. But she wasn't dirty in the sense that Jack MacLean and your friend Billy Geddes are.'

'What about Cowan?'

'It's not like the Education Directorate has a history of violence. Everyone just thought he was a touch crazy.'

Which reminded me. 'You know they call you Crazy Davie?'

'Behind my back, aye.'

'I wanted to be sure.'

'Guess what they call you.'

'Do I want to know?'

'I don't care. Quint the Quizzer.'

'Boring.'

'It could have been worse. Quint the Qunt?'

'Ha. The rain's stopped,' I said. 'Maybe that's a good omen.'

It started again as we reached Moray Place.

'Go easy on the guardswomen,' I said, getting out.

'Go easy on the medical guardian,' he said with a wide grin.

For once I decided to let him have the last word.

Sophia opened the door herself.

'I assumed you'd be making an appearance. I've sent the staff away for the night.'

'But not your daughter.'

Maisie was barrelling down the stairs with a human skull in her hands.

'Look, man with the silly name.'

'Hello, girl from a ghost story.'

She laughed. 'We've been doing anatomy.'

'Really?'

'She insists,' Sophia said. 'Come on, young lady. It's time for bed.'

'Can I put the skull on my pillow?'

Sophia sighed. 'If you have to.'

'Good night,' I called.

'Good night, ladies. Good night, sweet ladies,' was the response from Maisie.

I was taken aback. Had she been reading *Hamlet*? Or T. S. Eliot? And had I just had a sex change? I went into the lounge to check.

Sophia reappeared half an hour later. 'I presume we're celebrating. There's champagne in the fridge.'

'Guardian! Have you been on the take?'

'Gift from the chief medical officer of Inverness. I wonder if he's still alive.'

'Didn't sound good up there the last I heard.'

I followed her into the kitchen and we consumed the wine without much talk.

Sophia got up. 'There's beef in the oven, but you've got time to tell all.'

So I did, opening the bottle of red wine she put on the table halfway through.

'I can't believe that Doris could do all that,' she said when I'd finished.

'I was surprised too, though you know my default setting for guardians is "don't trust".'

'I always thought Brian Cowan was an intellectual who liked to rant, not a fighter.'

'Anyone can become whatever they want.'

'Thank you very much.' She took my hand. 'Who would you want to be?'

'There's no finer place to be than in my head.'

'Such conceit.' She leaned over and kissed me on the lips.

I managed to break off. 'There's just one thing.'

'Oh, yes, man who has everything?'

'*You* took the truth drug.'

Her fingernails dug into the back of my hand and she drew her head back.

'How did you know?'

'It never appeared again. If someone working with Cowan or Guardian Doris had stolen it, it would have been used.'

'You might not have been able to tell.'

'No,' I agreed, 'if the people it killed had been hidden away. All right, call it a deduction. You take the Hippocratic Oath seriously, unlike some medical personnel I've known over the years. It's impossible for you to countenance using a drug that induces death without warning.'

'Yes,' she said, head down. 'You're right.'

I took her hand. 'I don't blame you. Well, I do. You could have told me.'

'You would have pestered me to use it on the people you brought in.'

'True. Where is it now?'

'In the city's sewers.'

'Good.'

'Can we eat?'

I suddenly realized how ravenous I was. Dinner was a gluttonous affair.

In the middle of the night, I woke up. We had made sweet love and Sophia was asleep, the breath whistling almost soundlessly between her parted lips. I got up and went to the window, drawing the curtain a couple of inches.

Lights shone above the doors of the guardians' residences and the street lamps, but there was no illumination from any of the windows. The members of the city's governing body were asleep, perchance to dream of more citizen-unfriendly schemes. Would Calder survive as senior guardian? I suspected so; the same went for Jack MacLean, with Billy no doubt remaining as his SPADE. But should they? They'd allowed two of their colleagues to disrupt public order, ultimately in a big way, playing deaf and dumb throughout. All they seemed to care about was building ties with outsider states so that Edinburgh could become part of a reconstructed Scotland. Did I want that? My head said yes. If the other cities and regions got together, we would be left behind by remaining independent. But my heart was another matter. Like the guardians who had revolted, like Peter Stewart, I loved Edinburgh as it had been for three decades, despite its numerous failings. In a new Scotland people like Hel Hyslop would keep order. There would be no place for mavericks like me.

Things might be quiet again in the 'perfect city' for now, but it was only a matter of months till the referendum. I had the feeling there would be plenty of work for me and Davie and Sophia. At least they were two people I could trust; three if I counted my father. Then there was Jimmy Taggart. And the many Guard personnel who'd remained loyal. Maybe things weren't so bad.

I got back into bed. As I drifted away, I heard the old bluesman Smokey Hogg's 'Dark Clouds', quickly followed by Leroy Carr's 'Hurry Down Sunshine'. Maybe the Big Wet would finally end tomorrow, but I wasn't holding my breath.